THE HAUNTS OF MEN

and Other Tales of Love & War

ROBERT W. CHAMBERS

THE HAUNTS OF MEN AND OTHER TALES OF LOVE & WAR

Published by Stark House Press
1315 H Street
Eureka, CA 95501, USA
griffinskye3@sbcglobal.net
www.starkhousepress.com

THE HAUNTS OF MEN
Originally published by Frederick A. Stokes Company, New York, 1898,
and copyright © 1898 by Robert W. Chambers and the publishers.

THE KING IN YELLOW
Three stories. Originally published by F. Tennyson Neely, Chicago & New
York, and Chatto and Windus, London, 1895, and copyright © 1895 by the
publishers.

THE MAKER OF MOONS
Three stories. Originally published and copyright © 1896 by G. P. Putnam's
Sons, New York & London.

BARBARIANS
Chapters 1-3. Originally published by D. Appleton and Company, New
York & London, 1917, and copyright © 1917 by Robert W. Chambers.

All rights reserved under International and Pan-American Copyright
Conventions.

ISBN-13: 978-1-944520-59-5

Book design by Mark Shepard, SHEPGRAPHICS.COM
Cover art by "G. W. E." from the original hardback edition
of *The Haunts of Men.*
Proofreading by Bill Kelly

First Stark House Press Edition: January 2018

THE HAUNTS OF MEN

"It happened so unexpectedly, so abruptly, that she forgot to scream…"

A woman watches a regiment of soldiers trample her garden as war comes to her front door in "The God of Battles." Three soldiers trade shots across the river and discover a common bond in "Pickets." A Union officer finds unexpected aid and unintentional betrayal in "Smith's Battery." A forgotten lover in disguise is a witness to tragedy in "Collector of the Port." A timid art student has his horizons broadened when he seeks a bit of experience in the Latin Quarter in "Another Good Man."

These stories and many others represent Robert W. Chambers at the beginning of his career, when— some would say—he was at the height of his storytelling powers. Here are tales that range from the Revolutionary War to the artist salons of Paris, and from a small upstate village in New York to the Alpine mountains of Europe. Tales of love and loss, of sacrifice and madness; comic tales of the Bohemian art world and grim stories of life during wartime.

Also included are seven additional stories from *The King in Yellow, The Maker of Moons* and *Barbarians*, further glimpses into the hearts and minds of men.

Table of Contents

"WHAT IS GENIUS?"

by Robert W. Chambers

An extract from *Literature in the Making* by Joyce Kilmer (Harper & Brothers, 1917):

I asked Robert W. Chambers, who has written more "best sellers" than any other living writer, what he thought of Flaubert's method of work.

He looked at me rather quizzically. "I think," he said, with a smile, "that Flaubert was slow. What else is there to think? Of course he was a matchless workman. But if he spent half a day in hunting for one word, he was slow, that's all. He might have gone on writing and then have come back later for that inevitable word."

"But what do you think of Flaubert's method, as a method?" I asked. "Do you think that a writer who works with such laborious care is right?"

"It's not a question of right or wrong," said Mr. Chambers, "it's a question of the individual writer's ability and tendency. If a man can produce novels like those of Flaubert, by writing slowly and laboriously, by all means let him write that way. But it would not be fair to establish that as the only legitimate method of writing.

"Some authors always write slowly. With some of them it's like pulling teeth for them to get their ideas out on paper. It's the same way in painting. You may see half a dozen men drawing from the same model. One will make his sketch premier coup; another will devote an hour to his; another will work all day. They may be artists of equal ability. It is the result that counts, not the method or the time."

"And what is it that makes a man an artist, in pigments or in words?" I asked. "Do you believe in the old saying that the poet - the creative artist - is born and not made?"

"No," said Mr. Chambers, "I do not think that that is the truth. I think that with regard to the writer it is true to this extent, that there must exist, in the first place, the inclination to write, to express ideas in written words. Then the writer must have something to express really worthy of expression, and he must learn how to express it. These three things make the writer - the inclination to say something, the possession of something worth saying, and the knowledge of how to say it."

"And where does genius come in?" I asked.

"What is genius?" asked Mr. Chambers, in turn. "I don't know. Perhaps genius is the combination of these three qualities in the highest degree.

"Of course," he added, with a laugh, "I know that all this is contrary to the opinion of the public. People like to believe that writers depend entirely upon an inspiration. They like to think that we are a hazy lot, sitting around and posing and waiting for some sort of divine afflatus. They think that writers sit around like a Quaker meeting, waiting for the spirit to move them."

"But have there not been writers," I asked, "who seem to prove that there is some truth in the inspiration theory? There is William de Morgan, for example, beginning to write novels in his old age. He spent most of his life in working in ceramics, not with words."

"On the contrary," said Mr. Chambers, "I think that William de Morgan proves my theory. He really spent all his life in learning to write - he was in training for being a novelist all the while. The novelist's training may be unconscious. He must have - as William de Morgan surely always has had - keen interest in the world. That is the main thing for the writer to have - a vivid interest in life. If we are to devote ourselves to the production of pictures of humanity according to our own temperaments, we must have this vivid interest in life; we must have intense curiosity. The men who have counted in literature have had this intense, never-satiated curiosity about life.

"This is true for the romanticists as well as the realists. The most imaginative and fantastic romances must have their basis in real life.

"I know of no better examples of this truth than the gargoyles which one sees in Gothic architecture in Europe. These extraordinary creatures that thrust their heads from the sides of cathedrals, misshapen and grotesque, are nevertheless thoroughly logical. That is, no matter how fantastic they may be, they have backbones and ribs and tails, and these backbones and ribs and tails are logical - that is, they could do what backbones and ribs and tails are supposed to do.

"In real life there are no creatures like the gargoyles, but the important thing is that the gargoyles really could exist. This is a good example of the true method of construction. The base of the construction must rest on real knowledge. The medieval sculptors knew the formation of existing animals; therefore they knew how to make gargoyles."

"How does this theory apply to poets?" I asked.

"I don't know," answered Mr. Chambers, "but it seems to me to apply to all creative work. The artist must know life before he can build even a travesty on life."

I called Mr. Chambers's attention to the work of certain ultra-modern poets who deliberately exclude life from their work. He was not inclined to take them seriously.

"There always have been aberrations," he said, "and there always will be. They're bound to exist. And there is bound to be, from time to time, attitudinizing and straining after effect on the part of prose writers as well as poets. And it is all based on one thing - self-consciousness. It is self-consciousness that spoils the work of some modern writers."

I asked Mr. Chambers to be more specific in his allusions.

"I cannot mention names," he said, "but there are certain writers who are always conscious of the style in which they are writing. Sometimes they consciously write in the style of some other men. They are thinking all the while of their technique and equipment, and the result is that their work loses its effect. A writer should not be convinced all the while that he is a realist or a romanticist; he should not subject himself deliberately to some special school of writing, and certainly he should not be conscious of his own style. The less a writer thinks of his technique the sooner he arrives at self-expression.

"It's just like ordinary conversation. A man is known by the way in which he talks - that is his 'style.' But he is not all the while acutely conscious of his manner of talking - unless he has an impediment in his speech. So the writer should be known by his untrammeled and unembarrassed expression."

I asked Mr. Chambers what he thought of the idea that the popularity of magazines has vitiated the public taste and lowered the standard of fiction.

"I do not think that this is the case," he said. "I do not see that the custom of serial publication has harmed the novel. It is not a modern innovation, you know. The novels of Dickens, Thackeray, and George Eliot had serial publication. But I do believe that the American public reads less fiction than it did a generation ago, and that its taste is not so good as it was."

This was a surprising statement to come from an author whom the public has received with such enthusiasm, so I asked Mr. Chambers to explain.

"Of course the magazines are mechanically better today than they were a generation ago. Then we had not the photogravure and the half-tone and the other processes that make our magazines beautiful. But we had better taste and also we had more leisure.

"I remember when one of the most widely read of our magazines was a popular science monthly, which printed articles by great scientists on biological and other topics. That was in the days when Darwin was announcing his theory of evolution - the first great jolt which orthodoxy received. People would not take time to read a magazine of that sort now. They are so occupied with business and dancing and all sorts of occupations that they have little leisure for reading."

Mr. Chambers stopped talking suddenly and laughed. "I'm not a good man for you to bring these questions to," he said, "because I never have had any special reverence for books or literature as such. I revere the books that I like, not all books."

"And have you such a thing as a favorite author?" I asked.

"Yes," said Mr. Chambers. "Dumas."

During the 1870's Mr. Chambers was an art student in Paris, and he has many interesting memories of the French and English writers and painters who have made that period memorable. He knew Paul Verlaine (whose poetry he greatly admires), Charles Conder, and Aubrey Beardsley.

"I knew many of the Beaux Arts crowd, because my brother was a student of architecture at the Beaux Arts. And they were a decent, clean crowd - they were not 'decadents.' I do not take much stock in the pose of 'decadence,' nor in the artistic temperament. I never saw a real artist with the artistic temperament. I always associated that with weakness."

Mr. Chambers, although he has intimate knowledge of the Quartier Latin, has little use for "Bohemia."

"What is Bohemia?" he asked. "If it is a place where a number of artists huddle together for the sake of animal warmth, I have nothing to say against it. But if it is a place where a number of artists come to scorn the world, then it is a dangerous thing. The artist should not separate himself from the world.

"These artistic and literary cults are wrong. I do not believe in professional clubs and cliques. If writers form a combination for business reasons, that is all right, but a writer should not associate exclusively with other writers; he should do his work and then go out and see and talk to people in other professions. We should sweep the cobwebs from the profession of writing and not try to fence it in from the public."

Before I left, I mentioned to Mr. Chambers the theory that literature is better as a staff than as a crutch, as an avocation than as a vocation. This, like the "inevitable word" theory, is greatly beloved by college professors. Mr. Chambers said:

"I disagree utterly with that theory. Do you remember how Dr. Johnson wrote Rasselas? It was in order to raise the money to pay for his mother's funeral. I believe that the best work is done under pressure. Of course the work must be enjoyed; a man in choosing a profession should select that sort of work which he prefers to do in his leisure moments. Let him do for his lifework the task which he would select for his leisure - and let him not take himself too seriously!"

(Borrowed from Pornokitsch, March 25, 2014)

"How shall we seem, each to the other, when,
  On that glad day, immortal, we shall meet—
  Thou who, long since, didst pass with hastening feet—
I, who still wait here, in the haunts of men?"

THE HAUNTS OF MEN

ROBERT W. CHAMBERS

To Elsa

As a Black Veil of Lace,
Parted in sombre grace,
Shadows a pallid face,
So shall the Veil of Night,
Dimly withdrawn,
Shadow the coming Dawn.

Changed are the ashen skies,—
The clearer blue
Deep mirrored in thine eyes
Is changing too.

If the dim Dawn be fair,
Can its pale flames compare
In glory to thy hair?
What, in the jewelled skies,
Matches the dyes
In thine uplifted eyes!

Out from the splendid night
Bright as a spirit's flight
Thou com'st with the Light.
And in the East the World spins, grey and old,
And in the West wait Life and Death; behold!

Bend down with me; behold!
This is the World,—
This tattered scroll unrolled,—
This chart unfurled.
Here at thy feet,
The Seven Oceans part and meet.

Trace with thy finger tips
The round World round,
Free as a shadow slips
Over the ground.
The World sleeps there
Steeped in the shadow of thy hair.

THE GOD OF BATTLES

Sovereign of the world.... these sabres hold another language to-day from that they held yesterday. —VATHEK.

It happened so unexpectedly, so abruptly, that she forgot to scream. A moment before, she had glanced out of the pantry windows, dusting the flour from her faded pink apron, and she saw the tall oats motionless in the field and the sunlight sifting through the corn. In the heated stillness a wasp, creeping up and down the window pane, filled the dim house with its buzzing. She remembered that,—then she remembered hearing the clock ticking in the darkened dining-room. It was scarcely a moment; she bent again over her flour pan, wistful, saddened by the summer silence, thinking of her brother; then again she raised her eyes to the window.

It was too sudden; she did not scream. Had they dropped from the sky, these men in blue,—these toiling, tramping, crowding creatures? The corn was full of them, the pasture, the road; they were in the garden, they crushed the cucumbers and the sweet-peas, their muddy trousers tore tender tendrils from the melon vines, their great shoes, plodding across the potato hills, harrowed the bronzed earth and levelled it to a waste of beaten mould and green-stuff. They passed, hundreds, thousands,—she could not tell,—and at first they neither spoke nor turned aside, but she heard a harmony, subtile, vast as winds at sea,—a nameless murmur that sweeps through brains of marching men,—the voiceless prophecy of battle.

Breathless, spellbound, she moved on tiptoe to the porch, one hand pressed trembling across her lips. The field of oats shimmered a moment before her eyes, then a blue mass swung into it and it melted away, sheered to the earth in glimmering swathes as gilded grain falls at the sickle's sparkle. And the men in blue covered the earth, the world, her world, which stretched from the orchard to Benson's Hill.

There was something on Benson's Hill that she had never before seen. It looked like a brook in the sunshine; it was a column of infantry, rifles slanting in the sun.

Somebody had been speaking to her for a minute or two, somebody below her on the porch steps, and now she looked down and saw a boy, slim, sunburnt, wearing gauntlets and spurs. His dusty uniform glittered with gilt and yellow braid; he touched the vizor of his cap and fingered his sword hilt. She looked at him listlessly, her hand still pressed to her lips.

"Is there a well near the house?" he asked. After a moment he repeated the question.

Men with red crosses on their sleeves came across the grass, trailing poles and rolls of dirty canvas. She saw horses too, dusty and patient, tied to the front gate. A soldier, with a yellow ornament on his sleeve, stood at their heads, holding a red flag in one hand.

Something tugged gently at her apron, and, "show me the well, please," repeated the boy beside her.

She turned mechanically into the house; he followed, caking the rag-carpet with his boots' dry mud. In the woodshed she started and turned trembling to him but he gravely motioned her on, and she went, passing more swiftly under the trees of the orchard to the vine-covered well-curb.

He thanked her; she pointed at the dipper and rope; but already blue-clad, red-faced soldiers were lowering the bucket and the orchard hummed with the buzz of the wheel.

She went back to the porch, not through the house but around it. Across the little lawn lay crushed stalks and dying flowers; the potato patch was a slough of muddy green.

Soldiers passed in the sunshine. She began to remember that her brother, too, was a soldier, somewhere out in the world; he had been a soldier for nearly a week, ever since Jim Bemis had taken him to Willow Corners to enlist. She remembered she had cried and gone into the pantry to make bread and cry again. She remembered that first night, how she had been afraid to sleep in the house, how at dusk she had gone into the parlour to be near her mother. Her mother was dead, but her picture hung in the parlour.

Soldiers were passing, clutching their rifle butts with dirty hands, turning toward her countless sun-dazzled eyes. The shimmer of gun-barrels, the dancing light on turning bayonets, the flicker and sparkle on belt and button dazed and wearied her.

Somebody said, "We're the boys for the purty girls! Have ye no eyes for us, lass?"

Another said, "Shut up, Mike, she's not from the Bowery;" and, "G'wan ye dead rabbit!" retorted the first.

A flag passed, and on it she read "New York," and another flag passed, dipped to her in grim salute, while the folds shook out a faded "Maine."

She began to watch the flags; she saw a regiment plunge into the trampled corn, but she knew it was not her brother's because the trousers of the men were scarlet and the caps hung to the shoulders, tasselled and crimson.

"Maryland, Maryland, Maryland, 60th Maryland," she repeated, but she did not know she spoke aloud until somebody said: "It's yonder," and a blue sleeve swept towards the west.

"Yonder," she repeated, looking at the ridge, cool in the beechwoods' shadow.

"Is it the 60th Maryland you want, Miss?" asked another.

"Silence," said an officer, wheeling a sweating horse past the porch.

She shrank back, but turned her head toward the beechwoods. As she looked a belt of flame encircled the forest, once, twice, again and yet again, and through the outrushing smoke, the crash! crash! crash! of rifles echoed and re-echoed across the valley.

All around her thousands of men burst into cheers; a deeper harmony grew on the idle breeze—the solemn tolling of cannon. The flags, the bright flags spread rainbow wings to the rising breeze; they were breasting the hills everywhere. The din of the rifles, the shouting, the sudden swift human wave, sweeping by on every side, thrilled her little heart until it beat out the long roll with the rolling drums.

In the orchard the rattle of the bucket, the creak and whirr of the well-wheel, never ceased. A very young officer sat on his horse, eating an unripe apple and watching the men around the well. The horse stretched a glossy neck toward the currant bushes, mumbling twigs and sun-curled leaves. A hen wandered near, peering fearlessly at the soldiers.

The girl went into the kitchen, reached up for her sun-bonnet, dangling on a peg, tied it under her chin, and walked gravely into the orchard. The men about the well looked up as she passed. They admired respectfully. So did the very young officer, pausing, apple half-eaten; so perhaps did the horse, turning his large, gentle eyes as she came up.

The officer wheeled in his saddle and leaned toward her deferentially, anticipating perhaps complaint or insult.

In Maryland "Dixie" was sung as often as "The Red, White, and Blue."

Before she spoke she saw that it was the same officer who had asked her about the well; she had not noticed he was so young.

"I am sorry," he said,—and, as he spoke, he removed his cap—"I am very sorry that we have trampled your garden. If you are loyal, the Government will indemnify you—"

The sudden crash of a cannon somewhere among the trees drowned his voice. Stunned, she saw him, undisturbed, gather his bridle with a deprecatory gesture. His voice came back to her through the ringing in her ears: "We do not mean to be careless, but we could not turn aside, and your farm is in the line of advance."

Her ears still rang, and she spoke, scarcely hearing her own voice: "It is not that—I am loyal—it is only I wish to ask you where my brother's regiment—where the 60th Maryland is."

"The 60th Maryland—oh—why it's in King's Brigade, Wolcott's Division; I think it's yonder." He pointed toward the beechwoods.

"Yonder? Where they are firing?"

Again the cannon thundered and the ground shook under her. She saw him nod, smiling faintly. Other mounted officers rode up; some looked at her curiously, others glanced carelessly; the attitudes of all were respectful. She heard them arguing about the water in the well and the length of the road to Willow Corners. They spoke of a turning movement, of driving somebody to Whitehall Station. The musketry on the hill had ceased; the cannon, too, were silent. Across the trampled corn a regiment moved listlessly to the tap, tap of a drum. On the road that circled Benson's Hill, mounted soldiers were riding fast in the dust; several little flags bobbed among them; metal on shoulder and stirrup flashed through the dust, burnished by the mid-day sun.

She heard an officer say that there would be no fighting, and she wondered, because the musketry began again, little spattering shots among the beeches on the ridge, and behind the house drums rolled and a sudden flurry of bugle music filled the air. Other officers rode up, some escorted by troopers who bounced in their saddles and grasped long-staffed flags, the butts resting in their stirrups.

She reached up and bent down an apple bough, studded with clustered green fruit. Through the leaves she looked at the officers.

The sunshine fell in brilliant spots, dappling flag and cap and the broad backs of horses; there was a jingle of spurs everywhere. The hum of voices and the movement were grateful to her, for her loneliness was not of her own seeking. In the pleasant summer air the distant gunshots grew softer and softer; the twitter of a robin came from the ash-tree by the gate.

Out on the road by Benson's Hill, the cavalry were still passing, the little flags sped along, rising and falling with the column, and the short clear note of a trumpet echoed the robin's call.

But around the house the last of the troops had passed; she could see them, not yet far away, moving up among the fields toward the ridges where the sun burned on the bronzing scrub-oak thickets. The officers, too, were leaving the orchard, spurring on, singly or in groups, after the disappearing columns. From the main road came a loud thudding and pounding and clanking; a battery of artillery, the long guns slanted, the drivers swinging their thongs—passed at a trot. After it rode soldiers in blue and yellow, then waggons passed, ponderous grey wains covered with canvas, and on either side clattered more mounted troopers, their drawn sabres glittering through the heated haze.

She stood a moment, holding the apple bough, watching the yellow dust hanging motionless in the rear of the disappearing column. When the last wain had creaked out of sight and the last trooper had loped after it, she turned and looked at the silent garden, trodden, withered, desolate.

She drew a long breath, the apple bough flew back, the little green apples dancing. A bee buzzed over a trampled geranium, a robin ran through the longer grass and stopped short, head raised. Beyond Benson's Hill a bugle blew faintly; distant rifle shots sounded along the ridge; then silence crept through the sunlit meadows, across the levelled corn, across dead stalks and stems, a silence that spread like a shadow, nearer, nearer, over the lawn, through the orchard to the house, and then from corner to corner, dulling the ticking of the clock, stifling the wasp on the window, driving her before it from room to room.

On the musty hair-cloth sofa in the parlour she lay, flung face down, hands pressed to her ears. But silence entered with her, stifling the sob in her throat.

When she raised her head it was dusk. She heard the murmur of wind in the trees and the chirr of crickets from the fields. She sat up, peering fearfully into the darkness, and she heard the clock ticking in the kitchen and rustle of vines on the porch. After a moment she rose, treading softly, and felt along the wall until her hands rested on her mother's picture. Then, no longer afraid, she slipped silently across the room, and through the hallway to the pantry.

It was nearly moonrise before she had cooked supper; when she sat down alone at the long table, the moon, yellow, enormous, stared at her through the window.

She sipped her tea, turned the lamp-wick a trifle lower, and ate slowly. The little grey dusk moths came humming in the open window and circled around her. The porch dripped with dew; there was a scent of night in the air.

When she had sat silent a little while dreaming over the sins of a blameless life, there came to her, peace, so sudden so perfect, that she could not understand. How should she know peace? What thought of the past might bring comfort? She could just remember her mother,—that was all. She loved her picture in the parlour. As for her father, he had died as he had lived, a snarling drunkard. And her brother? A lank, blue-eyed boy, dissipated, unwholesome, already cursed with his father's sin—what comfort could he be to her? He had gone away to enlist; he was drunk when he did it.

She thought of all these things, her finger tips resting on the edge of the table. She thought too—of the soldiers passing, of the rippling crash of rifles, the drums, the cheering, the sunlight flecking the backs of the horses in the orchard.

There was a creak at the gate, a click of a latch, and the fall of a foot on the moonlit porch. She half rose; she was not frightened. How she knew who it was, God alone knows, but she looked up, timidly, understanding who was coming, knowing who would knock, who would enter, who would speak. And yet she had never seen him but once in her life.

All this she knew,—this child made wise in the space of time marked by the tick of the kitchen clock; but she did not know that the memory of his smile had given her the peace she could not understand, she did not know this until he entered, dusty, slim, sunburnt, his yellow gauntlets folded in his belt, his cap and sabre in his hand. Then she knew it. When she understood this she stood up, pale, uncertain. He bowed silently and stepped forward, fumbling with his sabre hilt. She motioned toward a chair.

He said he had a message for the master of the house, and glanced about vaguely, noting the single place at table and the single plate. She said he might give the message to her.

"It is only that—if I do not inconvenience you too much—" he smiled faintly,—"if you would allow me,—well, the truth is I am billeted here for the night."

She did not know what that meant and he explained.

"The master of the house is absent," she said, thinking of her brother.

"Will he return to-night?" he asked.

She shook her head; she was thinking that she did not want him to go away. Suddenly the thought of being alone laid hold of her with fresh horror.

"You may stay," she said faintly. He bowed again. She asked him if he cared for supper, with a gesture toward the table, and when he thanked her she took courage and told him where to hang his cap and sabre.

There was a small room between the parlour and the dining-room. She offered it to him, and he accepted gratefully. While she was in the kitchen, toasting more bread, she heard him go to the front door and call. There came a clatter of hoofs, a quick word or two, and, as she re-entered the dining-room, he met her. "My orderly," he explained, —"he may sleep in the stable, may he not?"

"My own bed-room is all I have here," she said.

"Not—not the one you gave me!" he asked.

She nodded. "You may have it,—I often sleep in the parlour,—I did when my brother was home."

"If I had had any idea—" he burst out. She stopped him with a gesture; but he insisted and at last he had his own way. "If I may sleep in the parlour, I will stay," he said, and she nodded and seated herself at the table.

He ate a great deal; she wondered a little, but nodded again at his excuses, and insisted that he must have more tea. She watched him; the lamplight fell softly on his boyish head, on his faint moustache, and bronzed hands. He ate much bread and butter and many eggs; he spoke about his orderly and the horses, and presently asked for a lantern. She brought him one; he lighted it.

When he had gone away with his lantern, she rested her white face in her hands and looked at his empty chair. She thought of her brother, she thought of the village people who leered askance when she was obliged to go to the store at Willow Corners. The mention of her father's name, of her brother's name in the village aroused sneers or laughter. As long as she could remember the one great longing of her life had been to be respected. She had seen her father fall at night in the village street, drunk as a hog; she had seen her brother reel across the fields at noonday. She knew that all the world knew—her world—that she was merely one of a drunkard's family. She never spoke to a neighbour, nor did she answer when spoken to. She carried her curse,—and her longing,—supposing that she was a thing apart. In the orchard at midday a man, a young boy, a soldier, had spoken to her and looked at her in a way she had never known. All at once she realised, dreaming there in the lamplight, that she was a woman to him, like other women; a woman to be spoken to with deference, a woman to be approached with courtesy. She had read it in his eyes, she had heard it in his voice. It was this that brought to her a peace as gracious, as sweet, as the eyes that had met her own in the orchard.

He was coming back from the stable now,—she heard his spurs click across the grass by the orchard. And now he had entered, now he was there, sitting opposite, smiling vaguely across the table. A rush of tears blinded her and she looked out into the night where the yellow moon stared and stared.

She found herself in the parlour after a while, silent, listening to his voice; and all about her was peace, born of the peace within her breast.

He told her of the war. She had never before cared, but now she cared. He spoke of long marches, of hunger and of thirst, with a boyish laugh, and she laughed too, not knowing how else to show her pity. He spoke of the Land, and now, for the first time, she loved it; she knew it was also her Land. He spoke of the flag and what it meant. In her home she had no symbol of her country, and she told him so. He drew a penknife from his pocket, cut a button from his collar, and handed it to her. On the button was an eagle and stars, and she pinned it over her heart, looking at him with innocent eyes.

She told him of her mother,—she could not tell much but she told him all she remembered. Then, involuntarily, she told him more,—about her life, her hopes long dead, her brother bearing his father's name and curse. She had not meant to do this at first; but as she spoke she had a dim idea that he ought to know who it was that he treated with gentleness and deference. She knew it would not change anything in him, that he would be the same. Perhaps it was a vague hope that he might advise her,—perhaps be sorry, she could not analyse it, but she felt the necessity of speaking.

There is a time for all things except confession. But, to the lonely soul, long stifled, time is chosen for confession when God sends the opportunity.

She spoke of honour as she understood it; she spoke of dishonour as she had known it.

When she was silent, he began to speak, and she listened breathlessly. Ah, but she was right! The God of Battles had sent to her a messenger of peace. Out of the smoke and flame he had come to find her and pity her. Through him she knew she was worthy of respect, through him she learned her womanhood, from his lips she heard the truths of youth, which are truer than the truths of age.

He sat there in the lamplight, his gilt straps gleaming, his glittering spurs ringing true with every movement, his bronzed young face bent to hers. She knew he knew everything that man could know; she drank in what he said, humbly. When he ceased speaking, she still looked into his eyes. Their brilliancy dazzled her; the lamp spun a halo behind his head. Wondering at his knowledge, she wondered what those things might be that he knew and had not told. He was smiling now. She felt the power and mystery of his eyes.

It is true that he had not told her all he knew,— although what a boy of eighteen knows is soon told. He had not told her that her brother lay buried in a trench in the beech-grove on the ridge, shot by court-martial for desertion in the face of the enemy. Yet that was the very thing he had come to tell her.

About midnight, when they had been whispering long together, he told her that her brother was dead. He told her that death with honour wiped out every stain, and she cried a little and blessed God,—the God of Battles, who had purified her brother in the flames of war.

And that night, when he lay asleep on the musty hair-cloth sofa, she crept in, white, silent, and kissed his hair.

He never knew it. In the morning he rode away.

PICKETS

"Hi, Yank!"

"Shut up!" replied Alden, wriggling to the edge of the rifle-pit. Connor also crawled a little higher and squinted through the chinks of the pine logs.

"Hey, Johnny!" he called across the river, "are you that clay-eatin' Cracker with green lamps on your pilot?"

"Oh, Yank! Are yew the U. S. mewl with a C. S. A. brand on yewr head-stall?"

"Go to hell!" replied Connor sullenly.

A jeering laugh answered him from across the river.

"He had you there, Connor," observed Alden with faint interest.

Connor took off his blue cap and examined the bullet hole in the crown.

"C. S. A. brand on my head-stall, eh!" he repeated savagely, twirling the cap between his dirty fingers.

"You called him a clay-eating Cracker," observed Alden; "and you referred to his spectacles as green lanterns on his pilot."

"I'll show him whose head-stall is branded," muttered Connor, shoving his smoky rifle through the log crack.

Alden slid down to the bottom of the shallow pit and watched him apathetically.

The silence was intense; the muddy river, smooth as oil, swirled noiselessly between its fringe of sycamores; not a breath of air stirred the leaves around them. From the sun-baked bottom of the rifle-pit came the stale smell of charred logs and smoke-soaked clothing. There was a stench of sweat in the air and the heavy odour of balsam and pine seemed to intensify it. Alden gasped once or twice, threw open his jacket at the throat, and stuffed a filthy handkerchief into the crown of his cap, arranging the ends as a shelter for his neck.

Connor lay silent, his right eye fastened upon the rifle-sight, his dusty army shoes crossed behind him. One yellow sock had slipped down over the worn shoe heel and laid bare a dust-begrimed ankle.

In the heated stillness Alden heard the boring of weevils in the logs overhead. A tiny twig snapped somewhere in the forest; a fly buzzed about his knees. Suddenly Connor's rifle cracked; the echoes rattled and clattered away through the woods; a thin cloud of pungent vapour slowly drifted straight upward, shredding into filmy streamers among the tangled branches overhead.

"Get him?" asked Alden, after a silence.

"Nope," replied Connor. Then he addressed himself to his late target across the river:

"Hello, Johnny!"

"Hi, Yank!"

"How close?"

"Hey?"

"How close?"

"What, sonny?"

"My shot, you fool!"

"Why, sonny!" called back the Confederate in affected surprise, "was yew a shootin' at me?"

Bang! went Connor's rifle again. A derisive catcall answered him, and he turned furiously to Alden.

"Oh, let up," said the young fellow; "it's too hot for that."

Connor was speechless with rage, and he hastily jammed another cartridge into his long, hot rifle, while Alden roused himself, brushed away a persistent fly, and crept up to the edge of the pit again.

"Hello, Johnny!" he shouted.

"That you, sonny?" replied the Confederate.

"Yes. Say, Johnny, shall we call it square until four o'clock?"

"What time is it?" replied the cautious Confederate; "all our expensive gold watches is bein' repaired at Chickamauga."

At this taunt, Connor showed his teeth, but Alden laid one hand on his arm and sang out: "It's two o'clock, Richmond time; Sherman has just telegraphed us from your State-house."

"Wa-al, in that case this crool war is over," replied the Confederate sharpshooter; "we'll be easy on old Sherman."

"See here!" cried Alden; "is it a truce until four o'clock?"

"All right! Your word, Yank!"

"You have it!"

"Done!" said the Confederate, coolly rising to his feet and strolling down to the river bank, both hands in his pockets.

Alden and Connor crawled out of their ill-smelling dust wallow, leaving their rifles behind them.

"Whew! It's hot, Johnny," said Alden pleasantly. He pulled out a stained pipe, blew into the stem, polished the bowl with his sleeve, and sucked wistfully at the end. Then he went and sat down beside Connor who had improvised a fishing pole from his ramrod, a bit of string, and a rusty hook.

The Confederate rifleman also sat down on his side of the stream, puffing luxuriously on a fragrant corn-cob pipe.

Presently the Confederate soldier raised his head and looked across at Alden.

"What's yewr name, sonny?" he asked.

"Alden," replied the young fellow briefly.

"Mine's Craig," observed the Confederate; "what's yewr regiment?"

"Two hundred sixtieth New York; what's yours, Mr. Craig?"

"Ninety-third Maryland, *Mister* Alden."

"Quit that throwin' sticks in the water!" growled Connor; "how do you s'pose I'm goin' to catch anythin'?"

Alden tossed his stick back into the brush-heap and laughed.

"How's your tobacco, Craig?" he called out.

"Bully! How's yewr coffee 'n 'tack, Alden?"

"First-rate!" replied the youth.

After a silence he said: "Is it a go?"

"You bet," said Craig, fumbling in his pockets. He produced a heavy twist of Virginia tobacco, laid it on a log, hacked off about three inches with his sheath knife, and folded it up in a big green sycamore leaf. This again he rolled into a corn-husk, weighted with a pebble, then stepping back, he hurled it into the air, saying: "Deal squar, Yank!"

The tobacco fell at Alden's feet. He picked it up, measured it carefully with his clasp-knife, and called out: "Three and three-quarters, Craig. What do you want, hard-tack or coffee?"

"'Tack," replied Craig: "don't stint!"

Alden laid out two biscuits. As he was about to hack a quarter from the third he happened to glance over the creek at his enemy. There was no mistaking the expression in his face. Starvation was stamped on every feature.

When Craig caught Alden's eye, he spat with elaborate care, whistled a bar of the "Bonny Blue Flag," and pretended to yawn.

Alden hesitated, glanced at Connor, then placed three whole biscuits in the corn husk, added a pinch of coffee, and tossed the parcel over to Craig.

That Craig longed to fling himself upon the food and devour it was plain to Alden, who was watching his face. But he didn't; he strolled leisurely down the bank, picked up the parcel, weighed it critically before opening it, and finally sat down to examine the contents. When he saw that the third cracker was whole, and that a pinch of coffee had been added, he paused in his examination and remained motionless on the bank, head bent. Presently he looked up and asked Alden if he had made a mistake. The young fellow shook his head and drew a long puff of smoke from his pipe, watching it curl out of his nose with interest.

"Then I'm obliged to yew, Alden," said Craig ; "'low, I'll eat a snack to see it ain't pizened."

He filled his lean jaws with the dry biscuit, then scooped up a tin-cup full of water from the muddy river and set the rest of the cracker to soak.

"Good?" queried Alden.

"Fair," drawled Craig, bolting an unchewed segment and choking a little. "How's the twist?"

"Fine," said Alden; "tastes like stable-sweepings."

They smiled at each other across the stream.

"Sa-a-y," drawled Craig with his mouth full, "when yew're out of twist, jest yew sing out, sonny."

"All right," replied Alden. He stretched back in the shadow of a sycamore and watched Craig with pleasant eyes.

Presently Connor had a bite and jerked his line into the air.

"Look yere," said Craig, "that ain't no way foh to ketch 'red-horse.' Yew want a ca'tridge on foh a sinker, sonny."

"What's that?" inquired Connor suspiciously.

"Put on a sinker."

"Go on, Connor," said Alden.

Connor saw him smoking and sniffed anxiously. Alden tossed him the twist, telling him to fill his pipe.

Presently Connor found a small pebble and improvised a sinker. He swung his line again into the muddy current with a mechanical sidelong glance to see what Craig was doing, and settled down again on his haunches, smoking and grunting.

"Enny news, Alden?" queried Craig after a silence.

"Nothing much—except that Richmond has fallen," grinned Alden.

"Quit foolin'," urged the Southerner; "ain't thar no news?"

"No. Some of our men down at Long Pond got sick eating catfish. They caught them in the pond. It appears you Johnnys used the pond as a cemetery, and our men got sick eating the fish."

"That so?" grinned Craig; "too bad. Lots of yewr men was in Long Pond, too, I reckon."

In the silence that followed, two rifle-shots sounded faint and dull from the distant forest.

"'Nother great Union victory," drawled Craig. "Extry! extry! Richmond is took!"

Alden laughed and puffed at his pipe.

"We licked the boots off of the 30th Texas last Monday," he said.

"Sho!" exclaimed Craig. "What did you go a lickin' their boots for?—blackin'?"

"Oh, shut up!" said Connor from the bank, "I can't ketch no fish if you two fools don't quit jawin'."

The sun was dipping below the pine-clad ridge, flooding river and wood with a fierce radiance. The spruce needles glittered, edged with gold; every broad green leaf wore a heart of gilded splendour, and the muddy waters of the river rolled onward like a flood of precious metal, heavy, burnished, noiseless.

From a balsam bough a thrush uttered three timid notes; a great gauzy-winged grasshopper drifted blindly into a clump of sun-scorched weeds, click! click! cr-r-r-r!

"Purty, ain't it," said Craig, looking at the thrush. Then he swallowed the last morsel of muddy hard-tack, wiped his beard on his cuff, hitched up his trousers, took off his green glasses, and rubbed his eyes.

"A he-cat-bird sings purtier though," he said with a yawn.

Alden drew out his watch, puffed once or twice, and stood up, stretching his arms in the air.

"It's four o'clock," he began, but was cut short by a shout from Connor.

"Gee-whiz!" he yelled, "what have I got on this here pole!"

The ramrod was bending, the line swaying heavily in the current.

"It's four o'clock, Connor," said Alden, keeping a wary eye on Craig.

"That's all right!" called Craig; "the time's extended till yewr friend lands that there fish!"

"Pulls like a porpoise," grunted Connor, "damn it! I bet it busts my ramrod!"

"Does it pull?" grinned Craig.

"Yes,—a dead weight!"

"Don't it jerk kinder this way an' that," asked Craig, much interested.

"Naw," said Connor, "the bloody thing jest pulls steady."

"Then it ain't no 'red-horse,' it's a catfish!"

"Huh!" sneered Connor,—"don't I know a catfish? This ain't no catfish, lemme tell yer!"

"Then it's a log," laughed Alden.

"By gum! here it comes," panted Connor; "here, Alden, jest you ketch it with my knife,—hook the blade, blame ye!"

Alden cautiously descended the red bank of mud, holding on to roots and branches, and bent over the water. He hooked the big-bladed clasp knife like a scythe, set the spring, and leaned out over the water.

"Now!" muttered Connor.

An oily circle appeared upon the surface of the turbid water,—another and another. A few bubbles rose and floated upon the tide.

Then something black appeared just beneath the bubbles and Alden hooked it with his knife and dragged it shoreward.

It was the sleeve of a man's coat.

Connor dropped his ramrod and gaped at the thing: Alden would have loosed it, but the knife-blade was tangled in the sleeve.

He turned a sick face up to Connor.

"Pull it in," said the older man,—"here, give it to me, lad—"

When at last the silent visitor lay upon the bank, they saw it was the body of a Union cavalryman. Alden stared at the dead face, fascinated; Connor mechanically counted the yellow chevrons upon the blue sleeve, now soaked black. The muddy water ran over the baked soil, spreading out in dust-covered pools; the spurred boots trickled slime. After a while both men turned their heads and looked at Craig. The Southerner stood silent and grave, his battered cap in his hand. They eyed each other quietly for a moment, then, with a vague gesture, the Southerner walked back into his pit and presently reappeared, trailing his rifle.

Connor had already begun to dig with his bayonet, but he glanced up at the rifle in Craig's hands. Then he looked suspiciously into the eyes of the Southerner. Presently he bent his head again and continued digging.

It was sunset before he and Alden finished the shallow grave, Craig watching them in silence, his rifle between his knees. When they were ready they rolled the body into the hole and stood up.

Craig also rose, raising his rifle to a "present." He held it there while the two Union soldiers shovelled the earth into the grave. Alden went back and lifted the two rifles from the pit, handed Connor his, and waited.

"Ready!" growled Connor, "aim!"

Alden's rifle came to his shoulder. Craig also raised his rifle.

"Fire!"

Three times the three shots rang out in the wilderness, over the unknown grave. After a moment or two Alden nodded good night to Craig across the river and walked slowly toward his rifle-pit. Connor shambled after him. As he turned to lower himself into the pit he called across the river; "Good night, Craig!"

"Good night, Connor," said Craig.

AN INTERNATIONAL AFFAIR

"...Brown-bear clam' de ole fence rail,
Rabbit holler; "Whar yoh tail?"
Banjo Song.

I.

When the gunboats entered Sandy River, Cleland's regiment was ordered to garrison and reconstruct the forts at the Landing, evacuated by the Confederate troops as soon as the gunboats crossed the bar.

The gunboats tossed a few shells after the leisurely retreating Confederates, then dropped anchor below the Landing, and waited for something to turn up. A week later they steamed out of the river, promptly stuck on the bar, churned and thrashed and whistled and signalled, and finally slid out into blue water where a blockade runner tempted them into a chase that contributed to the amusement of the Southern Confederacy.

By Thanksgiving time, Cleland's regiment had finished the forts at Sandy Landing. Cleland did it because he was told to, not because either forts or town were of the slightest military value to anybody. The Landing itself was a skunk-haunted village, utterly unimportant as supply depot, strategical pivot, or a menace to navigation. It was a key to nothing; its single railway led nowhere, its whisky was illegal, illimitable, and atrocious.

Cleland's report embodied all of this. He was ordered to hold his ground, establish semaphores, and plant torpedoes. So he built his semaphores as directed, planted torpedoes, and reported. Twenty-four hours later orders came to go into winter-quarters. Then he was notified that he was to be reinforced, so he built barracks for two more regiments, as directed, and wondered what on earth was coming. Nothing came except the two regiments; one arrived on the first of December, by rail,—an Irish regiment;—the other turned up a week later in two cattle trains, band playing madly from the caboose. It was a German regiment full of strange oaths—and aromas.

Now Cleland was enlightened; he understood that the Landing was to be used as a species of cage for these two foreign regiments, raised, Heaven knows where, and destined to prove a nuisance to any army that harboured them. The Irish possessed an appalling record of pillage, bravery, and insubordination. The German regiment, raised "to march mit Siegel," had an unbroken record of flight to its discredit. It had run at Grey's Ford, at Crystal Hill, at Yellow Bank, and at Cypress-Court-House. It fled cheerfully, morning, noon and night; its band stampeded naively and naturally; it always followed its band, adored by all; and the regiment bore no rancour when scourged in general orders. Fallbach was its colonel,—known to the sarcastic and uninstructed as Fallback,—a rosy, short-winded, peaceful Teuton, who ran with his regiment every time, and always accepted censure with jocular resignation.

"Poys will pe poys, ain't it?" he would say with a shrug; "Der band iss a fine band alretty. Dot trombone iss timid, and der poys dey follow der trombone."

When Cleland understood that the authorities had rid themselves of the two regiments by interring them at Sandy Landing, he wrote a respectful protest, was snubbed and ordered to begin housekeeping for the winter, which meant that his regiment was now on police duty, stationed at the Landing to keep the peace between the Germans and their Irish neighbours.

Trouble began promptly; Bannon, colonel of the 1st Irish, met Fallbach of the 1st Jägers, and mispronounced his name with an emphasis unmistakable. An hour later the two regiments knew the war was on and made preparations accordingly. Hogan of the 10th company, crossing the street, hustled Franz Bummel of the Jägers and called him a "dootch puddy-fud!"

Quinn, listening to the Jägers' band concert that afternoon, whistled "Doolan's Wake," and imitated Fritz Klein's piccolo, aided and abetted by Phelan and McCue. That night there were three scuffles and a fight, and the provost-marshal had his work cut out for him.

Little by little the two regiments were installed in distant sections of the town. Cleland dealt justice untempered with mercy, and the rival regiments understood that their warfare would have to be carried on by stealth.

When Phelan, Quinn, Hogan, and McCue were released from the guard-house, they rejoiced with their comrades of the 10th company, and prepared future calamity for the Jägers. But Fate was against them. Their regimental fetish, a strong young goat, disappeared, and that night the Jägers were reported to have revelled in a strangely suggestive stew.

A day or two later, Quinn, fishing for suckers in the Sandy River, was assaulted by three Jägers, his fishpole and three fish confiscated, and he himself ducked amid grunts of universal satisfaction.

The fury of the 10th company passed all bounds when Quinn was relegated to the guard-house for conduct unbecoming a soldier; but the Teutons never strayed from their barracks except in force, and, as night leave was forbidden both regiments, the 10th company hesitated to inaugurate riot by daylight.

Quinn, squatting in the guard-house found plenty of leisure to hatch revenge. He did not waste thought on mere individual schemes for assault and battery; he meditated a master stroke, a blow at the entire regiment calculated to tear every Teuton bosom. The two objects most cherished by the Jägers were their cat and a disreputable negro who cooked for the colonel. How to combine damage to these centres of Teutonic affection occupied Quinn's waking hours. To kidnap the cat; that was not enough,—the Teutons must be beguiled into eating their cat—and liking it too. How? Quinn sucked at an empty pipe and brooded. Bribe the negro Cassius, first to kidnap the cat, then to cook it? Quinn writhed maliciously at the prospect; he hated Tom, the black and white cat who sang every night on the Jägers' barrack roof—sang to each individual star in the firmament to the indignation of every Irishman in Sandy Landing.

When Quinn emerged from the guard-house he took council with Phelan and McCue; and that evening Hogan was despatched to tempt Cassius with promises and a little cash.

The affair was easier than Hogan had dared hope; Cassius took the cash and promised to betray, and Hogan, lips compressed, to stifle all outward mirthful symptoms, went back to the barracks where Quinn, Phelan, and McCue sat waiting in pessimistic silence.

"He'll not kill the cat," said Hogan, "he'll fetch ut in a bag to the shanty foreninst the hill,—d'ye mind the hut, McCue?"

"I do," said McCue impressively.

"Thin be aisy," continued Hogan; "we'll skin ut an' co-ook ut an' the naygur can take the stew to thot Dootch runaway sodger, Fallback, bad cess to him an' his! Pass th' potheen, McCue."

"Sure there's not stew in wan cat for all!" objected Phelan.

"There is! There is," said Quinn: "there's cats in town to be had for the askin', an' nary a Dootchman will starve! Usha! but they'll be crazy, th' omadhouns!"

"'Twill choke them," said Phelan.

"Did they choke wid the goat they shtole?" demanded McCue angrily.

"I met Bummel an' Klein," continued Quinn: "'Sure,' I sez, ' 'tis dhirty thricks ye play on the Irish.' 'Phwat's that?' sez Klein. 'Ye ate our goat,' sez I. Wid that they grinned an' me phist hurrt wid the timptayshun of Bummers nose."

"'Sure,' sez I, ' 'tis frinds we should be!' 'Sorra th' day!' sez Klein. 'Phwy not?' sez I. 'Ye hate us an' bate us,' sez Klein; 'I'll not thrust ye, Mike Quinn.' 'Take me hand,' sez I, extindin' me fingers; wan touch of nature, me lad! 'Tis a crool war entirely, an' it's frinds we'll be, an' no favor!' 'Prove ut,' sez he. 'I wull,' sez I, 'an' be th' same token 'tis huntin' we go this day week, so look fur a Christmas dinner to shame the Pope's cook.' 'A dinner,' sez he, 'wid th' town betchune us!' 'Ye'll dine wid us, yet,' sez I.

'An' how,' sez he, a lickin' the chops av him. 'Whin ye dine wid the Irish ye should have a long spoon,' sez I, laughin' friendly like.

'We'll sind ye a shtew, me b'y, if God sinds us the rabbits.' "Thin," continued Quinn, "we parrted genteel; an' they'll hear we have lave to hunt on Christmas day—musha, bad luck to th' Dootch scuts!—'tis cats they'll be eatin' this blessed hour come Christmas, an' may the howly saints sind them the black cramp of Drumgoole!"

II.

Christmas eve, while Hogan and Phelan lay slumbering, and Quinn and McCue walked their rounds, gloating over revenge, Cassius the disreputable sat in the kitchen of the Jäger barracks counting the advanced payment of cash received from Hogan, and leering at the black and white tom-cat who dozed peacefully by the dying fire.

"Pore ole Torn," muttered Cassius guiltily, "hit's gwinter 'sprise dishyere kitty. 'Spec ole Tom gwinter git riled."

The cat opened its yellow eyes.

"Gwinter 'sprise ole Tom," repeated Cassius, compassionately pursing up his lips.

The cat began to purr.

"Pore ole Tom," sighed the darkey, tremulous with remorse.

The cat rose and began to march around, purring and hoisting an interrogative tail.

Cassius continued to bemoan Tom's fate and recount the money until he had hardened his heart sufficiently. Finally he pocketed the coins, wiped his eyes, and approached the cat with seductive caution. Tom permitted caresses, courted further endearments, and suffered himself to be seized and dropped into a potato sack. But, once imprisoned, he scrambled and squalled and clawed until Cassius, unable to bear the sight and sound of Thomas's distress, deposited the sack in the pantry and fled from the barracks to the street.

Guilt weighed heavily on the darkey's soul; he shuffled along, battling with conscience, trying to think of some compromise to save the cat and his money at the same time. Moonlight flooded hill and valley; he heard the sentries calling from post to post, the stir of the horses in the artillery stables across the square, the creaking of leafless branches overhead. He went around to the chicken coop; he often went there to enjoy the thrill of a temptation that he dared not succumb to, also to keep stray cats from doing murder on their own account. For, though he dared not steal a single chicken, he could at least have the bitter pleasure of foiling the feline marauders of Sandy Landing. This he was accustomed to do with a tin box, placed on its side, a trip-stick, a string, and a bit of bone for bait. Cat after cat he had trapped and committed to the depths of Sandy River, highly commended by his colonel and the rank and file of the Jägers. Now, as he stepped softly around the corner, his eyes fell on a black and white object, stealing toward the window where the long tin box stood temptingly baited. The next instant the trip-stick clicked, the weighted box-lid fell and snapped, and Cassius seized the box with a chuckle of triumph.

"Cat! Cat!" he repeated, addressing the frantic inmate of the box, "down' yoh count yoh chickens fore dey's hatched!—"

Cassius stopped short, pulsating with a new idea. Why sacrifice Tom when here was a victim ready at hand, doubtless provided by Providence in the nick of time to save a poor darkey from treachery? And it was a kind of treachery that even Cassius found uncongenial.

"Pit-a-pat! Pit-a-pat!" mocked Cassius derisively listening to the manoeuvres of the imprisoned victim; "Stop dat scratchin' on de box! He! He! He! I'se gwineter let ole Tom outen de bag,—pore ole Tom! Dishyere nigger ain't no Judas! Lan's sakes!—dat ole cat smell kinder funny!"

He wrinkled his nose, sniffed, turned a pair of startled eyes on the big box under his arm, then a sickly smile of intelligence spread over his face and he placed the box gently on the ground.

"Had mah s'picions 'bout dat black an' white kitty-cat," he muttered.

The animal inside scratched and writhed and scrambled.

"Lan's sake!" chuckled Cassius, grinning from ear to ear, "'spec dat ole pole-cat gwine twiss he tail off'n 'bout two-free minutes! Yah! yah!—he! he! yiah—ho!"

And, as he entered the servant's quarters he smote his knees and shook his head, and laughed and laughed and laughed.

About midnight he took his banjo from the nail, thumbed it, and began to croon to himself:

> Bob-cat he caynt wag he tail–
> Ain got no tail foh to wag!
> Brown-bear clam' de ole fence rail,
> Rabbit holler; "Whar yoh tail?"
> Bob-cat larf like he gwinter bus';
> Pole-cat stop for to see de fuss,
> De bob-cat scoot, de bear turn pale,
> An' de rabbit he skip froo de ole fence rail.
>
> "Ef yoh wanter see a tail, "sez de pole-cat; "see!
> "Mah tail's long 'nuff foh mah folks an' me!"

III.

About three o'clock on Christmas afternoon, Hogan's rifle exploded prematurely and killed a rabbit. The intense astonishment of McCue, Quinn and Phelan nerved Hogan for more glory, and he fired at every tuft of hill-weed until his cartridges were gone, and his temper too.

"Bad cess to me goon!" he shouted, "'tis twisted it do be, an' I'll thank ye for th' loan av yere piece, McCue."

"G'wan," said McCue, "'till I show ye a thrick!"—and he blazed away at a rapidly vanishing cottontail and missed. Occasionally, firing by volleys, they scored a rabbit to four rifles, and, at sunset, McCue spread out a dozen or so cotton-tails on the newly fallen snow before the door of the hill shanty. Phelan wiped his brow with the back of his fist.

"Phwere's th' naygur?" he demanded.

Hogan looked at his watch and began to swear, just as Cassius appeared over the hilltop, a tin box under his arm, and on his face a smile of confidence.

"Have ye th' ould Tom!" demanded Quinn, as Cassius shuffled up and, depositing the tin box on the doorstep, looked cheerfully around.

"Evenin', gemmen, evenin'," said Cassius, licking his lips and leaning down to pinch the fat rabbits lying in a row; "Kinder cold dishycre Chris'mus, gemmen. 'Spec we gwinter 'sperience moh snow—"

"Have ye the cat?" repeated Quinn sternly.

"'Cose I has" said Cassius indignantly, "an' I'se come foh de cash—"

"Phwat's that!" snarled Hogan.

"Hould a bit!" interposed Quinn; "is the tom in the box now?"

"'Cose he is," repeated Cassius; "yaas, dasser mighty fine kitty, dat is! Hit ain't no or'nary cat, hit ain't,—no sah. Dasser pole-cat, sah, dat is!"

"'Tis a Dootch cat!" said Phelan.

"Sure Poles is Dootch, too," observed McCue; "Phwat are ye waitin' for I dunno?" he added, scowling at the darkey.

"I'se lingerin' foh mah cash," said Cassius.

"G'wan!" said Phelan briefly.

Cassius turned an injured face from one to the other. There was a hostile silence. Phelan produced a flour sack and threw the rabbits into it, one by one.

"'Scuse me, gemmen," began Cassius,—when an exclamation from Quinn silenced him and drew the attention of all to a black-and-white object advancing across the snow toward the shanty.

"Lan's sake!" muttered Cassius, "pole-cat in de box gwineter draw all de pole-cats in dishyere county!"

"'Tis a rabbit!" said McCue, seizing his gun.

"It's a cat!" said Hogan, "d'yez mind th' tail of ut!"

"Dat ain't no cat," said Cassius contemptuously, "dasser skunk."

"Skoonk is it? An phwat's a skoonk, ye black mutt?" demanded Mc-Cue. At the same instant Phelan fired and missed; Quinn, paralysed with buck-fever, clutched his rifle, mouth agape, while Hogan, in an access of excitement, began shouting and kicking the darkey from snowdrift to snowdrift.

"Now will ye grin!" he yelled; "G'wan home ye omadhoun!—"

"Leggo mah wool!" retorted the darkey, and rose from the snow with sullen alacrity: "Wha' foh yoh yank mah kinks?"

"Faith then, fur luck an' bad-luck," said Hogan and followed McCue into the deserted shanty.

A moment later, Quinn and Phelan came back after an eager but fortunately fruitless quest for the game, and McCue and Hogan issued from the shanty, bearing the tin box, ready to return to the barracks.

"Me heavy hand on th' naygur!" growled McCue: "he's gone, where?—I dunno, but he'll carry the bag o' rabbits or me name's not McCue! Call him, Hogan."

"Come out, ye bat-o'-th'-bog, ye! Where are ye now!—the Red Witch o' Drumgoole follow ye!" shouted Hogan, tramping around the shanty and poking under the steps.

"Lave th' black scut," said McCue with dignity, "I'll carry the sack. Have ye th' sack?" he added, turning to Phelan.

"I have not," said Phelan, "'twas there foreninst the shanty."

"Now the red itch o' Drumgoole on him!" shouted McCue. "Usha, musha, he's gone wid the sack, an' divil a bit or a sup av a shtew ye'll eat the night! Sorra the rabbit he's left!—me heavy hand on him an' his!— may the saints sind him sorrow this blessed night!"

"We have th' ould tom in th' box," said Quinn, with a significant flourish of his rifle.

"There's no luck in it—Care killed a cat, an' worrit the kittens. Begorra!—I'll kill no cat at all, at all!" replied McCue superstitiously.

"May the Dootch robbers choke whin they sup this night!" shouted Phelan; "Wirra the day I set eye on the naygur an' his Dootch whippets!"

"They'll have no luck, mark that!—McCue!" said Hogan: "We've their Tom in a box an' they'll have no luck!"

They gathered up their rifles in silence; McCue carried the box; one by one they filed down the darkening hillside toward the village where already a lantern or two glimmered along the stockade and the bugles were sounding the evening call.

When the sportsmen reached the barracks, and it became known that the Jägers' tom-cat had been captured, the regiment went wild with enthusiasm. It was decided not to open the box at once, because the cat might hastily migrate toward the familiar barracks of the Jägers; but Quinn, the prime mover in the capture of Thomas, was selected a delegate of one to present the box to Colonel Bannon as a surprise and a Christmas gift from the whole regiment.

So, that night, the regiment ate their Christmas dinner in eager anticipation, and their hilarity was scarcely marred by Hogan's report that the Jägers' barracks resounded with a joyous din of feasting and song.

"May th' banshee worrit thim! Let them be wid their futther—an'—mutther! May the red banshee sup with them in hell!" said Quinn as he rose in obedience to the orderly who said the Colonel would receive him.

He took the tin box gingerly, for the animal inside was very lively, and he followed the orderly to the door of the messroom in the officer's quarters.

Here the orderly left him a moment but returned directly and whispered:

"The colonel knows it's the Dootch cat ye have,—but ye'll say ye bought it. Sure he's a dacent man, is Colonel Bannon, an' no love lost betwixt him an' Fallback. Are ye ready now?"

"Yis," said Quinn firmly, forage cap in one hand, box in the other: "is the rigiment outside on the parade?"

"It is, an' ready to cheer."

"Then in I go," said Quinn.

The colonel sat at the head of the table, flanked by his staff and line officers. His face, a little red with Christmas cheer, was gravely composed for the occasion. His officers, to a man, beamed with anticipation.

"Quinn," said the Colonel.

"Sorr," said Quinn, standing at attention.

"This is a very pleasant occasion," said the Colonel, "and I am gratified that my men have remembered their colonel upon this blessed day. I am told you have a surprise for me, Quinn."

"Yis sorr,—a cat, sorr."

"A cat!" said the Colonel in affected surprise.

"We've lost our goat, sorr, but we'll conshole our sorrow wid a cat, sorr—Colonel Bannon's cat if you plaze, sorr."

The Colonel's eyes twinkled.

"'Tis a dacent kitty, sorr," said Quinn, undoing the rope that held the lid; "a Dootch Kitty they do say from Poland, sorr, where we sint for a dozen an' this is the pick o' them."

The Colonel suppressed a smile; the officers gurgled.

"I have the spachless honor, sorr," said Quinn, placing the box on the table before the Colonel,—"I have the unmintionable deloight in presinting to our beloved Colonel in the name av his beloved rigiment, this illegant kitty!"

And he took off the lid.

There was a silence. Suddenly a long slender black and white creature sprang from the box to the table, flourishing a beautiful bushy tail; there came a yell, a frightful stampede, a crash of glass, a piteous shriek from the Colonel under the sofa: "Quinn! Quinn! Ye murtherin' scut! 'Tis a skoonk! Usha, but I'll have yer life fur this night's work!"

And Quinn, taking his nose firmly in both hands, pranced away like one demented—fled for his life through the falling snow of that blessed Christmas night.

In the barracks of the Jägers was song and jest and Christmas cheer:— shouting and feasting and heart-friendships, and the intermittent din of trombones.

Cassius, feeding to repletion in the kitchen with a bowl of rabbit stew between his knees, paused to hold his aching sides because it hurt him to laugh when he ate. Beside him on the floor, Thomas licked his whiskers, and yawned and stared into the dying fire.

SMITH'S BATTERY

A new warre e're while arose —*LOVELACE.*

Impotent Pieces of the Game He plays
Upon this Checker-board of Nights and Days;
Hither and thither moves, and checks, and slays,
And one by one back in the Closet lays.
                          FITZGERALD.

I.

On the evening of the 15th the cavalry left by moonlight, riding along the railroad toward Slow-River-Junction. The bulk of the infantry followed two days later, leaving behind them "The Dead Rabbits,"—a New York regiment,—a squad of cavalry, and Smith's four-gun battery, to garrison a hamlet inhabited principally by mosquitoes.

The hamlet of Slow-River contained a red brick church, some houses, a water-tank, and a race-track. The "Dead Rabbits" established their warren in the race-track sheds, the cavalry guarded the railway and water-tank, and Smith's battery decorated the graveyard around the red brick church.

The inhabitants of Slow-River, barring the mosquitoes, had mostly disappeared toward Dixie before the arrival of Wilson's division. When Wilson moved on toward the Junction, leaving behind him the "Dead Rabbits,"—and Smith's Battery to take care of them—the non-combatant population of Slow-River numbered two,—not including an Ethiopian of no account.

Smith, of Smith's Battery, had constituted himself an inquisition of one. The Reverend Laomi Smull, pastor of the brick church took the oath of allegiance and smacked the Book with moist thick lips. Mrs. Ashley, the remaining inhabitant of Slow-River, widow of a Union officer killed in the early days of the war, took the oath earnestly, then told Smith who she was and received his apologies with sensitive reserve.

"I wished to take the oath," she said: "I have not had my country brought so near for many months."

The Reverend Laomi Smull, clasped his soft fingers together and surveyed the firmament while Mrs. Ashley brushed the tears from her blue eyes. When she thanked Smith for the privilege of publicly acknowledging her country, the Reverend Laomi nodded and closed his small eyes as though in ecstatic contemplation of a soul regenerated.

"Where's the nigger?" inquired Smith when Mrs. Ashley had gone back to her cottage below the church.

"Do you refer to our unfortunate coloured brother?" suggested the reverend gentleman.

"Oh yes—of course," said Smith, fidgeting with his sabre.

"Abiatha is angling from the bridge," said Smull wagging his double chin till his collar creaked.

"What is he fishing for," inquired Smith, who was an angler.

"Fish," said the Reverend Laomi, and entered his church with more agility than his fat bulk appeared to warrant.

At the door he turned to cast one last sly glance at the firmament.

Smith, distrustful, and of the earth earthy, walked back to the graveyard, lifting his sabre to prevent the clanking of the scabbard on fallen gravestones.

"Look out for that pastor," he said to Steele: "if I know a copperhead from a copper kettle he's one with double fangs."

"You think he may play tricks?" asked Steele, toasting a rasher of bacon on the coals before his feet.

"Yes, I do. He'll get no passes from me, I can tell you. I'm going up into the church tower. Is there a bell there?"

"A cracked one," said Steele.

"I'll take the clapper out," observed Smith. He accepted a bit of bacon from Steele, laid it on a morsel of hardtack, munched silently for a few minutes, then washed his breakfast down with a tin of coffee, returned Steele's salute, and entered the church through the vestry. Climbing the belfry ladder on tiptoe, cap in hand, he could not prevent the ladder from creaking. So, when he stepped out on the loosely laid planks beside the bell, he found the Reverend Laomi Smull leaning on the belfry-ledge, preoccupied with the sky.

"Oh," said the reverend gentleman with a start, "is it my young friend, Captain Smythe?"

"Smith," said the officer dryly, and felt in the bell for the iron clapper.

"Where is the clapper?" he added turning on Smull.

The Reverend Laomi regarded him calmly.

"I do not know," he said.

To search the person of the minister was Smith's first impulse; Smull divined it and smiled sadly.

"He's thrown it from the tower where he can find it," thought Smith. Then he drew a jackknife from his blouse, cut the two bell-ropes and let them drop to the tiled floor far below. The thwack of the ropes echoed through the silent church; Smith apologised for the military precaution and stepped to the tower parapet. There he could look out over the ravaged country toward the Junction where rumour reported an ominous concentration of Union troops. He could see the water-tower and the railroad and cavalry patroling the embankment in the morning sunshine. He could see the weather-stained sheds of the race-track where the "Dead Rabbits" prowled, a nuisance and sometimes a terror to everybody except the enemy. Behind him he heard the Reverend Laomi pattering about over the loose planks that formed the belfry flooring.

"I shall station a signal officer here," he said without turning.

"Sir," stammered the minister.

"I am sorry," said Smith impatiently: "we need the church more than you do."

"I agree with you," said Smull in a peculiarly soft voice.

"I am sorry to exclude you—" began Smith turning,—and those words had wellnigh been his last, for one leg slipped through an unexpected fissure between the planks, and he clutched a beam beside him and drew himself up, deadly pale.

He looked at Smull; the clergyman overwhelmed him with congratulations on his escape from pitching headlong to the tiled floor below. He spoke of the mercy of Providence, of the miracles of the Most High; he deplored the condition of the belfry floor; he reproached himself for not noticing the fissure.

"I did not notice it either—when I came up," said Smith.

He followed Smull down the ladder and out of the church, returning the reverend gentleman's salute gravely. Then he ordered Steele to use the church for barracks and march his men in without delay.

"Into the church?" repeated Steele.

"I guess Union soldiers won't desecrate this church or any other church," said Smith savagely, and turned on his heel.

On his way to the river he passed Mrs. Ashley's cottage; she was hanging a home-made flag over the porch; the stars and stripes were not symmetrical, but they were stars and stripes.

She stood on the top of a ladder, hammering tacks and holding the red, white, and blue folds in her pretty mouth. Occasionally she hammered one pink-tipped finger instead of a tack; at such moments she repeated, "Oh dear!"

Smith, cap in hand, offered to hold the ladder; Mrs. Ashley thanked him and continued to hammer serenely, until she remembered her ankles and descended precipitately. Then Smith climbed the ladder, drew out all the tacks Mrs. Ashley had hammered in, rehung the "symbol of light and law," draped and nailed it with military rigidity, and descended, covered with perspiration and mosquito bites.

Mrs. Ashley, cool and sweet in a white gown and black sash, thanked him and offered him a cup of tea under the magnolias. He accepted and sat down, sabre between his knees, to mop his face and evade mosquitoes until she returned with two cups of cold tea, creamless and sugarless.

"I have some limes—if you wish,—Captain Smith," she ventured, holding out the golden-green fruit in her smooth palm.

He thanked her and squeezed a lime into his tea.

Overhead, among the magnolia blossoms, the summer harmony had already begun with the deep symphony of bees; butterflies hovered under the perfumed branches; a grasshopper clicked incessantly among the myrtle vines.

Mrs. Ashley rested her chin on her wrist and looked at nothing. A breeze began to stir the folds of the draped flag over the porch; the crimson stripes undulated, the stars rose and fell.

"We hear nothing in Slow-River," said Mrs. Ashley: "has anything important happened, Captain Smith?" Her voice was almost inaudible.

"Nothing important. The last battle went against us."

"Will there be a battle here?"

"No—I don't know—I have no reason to suppose so," he said with conscientious precision. "If by any possible chance the rebel cavalry should ride around our army we might be visited here, but," he added, "the contingency is too remote for speculation."

"Too remote for speculation?" repeated Mrs. Ashley under her breath.

Smith looked up at her—he had been watching a file of ants bearing off minute crumbs from the biscuit he was nibbling. Smith's shoulder-straps were too recent to admit of trifling, and he had an instinct that Mrs. Ashley considered him young.

"Too remote for speculation," he repeated, and touched the down on his upper lip with decision. The faintest flicker of amusement stirred Mrs. Ashley's blue eyes.

They spoke of the war, of battles on land and sea, of sieges and blockades, of prisons and of death. Listening to her passionless voice he forgot his shoulder-straps for a while. She noticed it. She spoke now as a very young hostess to a distinguished guest, and he appreciated it. Little by little they dropped into the half frank, half guarded repertoire peculiar to conventional civilisation; he recognised her beauty; she conceded his gallantry; the bees buzzed among the magnolias; the warm breeze stirred the flag.

Sitting there with white fingers interlaced, and blue eyes demurely fixed on his, she wondered at the pains she took to wind him around the least of those white fingers of hers. Yet there was reason enough for her; her reason, in concrete form, skulked up-stairs under a mound of bedclothes,— a sallow faced, furtive young man, reported killed at Bull Run,—a deserter from the Union army, a Rebel at heart, too cowardly to back his convictions,—the blight and sorrow and curse of her young life—her husband.

From the day of their marriage, she had found him out and loathed him, yet, when he marched with a loyal regiment, she had bade him God-speed.

When the news came from Bull Run she had wept and forgiven him the past, because he had been good to her in death,—he had left her the widow of a Union soldier. His apparition in Slow-River almost killed her. The Reverend Laomi Smull sarcastically bade her rejoice and put off her widow's weeds. She did neither.

Suddenly Wilson's advance was signalled from the hills beyond the river; the population of Slow-River fled Dixie-ward,—all except young Ashley, who lay sleeping off a debauch in his own gutter. The Reverend Laomi preferred to remain for several reasons. Hours after the Union cavalry dashed into the village, Ashley awoke to consciousness. When he comprehended what had happened he crawled into bed and cursed his wife and his luck and the Union Army impartially.

With what loathing did she aid in concealing him! With what desperation did she evade questions and intrusive patrols and the quiet questions of officers, courteous young fellows in blue, who accepted her word of honour with a bow and went away, deceived by a loyal woman—the wife of a coward and traitor—for that traitor's sake.

But she must play the frightful comedy to the end; she was doing it now, smiling back at Smith with eyes that caressed; with death in her heart.

When he rose to go she dropped him the quaintest and stateliest courtesy that can be dropped by a girl of twenty. His cap swept the tall grass-blades; Southern chivalry is infectious. So he passed on his way to the river.

Five minutes later the Reverend Laomi Smull appeared at the gate, smirked at the young wife, entered the cottage, and ascended the stairs with a paradoxical nimbleness that displayed two white cotton socks and inadequate attention to personal ensemble.

II.

Smith pursued his way to the river through a weed-tangled path choked with rank marshy stalks, mint, elder, and wild lady-slipper. The little brown honey-bees hummed from bud to bud; dragon-flies, balanced in mid-air on quivering wings, selected plump mosquitoes from the cloud that wavered above Smith's head, and darted so close to his ears that he dodged like a new recruit at a bullet. When he came to the narrow sluggish river, where a footbridge swayed in the amber eddies, he took his cigar from his mouth and his Bible from his pocket.

A dilapidated individual of African descent, legs dangling over the water, fishpole clasped in both black fists, glanced up at the young officer and said: "Mohnin' suh!" Smith nodded, looked hard at the darkey, shrugged his shoulders, and restored the cigar to his lips and the Bible to his pocket.

"What are you fishing for, Uncle?" he asked.

"Fishin' foh bass, suh," replied the dilapidated one.

"Catch any?"

"I done cotch free bass an' a tarrypin turkle, suh."

"Want to sell them?"

"No, suh,"

"Going to eat them all yourself, Uncle?"

"I's gotter right ter," said the angler combatively.

Smith glanced down on the river sand where, anchored to a string, three plump bass floated out in the current.

"Are you going to eat the terrapin, too, Uncle?"

"Co's I is," sniffed the darkey; "I's gotter right ter."

"Let's see it," said Smith.

The angler climbed down to the strip of sand, picked up the terrapin, and held it out to Smith.

"How much?" asked Smith.

"Two dollahs, suh."

Smith paid the money grimly, picked up the terrapin, and stood a moment watching the darkey climb back to his perch on the footbridge.

"You'll leave your footprints on the sand of time," said Smith; "you'll be in Wall Street in a month—or in Sing-Sing."

"Wha's dat yoh's a-sayin' 'bout leabin' shoeprints on de san's ob time, suh?" asked the sable one, much interested.

"Nothing. If you get any more terrapin, bring them to the artillery camp. What's your name, Uncle?"

"Nuffin', suh?"

"No name?"

"No suh, Jess 'Biah, suh."

"Oh—Alcibiades? No? Then Abiatha?"

"Yaas, suh."

"Whose darkey are you?"

"Mis' Ashley's niggah, suh."

"Oh! And the fish are for Mrs. Ashley?"

"Yaas, suh. Gwineter tote 'em back foh dinner, suh."

"Then," said Smith, "take back your terrapin too, you rascal! How dare you sell your mistress's property!"

'Biah watched the terrapin fall on the sands again, then he ruefully fished out the two dollars from some rent in his ragged coat. For a moment he struggled to tell the truth,—that Mrs. Ashley, in the present state of her finances, would rather have twenty-five cents than a dozen terrapins. Perhaps he feared Mrs. Ashley's wrath, perhaps a spark of Mrs. Ashley's pride had lodged beneath his own shirtless bosom. He said nothing, but rose, holding his fishpole in one hand, and sidled along the footbridge toward Smith, money clutched in one outstretched fist.

Smith glanced at the four silver half-dollars.

"Keep them and buy a coat, 'Biah," he said, relighting his cigar. At the same instant a big bass seized 'Biah's hook and made off with it, and 'Biah, losing his balance, dropped the silver coins into the river. Then the tattered African lost his head, too; for a minute, bass, darkey, pole, and line became a blurr on the bridge, on the sands below, and finally in the water.

When 'Biah emerged, he had the bass by the gills; later he fished out pole and line, while Smith, wading through the shallows in his cavalry-boots, poked about for the lost coins with the butt of his sabre-scabbard.

Ten minutes later 'Biah had recovered three of the half dollars. Smith had found something else,—a bundle of soaked clothes bearing United States army buttons and a second lieutenant's shoulder straps.

Instinctively he tossed the soaked packet into the alders and walked carelessly back to the footbridge where 'Biah, absorbed in disentangling his tackle, breathed hard and deep and muttered maledictions on "dat ole bull-bass what fink he know a heap moh'n ole 'Biah."

"Done drap mah hook in de hole," he puffed; "gwine ter gitter hook an' tote mah fish, suh. Mohnin', suh, mohnin',"; and 'Biah scrambled to his feet and shuffled back along the weed-grown footpath that led to Mrs. Ashley's cottage.

When the negro had disappeared, Smith leaped lightly to the sand below, parted the alders, found the bundle of clothes, and cut the cord with his sabre.

"New clothes," he muttered: "not a patch, not a rag—hello—what's this?"

He drew a soaked bit of paper from the breast-pocket of the jacket, and, standing in the alders, read the pencilled memorandum.

It was a receipt signed by the Reverend Laomi Smull for pew-rent received from Anderson Ashley. But what troubled Smith was the date, for, if Mrs. Ashley's husband had been killed at Bull Run, how could he be renting pews from the Reverend Laomi in Slow-River? Smith examined the paper closely; it read:

"Received from Anderson Ashley, Esquire, $3.75, pew-rent for Mr. and Mrs. Anderson Ashley."

The date, two months back, startled him. As he stood, holding the paper, staring vacantly at the motionless leaves on the alders, far away he heard the noon call from the artillery bugles, taken up by the cavalry trumpets at the water-tank, and passed on to the infantry around the race-track. He shoved the wet clothes under a fallen log, opened the Bible in his pocket, placed the folded receipt between the leaves, and, carrying the Bible in one hand, sword in the other, went back along the tangled footpath toward Mrs. Ashley's cottage.

III.

When the Reverend Laomi Smull displayed unexpected agility on Mrs. Ashley's staircase, Ashley himself, hearing the ascending footsteps, cowered under the bed quilts and turned cold to the marrow of every bone.

"It's me," said the reverend gentleman, entering the bed-room and waving his fat hands at the pile of quilts under which Ashley squirmed in fear: "it's me, Ashley," he repeated, disregarding the finer points of grammatical construction: "Moseby's men is in the hills and I don't know what to do."

Ashley's dissipated face emerged from the bedcovers. Fear stamped every feature with a grimace that amused Smull.

"What did you say about Moseby's men?" stammered Ashley.

"They're in the hills across the river," repeated Smull: "I seen smoke on Painted Rock."

"It's a blockade still," suggested Ashley.

"No it ain't," retorted Smull; "it's green wood burnin'—don't I know a still, hey? It's Confederate cavalry, an' they've ridden around the Yankee army, that's what they've done."

Ashley protruded his long pallid neck, looked around like an alarmed turkey, in a weed patch, and finally stared at Smull.

"What are you going to do?" he asked.

The fat cunning on Smull's face was indescribable.

"Do?" repeated Smull.

"Yes, do! Didn't Moseby tell you to ring the church bell on Sunday as many times as there was Yankee companies in Slow-River? Didn't he tell you to hang out your washing according to code,—a shirt, 'come,' two shirts 'run,' a red undershirt, 'run like the devil'—say, didn't he and you fix up the code?"

Smull's small eyes rested on the door, then on Ashley.

"The Yankee Battery Captain came to look at the bell. I threw the clapper out into the bushes," he said.

After a moment he added: "He came near falling through the plank floor. Frightened me to death—most."

Ashley's eyes met his; Smull raised a fat white hand to conceal the expression of his mouth.

"That's all very well," said Ashley petulantly, "but I reckon you'd better go. If I'm caught I'm toted out to a shootin' match—and I'll be the target too."

This observation appeared to start a new train of thought in Smull's mind. And, as he cogitated, his expression changed from sly malice to complacence, and then to that sanctimonious smirk with which, in the garden below, he had greeted Mrs. Ashley.

"Ashley," he said gravely, "I can't give no signals to Moseby, nohow. I regret," he continued piously, "I regret and see the error that the South has made in this here unchristian war."

Ashley started and fixed his bloodshot eyes on Smull, who immediately raised his own to the ceiling and addressed it unctuously: "This here unchristian war to disrupt the sacred union of the States is a offence against God and man, my young friend, and I now am brought to see, by God's grace, the sin of secession an' slavery, an' Jefferson Davis an' his wicked ways. Surely the wicked shall perish and be cut down like the grass; in the morning it flourisheth and groweth up, in the evenin' it is cut down an' withereth, my young fren'."

Ashley had grown paler and paler; his fingers clutched at the bedclothes, and he watched Smull's increasing exaltation with a horror that pinched every feature in his face.

"No!" bawled Smull: "no! no! I have took the oath of allegiance to these here United States! Blessed is the merciful, for they shall obtain mercy!"

"Shut up!" gasped Ashley, "do you want to have the Yankee provost here?"

Smull raised his hands and wept on; "Behold I am utterly enlightened! Blessed are the meek for they—"

"Stop!" shrieked Ashley, starting up in bed.

Smull glanced sharply at him, then sat down with a sigh.

"Are you going to give me up to the provost-marshal because you took the oath?" quavered Ashley, beside himself with fright and fury.

"No," said Smull wagging his double chin and meeting Ashley's glance squarely; "no, I will not bring the centurions for fear they utterly destroy thee with the sword."

Ashley, sweating with terror, looked at the reverend gentleman and wondered whether he could kill him without undue disturbance. That fat neck could not be strangled with Ashley's slender fingers; the revolver under the pillow was surer—and surer still to bring the Yankee soldiers pell-mell into the house. He had been jealous of Smull when that gentleman made his weekly call on Mrs. Ashley. He, besotted as he was, noticed the expression of Smull's small eyes when Mrs. Ashley entered the room, her innocent heart filled with plans for charities suggested by the minister. Would the

Reverend Laomi like to see Mrs. Ashley a real widow? Would he even aid fate toward the accomplishment of her widowhood?

"What the hell made you holler like that!" stammered Ashley fiercely. "Damn you," he added, "if the Yankees had come into this room, you would have left it feet first an' fit for a hole in the ground?"

The Reverend Laomi Smull looked sadly at the young man. There were tears on his fat cheeks.

"Yes, I tote a gun," sneered Ashley, tapping the pillow under his head. "Don't be a fool. Hang out your shirt and let Moseby come and clean out these Yankees, for God's sake, before they shoot me and hang you on my evidence."

"Moseby's men can't face cannon," observed Smull with sudden alacrity.

"Then lock the cannoniers in the church when Moseby signals. You can do it; you've got the keys, haven't you?"

Smull nodded.

"They'll come at night, of course; you can go and whine hymns in the church by special permit, and lock the door when the first carbine goes off."

"And the bell on Sunday?" inquired Smull: "the clapper's gone, the ropes are cut, and the Yankee Battery Captain wouldn't let me ring it nohow."

"Never mind the bell. If Moseby sees the shirt he'll attack by night, unless he's in force. If the whole Confederate cavalry has ridden around Wilson, then he'll come by day and send the Yankees packing, battery or no battery. All you've got to do is to hang out that shirt. Now go away, d'you hear?"

Smull rose and walked softly to the door.

"And," added Ashley, "if you play tricks on me you'll hang on my evidence."

Smull opened the door.

"And you'll not get my wife anyway, damn you!" finished Ashley triumphantly from the bed.

Smull turned and looked at him, then went out, quietly closing the door behind him.

At the foot of the stairs he met Mrs. Ashley, and he smirked and opened his thick moist lips to speak, but the young wife's face startled him and he closed his mouth with a snap of surprise.

"You intend to betray my husband," she said breathlessly.

"You have been listening at your husband's door," he retorted savagely.

She clenched her small hands: "What of it! With cowards and traitors and hypocrites as guests, honest people need be forewarned! Shame on you! Shame on your cloth! Shame on your oath of allegiance! You'll sell my husband to steal his wife! You'll break your oath to bring the rebel cavalry down on us!"

She brushed the tears from her eyes with both trembling hands.

"God knows," she said, "I thought I was right to hide my husband, and I think so now. Yet, if he or you betray these soldiers I shall denounce you both to the first picket!"

"Madame," began Smull in thick persuasive tones, "you wrong me—"

"Leave this house!" she said, trembling.

The Reverend Laomi bowed low, raised his eyes to the sky, sighed, and stepped out into the garden. There, before he could rearrange his expressive features, Smith met him face to face and returned the clergyman's disconcerted salute gravely.

"One moment, my dear young friend," stammered Smull.

Smith wheeled squarely in his tracks and stood rigid. Smull hesitated, passed a fat tongue over his lips, and weighed the chances. The next moment he made up his mind, glanced at the door, saw Mrs. Ashley entering the house, then leaned swiftly toward Smith and whispered.

Smith drew himself up sharply; the Reverend Laomi Smull turned and left the garden, head bowed on his breast as though in anguish of spirit. A few minutes later he brought a wash basket out of his house and pinned a single shirt to the line with a wooden clothespin. Then he ran to the woods, as fast as he could, and squatted under a rock where a tangle of brambles fell like a curtain to screen him from the eyes of the impious, indiscreet, and importunate.

IV.

Smith, holding his sabre very stiffly, raised the bronze knocker on Mrs. Ashley's door and rapped three times. Then he loosened the chin-strap of his forage-cap; drew off both gauntlets, folded them, and placed them in his belt.

As he waited for admittance he saw the flag over the porch, motionless in the still air; he heard the wild bees' harmony overhead, he heard the rustle of a summer gown behind the door. But the door did not open. He waited. A burr stuck to the crimson stripe on his riding breeches; he flicked it off with his middle finger. Presently he knocked again, once; the door opened, and Mrs. Ashley came out, smiling faintly.

"I hope you want another cup of tea," she said with the slightest gesture toward the table under the magnolias where the two chairs still stood as they had left them in the morning.

He attended her, cap in hand, to the table; when she was seated, he stood beside her.

"Is it tea, Captain Smith?" she asked, looking up at him.

He grew suddenly red, but did not reply.

"What is it then?" she repeated, smiling: "not the mere honour of my poor presence I am sure. But, as a gallant officer, you must contradict me, Captain Smith."

Fear whitened her lips that the smile had not left; she faced him with the coquetry of desperation; and the pathos of it turned him sick at heart.

"I brought the Bible to you," he said; "it is the one you swore on—the oath of allegiance. You kissed it."

She inclined her throbbing head and took it.

"Open it," he said.

She obeyed. The wet bit of folded paper caught her eyes and she held it out to Smith, saying: "This is yours."

"No!" he said, "it is yours."

She glanced swiftly up at him, caught her breath; and sat motionless, the paper clutched nervously in her fingers.

"Read it," he said in a scarcely audible voice.

She opened it; one glance was enough. Then she dropped it on the grass at her feet. Presently he stooped and recovered it.

"Yes," she said, obeying his eyes' command, "my husband is not dead. What of it?"

"Where is he?"

She was silent.

"A deserter."

"Yes."

"A traitor."

"Yes."

Smith walked to the gate, looked down the road toward the church where the artillery pickets paraded, naked sabres drawn. Then he came back.

"You are under arrest," he said, looking at the ground.

She turned a bloodless face to his, and raised one slender hand to her forehead.

"Do you doubt my loyalty?" she stammered.

He turned his back sharply.

"My loyalty?" she repeated as though dazed.

He was silent.

"But—but you administered the oath—you saw me kiss the Book," she persisted with childlike insistence.

"And your husband?" he asked, turning abruptly.

"What of him!" she cried, revolted; "I am myself!—I have a brain and a body and a soul of my own! Do you think I would damn my soul with a kiss on that Book! Do you think if I were a Rebel I would deny it to save my body?"

"You have denied it," he said. He took the Bible from her hand and opened it at a marked page:

"By their acts ye shall know them," he read steadily, then closed the Book and laid it on the table. Their eyes met; the anguish in his bore a message to her that pleaded for forgiveness for what he was about to do.

"Not *that!*—" she stammered, half rising from the chair.

He turned, drew out a handkerchief, and signalled the artillery picket, flag-fashion. Then, before he could prevent it, she was on her knees to him, there on the grass, her white face lifted, speechless with horror.

"For God's sake don't do that," he said, trying to raise her, but she clung to him and pushed him toward the gate murmuring, "Go! Go!"

Furious at the agony he was causing her, tortured by the agony it cost him, he held her firmly and told her to be silent.

"Your husband is hidden in that house," he said: "he is attempting to add to his treason by communicating with the Rebel cavalry. He tried to force your own pastor, at the point of a pistol, to hang a red shirt on his clothesline, which means 'attack!' The pastor is a good man; he had taken the oath; such villainy horrified him. To save his life in the room above he consented to hang out a signal, but the signal he hung out is a white shirt which means 'retreat.' There it is!"

He pointed angrily at the white shirt hanging on the minister's clothesline down the road.

"Now," he said, "let me do my duty."

He took her by the wrists, and looked straight into her eyes, adding:

"I'd rather be lying dead at your feet than doing what I've got to do."

"But," she cried, struggling to free herself, "but the signal! Can't you understand? The man lied! He lied! He lied! The white rag means 'attack!'"

Stupefied, he dropped her wrists and stepped back.

"Run to your battery!" she wailed, "run! run! Can't you understand! They're coming! They'll kill you!"

Scarcely had she spoken when a rifle-shot rang out from the race-track, another, another, then a scattered volley.

An artillery guard approached the garden, halted, turned, then scattered pell mell toward the church. The next moment Smith was running for his battery and shouting to Steele, who, mounted, cantered among the gravestones, and hurried the panic-stricken cannoniers to their stations.

A frightful tumult arose from the race-track, where the "Dead Rabbits," taken utterly unprepared by a cloud of Confederate cavalry, ran like rabbits very much alive. Through them galloped the Confederate riders, heavy sabres dripping to the hilt. The Union cavalry at the water-tank was overwhelmed; the gray-jacketed troopers, shouting their "Hi! yi! yi! yi!"

wheeled into the village, shaking a thousand glittering sabres; but here they met a blast of cannister from the churchyard that sent them reeling and tumbling back to the race-track, now swarming with the entire Confederate division.

Smith's battery, limbered up, filed out of the churchyard, while Smith, looking annihilation in the face, saw the last of the "Dead-Rabbits" legging it for the woods. He turned with a groan to Steele, and Steele said, "Ride for it, if we're to save the guns! The whole rebel cavalry is here!"

Bullets began to sing into the bewildered column; the cannoniers struggled with the horses and swore. Suddenly a shell fell squarely on the church tower and burst.

"They've got artillery; we're goners!" shouted a teamster.

Smith drew his sabre and raised it high above his head: "Battery forward!" he cried: "by the left flank! Gallop!"

"God help us," gasped Steele.

Team after team dashed into position, dropped their guns, and wheeled into station behind. Smith dismounted and, standing by gun No. 1, began to make calculations, pad and pencil in hand. Presently he gave his orders; a shrapnel shell was rammed home, the screw twisted to the elevation, then:

"Fire!"

A lance of flame pierced the white cloud, the shell soared away toward the race-track and burst beyond it.

Before gun No. 2 could be fired, a roar broke from the wooded heights close to the left, and a flight of shells struck Smith's battery amidships. For a moment it was horrible; teams were butchered, guns dismounted, cannoniers torn to shreds.

"Steele, bring that limber up!" shouted Smith; "they shan't have every gun!"

Steele seized the bridle; the terrified animals lashed out right and left, threatening to kick the traces to bits. A cannonier tried to hook up the gun but fell dead under the limber. A caisson blew up, hurling a dozen men into the air and stunning as many more. With blackened face and jacket, Steele reeled toward the gun again but fell on his face in the long grass.

"Bring off that gun!" shouted Smith, standing straight up in his stirrups. Crack! went the wheel, and the gun sank to its axle. Then Smith sprang from his horse and helped the gunners take the spare wheel from the caisson, roll it up over the grass, and mount it on the broken pieces. Smith hammered it on the axle, then drove home the linchpin, brushed the sweat from his half-blinded eyes, and looked around.

What he saw was the wreck of three guns and caissons, the blackened fragments of gunners and horses, and a mess of trampled grass; and beyond, between his single gun and the race-track, a long gray line, glittering with naked steel, sweeping straight upon him.

Of his battery there remained three men with him; the others were lying dead around Steele or stunned and mangled somewhere in the rank grass.

Scarcely conscious of what he did, he helped his three gunners hook the gun to the limber, then mounted and followed the gun back into the village through a constantly increasing rain of bullets. One of his men fell to the earth.

"I guess the whole Rebel army's here," he said, as though speaking to himself: "I guess I'd better get this gun to the Junction damn quick."

In front of Mrs. Ashley's cottage, as the cannon passed, Ashley, in his shirt-sleeves, fired from the window point-blank at a cannonier and shot him out of his saddle. The dead man's clutch on the team's bridle brought the gun to a halt, and the remaining gunner sprang from his saddle with an oath and dashed into the house, sabre unsheathed.

"Come back!" shouted Smith, reining in; "man! man! we've got to save the gun! Come back!" He climbed from his own saddle into the saddle of the nigh battery horse and seized the heavy rawhide. A bullet broke his wrist as he lifted it.

There was a struggle going on in the room from which Ashley had fired, but Smith did not see it; his head swam and he looked at his gun with sick eyes. For a second all round grew black, then he found himself rising from his horse's neck, and, in the road beside him, he saw Mrs. Ashley and 'Biah, holding the bridles he had dropped.

"They've hit me, I can't guide the team," he said vacantly. "I've got to save the gun, you know."

His eyes fell on the dead body of her husband, lying where it had been flung from the window among the flowers below.

"He's dead," said Mrs. Ashley; "I can't stay. Don't leave me! I can sit a horse if you will let me. I'll go with you. Don't refuse me!"

She sprang into the limber seat and clutched the railing with both hands; 'Biah followed with a howl of terror. There was a whip there; she swung the heavy rawhide and, seizing a horse by the mane, drew herself forward to the saddle, calling; "here they come! Gallop! gallop!"

With a plunge the six horses leaped forward, and tore down the road, Smith swaying in his saddle with a broken arm, the young girl, enveloped in a torrent of dust, riding the nigh horse of the wheel-team, limber and gun swaying and crashing on behind, 'Biah bouncing, jouncing, and howling intermittently.

"Guide!" called Smith faintly: "I can't."

She seized the bridles and lashed the horses. 'Biah shrieked.

"There are soldiers ahead!" she cried to him,—"Rebel infantry! They're going to fire!"

"Drive over them!" he gasped.

With a rumble, a roar, and a tearing crash, the train broke into the shouting mass of men, the scurrying wheels crunched on something, there came a flash of rifles, and Smith staggered. Before his eyes all was a bluer; he still heard the hoofs clink, the chains clash, the wheels thump and pound. Gun and limber struck an opposing body and leaped into the air; Smith's glazing eyes opened; he clung to his mount and attempted to turn.

He tried to say: "Is the wheel broken?"

She could not reply, nor did she dare turn her head to that heap in the road already far behind. Terror sealed her lips—had sealed her lips when, through the dust ahead, she saw Smull, almost under the head team's hoofs, start to run, then go down to death beneath her very eyes.

Six wild horses, a runaway limber and gun, two half-dead creatures hanging to the saddles, and a frantic darkey on the limber,—that was all of Smith's battery that tore into the Junction to the horror of Wilson and the scandal of the rank and file.

It all happened years ago; too long ago to fix the year or the date. Perhaps the incident is recorded in the archives of the Nation. Perhaps not. At all events when they had picked some stray bullets out of Smith and set his wrist in splints, he went North on furlough.

I think Mrs. Ashley went with him; and 'Biah being of no account, toted their luggage and breathed hard.

AMBASSADOR EXTRAORDINARY

> Alas! he's gone before,
> Gone to return no more,
>
> Whose well-spent life did last
> Full ninety year and past,
>
> Crowned with Eternal bliss
> We wish our souls with his.
> *Ancient Epitaph*
>
>
> Sing again the song you sung
> When we were together young—
> When there were but you and I
> Underneath the summer sky.
> GEORGE WILLIAM CURTIS.

I.

It was the season when our beloved motherland undergoes a quadrennial Caesarian operation and presents a new president to a pardonably hysterical people.

Installed in the several departments of the national incubator, newly hatched cabinet officers, destitute of the Roman Augur's sense of humour, met around the "Oracle," and parted, without the shadow of a smile; brand-new heads of departments gazed solemnly at each other, government clerks cast owlish eyes on brand-new chiefs, gloomily alert for new cues.

The Ambassador to England was named, and sent forth; at parting the President intimated to him that he was a statesman; they shook hands and looked into each other's eyes; neither relaxed a muscle. The Ambassador to Germany departed; the Ambassador to Russia followed. Other statesmen-patriots expatriated themselves with serious alacrity; a Minister descended on Brazil, another on Spain, another on Belgium; no guilty land escaped.

When His Excellency the United States Ambassador to France presented his credentials to the President of the French Republic, the guard at the Elysée presented arms, a nurse-maid wheeling a baby-carriage stopped to look, and there was a paragraph in the *Figaro* several days later.

In the Latin Quarter the American students discussed the new Ambassador.

Selby said to Severn: "There's a new Ambassador, you know; I hear he's red-headed."

Severn said to Rowden: "There's a new Ambassador, you know. I understand his family have red hair."

Rowden observed to Lambert: "I am told that the new Ambassador's daughter has red hair."

That morning the pale April sunshine, slanting through the glass-roofed studio in the rue Notre Dame, awoke Richard Osborne Elliott from refreshing slumbers. That young man, in turn, aroused Foxhall Clifford from a lethargy incident on a nuit blanche and a green table.

"Black can't turn up every time; red is bound to assist the lowly," muttered Clifford on his pillow.

At that moment Elliott, reading the *Figaro*, encountered the paragraph concerning the new Ambassador.

"Red is going to assist us," he remarked; "they say he has red hair."

"Who?" yawned Clifford.

An hour later Elliott, swathed in a blue crash bath-robe, sat in the studio sipping his morning coffee and perusing the feuilleton in the *Figaro*.

His comrade entered a moment later carrying a pair of shoes, and sat down on the floor.

"New Ambassador," repeated Clifford, lacing his patent leathers; "what do I care for Ambassadors!"

"They're good to know," observed Elliott, "they give receptions."

"Yes," sneered Clifford, "fourth of July receptions, where everybody waves little flags at every body else. I've seen trained birds do that."

"Ambassadors," insisted Elliott, "can get you out of scrapes. If you're broke they can send you home. You're not much of a patriot anyway."

"Yes, I am," snapped Clifford, "I'm loyal to the spinal marrow, but I draw the line at our diplomats."

He laced the other shoe, tied it, straightened up and rose, kicking out gently first with one leg then with the other until his trousers fell over each instep with satisfying symmetry.

"Patriot?" he went on, "I am too patriotic to countenance the status quo at our consulate, where the United States Consul sits in his shirt-sleeves and practises at a cuspidor, and where you can't get a consular certificate without being bullied by an insolent roustabout! So your new Ambassador," he continued reflectively, "can go to the devil!"

"Now you're too hasty," said Elliott; "Ambassadors are not consuls." He added dreamily, "His Excellency has a daughter—I understand."

Clifford, loitering before the mirror, unconsciously gave a smarter twist to his tie, and buttoned the snowy waistcoat in silence. When he was ready, gloved, hatted, and faultlessly groomed, he selected a blossom from a pot of fragrant pinks on the window and drew it through the lapel of his morning coat.

"Going to see Jacquette?" asked Elliott, pouring out more coffee.

"No," replied Clifford. He hummed a bar of a wedding march, strolled to the great glass window, mused a moment, sighed, whistled softly, and sighed again. There was a cock-sparrow out in the garden, hopping around, chirping and trailing his dusty wings through the gravel. A lady sparrow pecked him at intervals. The innocent courtship of the little things stirred Clifford with amorous wistfulness. He flattened his nose against the window glass and watched them, gently humming:

> "The fox and the bear,
> The squirrel and the hare,
>   The dickey-bird up in the tree,
> The roly-poly rabbits,
> So amazing in their habits,
>   They all have a mate but me,
>   But me!
>
> They all—
> They a—a—a—ll—
>   Oh, they all have a mate but me!"

Elliott listened scornfully.

"Why," said Clifford, twisting suddenly around, "should I go to school and paint Italian models—on a day like this?"

"You haven't been to the atelier in a week," said Elliott morosely. "Oh, I know what you're going to say!"

"No, I'm not," retorted Clifford.

"You are! You're going to tell me that you've seen the most wonderful girl in the Luxembourg, who must be some foreign countess! Don't I know! Haven't I heard it a thousand times? And hasn't the countess always turned up with you at some cheap restaurant?"

Clifford sat down on a camp-stool and pointed his cane toward the floor. Squinting along it at a spot of sunlight on the velvety Eastern rug, he listened in silence to Elliott's reproaches.

"Have you finished?" he asked.

Elliott girded up his bath-robe and moved off.

"Because," continued Clifford, "I have a proposition to make."

"Make it then," said Elliott, scowling.

"Well, sit down."

Elliott squatted Turk fashion on a divan, saying bitterly, "Last week you moaned and protested that you had been wasting your time. Now go on with your proposition,—but I'll not be a party to any new infatuation, let me tell you—"

Clifford began to walk up and down the studio, gloved hands clasped behind his back, head thoughtfully bent as far as his collar permitted. As he walked he twiddled his cane.

"Well?" inquired Elliott sarcastically.

Clifford came up to him and stood a moment in silence. Then he said: "Elliott, suppose we get married to twins?"

"Married!" bawled Elliott in angry astonishment.

"Irretrievably," continued Clifford gently, "suppose we go into the thing thoroughly. Suppose we become respectable!"

"I am," broke out Elliott, but the other held up five expostulating gloved fingers.

"In a way—yes, in a way. But do you know what I think? I think no man is absolutely and hopelessly respectable unless he has a wife!—Elliott, a wife—a little wifey—"

"Rubbish!" replied Elliott, rising from the divan. "And let me inform you I don't want a wife. I'm well enough as I am—if anybody should ask you. Let go of my bath-robe; I'm going to paint."

"Think," urged Clifford,—"think of being really and legally married— think of the joyful anguish—no more suppers, no more Bullier, no more tzing! la! la!—"

He removed his silk hat, skipped playfully, and pretended to kick it.

"But," he continued, with sudden soberness, "a wife—a little wifey is recompense for all pleasure—"

"Antidote, you mean—"

"No, I don't! Joy is born from the nuptial blessing. I desire to wed—"

"Who? What?"

"A lovely, spirituelle, delicate vision—unworldly and—er—passably provided for—"

"By you?"

"Partly by me—partly by an adoring father,—a fine silvery-haired old patrician, borne down by the weighty cares of his millions—do you know any of that kind, Elliott?"

"I know some silvery-haired patricians."

"Tottering under the weight of millions?"

"Yes."

"With daughters?"

"Never asked 'em."

"What about the new Ambassador? You said his daughter—"

Elliott laughed:

"Oh, he's tottering under millions, but his hair is red and I think that hers—"

"You annoy me," said Clifford, and left the studio. He paused in the garden, sniffed at the lilacs, eyes raised in contemplation of the firmament.

"Nevertheless," he said to himself, "red hair or silver hair—I'm not bigoted on the silver question. And," he added with sprightly humour, "it's 16 to 1 I call on his Excellency before the week is out."

II.

His Excellency the United States Ambassador was a sheep-faced old gentleman who became hopelessly mixed up in some railroads and escaped with impaired health and most of the stock. Wheat hit him hard a year later, and oil nearly ended him, but he became entangled in trolley wires and put them underground to save future annoyance to his legs. This naturally set him on his feet again; and he went to Washington where there is honour among—financiers, and where they practise statesmanship as she is taught. When his wife died and his daughter Amyce began to go to school, his future Excellency bobbed up and down in Congress with the caprice and abruptness of a bottled imp. The see-saw continued year after year; sometimes he had a bill passed, sometimes he blocked a bill; now and then he got other people's money, now and then other people got his money; but it evened up in the end like dominoes—if you play long enough.

Then came the new administration, the stampede for office. Before his future Excellency made up his own mind, fate shoved him into the front rank, and he asked for the French mission and the odds were against him. The President weighed him—the scales of the mint are exquisitely adjusted—and, separating the dross from the pure metal, the mind from the material, the President found him available for the diplomatic mission and told him he might have it. So he took it and went.

His Excellency's income permitted him to keep up his establishment in the rue de Sfax. Two neat attachés, military and naval, played croquet with him; his first secretary read Ollendorf to him, his daughter played hostess on national holidays, and Massenet every morning from ten to twelve. From three to four she swung in a hammock in the garden, and read Henry James.

It was at that hour and under those circumstances that Clifford first met Amyce. He was permitting his Excellency to beat him at croquet on the lawn; he loathed the game with a loathing untranslatable. He sat on the butt-end of his mallet, watching his Excellency pattering about from stake to stake, adjusting the balls with a chuckle, stooping to peer through wickets, calculating angles and split-shots.

His Excellency's heavy, sheep-like face with its silvery tuft of side-whiskers was ruddy and minutely shaved. Always scrupulously dressed, he had the air of having been neatly attired by a doll's costumer, then varnished. There was something about the old gentleman that recalled the irresponsible inertia of a manikin,—something, when he moved that resembled the automatic trot of a marionnette. He left an impression of not being responsible for either his clothes or his movements, but mutely referred you to his maker for guarantees that both were O. K. His hair was the glossy white that red hair frequently changes to; his eyes were pale hazel, lambent and vitreous as the eyes of a middle-aged sheep. His upper lip, also, seemed as though it were intended for cropping short grass.

He had taken to Clifford at once; he introduced him to the naval attaché and to the military attaché, to the first, second, and third secretaries of the Embassy. He did this partly because Clifford came armed with three good letters of introduction, partly because the United Service began to fight shy of the croquet-ground, and a substitute was necessary.

He did not, however, present him to his daughter; in fact Clifford had never even caught a glimpse of her, although on two occasions he had been bidden to dine at the Embassy. Stanley of the cavalry, the military attaché, had been pumped by Clifford without result. All he learned was that the young lady sometimes dined by herself.

However, that afternoon in early May, as Clifford sat glum and impatient on his mallet, and the Ambassador trotted about mauling the lawn, a young lady suddenly appeared under the trees by the hammock, glanced nonchalantly at his Excellency, languidly surveyed Clifford, and then, placing a hammock-pillow where it would do the most good, sat down in the hammock. It was gracefully done; she appeared to dissolve among a cloud of delicate draperies; her head indented the feather cushion; one small patent-leather toe glistened in the sunlight.

"She *is* red-haired," was Clifford's first thought; the next was: "She is a beauty,—oh, my conscience!"

She was. Her eyes were those great tender grey eyes that must have been forgotten when Saint Anthony was tortured; her skin was snow and roses. But her hair, her splendid, glistening hair, heavy and red gold!—dazzling as sunlight on floss-silk!

"It's your shot," said his Excellency for the third time.

The Ambassador won the game; he proposed another and Clifford assented with a sickly smile. Inwardly he swore that he would be presented, willy-nilly, even though he had to drag his Excellency to the hammock.

"Confound him," he thought; "have rumours of my reputation in the Quarter penetrated my country's Embassy?"

They had not; yet, it was exactly because Clifford was an artist and inhabited the Latin Quarter that the Ambassador avoided taking him to the bosom of his family. Vague and dreadful stories had been afloat in the Embassy concerning the Quarter. His Excellency had read *Trilby* too. This may have weighed with him; he had that distrust of art and artists prevalent among Anglo-Saxons. He also had the Anglo-Saxon desire to explore the Quarter for him self, one day,—if all was true as rumour had it. Therefore Clifford was doubly welcome, for his croquet, and for what the future promised when his Excellency needed a companion to the veiled mysteries of the Rive Gauche. So, on the whole, Clifford was a good man to amuse him, but not at all the kind of man to amuse Amyce.

But Fate, busy, as usual, with other people's business, began to meddle with the hammock cords where Amyce swung serenely reading Henry James.

Amyce rose just in time; there came a rapid unravelling of cords, and the collapsed hammock fell with a flop.

Flushed at the nearness of undignified disaster, Amyce shook out her fluffy skirts, Henry James tightly clasped in one hand, and looked appealingly at his Excellency.

The Ambassador started to rehang the hammock; Clifford said: "Permit me—"

"Not at all," returned the Ambassador,—but that was where he collided with Fate.

Amyce smiled and looked relieved; Clifford re-hung the hammock; Amyce thanked him. Then there was a pause during which both looked expectantly at his Excellency.

The Ambassador sullenly did his duty and took Clifford back to the lawn and beat him five games of croquet. But even this triumph was wet-blanketed, for Amyce, holding Henry James to her chin, came out to the lawn to "watch papa" and "encourage" papa," and condole with Clifford for his bad fortune. Only he knew how good that fortune had been—and, perhaps, she suspected it.

Amyce suggested tea on the lawn; his Excellency began to object, but Fate was there and took another fall out of his Excellency, for Amyce had already ordered it, and a servant appeared with tables and trays on the porch.

The Ambassador cropped thin slices of bread-and-butter; Amyce poured tea; Clifford, in a daze of love, saw everything through pink haze. From this dream he was abruptly roused by the advent of Captain Stanley of the cavalry. He saw Amyce feed the brute with tea; he heard her laugh softly when the Captain told some imbecile story or imitated Count Fantozzi. He measured the Captain, he accorded him six feet two, a pair of superb legs, and a cavalry moustache.

"Granted him cards and spades," thought Clifford, "I'll beat him yet. I know I can."

He was an honest youth with no more vanity than you or I.

III.

In the Quarter, Clifford's attitude became unbearable. Rumours were afloat that he had outgrown the Quarter and its simple lurid pleasures; that he had put away childish things; that he consorted exclusively with the ostentatious great. When garden parties were given at the English Embassy, Clifford's name figured among the guests,—and the Quarter read it in the *Figaro* and chafed.

Elliott, incredulous at first, observed the absence of Clifford from all Quarter rites with astonishment and grief. The studio grew lonelier and lonelier. Elliott drank cocktails and brooded.

"See here," he blurted out, one day, "how long are you going to keep this up?"

"What?" replied Clifford, placing violets in his buttonhole.

"This confounded pose of yours—this tolerating the Quarter—this Embassy nonsense!"

"I prefer it to Bullier," said Clifford—"or," he added maliciously, "to the 'Bal à l' Hôtel-de-Ville.'" Then he put on his gloves, humming:

> "Des chapeaux melon et des chapeaux rond!"
> Dame? c'est pas d'la petite bière!—eu!
> Tous ces gueux là
> Ils ont pigé ça
> 'A la Belle Jardinière!—eu!"

Elliott arose in fury.

"Very well," he said, "go and eat thin bread-and-butter and talk to fat princesses!—go and learn baccarat from that yellow mummy Fantozzi!—go and play imbecile croquet games with his Excellency and marry his daughter and live in the Parc Monçeaux. But you'll regret it! oh yes, you'll be sorry. And you'll think of the Luxembourg and of Jacquette and the old studio, and you'll hear a nursery full of babies squawling and you'll see

Fantozzi leering at your wife and—"

Clifford looked around with gently raised eyebrows.

"I won't be back to dinner," he said amiably.

"Where are you going—dressed like that!" burst out Elliott with new violence.

"Going to shoot pigeons in the Bois."

They stood for a while in silence. Presently Elliott arose, went over to his manikin, and began to dress it; the manikin at present was doing duty as a French fireman for Elliott's great picture, "Saved!"

He mechanically placed the brass pot-helmet on the manikin's papier-mâché head, twisted the neck viciously, straightened out a sawdust stuffed arm, placed a rope in the hand, and closed the jointed fingers. Then he hauled out his easel, opened his colour box, and clattered the brushes.

Clifford watched him.

Elliott set his palette rainbow fashion, touched the canvas with the tip of his third finger, rolled a badger brush in rose-dorée, and began to glaze.

"Don't glaze yet," said Clifford.

"Why?" snapped Elliott without turning.

"Because you make the flames too pink."

"What do you know about flames or pictures or glazing?" said Elliott bitterly. "Go and shoot pigeons and get married."

Clifford went out haughtily; yet there was an unaccustomed pang in his breast. He suddenly realised how utterly out of it he was; he began to comprehend that he was afloat on the Rubicon in a very leaky boat. There was nothing to warrant his hopes of Amyce except a superb self-confidence. He saw he was alienating the Quarter;—he noticed it now, as he walked, when Selby passed with a constrained smile, when Lambert bowed to him with unaccustomed rigidity, when, as he crossed the Luxembourg, Jacquette, passing with Marianne Dupoix, averted her pretty eyes.

He knew that an announcement of his engagement would be followed by excommunication from the Quarter. He had intended, in the event of betrothal, to confine his Quarter visits to Elliott and Selby and Rowden, but the prospect of involuntary exclusion had small attraction for him. He thought of Jacquette; the odour of violets from a street flower-stand recalled her.

He was in a bad humour when he reached the Tir aux Pigeons. Before he entered he saw Captain Stanley laughing on the lawn with Amyce. That, and the apparition of Fantozzi, completed his irritation and his score at the traps was ridiculous.

"You play croquet better," observed his Excellency, at his elbow.

That was the last straw, and Clifford forced a smile and went across the lawn.

"What was your score?" asked Amyce, looking up at him from the shade of her white parasol. He was compelled to confess it.

Fantozzi, interrupted in the recountal of recent personal experience with an electric tram-car, raised his eyebrows superciliously.

"Pooh," said Captain Stanley, "everybody gets out of form at times."

Clifford looked gratefully at his generous rival; Amyce also raised her eyes to the well-knit military figure. Generosity is sometimes its own reward—sometimes it even receives perquisites.

Fantozzi continued his dramatic recital of the discourteous tram-car.

"I would come in a tram electrique—Mademoiselle—behold me on the corner street!—the tram approach!—I nod my head!—he do not hear me—"

"Couldn't hear you nod your head?" inquired Stanley sympathetically.

"Wonder his brains didn't rattle," muttered Clifford to himself.

"I nod! I nod!" repeated Fantozzi with mercurial passion; "I permit myself to make observation to stop! Cease! arrest ze tram! He regard me insolent! the tram vanishes itself! I am left on the corner street! The miserable laugh!"

"Are you sure you called to the motor-man to stop?" asked Stanley gravely.

"Parbleu! I did say stop! I said it! I did hear myself say it!"

"Mr. Clifford," said Amyce, "who is shooting?" She raised her lorgnettes: "Oh, Count Routier! Do you know I am not pleased to see little birds shot. Captain Stanley, it is your turn next. Have you no pity for those poor pigeons?"

"Monsieur Clifford had," said Count Fantozzi.

Amyce frowned a little; Fantozzi, prepared to laugh at his own wit, winced at the silence.

"Well," said Stanley, "I must go and perform. Shall I miss every bird—is it your pleasure?" he added, looking at Amyce.

Amyce smiled, her face was an enigma.

"Do as you please, I wish you good fortune in any event," she said.

Fantozzi pretended to shudder for the pigeon victims; Stanley walked thoughtfully across the lawn; Clifford, on fire with mixed emotions of jealousy and love, pretended to be absorbed in the shooting. He glanced indifferently at the gaily-dressed groups on the green, recognised some people and bowed, returned the salutes of other people who recognised him, and finally sat down on a camp-stool near Amyce.

Others were joining the group; a lieutenant of hussars, in sky-blue and silver, a brilliant-eyed diplomatic group from Brazil, one or two tall Englishmen, scrubbed pink, and finally his Excellency the United States Ambassador.

Clifford loathed them all; yet, Amyce was very kind to him. While Captain Stanley stood shooting, she scarcely glanced at the traps, and when that sober-faced young cavalryman sauntered back and confessed he had killed every bird, she scarcely raised her eyebrows. Was it displeasure?

"It is but a sport brutal," whispered Fantozzi close behind her.

"Like your bull-fights," said Clifford, seriously. He and Stanley were quits. It was war with Fantozzi.

The Spanish attaché with the Italian name glared blankly at Clifford who returned his glance wickedly.

"Croquet is better sport," bleated his Excellency, accepting a glass of champagne and a thin slice of bread-and-butter.

Clifford's turn came again at the traps; he missed right and left. He heard Fantozzi laugh. When he came back Amyce had gone away with his Excellency and Captain Stanley. However, Fantozzi was there and Clifford succeeded in picking a quarrel with him and followed it with a smile and the slightest touch on the Count's shirt front.

Fantozzi turned a delicate green, then crimson. Then he went away to the club-house and called for a cab, and drove to his Embassy at a speed that interested pedestrians along the Champs Elysée.

Clifford withdrew a little later to the Café Anglais where he sullenly brooded and dined too freely. About nine o'clock, he went to see Stanley; at half-past ten a handsome young Spaniard called to pay his respects and bring courteous greetings from Fantozzi.

Clifford left the Spaniard and Stanley deeply interested in each other's society, and took a cab to the United States Embassy, where, as an artist, he was to oversee the decorative preparations for next evening's garden-party. His Excellency had requested it; Amyce appeared pleasantly cordial; so Clifford went to direct the hanging of lanterns and gaily-coloured scarfs, and, incidentally to propose marriage to his Excellency's only daughter.

His Excellency was smoking a cigar on the lawn as Clifford entered, mentally thanking all the saints that it was too late to play croquet. Servants moved through the shrubbery; a few lanterns threw an orange light among the chestnut branches.

His Excellency was in good humour; he pattered about, as though driven by improved mechanism; he chuckled at times that irritating chuckle incident to victory at croquet.

"We'll have electric lights next week," he said; "ever play croquet by moonlight?"

"There is no moon to-night," said Clifford, triumphantly.

"I know it," sighed his Excellency.

Presently the Ambassador exhibited a desire to interfere with Clifford's directions to the servants; he insisted on mounting a ladder and fussing with a string of crimson lanterns. The first, second, and third Secretaries of the Embassy were summoned to steady the ladder; Clifford saw an opportunity and seized it.

Amyce, who had been standing on the porch, observed Clifford's advance with mixed sentiments.

"Are all the lanterns hung?" she asked.

"No," said Clifford, "his Excellency has proposed modifications."

"Man proposes—" began Amyce, gaily, then stopped.

The silence was startling.

Presently Amyce picked a rose from the vine at her elbow.

"Is it mine?" asked Clifford.

"Yours? I—I don't know."

She held it a moment, then he took it.

"And the giver?" he whispered.

"I—I don't know," said Amyce.

"Then," said Clifford, "I shall take her—as I took the rose;" and he moved toward her up the steps.

At that moment Fate, who had been listening as usual, somewhere among the shadows, took a hand in the proceedings; there was a crunch of footsteps on the gravel walk, the dim glimmer of a cigar, and Captain Stanley entered the house, bowing pleasantly to Amyce and casting a look at Clifford that meant, "Follow me."

Before Clifford could move, Amyce passed him with a pale smile and crossed the lawn toward the lantern-hangers.

His emotions were indescribable; he damned Stanley, then, buoyed with the intoxicating thought that Amyce had not refused him, he went into the house and found Stanley waiting in the smoking-room.

"Well," said Clifford ungraciously.

Stanley appeared a trifle surprised but said: "I'm sorry you are in this mess, old fellow. Fantozzi naturally wants a shot at you."

An unpleasant sensation passed through Clifford; Fantozzi and his shot were repulsive at the moment.

"When?" asked Clifford.

"To-morrow at sunrise. I've notified Bull."

Clifford grew angry: "Then he can have his shot," he said savagely, and sat down for a conference, interrupted about eleven o'clock by his Excellency.

The Ambassador was in no mood for bed. Perhaps something in the lighted lanterns had roused the long smouldering spark of revelry, dormant in every masculine bosom. Being an Anglo-Saxon he knew of no lighter gaiety than heavy drinking. He began to tell stories—quite pointless tales—and he would not let Clifford go, and he spoke vaguely of wonderful brands of whisky past and whisky to come. He sat there, his limpid hazel eyes meeker than any lambkin's, a carefully dressed lay-figure, irresponsible to God and man, and for whom nobody was responsible except his Constructor.

About midnight he became entirely automatic; his eyes seemed to plead for somebody to wind him up and set him going again.

"When he gets this way he has a tendency to wander," whispered Stanley; "I usually lock him in his room; if I didn't he'd be all over town—like an escaped toy."

Clifford went out on the porch; Stanley followed.

"At sunrise," said Clifford soberly. "Will you call for me in a carriage?"

"At sunrise," replied Stanley offering his hand.

Then Clifford went away, and Stanley, lingering to watch him to the gate, walked slowly back to the smoking-room.

To his horror his Excellency had disappeared. The west porch door swung wide open.

"He'll be all over Paris!" groaned Stanley smiting his head with both hands.

IV.

Clifford did not go back to the studio; he took a long drive in a cab to steady his nerves. He alternately thought of Amyce, of Fantozzi, of his Excellency's incoherent stories, of Elliott and the studio,—and, perhaps, of Jacquette. Two hours before dawn he found himself standing in front of Sylvain's; and, wondering why he had wandered there, he went in and upstairs. The long glittering room reeked with cigar smoke; voices rose harshly from the disordered tables; a piano tinkled faintly on the floor above. He looked at his watch; it lacked an hour of the appointed time when he was to meet Stanley with the carriage at the studio. He turned toward the portal impatiently; somebody entered as he opened the leather doors; he glanced up and met his Excellency face to face.

His Excellency began a mechanical trot into the room; Clifford involuntarily detained him and the Ambassador stopped obediently as though somebody had arrested his running-gear. He examined Clifford with mild vitreous eyes as though he had never before seen him. He was perfectly docile, perfectly contented to be started again in any new direction. He needed a few repairs; Clifford saw that at once. It would never do to send his Excellency home with such a hat and collar and tie; the personnel at the Embassy must never see his Excellency in such disorder.

"Come," said Clifford gently. There was a cab at the door; he stowed his Excellency away in one corner and followed, ordering the cabby to hasten to the studio in the rue Notre Dame. There was not much time to lose when they reached the studio. Clifford attempted to adorn his Excellency with clean linen, but found that it might take some hours as the machinery had run down and the Ambassador evinced an unmistakable inclination to slumber. He seated his Excellency in an arm-chair, and hurriedly changed his own evening dress for morning clothes. Then he went up to Elliott's bedroom, but that young man's bed was untenanted and undisturbed. The Ambassador slept peacefully in the studio; after a moment's thought Clifford scribbled a note:

"DEAR ELLIOTT:—
When you come in please give this gentleman clean linen and a new hat and brush his clothes and send him to the United States Embassy p. d. q.
"Yours,
"CLIFFORD."

As he finished he heard carriage-wheels in the street outside and he thrust the note into his Excellency's hat-band, jammed the hat on the slumbering diplomat's head, and hurried out to the street where Stanley and Bull were waiting in the dim grey of the coming dawn.

"Not had coffee!" exclaimed Bull; "nonsense, it's traditional!"

"We'll take it at St. Cloud," said Stanley. "Are you ready, old fellow?"

The carriage door slammed, the wheels rattled faster and faster.

"By the way," said Clifford, "his Excellency paid me a visit this morning. I'll see he gets home in good shape."

"Thank heaven!" cried Stanley; "I've been hunting him all night!"

A moment later he looked earnestly at Clifford: "Is your hand steady?"

"Yes," said Clifford pleasantly.

"You'd better shoot closer than you did at the pigeons," suggested Bull.

"Why? Is Fantozzi a good shot?"

"Rotten," said Stanley.

"He's the more to be feared then," observed Bull cynically.

"Why, you know," confessed Clifford with a frank smile, "I feel certain that I'm not going to be hit. I was nervous last night, but not on that account."

And he smiled confidently, thinking of Amyce.

"But," insisted Bull, "are you going to hit your man?"

"Perhaps. What bosh it all is, anyway," laughed Clifford.

V.

It was not yet sunrise when Elliott, entering the studio with Selby, lighted the gas and started to prepare for bed. As Elliott turned up the gas Selby encountered the owl-like eyes of his Excellency, blinking, limpid, vacant.

"What's that?" he said nervously. But when he saw the evening dress, the disordered tie, the hat, he approached the Ambassador curiously. Presently he reached up, slipped the note from his Excellency's hat-band, opened it, read it in silence, then passed it to Elliott without a word.

"May I ask who you are?" said Elliott. His Excellency bleated and waited for somebody to set him in motion, with placid confidence. Elliott frowned. This then was one of those who had lured Clifford from the fold!—this wicked old creature, apparently paralysed by depravity, planted in an arm-chair! His ruffled hat accused him! His crumpled tie, coyly peeping from behind one ear, convicted him!

"Call a cab," said Elliott thickly.

His Excellency betrayed no emotion; his round eyes followed Elliott's movements with trustful tranquillity. When Selby returned, saying the cab was there, Elliott assisted the Ambassador to his feet; but, what was his surprise and indignation to see that his Excellency was entirely capable of movement. For, once set in motion, the Ambassador began trotting all about the room with perfect solemnity and, apparently with keen satisfaction.

"I beg your pardon," said Elliott coldly, "your cab is waiting." He might as well have talked to the statues in the Louvre. Then he lost his self-control and, taking his Excellency by one sleeve he led him to the arm-chair and seated him.

"Aged man," he said, "are you not mortified? You have dragged my comrade into your depraved society! You've taken him away from the Latin Quarter, you've stuffed his head full of marriage nonsense, of ambition, of desire for wealth and position. How dare you come here and ask for a hat and a collar!"

"Do you intend to ruin Clifford at baccarat?" demanded Selby.

"Or marry him to anybody?" added Elliott hoarsely.

"Who are you?" cried Selby; "are you a corrupt diplomat? Or are you merely a wicked old man on a spree?"

"He can't wear that hat; it won't stay on," observed Elliott. Selby took a woman's bonnet from the manikin, placed it on his Excellency's head and tied the strings under his chin. Elliott threw Clifford's covert-coat over his Excellency's shoulders.

"That bonnet will keep him from catching cold," he said, "it may teach him a lesson, too, when his wife sees it."

His Excellency unmoved, serene, surveyed Elliott from under his bonnet.

"Come," said Selby, and they set the Ambassador in motion again, out the door, along the garden to the street where the cab stood. The cabby stared a little, but Elliott said grimly: "Take him to the United States Embassy with Mr. Clifford's compliments. And leave word that he can keep the bonnet for future use."

About that time, several miles away in the forest of St. Cloud, Clifford was taking careful aim at Fantozzi's anatomy, and Fantozzi was returning the attention. A moment later two insignificant reports broke the silence; both men, very pale, stood motionless; two tiny shreds of smoke floated upward through the tender foliage above.

Captain Stanley turned to Fantozzi's second, they conferred for a moment, then Stanley turned away to avoid a smile and went hastily up to Clifford.

"He says he doesn't want another shot; he says honour is satisfied; look out, I believe he's preparing to embrace you!"

In vain Clifford attempted to shun the fervid reconciliation, in vain he dodged Fantozzi's tears and hugs. Fantozzi would not leave him, not he! Clifford dexterously escaped a kiss aimed at his cheek.

There were compliments from seconds, from the surgeon, from the principals. Undismayed, Stanley tackled the procés-verbal. Bull locked up his instruments, the carriages were summoned by handkerchief signal; the duel was at an end. Gaily they drove back to breakfast—a red-hot Spanish breakfast at Fantozzi's apartments. They toasted each other, they toasted the two nations, Spain and the United States.

Stanley, obliged to report at his Embassy, excused himself and promised to return. The breakfast continued; Fantozzi played exquisite Spanish airs on the guitar between courses; his handsome attaché accompanied him on the piano.

Bull, tactless to the back-bone, sang "Cuba Libre," but nobody cared and everybody laughed. Afternoon came; they still breakfasted. Fantozzi insisted on a bout with the foils; Clifford accepted; they broke a handsome vase and some saucers.

About four o'clock, while Bull was singing "Cuba Libre" for the eleventh time by special request, Stanley entered, glanced gravely around, and motioned Clifford to come outside. Clifford went, closing the door behind him, troubled by the stony solemnity of Stanley's visage.

"What's up?" he inquired.

"This," said Stanley with inscrutable eyes. "His Excellency was sent home in a cab this morning, wearing a woman's bonnet and your covert-coat!"

"What!" gasped Clifford.

"Also with your compliments and a request that his Excellency keep the bonnet for future use."

Cold sweat broke out on Clifford's brow.

"It's Elliott!" he moaned. "It's Elliott's work! Oh, Heaven, he didn't know what he was doing!"

Stanley was silent.

"I'll go to the Embassy," cried Clifford, "I'll go now."

"Better not," said Stanley kindly.

There was a pause.

"Does—does she know?" faltered Clifford.

"Yes," said Stanley.

"And—and she—*she* believed I did it!"

"No—I told her you were incapable of such a thing. But she is perhaps a little prejudiced—that is—I mean—you understand, I found her much distressed."

Clifford raised his eyes, searching the handsome young face before him. Something in that face made his heart turn to water.

"Stanley!" he blurted out, "it isn't *you*, is it, she has promised to marry—"

"Yes," said Stanley slowly.

Clifford went and leaned over the banisters. After a long time he straightened up, mopped his brow with his handkerchief, smiled, and came up to Stanley holding out his hand.

"Before I take it I want to say that this incident had nothing to do with it," said Stanley; "I proposed and was accepted at the pigeon match."

Clifford was staggered for a moment; then he recovered and held out his hand again.

"She is one in a million," he said cordially, thinking to himself, "and the rest of the millions are just like her, oh, Lord! just like her!"

Stanley grasped his hand; they stood looking at each other with kindly eyes. Fantozzi's voice came through the closed door:

> "Espagne! Espagne!
> Bravo! Toro!"

Somewhere in there Bull still chanted "Cuba Libre!" Presently they bowed to each other, shook hands again, and parted.

"My compliments to His Excellency and to Miss Amyce," said Clifford. Then he went in and took leave of Fantozzi and the others despite their united protests. An hour later he entered the studio, fell upon Elliott and beat him madly. They fought like schoolboys until tired; perspiring and breathless, they retreated to separate sofas and panted.

"Confound you!" gasped Elliott, "what do you mean by it?"

"I mean that I forgive you," said Clifford grimly; "go to the devil!"

They smiled at each other across the studio.

"Was *that* the Ambassador, then?" asked Elliott.

"It was,—Ambassador Extraordinary and Minister Plenipotentiary."

"He isn't red-headed," suggested Elliott, "your Ambassador Extraordinary."

"Nevertheless," said Clifford "he is a most extraordinary Ambassador. Where shall we dine?"

"In the Quarter?"

"In the Quarter."

"With me?"

"With you."

"And Colette and Jacquette?"

"And Colette and Jacquette."

Elliott, choking with emotion, nodded, and picked up a ruffled silk hat from the floor.

"His Excellency's," said Clifford softly, and hung it over an easel.

YO ESPERO

God be merciful to me, a sinner. Thou hast already been merciful to the virtuous by making them so. —*Arabian Prayer*.

I.

"Good morning," said the young fellow, lifting his cap.

"Good morning," said the girl.

It was the third time they had met; they had never before spoken. The young fellow buttoned his tweed jacket to the throat, glanced over the wooden railing of the foot-bridge, and then looked up at the sky. The sky was pale blue, fleckless and untroubled save for a shred of filmy vapour floating all alone in the zenith;—that was all, except the gilt incandescent disc of the sun;—all, except a speck, high in the scintillating vault, that circled slowly, slowly southwards, and vanished in mid-air.

The speck was a buzzard.

The young fellow turned from the glimmering water and looked diffidently at the girl. She bent her grey eyes upon the stream.

"Would you mind telling me whether there are trout in this river?" he asked, moving a step toward her.

She raised her head instantly, smiling.

"Gay Brook was a famous trout stream—once," she answered.

"Then I suppose there are a few still left in it," he asked, also smiling.

"But," continued the girl, "that was very, very long ago." She was looking again at the water, pensively.

"How long ago?" he persisted, drawing a little nearer.

"About seventy-five years ago," she replied without raising her head; "Buck Gordon says so. Do you know Buck Gordon? His boys are the telegraph agents at the station above. I don't know the Gordon boys; I have spoken twice with old man Gordon. I do not suppose," she continued reflectively, "that there has been a trout in Gay Brook for fifty years. Do you know why?"

"No," he said, "but I should be glad to know."

He had drawn a little nearer and now leaned on the wooden railing of the bridge, his back to the water, his hands in his pockets. A leather rod-case was slung over one shoulder. The southern sun crisped the edges of his short hair and shorter moustache.

"The reason," said the girl, gazing dreamily into the stream again,—"the reason is because they cut off so much timber in the mountain notch yonder that now the freshets come every spring, and for weeks the water is nothing but yellow mud. Trout can't live in mud,—can they?"

After a silence he said: "And so there are no more trout." She shook her head. The sun burnished her dark hair and tinged the delicate contour of cheek and throat with a warmer flush. Her white cambric sunbonnet swung from her waist by both strings. Presently she put it on and turned toward him, holding the tips of the strings between the forefinger and thumb of her left hand. Her right hand lay indolently along the grey railing of the bridge. It was dimpled and tanned to a creamy tint.

"I have seen you three times here at the bridge," she observed.

"And I have seen you," he said; "I wish I had spoken before."

She tore a tiny splinter from the sun-bleached railing and dropped it into the water. It danced away through the trembling sunbeams.

"I wondered why you came to fish in Gay Brook," she went on; "I might have told you that there are nothing but minnows here;—I nearly did tell you—"

"I wish I had asked the first time we—I saw you," he said; "it would have saved me no end of disappointment. Why did you not tell me?"

"Because—you didn't ask me. I might have told you anyway if I had not seen that you were from the North."

"You dislike Northern people?"

"I? Oh, no,—I don't know any."

"But you say that if—"

"I mean that I do not understand Northern strangers."

The young fellow looked at her curiously.

"Why, I thought you also were from the North," he said; "you do not speak with a Southern accent—"

"I am from Maryland, but I have lived here in North Carolina nearly all of my life. The reason that I do not speak with a Southern accent is because my uncle is from the North and I have lived alone with him,—ever since I can remember."

"Here?"

"Yes. I am very glad you spoke to me. When do you go away to the North again?"

The young fellow touched his short moustache and gave her a sharp glance. His sunburned cheeks were tinged with a faint colour.

"I am very glad too," he said; "I find it a bit lonely at the hotel."

"The hotel," she repeated; "there are two hundred people there."

"And I am lonely," he said again.

"You can't be,—how can you be?" she persisted, raising her grey eyes to his.

"Because," he replied; "I haven't anything in common with any of them,—except Tom O'Hara."

"I don't understand," she insisted. "It seems to me that if I had the happiness of being with a great many people I should have all in the world that long for. I have nobody,—except my uncle."

"You have your friends," he said.

"No, nobody except my uncle. I do not count Zeke, and the boys."

"Zeke?"

"Zeke Chace."

"Oh," he said; "I've heard of him. He runs the blockade, doesn't he?"

"Does he?" she asked demurely.

He laughed and rested his head on his wrist, looking into her face. Her face was half hidden in the shadow of her sunbonnet, so she met his gaze placidly.

"Doesn't Zeke Chace run the blockade?" he repeated.

"What blockade?" she asked. Her grey eyes were very round and innocent.

"Have you never heard of blockade whisky?" he insisted.

She had to laugh.

"I might have heard something about it," she admitted.

His pleasant serious face questioned hers and her lips parted in the merriest laugh again.

"How silly!" she cried; "everybody has heard of blockade whisky."

"Oh," he said, "I have often asked, but the people around here won't talk about it!"

"Perhaps they take you for a Revenue Officer," she ventured gravely.

"Very probably," he answered.

At this she laughed outright. It occurred to him that she was making fun of him and he glanced at her again sharply.

"How do you know that I am not a Revenue Officer?" he asked.

Her laughing eyes met his.

"Can you tell a coon from a possum?" she asked in return.

"I? Of course."

"So can I," she said, trying hard to look serious. After a moment they both laughed outright.

"You have teased me unmercifully," he said; "don't you think you ought to tell me where I can catch a trout or two?"

"Then I will," she answered impulsively, moving a step nearer; "but Zeke won't like it. There are trout in the Buzzard Run."

"The Buzzard Run?"

"It's yonder, behind Mist Mountain. Zeke won't like it," she repeated.

"Why? Does Zeke fish too?"

"Zeke? Hm! Not exactly. Never mind,—I shall tell Zeke about you and nobody will bother you. But you must be a little careful; there are snakes on Mist Mountain."

"Not dangerous snakes,—are there?"

"I don't know what kind you are used to," she said; "there are rattlers in the rocks on Mist Mountain."

After a pause he asked her if there were many rattlesnakes there.

"Sometimes one sees two or three, sometimes none at all," she answered. "They give you warning; they run if you let them. It might be better if you kept to the path. There is a path all the way."

"Then I'll stick to it," he said lightly; "I suppose it's too late to go to-day." He looked at his watch and raised his eyebrows. "Why, it's twelve o'clock!" he exclaimed.

She refused to believe it and bent her dainty head over his shoulder to see.

"Dear me!" she cried, "uncle will question me!"

They stood looking at each other with new-born awkwardness. She took one short step backward.

"Are you going?" he asked, scarcely conscious of what he said.

"Why, yes,—I must."

He leaned over the bridge railing and looked at the crinkling ripples. After a while she also bent over, resting her elbows on the railing. A brilliant green beetle ran across the bleached board, halted, spread its burnished wings, and buzzed away across the stream. A small fluffy honey-wasp alighted between her elbows and crept quickly into a hole in the splintering plank.

"Yes," she repeated, "I must go."

He raised his head and looked her frankly in the eyes:

"I should like to see you again," he said.

"Really? Oh, I suppose I shall pass the bridge again before you go."

"How do you know? Suppose I should go tomorrow?"

"You said you were going fishing to-morrow, didn't you?"

"Why no,—I didn't say so," he said eagerly; "I would rather talk with you."

"Why don't you go fishing?"

"I would rather talk to you," he repeated.

"What shall we talk about—blockade whisky?"

They both laughed. He had moved up beside her again.

"I want to see you again," she said, "I think you can see that I do. I could come to the bridge tomorrow. I would rather the people at the hotel did not know. My uncle has forbidden me to speak to anybody except Zeke and the boys. When I was a child I did not feel very lonely; now I have the greatest longing to know people—girls of my own age. I dare not."

"Have you no girl friend at all?"

"No. I should like to know older women too. At night in bed I often cry and cry—there!—I should not tell you such things—"

"Tell me," he said soberly.

But she only smiled and shook her head saying; "It is lonely at Yo Espero."

He looked into her grey eyes; they troubled him.

"I dare not wait any longer," she said,—"goodbye,—will you come to-morrow?"

"Here? Yes. Shall I come early?"

"Oh, yes."

"At seven?"

"Yes."

He offered her his hand but she did not take it.

"Wait," she said, "I do not know your name,—no,—don't tell me now,—let me think a little of what I have done. If I come to-morrow—then you may tell me."

He watched her hurry away up the woodland path that leads to Yo Espero. When she was gone he stood still, idly tearing dried splinters from the bridge railing.

II.

The piazzas of the Diamond Spring Hotel were empty; the guests came trooping through the great square hall and into the big dining-room to be fed.

Young Edgeworth arrived late and silently took his seat, bowing civilly to his neighbours.

There were fifteen people at his table, including the Reverend Dr. Beezeley, who presided, flanked by his wife, his progeny, and a bottle of Diamond Spring water. Near to the Reverend Orlando Beezeley sat another minister, a little pink gentleman with bulging eyes. His name was Meeke and he looked it. But he wasn't.

Now the Reverend Orlando Beezeley and Dr. Samuel Meeke were both of a stripe, differing on one or two obscure questions. One reverend gentleman was a pillar of the "Pure People's League;" the other wore the badge of the "Charity Band." And they squabbled.

For their leagues, their bands, and their squabbles, Edgeworth cared nothing. He believed that all people should be allowed to worship God in their own fashion,—even by squabbling if they chose. He was disposed to be courteous to the two ministers and their wives and young. It was difficult, however, partly because they were inquisitive, partly on account of the Reverend Orlando's personal habits, which were maddening. He put his fingers into everything, including his mouth; they were always sticky, and this, combined with cuffs that came too far over his knuckles, oppressed Edgeworth. The Reverend Orlando's fingers were obtrusive. When he walked they spread out, perhaps to stem the downward avalanche of cuff. He also twiddled them when he had no other use for them, and Heaven knows he put them to uses for which they were never intended.

All this interfered with Edgeworth's appetite and he shunned the Reverend Orlando Beezeley. Once, at the table, the minister asked him why he didn't go to the Sunday services which he, Dr. Beezeley, held in the hotel parlours, and when Edgeworth said it was because he didn't want to, the Reverend Orlando sniffed offensively. For a week the atmosphere was surcharged with unpleasantness; but one day Dr. Beezeley asked Edgeworth what he did for a living, and Edgeworth pleasantly told him that it was none of his business. The atmosphere at once cleared up and the Reverend Orlando became irksomely affable. This was because he was afraid of Edgeworth and disliked him.

Therefore, when Edgeworth entered the dining-room and slipped quietly into his chair, Dr. Beezeley said: "Hey! been a-fishin?"

"No," said Edgeworth.

"Where've you been then?" urged Mrs. Beezeley, devoured by curiosity. She had contracted this disease in the little Boston suburb where she lived, and she had infected her whole family.

"I have been out," said Edgeworth pleasantly.

Dr. Samuel Meeke, who had pricked up his ears, relapsed into a dull contemplation of Mrs. Dill again.

But Mrs. Beezeley was not defeated. She turned to the pallid lady beside her, Mrs. Dill, and said in a thin high voice: "Pass the trout to Mr. Edgeworth; he can't seem to catch any—even off the old foot-bridge."

Edgeworth was intensely annoyed, for it was plain that some of the Beezeley brood had been spying. He looked at Master Ballington Beezeley who grinned at him impertinently.

His father was busy feeding himself with mashed potato, but he observed his heir's impudence and was not displeased.

"I seen you," cried the youthful Beezeley, writhing with the pressure of untold secrets,—"you was mashin' a country-girl, Mister Edgeworth,—I seen you!"

"Te-he!" tittered Mrs. Dill.

"'I *saw* you,' would perhaps be more correct," said Edgeworth; "unless perhaps your parents have instructed you to the contrary—"

"Ballington!" cried Mrs. Beezeley, turning red, "how dare you use such grammar?"

Edgeworth surveyed the defeat of the Beezeleys without any particular emotion.

Mrs. Dill attempted to save the day but choked on an olive and was assisted from the room by Dr. Samuel Meeke. Then the Beezeleys made Mrs. Meeke wretched with significant looks and smiles and half-suppressed coughs, until she rose to find out why Mrs. Dill and her husband did not return. Poor little woman! her bosom friend, Mrs. Beezeley, had long ago quenched for her what little comfort in life she ever knew.

When the Reverend Orlando Beezeley had fed to repletion, he removed the napkin from his chin, cleared his throat, picked his teeth, and finally took himself off to the piazza.

"I can't stand this table full much longer," muttered Edgeworth to himself, and he called to the head waiter, a majestic personage of colour, and also a Baptist deacon.

"Deacon," said he, "give me a place at another table to-night, can you?"

"Sho'ly, Sho'ly, Mistuh Edgewurf," said the majestic one; "might you prefer to be seated at Mis' Weldon's table, Mistuh Edgewurf?"

Edgeworth looked across at Mrs. Weldon and then at her pretty daughter, Claire.

"Go over and ask Mrs. Weldon whether she objects," he said.

Mrs. Weldon did not object and neither did Claire, so Edgeworth walked over and said some polite things which he forgot a minute afterward. So did Mrs. Weldon. I am not sure about Claire.

When Edgeworth went out on the veranda to smoke his pipe, a young fellow in tweeds and scarlet golf-jacket, who was sitting astride the railing said: "Hello, Jim, it's all over the hotel that you're sweet on some country girl."

"Tommy," said Edgeworth, in a low pleasant voice, "go to the devil!"

O'Hara smiled serenely.

"I suppose it's that Beezeley whelp, eh, Jim?"

"I fancy it is. A fellow can't brush his hair but it's reported in Diamond Springs."

"Oh, there's truth in it then," laughed O'Hara.

"That," said Edgeworth, "is none of your confounded business;" and they strolled off together, arm in arm, smoking placidly.

"These Beezeleys," said O'Hara, "are blights on the landscape. They ought to be exterminated with Paris-green."

"Or drowned in tubs," said Edgeworth.

"Like unpleasant kittens," added O'Hara.

"Come," said Jim Edgeworth, "what was that yarn you wanted to spin for me this morning?"

"Yarn? 'Tis no yarn," said O'Hara; "it's the truth and it troubles me. Sit down here on the grass till I tell you. Look at the veranda, Jim; it's like a circus with the band playing."

"The girls' frocks are very pretty; I like lots of colour," said Edgeworth.

"There's plenty in Claire Weldon's cheeks," observed O'Hara, gloomily.

"It's natural," said Jim.

"It was before you came. Now she puts more on in your honour;—confound it, man, can't you see the lass is forever making eyes at you?—and, Jim, it's death to me!"

Edgeworth stared at him.

"Oh, you're blinder than the white bat of Drumgilt!" said O'Hara; "you've eyes in your head, but they're only there for ornament. Didn't you know I am in love with Claire Weldon now?"

"Why no," said Edgeworth, "are you really, Tommy?"

"Am I really, Tommy? Faith, I thought even the fish in Gay Brook knew it."

"Well," laughed Edgeworth, "go in and win, then!"

"Do you mean it?" said Tommy gravely.

"Mean it? My dear fellow, why shouldn't I?" O'Hara beamed upon him and grasped his hand.

"There!" he cried, "I knew it! I've told her ye didn't care tuppence for any lass, and if she didn't take me she'd be doin' herself but ill service."

Edgeworth burst into fits of laughter. "Is that the way you woo a girl, Tom O'Hara?"

"There are ways and ways," said O'Hara doggedly.

"How about Sir Brian?" asked Jim, checking his mirth.

Sir Brian was Tommy's father. The several thousand miles that separated father and son did not lessen Tommy's uneasiness concerning his father's approval.

"I can't help it," said Tom; "if he disowns me I'll go to work, that I will! and Claire knows it."

"They say," said Edgeworth, "that the O'Haras always get what they want."

"They do. My grandfather loved a lass who died, so he blew out his brains and caught her in heaven."

"Hm!" coughed Edgeworth.

"Do you know to the contrary?" demanded O'Hara.

"No," said Jim, "I'll have to wait a bit to verify this story. Have you any tobacco? Thanks, my pipe's out. Look at the sky, Tom; it's pretty, isn't it?"

They sprawled on their backs and kicked up their heels; two bronzed young athletes,—as trim a pair as one might see anywhere betwixt the poles of this planet.

"Hark," said Edgeworth, "hear Beezeley and Meeke squabbling over their Maker. Do you suppose He hears them? He is so very far away. Hark how they wrangle over their future blessedness. I should think they would be ashamed to have God hear them.”

“Beezeley says he believes in hell, but doesn’t want to go there,” said O’Hara, lazily.

“There’s no hell,” said Edgeworth. He hadn’t lived long enough to know; he was nineteen.

O’Hara raised himself on one elbow and looked at him.

“No hell?” he asked.

“No.”

If he had seen the lines in O’Hara’s young face,—the faint marks about the eyes and mouth, he might have answered differently.

The afternoon sunlight lay warm across the level meadow. The locust trees were in full bloom, deep laden with heavy, drooping clusters of white blossoms. Every wandering breeze bore the penetrating sweetness of the locusts and the delicate odour of hemlock and pine. Great scarlet trumpet-flowers swayed in the May wind; from the nearer forest came the scent of dogwood and azalea. Over the greensward butterflies fluttered, little white ones, chasing each other among the dandelions, great swallow-tailed butterflies, yellow and black, flopping around the phlox, or pursuing a capricious course along the river bank. There were others too, gay comma-butterflies, delicate violet or blue swallow-tailed butterflies, and now and then a rare shy comrade of theirs, pale sulphur and grey, striped like a zebra, that darted across the flower-beds and flitted away to its dusky haunts among the shrub-oak and holly of the mountain sides. An oriole, gorgeous in orange and black, uttered a sweet call from the lower branches of an oak. A bluebird dropped into the lower grass under the bushes. Then a catbird began to sing and trill and warble until the whole air rippled with melody.

“’Tis a nightingale or I’m in Drumgilt!” said O’Hara, sitting up.

“It’s a male catbird,” said Edgeworth, rising; “come on, Tom!”

O’Hara picked himself up from the grass, scraped out his pipe, ran a grass-stem through it, and looked at the sun.

“We have loafed the whole afternoon away,” he said.

“I was anxious to kill time,” said Edgeworth. He was thinking of the girl at the bridge.

“Kill time! kill time!” said O’Hara impatiently,—”why, man, ‘tis time that kills us! I’m going to find Miss Weldon, and I’d be obliged to ye to stay away.”

“Bosh!” said Edgeworth, “you’re worth twenty like me.”

“That I am!” said Tom, “but I’ll be saying good night, lad! And for the love of me, stay away from Claire Weldon. You don’t want my curse?”

"Oh, no," laughed Edgeworth; "but I'm going to dine at their table. I asked the Deacon to fix it. I can't stand the holy alliance any longer."

"All right," said O'Hara, "when a girl has to see a man eat three times a day, she loses her illusions concerning him."

"What's that?" demanded Edgeworth.

But O'Hara swung off across the clover, whistling "Terry Bowen" and buttoning his scarlet golf-jacket with an irritating air of self-satisfaction.

"The mischief take Tom and his girls!" said Edgeworth to himself, but he looked after Tom and smiled, for he thought the world revolved about O'Hara. Still he began to be lonely again, now that O'Hara was gone.

"Why the deuce can't he spend a half hour now and then with me?" he muttered to himself; "what can he find to talk about all day to that one girl?"

III.

That night after dinner he found himself joining the procession upon the veranda, walking with a pretty girl whom he did not remember meeting, but, from whose conversation, he knew he must have danced attendance on somewhere or other.

In the half light of the mellow Japanese lanterns, he caught glimpses of familiar faces in the throng; Dr. Beezeley, unctuous and sticky-fingered, the faded Mrs. Dill with Dr. Samuel Meeke, poor little Mrs. Meeke, anxiously smiling when she caught the protruding eyes of her husband, Mrs. Weldon, gracious and serene, walking with some tall, heavy-whiskered Southerner, Tommy O'Hara conducting Miss Claire Weldon, with something of the determination that one notices in troopers who convoy treasure-trains. In and out of the lights they passed him, vague impressions, of filmy draperies and lantern-lit faces, with now and then a shadowy gesture or a sparkle of eyes in the twilight. Beyond, the dark foliage of sycamore and maple loomed motionless, with never a wind to stir the tender leaves, but the locust-trees, where the grape-like bunches of white blossoms hung, were all hazy with the quivering wings of dusk-moths. Slender sphinx-moths darted and turned and hovered over the phlox, grey wraiths of dead humming-birds, poised above phantom flowers. Below the fountain spray, drifting fine as a veil of mist across the shadowy blossoms of white iris, a hidden tree-frog quavered a sweet-treble, and on every twig-tip gauzy-winged creatures scraped resonant accompaniment.

"Of what are you thinking, Mr. Edgeworth?" asked the girl beside him.

He started slightly; he had quite forgotten her. He had been thinking of the girl at the bridge and the tryst next morning, but he said: "I was listening to the tree-frog. It means rain to morrow."

"I am very sorry," said the girl, "I was going to Painted Mountain on horseback. Shall we sit here a moment?" She shook out her skirts and seated herself, and he found a place on the veranda railing beside her.

"Painted Mountain?" he asked; "that is beyond Yo Espero, isn't it?"

"Yo Espero is on the southern slope. I heard such an interesting story about Yo Espero to-day; shall I tell you?"

He looked at her sharply, then nodded, saying: "Tell me first what Yo Espero means. It's Spanish, isn't it?"

"I don't know,—I suppose so. I believe it means '*I hope*.' The village,—there's only one house you know,—was named Yo Espero by the only inhabitant. They say he took the name from the label on the lid of an old cigar-box that he found among the rocks."

"Very unromantic and intensely American," said Edgeworth laughing.

"Ah, but wait,—there's more to come. The man who lives at Yo Espero has a niece, a beauty they say, and would you believe it, the man, her uncle, named her also Yo Espero!"

"Oh!" said Edgeworth musingly.

"Poor girl,—named from a cigar brand! It is wicked—don't you think so, Mr. Edgeworth?"

"Yo Espero," he repeated softly,—"I don't know, —Yo Espero."

"Her uncle calls her Io for short when he does not call her Yo Espero. He must be a brute. They say he knows things about the blockade too."

Edgeworth became interested.

"I have never seen the girl," she continued, "but Mrs. Weldon has, and she says the girl is simply a raving beauty. Dr. Beezeley tried to call on the uncle but was shown the door without ceremony. They say the man is well educated and from the North, but he won't allow anybody to enter his house or speak to his niece."

"Do you know his name?" asked Edgeworth.

"Mrs. Beezeley says it is Clyde. He is some broken-down Northern man of good family who has sunk low enough to mix himself up with the blockade. People say the Revenue Officers are after him and will get him sooner or later. I wonder what the girl will do then?"

"I wonder," repeated Edgeworth under his breath; "hello! here's Tommy O'Hara, the pride of Drumgilt!"

"And the Pride has had a fall," said O'Hara sentimentally;—"did—did you notice if Miss Weldon was passing this way, Jim? Ah, did you see her pass, Miss Marwood? With Colonel Scarborough? Oh, the mischief!"

"Come," laughed Miss Marwood, "we'll go and find them; Mr. Edgeworth doesn't care; he likes solitude—"

Edgeworth attempted to protest, but was bidden to go with them or stay, as he pleased. And he stayed,—to smoke and muse and ponder on the long dim porch while the dew dripped from the perfumed vines, and the great stars spangled the sky, and the million voices of the night sang of summers past and summers to come. And the burden of the song was always the same, Yo Espero, Yo Espero.

At seven o'clock next morning, Edgeworth stood on the little foot-bridge, leaning both elbows upon the wooden railing. Between his elbows was a fresh white cut in the weather-stained plank, from which a shaving of wood had recently been planed, and on this white space was printed in pencil:

"I shall not see you again."

He never doubted that the message was for him. He leaned idly upon the rail, reading and re-reading it. A fine warm rain, scarcely more than a mist, was falling through the calm air. The tiny globules powdered his cap and coat, shining like frost-dust.

Presently he fumbled in his pocket, found a jackknife, opened it, and deliberately shaved the writing from the plank. Then, in his turn he wrote:

"If you will not see me I shall go to-morrow."

"Let the Beezeley whelp read that and make the most of it," he muttered, turning away with an unaccustomed feeling of wistfulness.

What he longed for he did not know; perhaps for a little of O'Hara's society, so he lighted his pipe and started toward the hotel, his hands deep in his pockets, his tanned cheeks glistening with the fine rain.

After a few moments it occurred to him that he had put it rather strongly;—in fact it was an unwarranted and idiotic thing to write. Why in the world should he leave Diamond Springs because a girl whom he had met three times and spoken to once, refused to meet him again? He hesitated, mused a little, and finally resumed his course. Let it stay as it was; it mattered nothing to him anyway. He would leave the hotel,—he would leave the state too, for that matter, for he was sick and weary of the Carolinas, and of the big hotels, filled with invalids who sat in hot baths or drank bottles of nasty "waters." Would O'Hara go with him? He thought of Claire Weldon and frowned.

"She's spoiled O'Hara, that's what she's done!" he pondered bitterly.

When he came in sight of the hotel he saw Dr. Beezeley pottering about the croquet ground. When the reverend gentleman walked, his flat feet scraped the gravel and lapped over each other in front, like the toes of a Shanghai rooster.

"Hey!" said Dr. Beezeley, "been a walkin'?"

Edgeworth nodded.

"Want to play croquet?" asked Beezeley, looking at him over his glasses; "it ain't goin' to rain much more."

Edgeworth said he never played croquet. Beezeley straightened a wicket, hammered a painted stake, and sniffed.

His face, with the bunchy chop-whiskers cut a little close, reminded Edgeworth of the countenance of some big buck rabbit. The reverend gentleman also had other rabbit peculiarities, such as a perpetual appetite, a prehensile lip, and an enormous progeny.

O'Hara hailed him from the tennis courts and he went over, puffing his pipe moodily. But when he found that Tommy intended to invite two girls to make up doubles, Edgeworth flatly refused to play.

"Confound it, Tommy," he said, "you are good enough company for me, and I ought to be for you. What's the use of lugging in strangers every minute?"

"Ladies are never strangers," said Tom airily; "one of them is Miss Weldon."

"That's all right," said Edgeworth savagely, "but she can't play tennis. Is it a kindergarten you're setting up, Tom O'Hara? Call your caddy and come on to the links."

"Listen to the lad!" said O'Hara; "why, man, I'll go with you where you like and I'll do what you like,—only," he added, "I have an appointment to ride at ten—with Miss Weldon."

"Ride then," said Edgeworth with a scowl, and turned on his heel, leaving O'Hara a sadly puzzled man.

"What the mischief is the matter with me, anyhow?" muttered Edgeworth, striding wrathfully away across the meadow; "why can't I let Tommy alone with his girl. I'm making a nuisance of myself I fancy."

The restlessness which possessed him he did not even attempt to analyse. That it was caused by something or somebody outside of himself he was convinced.

"These people here," he thought, "are empty-headed and common— when they're not sanctimonious and vulgar. I'll be hanged if I'm going to spend the time talking platitudes to girls in golf gowns."

Of course it was their fault that he felt irritable and bored. He thought of his book, "The Origin of the Cherokee Indian," but the prospect of shutting himself in his room to drive a pen over reams of foolscap had small attraction for him. The rain had ceased, the heavy perfumed air, vague with vapour, oppressed him, and he looked up at the mountains, half veiled in mist. But climbing was out of the question,—he didn't know exactly why,—but it was clearly out of the question. He would not go fishing either; neither would he read. What was there left to do? Nothing, except to go back to the foot-bridge.

So when at last, by the highways and byways of cogitation, he had completed the circle, and had arrived at the point from which he started, he found that his legs had secured the precedence of his brain, for already they were landing him at the footbridge.

He was really a little surprised when he found himself there. He stepped to the railing to find his inscription. Somebody had shaved it off with a knife, and, in its place was written:

"Good-bye."

It was then that Edgeworth experienced a most amazing, not to say painful, sensation. It started in the region of the heart, and, before he was aware, it began to affect his throat.

"Good-bye."

He looked stupidly at the word, repeating it aloud once or twice. Presently he pulled out his knife and hacked away the writing with a misty idea that it might bother him less when it was obliterated. On the contrary it bothered him more than ever. A desire possessed him to go away, but, when he pictured himself in a train, rushing northward, the prospect was not as alluring as he felt it should be. Perhaps it was because he knew O'Hara would not go with him.

"The devil take Tom O'Hara!" he blurted out. The effect of this outburst did not soothe him; it did, however, frighten a small hedge-sparrow nearly to death.

He looked up at the sun-warped sign-post on the end of the bridge. It bore the following valuable information.

Hog Mountain	6 miles.
Buzzard Run	10 miles.
Red Rock	1 mile.
Yo Espero	3 miles.

"Yo Espero," he repeated aloud.

There was a step on the creaking planks behind him,—a light step,—but he heard it.

They faced each other for a moment in silence. The sun shone out of the mist above and tinged the edges of her hair with a mellow radiance.

"Come," she said, "we can't stay here."

"Where—then?"

Their eyes met. Her lips were slightly parted; perhaps she had walked fast, for her breast rose and fell irregularly. In that silent exchange of glances, each read, for one brief second, a line in the book of fate;—each read,—but whether they understood or not, God knows, for they smiled at each other and turned away, side by side into the forest.

IV.

"Yo Espero! Yo Espero!" Asleep, awake, the words haunted him, night and day they rang in his ears, "Yo Espero, Yo Espero." The brooks sang it; in the hot mid-day the cadence of the meadow creatures took it up; the orioles repeated it across the fields, the thrushes' hymn was for her alone: "Yo Espero, Yo Espero."

Days dawned and vanished, brief as the flash of a fire-fly wing. The locust-trees powdered the greensward with white blossoms, the laurel, dainty and conventional, spread its flowered cambric out to dry, and the dogwood leaves drifted through the forest like snowflakes.

O'Hara, the triumphant affianced of Claire, provoked the wrath of all unaffianced gods and men. He simply mooned. Guests arrived and guests left the Diamond Spring Hotel, but the Beezeleys stayed on for ever. There were captains and colonels and generals from the South; the names of Fairfax and Marmaduke and Carter and Stuart were heard in corridor and card-room. There were Rittenhouses and Appletons, and Van Burens, too, and the flat bleat of Philadelphia echoed the colourless jargon of Boston and the semi-civilized accent of New York.

It was the middle of May. The catbirds had ceased their music and now haunted the garden, mewing from every thicket. A crested blue jay, ominous prophet of distant autumn, screamed viciously at the great belted kingfishers, but wisely avoided these dagger-billed birds, and also the occasional cock-of-the-woods that flew into the oak-grove, and tapped all day on the loose bark.

Edgeworth loved all these creatures. A few weeks previous he hadn't cared tuppence for them. But now it was different; he felt at home with all the world; he smiled knowingly at the thrushes, he nodded gaily to the great blue heron, and laughed when that dignified but snobbish biped cut him dead. Flowers too he was on good terms with; he haunted the woods, now all ablaze with azaleas, he sat among blue and violet larkspurs and felt that he was among friends. The little wood-violets peeped up at him fearlessly; they knew he would never pick them; the big orange lady-slippers arranged themselves neatly, two by two, as he passed, but he laughingly disregarded their offers. True, the girl at his side,—for he never rambled alone,—was worthy of such self-sacrifice on the part of any lady-slipper, orange or maroon.

"Io," he said, as they lay in the forest on the heights above Diamond

Springs, "can you realise it all? I scarcely can. Was it yesterday, was it last week,—was it years ago that I said good morning to you there on our bridge?"

"Jim, I don't know."

Her hair had fallen down and she flung it like a glistening veil from her face. She lay full length across the soft pine needles, her scarlet lips parted, tearing bits of flame-colored azalea blossoms from a cluster at her belt.

"See the lizards," said Edgeworth sitting up beside her, "see them race over the dry leaves! There! They've run up a tree! Look, Io."

"I see," she said. But she was looking up at him.

He bent over her and kissed her, both hands clasped in hers.

"You didn't look at all," he said.

"Didn't I?" whispered Yo Espero.

It was true that she had not looked. When her eyes were not fastened upon his face, they were closed.

So he sat smiling down at her with her slim fingers twisted in his; and that shadow of wistfulness that ever hovers close to happiness, fell over his eyes. And he said: "Do you ever regret—anything—Io?"

She smiled faintly.

"No—nothing, dear."

"Nothing?"

"Nothing."

"Then you are happy."

"Yes."

What had she to regret? She loved him. To him she came, sick at heart for the companionship which she had never known. He had delivered her from her loneliness. First she listened to him with the fierce happiness of the lonely; then she idolized him; then she loved him. Love was all she had to give; and she gave it, even before he asked,—gave it without thought or regret.

"Do you know," he said, "that you have the prettiest hands in the world?"

"Have I?"

"Don't you know that your whole figure is exquisite?"

She raised one hand indolently and placed the fingers across his lips.

"What do I care,—if you love me?" she said.

"But I care," he said; "to think that you,—all, all of you,—with your beautiful eyes and your neck and your lips and these two little hands, are mine—all mine!—"

"And that brown hair above me—is mine,—isn't it?" murmured the girl; "I never asked you before, but don't—don't I own some of you too? I have given you all of myself."

It was little to ask;—the question was a new one though, and he suddenly began to wonder how much of him she did own. He looked at her half curiously as she lay there, her innocent face upturned, her young figure flung across the pine-needle matting of the forest. Her eyes told him she loved him; every line and curve of her sweet body solemnized the vow.

"Io," he said, "all of me that is worth owning you own."

"This hand?" she asked, locking her fingers in his.

"Both," he said.

"Everything? All—all?"

"All, Yo Espero."

"You never said so—before."

"I say it now; all! all! all!"

"We will go to Silver Mine Creek," said Yo Espero, "and we will fish there for a little fish. There are bass in the French Broad, and you shall catch them from the rifts below Deepwater Bridge. We will gallop on horseback to Sunset Sands and we will go to Bubbling Spring. All this will take time, you know, but you are never going away, are you? Hush! I could not live until sunrise. Then, in the fall, we will go across to the little Hurricane where there are deer. You shall shoot a great wild-turkey also! Dear me! What more can a man ask for? And then there are teal and mallard on the French Broad before the ice has bridged the Little Red Horse. You will love the South."

"Yes, dear," he answered, soberly; but his eyes were turned to the North.

"I know lots of springs in the forest," she said, watching his face.

"And blockade stills?" he smiled.

She laughed outright and sat up, gathering her heavy hair into a twist.

"There is one within a few steps of where we sit; you could never find it," she said, tauntingly.

"Oho!" he exclaimed, "whose?"

"Zeke's," said the girl, "I could go to it in two minutes,—hark!—was that a gunshot from the valley?"

"I think it was," he said, "it came from that way," and he pointed to the west.

"From Painted Mountain! Did it sound like a rifle, Jim?"

Her eyes were very bright. Two red spots glowed on either cheek.

"I don't know, dear," he said, "why?"

As he spoke he rose and stepped back two paces. And as he took the second step there came a whirr, a girl's scream, and a rattlesnake struck him twice above the ankle.

For one second the forest swam before his eyes; then a cold sweat started from the roots of his hair and he bent and picked up a stick, shaking in every limb. It was over in a moment; the snake lay dead, shuddering and twisting among the rocks, but it was Yo Espero who had crushed it, and now she turned to him a face as bloodless as his own.

"Wait!" she panted, "there's whisky at Zeke's!" and she sprang across the mountain-side and vanished among the thickets.

He bent over and tore down his stocking; then his head whirled and he sank trembling upon the ground.

As he lay there great throbs of pain swept through him in waves, succeeded by momentary numbness, but through the mist of faintness and the delirium of pain he heard the dead snake thumping among the leaves. Then all was one great thrill of agony, but, as his senses reeled again, a touch fell upon his arm and he heard her voice:

"Drink,—quickly—all—all you can!"

And he did, blindly, guided by her arm. She held the demijohn until his head fell back.

Then she knelt, ripped her own sleeve from wrist to shoulder and stared at her round white arm. Two blue marks, close together, capped the summit of a terrible swelling, and she cried out once for help. With all the strength that remained, she dragged the demijohn to her mouth and stretched out on the ground, the crystal clear liquor running between her teeth. She tried hard to swallow. Once she murmured, "I knew there was not enough for both,—I guess there isn't much left; I guess—it's—too late—"

After a minute or two she wandered in her delirium, but still she swallowed desperately until the demijohn rolled away from her nerveless grasp, and she seemed to lose consciousness. With the last spark of understanding left in her numbed brain, she turned over and stretched out, her lips crushed against his face.

Zeke found them. Whether it was the smell of blockade whisky, coupled with the absence of his demijohn, or whether it was Providence, cannot be successfully argued here. But he found them, and he carried them into his ramshackle cabin and laid them side by side across his mattress.

After he had looked at them for half an hour's absolute silence, he spat the remains of a hard-chewed quid into a corner, picked up his gun, and wended his way down the mountain-side to the Diamond Springs Hotel.

Here he was promptly arrested by two pale-faced Revenue Officers, and here, for the first time, he learned that Clyde, the tenant of Yo Espero on Painted Mountain, had been shot dead, two hours before, for resisting arrest at the hands of United States officers.

The hotel was in commotion, but when Zeke drawled out his story, panic reigned supreme, and the Beezeleys started in a body for Zeke's hut. How they got lost on the mountain and were frightened by snakes, and how Dr. Samuel Meeke headed a rescue party in their behalf, has no place in this story,—nor, I imagine, in any story. O'Hara went on Zeke's bond, and Zeke, followed by O'Hara and the proprietor of the Diamond Springs Hotel, started for the blockader's burrow. The proprietor's name was Eph Doom, but, unlike his namesake, nothing about him was sealed, not even his lips, and he chattered continually until Zeke drawled out: "O shet up, yew mewl o' misery!"

Once O'Hara spoke:

"You left them both lying across your bed, Zeke?"

"'Bout a foot apart," drawled Zeke.

But when O'Hara burst into the cabin, he cried:

"Thank God!" For they were in each other's arms.

And that is all there is to say.

Eph Doom recounts a great deal more; he tells how those two striplings, dazed by alcohol and numbed with poison, clung together blindly; he tells how he, personally, drove a shoal of Beezeleys and Meekes and Dills from the door of the cabin, and he relates with fire how young Edgeworth sat up, pale, trembling, and demanded that he, Ephraim Doom, should, as a Justice of the Peace, then and there instantly unite in holy wedlock James Edgeworth and Yo Espero Clyde: which he did not do, because O'Hara whispered: "Wait till he's sober."

How Zeke escaped the clutches of the law needs a story by itself.

How Dr. Samuel Meeke and Mrs. Dill—but that is scandal.

How Yo Espero and Edgeworth loved is all that concerns this story.

COLLECTOR OF THE PORT

"'Why do you limp?' asked the maid.
'I always stumble when the path is smooth,' said Love."

> I will grow round him in his place,
> Grow, live, die looking on his face,
> Die, dying clasp'd in his embrace.
> TENNYSON.

In winter the Port is closed, the population migrates, the Collector of the Port sails southward. There is nothing left but black rocks sheathed in ice where icy seas clash and splinter and white squalls howl across the headland. When the wind slackens and the inlet freezes, spotted seals swim up and down the ragged edges of the ice, sleek restless heads raised, mild eyes fixed on the turbid shallows.

In January, blizzard-driven, snowy owls whirl into the pines and sit all day in the demi-twilight, the white ptarmigan covers the softer snow with winding tracks, and the white hare, huddled in his whiter "form," plays hide and seek with his own shadow.

In February the Port-of-Waves is still untenanted. A few marauders appear, now and then a steel grey panther from the north frisking over the snow after the white hares, now and then a stub-tailed lynx, mean-faced, famished, snarling up at the white owls who look down and snap their beaks and hiss.

The first bud on the Indian-willow brings the first inhabitant back to the Port-of-Waves, Francis Lee, superintendent of the mica quarry. The quarrymen follow in batches; the willow-tassels see them all there; the wind-flowers witness the defile of the first shift through the pines.

On the last day of May the company's flag was hoisted on the toolhouse, the French-Canadians came down to repair the rusty narrow-gauge railroad, and Lee, pipe lighted, sea-jacket buttoned to the throat, tramped up and down the track with the lumber detail, chalking and condemning sleepers, blazing spruce and pine, sounding fish-plate and rail, and shouting at intervals until the washouts were shored up, windfalls hacked through, and landslide and boulder no longer blocked the progress of the company's sole locomotive.

The first of June brought sunshine and black flies, but not the Collector of the Port. The Canadians went back to Sainte Isole across the line, the white-throated sparrows' long dreary melody broke out in the clearing's edge, but the Collector of the Port did not return.

That evening, Lee, smoking his pipe on the headland, looked out across the sunset-tinted ocean and saw the white gulls settling on the shoals and the fish-hawks soaring overhead with the red sunglint on their wings. The smoke of a moss smudge kept the flies away, his own tobacco smoke drove away care. Incidentally both drove Williams away,—a mere lad in baggy blue-jeans, smooth-faced, clear-eyed, with sea-tan on wrist and cheek.

"How did you cut your hand?" asked Lee, turning his head as Williams moved away.

"Mica," replied Williams briefly. After a moment Williams started on again.

"Come back," said Lee; "that wasn't what I had to tell you."

He sat down on the headland, opened a jack-knife, and scraped the ashes out of his pipe. Williams came slowly up and stood a few paces behind his shoulder.

"Sit down," said Lee.

Williams did not stir. Lee waited a moment, head slightly turned, but not far enough for him to see the figure motionless behind his shoulder.

"It's none of my business," began Lee, "but perhaps you had better know that you have deceived nobody. Finn came and spoke to me to-day. Dyce knows it, Carrots and Lefty Sawyer know it,—I should have known it myself had I looked at you twice."

The June wind blowing across the grass, carried two white butterflies over the cliff. Lee watched them struggle back to land again. Williams watched Lee.

"I don't know what to do," said Lee, after a silence; "it is not forbidden for women to work in the quarry—that I am aware of. If you need work and prefer that sort, and if you perform your work properly, I shall not interfere with you. And I'll see that the men do not."

Williams stood motionless; the smoke from the smudge shifted west, then south.

"But," continued Lee, "I must enter you properly on the pay-roll; I cannot approve of this masquerade. Finn will see you in the morning; it is unnecessary for me to repeat that you will not be disturbed."

There was no answer. After a silence Lee turned, then rose to his feet. Williams was weeping.

Lee had never noticed her face; both sun-tanned hands hid it now; her felt hat was pulled down over the forehead.

"Why did you come to the quarry?" he asked soberly. She did not reply.

"It is men's work," he said; "look at your hands! You cannot do it."

She tightened her hands over her eyes; tears stole between her fingers and dropped, one by one, on the young grass.

"If you need work—if you can find nothing else—I—I think perhaps I may manage something better," he said. "You must not stand there crying—listen! Here come Finn and Dyce, and I don't want them to talk all over the camp." Finn and Dyce came toiling up the headland with news that the west drain was choked. They glanced askance at Williams, who turned her back. The sea-wind dried her eyes; it stung her torn hands too. She unconsciously placed one aching finger in her mouth and looked out to sea.

"The dreen's bust by the second windfall," said Dyce, with a jerk of his stunted thumb toward the forest. "If them sluice-props caves in, the timber's wasted."

Finn proposed new sluice gates; Lee objected, and swore roundly that if the damage was not repaired by next evening he'd hold Finn responsible. He told them he was there to save the company's money, not to experiment with it; he spoke sharply to Finn of last year's extravagance, and warned him not to trifle with orders.

"I pay you to follow my directions," he said. "Do so and I'll be responsible to the company; disobey, and I'll hold you to the chalk-mark every time."

Finn sullenly shifted his quid and nodded; Dyce looked rebellious.

"You might as well know," continued Lee, "that I mean what I say. You'll find it out. Do your work and we'll get on without trouble. You'll find I'm just."

When Dyce and Finn had shuffled away toward the coast, Lee looked at the figure outlined on the cliffs against the sunset sky,—a desolate, lonely little figure in truth.

"Come," said Lee; "if you must have work I will give you enough to keep you busy; not in the quarry either,—do you want to cripple yourself in that pit? It's no place for children anyway. Can you write properly?"

The girl nodded, back turned toward him.

"Then you can keep the rolls, duplicates, and all. You'll have a room to yourself in my shanty. I'll pay quarry wages."

He did not add that those wages must come out of his own pocket. The company allowed him no secretary, and he was too sensitive to suggest one.

"I don't ask you where you came from or why you are here," he said a little roughly. "If there is gossip I cannot help it." He walked to the smudge and stood in the smoke, for the wind had died out and the black flies were active.

"Perhaps," he hazarded, "you would like to go back to—to where you came from? I'll send you back."

She shook her head.

"There may be gossip in camp."

The slightest movement of her shoulders indicated her indifference. Lee re-lighted his pipe, poked the smudge, and piled damp moss on it.

"All right," he said, "don't be unhappy; I'll do what I can to make you comfortable. You had better come into the smudge, to begin with."

She came, touching her eyes with her hands, awkward, hesitating. He looked gravely at her clumsy boots, at the loose, toil-stained overalls.

"What is your name?" he said, without embarrassment.

"My name is Helen Pine." She looked up at him steadily; after a moment she repeated her name as though expecting him to recognise it. He did not; he had never before heard it, as far as he knew. Neither did he find in her eager, wistful face anything familiar. How should he remember her? Why should he remember? It was nearly six months ago that, snow-bound in the little village on the Mohawk, he and the directors of his company left their private Pullman car to amuse themselves at a country dance. How should he recollect the dark-eyed girl who had danced the "fireman's quad-rille" with him, who had romped through a reel or two with him, who had amused him through a snowy evening? How should he recall the careless country incident,—the corn popping, the apple race, the flirtation on the dark, windy stairway? Who could expect him to remember the laughing kiss, the meaningless promise to write, the promises to return some day for another dance, and kiss? A week later he had forgotten the village, forgotten the dance, the pop-corn, the stairway, and the kiss. She never forgot. Had he told her he loved her? He forgot it before she replied. Had he amused himself? Passably. But he was glad that the snow-plows cleared the track next morning, for there was trouble in Albany and lobbying to do, and a rival company was moving wheels within wheels to lubricate the machinery of honest legislation.

So it meant nothing to him, this episode of a snow blockade; it meant all the world to her. For months she awaited the letter that never came. An Albany journal mentioned his name and profession. She wrote to the company and learned where the quarry lay. She was young and foolish and nearly broken-hearted, so she ran away. Her first sentimental idea was to work herself to death, disguised, under his very eyes. When she lay dying she would reveal herself to him, and he should know too late the value of such a love. To this end she purchased some shears to cut her hair with; but the mental picture she conjured was not improved by such a sacrifice. She re-coiled her hair tightly and bought a slouched hat, too big.

When, arrived at the quarry, she saw him again, she nearly fainted from fright. He met her twice, face to face, and she was astounded that he did not recognise her. Reflection, however, assured her that her disguise must be perfect, and she awaited the dramatic moment when she should reveal herself—not dying from quarry-toil—for she did not wish to die now that she had seen him. No—she would live—live to prove to him how a woman can love—live to confound him with her constancy. She had read many romances. Now, when he had bade her follow him to the headland, she knew she had been discovered; she was weak with terror and shame and hope. She thought he knew her; when he spoke so coolly she stood dumb with amazement; when he spoke of Finn and Sawyer and Dyce she understood he had not penetrated her disguise, except from hearsay, and a terror of loneliness and desolation rushed over her.

Then the impulse came to hide her identity from him,—why, she did not know. Again that vanished when he called her to come into the smoke. As she looked up at him her heart almost stopped; yet he did not recognise her. Then the courage of despair seized her and she told her name. When at length she comprehended that he had entirely forgotten her—forgotten her very name—fright sealed her lips. All the hopelessness and horror of her position dawned upon her,—all she had believed, expected, prayed for, came down with a crash.

As they stood together in the smoke of the smudge, she mechanically laid her hand on his sleeve, for her knees scarcely supported her.

"What is it; does the smoke make you dizzy?" he asked.

She nodded; he aided her to the cliff's edge and seated her on a boulder. Under the cliff the sunset light reddened the sea. A quarryman, standing on a rock, looked up at Lee and pointed seaward.

"Hello!" answered Lee, "what is it? The Collector of the Port?"

Other quarrymen, grouped on the coast, took up the cry; the lumbermen, returning from the forest along the inlet, paused, axe on shoulder, to stare at the sea. Presently, out in the calm ocean, a black triangle cut the surface, dipped, glided landward, dipped, glided, disappeared. Again the dark point came into view, now close under the cliff where thirty feet of limpid water bathed its base.

"The Collector of the Port!" shouted Finn from the rocks.

Lee bent over the cliff's brink. Far down into the clear water he followed the outline of the cliff. Under it a shadowy shape floated, a monstrous shark, rubbing the rock softly as if in greeting for old acquaintance' sake.

The Collector of the Port had returned from the south.

II.

The Collector of the Port and the company were rivals; both killed their men, one at sea, the other in the quarry. The company objected to pelagic slaughter and sent some men with harpoons, bombs, and shark-hooks to the Port; but the Collector sheered off to sea and waited for them to go away.

The company could not keep the quarrymen from bathing; Lee could not keep the Collector from Port-of-Waves. Every year two or three quarrymen fell to his share; the company killed the even half-dozen. Years before, the quarrymen had named the shark; the name fascinated everybody with its sinister conventionality. In truth he was Collector of the Port,—an official who took toll of all who ventured from this Port where nothing entered from the sea save the sea itself, wave on wave, wave after wave.

In the superintendent's office there were two rolls of victims,—victims of the quarry and victims of the Collector of the Port. Pensions were not allowed to families of the latter class, so, as Dyce said to Dyce's dying brother: "Thank God you was blowed up, an' say no more about it, Hank."

There was, curiously enough, little animosity against the Collector of the Port among the quarrymen. When June brought the great shark back to the Port they welcomed him with sticks of dynamite, but nevertheless a sense of proprietorship, of exclusive right to the biggest shark on the coast, aroused in the quarrymen a sentiment akin to pride. Between the shark and the men existed an uncanny comradeship, curiously in evidence when the company's imported shark-destroyers appeared at the Port.

"G'wan now," observed Farrely, "an' divil a shark ye'll get in the wather, me bucks! Is it sharks ye'll harpoon? Sure th' company's full o' thim."

The shark-catchers, harpoons, bombs, and hooks, retired after a month's useless worrying, and the men jeered them as they embarked on the gravel train.

"Drhop a dynamite shtick on the nob av his nibs!" shouted Farrely after them—meaning the president of the company. The next day, little Caesar l'Hommedieu, indulging in his semi-annual bath, was appreciated and accepted by the Collector of the Port, and his name was added to the unpensioned roll in the office of the company's superintendent, Francis Lee.

Helen Pine, sitting alone in her room, copied the roll, erased little Caesar's name from the pay-roll, computed the total back pay due him, and made out an order on the company for $20.39. Then she rose, stepped quietly into Lee's office which adjoined her own room, and silently handed him the order.

Lee was busy and motioned her to be seated. Dyce and Finn, hats in hand, looked obliquely at her as she leaned on the window-ledge, face turned toward the sea. She heard Lee say, "Go on, Finn;" and Finn began again in his smooth plausible voice:

"I opened the safe on a flat-car, an' God knows who uncoupled the flat. Then Dyce signalled go ahead, but Henderson he sez Dyce signalled to back her up, an' the first I see was that flat hangin' over the dump-dock. Then she tipped up like a seesaw an' slid the safe into the water—fifty-eight feet sheer at low tide."

Lee said quietly: "Rig a derrick on the dump-dock, and tell Kinny to get his diving kit ready by three o'clock."

Finn and Dyce exchanged glances.

"Kinny he went to Bangor last night to see about them new drills," said Finn defiantly.

"Who sent him?" asked Lee angrily. "Oh, you did, eh?"

"I thought you wanted them drills," repeated Finn.

Lee's eyes turned from Finn to Dyce. There was, in the sullen faces before him, something that he had never before seen, something worse than sinister. The next moment he said pleasantly: "Well then, tell Lefty Sawyer to take his diving kit and be ready by three. If you need a new ladder at the dump-dock send one there by noon. That is all, men."

When Finn and Dyce had gone, Lee sprang to his feet and began to pace the office. Once he stopped to light his pipe; once he jerked open the top drawer of his table and glanced at a pair of heavy Colt's revolvers lying there, cocked and loaded. He sat down at his desk after a while and spoke, perhaps half unconsciously, to Helen, as though he had been speaking to her since Finn and Dyce left:

"They're a hard crowd—a tough lot—and I knew it would come to a crisis sooner or later. Last year they drove the other superintendent to resign, and I was warned to look out for myself. Now they see that they can't use me, and they mean to get rid of me."

She turned from the window as he finished; he looked at her without seeing the oval face, the dark questioning eyes, the young rounded figure involuntarily bending toward him.

"They tipped that safe off the dock on purpose," he said; "they sent Kinny to Bangor on a fool's errand. Now Sawyer's got to go down and see what can be done. I know what he'll say! He'll report the safe broken and one or two cash boxes missing, and he'll bring up the rest and wait for a chance to divide with his gang."

He started to his feet and began to pace the floor again, talking all the while:

"It's come to a crisis now, and *I'm* not going under! I'll face them down; I'll break that gang as they break stone! If I only knew how to use a diving kit—and if I dared—with Dyce at the lifeline—"

Half an hour later Lee, seated at his desk, raised his pale face from his hands and, for the first time, became conscious that Helen sat watching him beside the window.

"Can I do anything for you?" he asked pleasantly.

She held the order out to him; he took it, examined it, and, picking up a pen, signed his name.

"Forward it to the company," he said; "Caesar's family will collect it quicker than the shark collected Caesar."

He did not mean to shock the girl with cynicism; indeed it was only such artificial indifference that enabled him to endure the misery of the Port-of-Waves,—misery that came under his eyes from sea and land,—interminable hopeless human woe.

What could he do for the lacerated creatures at the quarry? He had only his salary. What could he do for families made destitute? The mica crushed and cut and blinded; the Collector of the Port exacted bloody toll in spite of him. He could not drive the dust-choked, half-maddened quarrymen from their one solace and balm, the cool, healing ocean; he could not drive the Collector from the Port-of-Waves.

"I didn't mean to speak unfeelingly," he said. "I feel such things very deeply."

To his surprise and displeasure she replied: "I did not know you felt anything."

She grew red after she said it; he stared at her. "Do you regard me as brutal?" he asked sarcastically.

"No," she said, steadying her voice: "you are not brutal; one must be human to be brutal."

He looked at her half angrily, half inclined to laugh.

"You mean I am devoid of human feeling?"

"I am not here to criticise my employer," she answered faintly.

"Oh—but you have."

She was silent.

"You said you were not aware that I felt anything."

She did not reply.

He thought to himself: "I took her from the quarry, and this is what I get." She divined his thought. She could have answered: "And you sent me to the quarry—for the memory of a kiss." But she did not speak.

Watching her curiously, he noticed the gray woollen gown, the spotless collar and cuffs, the light on her hair, like light on watered silk. Her young face was turned toward the window. For the first time it occurred to him that she might be lonely. He wondered where she came from, why she had sought Port-of-Waves among all places on earth, what tragedy could have driven her from kin and kind to the haunts of men. She seemed so utterly alone, so hopelessly dependent, so young that his conscience smote him, and he resolved to be a little companionable toward her, as far as his position of superintendent permitted. True, he could not do much; and whatever he might do would perhaps be misinterpreted by her, certainly by the quarrymen.

"A safe fell off the dock, to-day," he said pleasantly, forgetting she had been present at the announcement of the disaster by Finn and Dyce. "Would you like to see the diver go down?"

She turned toward him and smiled.

"It might interest you," he went on, surprised at the beauty of her eyes; "we're going to try to hoist the safe out of fifty odd feet of water—unless it is smashed on the rocks. Come down when I go at three o'clock."

As he spoke his face grew grave, and he glanced at the open drawer by his elbow, where two blue revolver barrels lay shining in the morning light.

At noon she went into her little room, locked the door, and sat down on the bed. She cried steadily till two o'clock; from two until three she spent the time in obliterating all traces of tears; at three he knocked at her door, and she opened the door, fresh, dainty, smiling, and joined him, tying the strings of a pink sun-bonnet under her oval chin.

III.

The afternoon sun beat down on the dump-dock where the derrick swung like a stumpy gallows against the sky. A dozen hard-faced, silent quarrymen sat around in groups on the string-pieces; Farrely raked out the fire in the rusty little engine; Finn and Dyce whispered together, glowering at Lefty Sawyer, who stood dripping in his diving suit while Lee unscrewed the helmet and disentangled the lines.

Behind Lee, Helen Pine sat on a pile of condemned sleepers, nervously twisting and untwisting the strings of her sun-bonnet.

When Sawyer was able to hear and be heard, Lee listened, tight-lipped and hard eyed, to a report that brought a malicious sneer to Finn's face and a twinkle of triumph into Dyce's dissipated eyes.

"The safe is smashed an' the door open. Them there eight cash-boxes is all that I see." He pointed to the pile of steel boxes, still glistening with salt water, and already streaked and blotched with orange colored rust.

"There are ten boxes," said Lee coldly; "go down again."

Unwillingly, sullenly, Lefty Sawyer suffered himself to be invested with the heavy helmet; the lines and tubes were adjusted, Dyce superintended the descent and Finn seized the signal cord. After a minute it twitched; Lee grew white with anger; Dyce turned away to conceal a grin.

When again Sawyer stood on the dock and reported that the two cash-boxes were hopelessly engulfed in the mud, Lee sternly bade him divest himself of the diving suit.

"What you goin' to do?" said Finn, coming up.

"Is it your place to ask questions?" said Lee sharply. "Obey orders or you'll regret it!"

"He's going down himself," whispered Dyce to Sawyer. The diver cast a savage glance at Lee and hesitated.

"Take off that suit," repeated Lee.

Finn, scowling with anger, attempted to speak, but Lee turned on him and bade him be silent.

Slowly Sawyer divested himself of the clumsy diving suit; one after the other he pushed the leaden soled shoes from him.

Lee watched him with mixed emotions. He had gone too far to go back now—he understood that. Flinching at such a moment meant chaos in the quarry, and he knew that the last shred of his authority and control would go if he hesitated. Yet, with all his heart and soul he shrank from going down into the sea. What might not such men do? Dyce held the life-line. A moment or two suffocation—would such men hesitate? Accidents are so easy to prove and signals may be easily misunderstood. He laid a brace of heavy revolvers on the dock.

As Dyce lifted the helmet upon his shoulders, he caught a last glimpse of sunlight and blue sky and green leaves—a brief vision of dark, brutal faces—of Helen Pine's frightened eyes. Then he felt himself on the dock ladder, then a thousand tons seemed to fall from his feet and the dusky ocean enveloped him.

On the dump-dock silence reigned. After a moment or two Finn whispered to Sawyer; Dyce joined the group; Farrely whitened a bit under his brick-red sunburn and pretended to fuss at his engine.

Helen Pine, heart beating furiously, watched them. She did not know what they were going to do—what they were doing now with the air tubes. She did not understand such things, but she saw a line suddenly twitch in Dyce's fingers, and she saw murder in Finn's eyes.

Before she knew what she was doing she found herself clutching both of Lee's revolvers.

Finn saw her and stood petrified; Dyce gaped at the level muzzles. Nobody moved.

After a little while Dyce's right hand twitched violently. Finn started and swore; Sawyer said distinctly; "Cut that line!"

The next instant she fired at him point-blank, and he dropped to the bleached boards with a howl of dismay. The crack of the revolver echoed and echoed among the rocks. Presently, behind his engine, Farrely began to laugh; two quarrymen near him got up and shambled hastily away.

"Draw him up!" gasped the girl with a desperate glance at the water.

Finn, the foreman, cursed and flung down his lines and walked away, cursing.

"Take the lines, Noonan," she cried breathlessly; "Dyce, pull him up!"

The great blank-eyed helmet appeared; she watched it as though hypnotised. When, dragging his leaden feet, Lee stumbled to the dock and flung one of the two missing cash-boxes at Dyce's feet, she grew dizzy and her little hands ached with their grip on the heavy weapons.

Sawyer, stupid, clutching his shattered fore-arm, never removed his eyes from her face; Dyce unscrewed the helmet, shaking with fright.

"There, you lying blackguard!" panted Lee, pointing to the recovered cash-box, "take them all to my office where I'll settle with you once and for all!"

Nobody replied. Lee, flushed with excitement and triumph, stripped off his diving-dress before he became aware that something beside his own episode had occurred. Then he saw Lefty Sawyer, bedabbled with blood, staring with sick, surprised eyes at somebody—a woman,—who sat huddled on a heap of sun-dried sleepers, sun-bonnet fallen back, cocked revolver in either hand, and, in her dark eyes, tears that flowed silently over colourless cheeks.

Lee glared at Dyce.

"Ask *her*," muttered Dyce doggedly.

He turned toward Helen, but Farrely, behind his engine, shouted: "Faith, she stood off th' gang or the breathin' below wud ha' choked ye! Thank the lass, lad, an' mind she's a gun whin ye go worritin' the fishes for the coompany's cash-box!"

That night Lee made a speech at the quarry. The men listened placidly. Dyce, amazed that he was not discharged, went back to nurse Sawyer, a thoroughly cowed man. Noonan, Farrely, and Phelan, retired to their shanty and got fighting drunk to the health of the "colleen wid the gun;" the rest of the men went away with wholesome convictions concerning their superintendent that promised better things.

"Didn't shanghai Dyce,—no he didn't," was the whispered comment.

Lee's policy had done its work.

As for the murderous mover of the plot, the plausible foreman, Finn, he had shown the white feather under fire and he knew the men might kill him on sight. It's an Irish characteristic under such circumstances.

Lee walked back from the quarry, realising his triumph, recognising that he owed it neither to his foolhardy impulse, nor yet to his mercy to Dyce and Sawyer. He went to the house and knocked at Helen's door. She was not there. He sat alone in his office, absently playing with pen and ruler until the June moon rose over the ocean and yellow sparkles flashed among the waves. An hour later he went to the dock and found her sitting there alone in the moonlight.

She did not repulse him. Her hour had come and she knew it, for she had read such things in romances. It came. But she was too much in love, too sincere to use a setting so dramatic. She told him she loved him; she told him why she had come to the Port-of-Waves, why she had remembered the kiss and the promise. She rested her head on his shoulder and looked out at the moon, smaller and more silvery now. She was contented.

Under the dock the dark waves lapped musically. Under the dock Finn, stripped to the skin, plunged silently downward for the one missing cash-box, trusting to his sense of touch to find the safe.

But what he found was too horrible for words.

"Hark," whispered Helen; "did you hear something splash?"

Lee looked out into the moonlight; a shadow, a black triangular point cut the silvery surface, steered hither and thither,—circled, sheered seaward, and was lost. Then came another splash, far out among the waves.

"The Collector of the Port," said Lee; "is making merry in the moonlight."

> *I' bruinait…. L'temps était gris,*
> *On n'voyait pas l'ciel … L'atmosphere*
> *Semblant suer au-d'ssus d'la ville,*
> *Tombait en bué su' la terre.*
> "FANTAISIE TRISTE."

THE WHISPER

As I entered the alley the bells of the dim city tolled for the passing night. Far in the black maze of filthy lanes and mist-choked streets a policeman whistled; I heard the distant din of an Elevated train, rushing through the fog, nearer, nearer, duller now, now smothered in the vapour which rolled from river to river, thick, heavy, stifling.

In the gloom of the alley a shadowy form loomed up and passed, leaving no sound of footsteps in my ears, but all around me the vapour became faintly tainted with opium and a flare of yellow light streamed out across the fog from an opening door. There was a momentary murmur of voices, the soft shuffle of felt-shod feet, the rustle of silken sleeves. A painted paper lantern swung from the doorway, dipped, and disappeared. I heard the deadened slam of the door and the black night veiled my eyes again.

An empty truck, with broken shafts buried in the mud of the gutter, blocked the sidewalk, and I crossed the greasy pavement to avoid it.

Around the pale flame of a gas lamp the fog spun an iridescent oval; the wet sidewalk glimmered underneath. Far down the reeking throat of the alley an arc-light shone like a grey star.

I raised my eyes to the dark house before me where from a rusting balcony a sign hung low above the doorway.

"This was her house," I said aloud to myself; but I passed on to the next house. Here I paused a moment, looking back at the bamboo sign dripping with fog, then turned and descended some wooden steps to an iron door. Before I could find the handle, wrought in bronze like a dragon's claw, the door flew open and I heard McManus' angry bellow; "Git t' hell outer here, yer dope suckin' yap!" and a Chinaman was hustled into the area beside me.

"Chin chin thlough hattee!" snarled the Chinaman, "walkee where dlam please!"

"I'll walkee you on yer neck!" growled McManus, and kicked the Chinaman half way up the steps.

"Dlam! Dlam! Dlam!" screamed the Chinaman, dancing with rage, but Charley, the bouncer, burst out of the door, and the Chinaman fled chattering like an infuriated ape.

I stepped into the low-ceilinged room and took a chair at a cherry-wood table beside the wall. Two young men sitting there said, "Hello, Jim!"

"Good evenin'," said McManus, leaning over the bar, "did you see me givin' de bounce to Wah-Wo?"

"Yes," I said, "when did he come back?"

"He jest come in. I told him to git an' he give me de ha-ha, so Charley trun him down. What t'hell, sez I, an' he gives me back talk! Say, I won't do a t'ing to him!"

One of the young men at the table beside me looked up from the Welsh-rabbit he was eating and called for ale. McManus brought it himself, a brimming pewter mug, and wiped his hands on his blue apron. Then he bawled for Charley to take my order.

"Sure," said Charley coming in from the street where he had been patiently waiting for a scrap, and he leaned with both fists on the table and winked pleasantly at the company. Lynde, of the "Herald," advised me to try a rabbit, and Penlow, of the "Tribune," spoke well of the chops, so I left it to Charley and he retired to the grill, whistling, "Oh I don't know!"

"It's a wonder to me," I said, hanging my wet mackintosh on a peg and kicking off my overshoes, "it's a wonder to me that Wah-Wo was discharged."

"There was no evidence to hold him," observed Lynde after a moment's silence.

Penlow lighted his pipe and rattled his mug on the table.

"No evidence," I repeated; "do you fellows doubt that Wah-Wo did it?"

"I suppose he did," said Penlow, "it was my scoop too."

"We may scoop yet," said Lynde, "the man's bound to be caught. What did they do with that young tough from Hell's Kitchen?"

"Sheehan? Oh, his alibi is good," said Penlow. "Mac, fill her up will you?"

McManus replenished the pewter and stood for a moment beside us as if undecided.

"Gents," began McManus, "youse is dead off—excuse me." He shifted his toothpick and rubbed his thumb on the polished bar.

"Wah-Wo ain't in it," he said contemptuously: "I give him de t'row-down,—fur why?—fur because I don't give de glad hand to no dope suckin' come-on—an' he's dopy. But he didn't do no dirt to the gal whut youse gents was stuck on—he ain't that kind. He give me the laugh an' I t'rowed him down, see? An' I won't do a t'ing but push his face in. See? "

"But," said Penlow, "her dog flew at him when he went to the house. Kerrigan, you know—'Happy Days Mike'—said that Wah-Wo tried to cut a girl in Doyers Street."

"Nit! I don't think," said McManus scornfully: "Kerrigan's a stuff—"

"Well, Mac," said Lynde, "what's your theory? You know as much about it as anybody. The girl came in here every night, didn't she? People say that she lived alone, but of course she had company when she wanted it. What's your idea, Mac?"

McManus looked out of the window and drummed on the bar with the blade of his oyster knife. Charley, clad in a blue checked jumper, arrived with some chops and ale. I unfolded my napkin and began my supper.

For a while I ate in silence, thinking of Wah-Wo and the dead girl.

Caithness of the Consolidated Press came in looking cold and ill, and we hastily made room for him at our table.

"You're sick," said Lynde sharply, "you ought to be in bed."

"I'm all right," said Caithness, glancing at us with his large dark eyes: "Mac, get me something hot."

I swallowed my ale and turned again to the chops, scarcely listening to the hum of voices beside me, for I was thinking again of the dead girl.

I had no doubt that Wah-Wo had killed her. Again and again I had seen his eyes fastened upon her as she sat chatting with us, here at this very table. The motive was clear to me. I had spoken of this to the others but they laughed at me. The District Attorney took no stock in it, either; the result was the discharge of Wah-Wo.

How could anybody but a Chinaman, crazed with jealousy and opium, harm the child? For she was a mere child, this pallid victim whose soul had mounted to the Judgment seat from the filth of Chinatown.

Pale, slim, childish, depraved, she had never haunted Chinese resorts nor, to my knowledge, had she ever touched needle to flame. She had shunned the women of the quarter. I seldom saw her speak to any man except the reporters and newspaper artists who came to McManus's for a midnight chop or rarebit.

Her acquaintance with us had been open and guileless. She chatted with us about our business, discussed the latest police shake-up or the newest Tammany scandal, gave us her views on politics and the City Hall, and glided away into the street again followed by her dog. Her dog! A great hulking brute, black as night, with sombre eyes and low hanging jowl,—a creature silent, unmoved except when she bent her pale face to his ear and whispered. Then and then only he would rise, shuffling from the sawdust floor under the bar, and stalk after her into the night.

He never paid the slightest attention to us. Calls, caresses, threats, left him unmoved.

"What is it you whisper into his ear, Lil?" we often asked, but she would only smile and answer: "His name."

And so, as none of us knew his name, we called him simply, "her dog."

It had been two months now since Lil was found on her bed with a bullet in her heart and the dog lying stolidly across her bare little feet. And after we had clubbed together and buried her, we were kinder to her dog.

Every night he came gravely into McManus' to lie down under the bar just as he had done when Lil sat there chatting with us.

At first McManus was afraid that the dog would "hoodoo the place," but he left the silent brute undisturbed, and, after a while, began to grow fond of it.

"That dog ain't no mutt," McManus would say as he stood behind the bar opening oysters; "no an' he ain't no rube! Say! he's in it all the time when Charley trims the steaks."

As I sat thinking of all these things and sipping my ale meditatively, I heard the iron door creak on its hinges and the knocker fall once. Then something heavy and hairy rubbed its body against the door outside. McManus stood up saying: "Here he comes, gents!"

Her dog entered.

Lynde held out his hand as the brute passed, and Penlow flung a bone on the floor. The dog noticed neither the caress nor the bone, but lay down under the bar and stretched his great limbs across the floor, sighing heavily.

"There is one thing certain," said Lynde, looking at the dog: "the man who killed the girl was in the habit of visiting her,—and that dog knew him."

"I also believe the murderer was known to the dog," said Penlow.

"The murderer," said Caithness, "was her lover."

"It is strange," said I, "that none of us suspects anybody except Wah-Wo."

"Why strange?" asked Caithness, then he added impatiently, "yes, it is strange! Do you think she would have looked at a Chinaman?"

"The Chinaman looked at her; I saw him," I replied.

"After all, she was a common girl of the street," said Penlow unaffectedly, "and I guess pride cut no figure with her."

"That is where you lie," said Caithness in a low voice.

There was a dead silence. Then Penlow said: "Did I understand you, Caithness?"

I rose and laid my hand on Penlow's arm, which was twitching though his face was calm.

"Are you crazy?" I said to Caithness.

"I think I am," said Caithness slowly, "I beg your pardon, Penlow."

Lynde turned his puzzled eyes from Penlow to Caithness and lifted his mug mechanically. Penlow straightened in his chair but said nothing, and I leaned back motioning McManus to remove the covers.

After a few moments the constraint became irksome. "Red," the tortoise-shell cat, mascotte of McManus and exterminator of mice by special appointment, had cornered a vicious rat in the backyard, and now came marching in to display the game for our benefit.

"Git!" said McManus with pardonable pride, "the gents here don't give a damn fur to see rats."

Charley hustled the cat out again and McManus assured us for the hundredth time that "Red" was the only cross-eyed cat in New York.

None of us had ever before seen a cross-eyed cat so we did not deny it, although I remonstrated with McManus concerning his pride in "Red's" ocular misfortune.

"What's that?" demanded McManus.

"I don't see why," said I, "a cat should be the more valuable because it happens to be afflicted with strabismus."

"Sure!" said McManus doggedly.

"No, I don't," I repeated.

"It's a mascot," said McManus.

"How do you know?"

"Did youse gents ever see another cross-eyed cat?" demanded McManus hotly.

We all said no.

"Then what t'hell do youse gents know about mascots?" he exclaimed triumphantly.

The constraint still weighed upon us, however, for Caithness had neither spoken nor smiled, and Penlow, it was easy to see, had not forgotten.

Lynde picked up a paper and ran it through, unaffectedly searching for his own matter; after a while Penlow did the same.

I looked at Caithness, and he felt my eyes, for presently he moved a little and passed his hand over his sunken cheeks.

"What's up?" I asked, dropping my voice and bending toward him.

"Nothing—why?"

"You look like the last rose of summer,—you've got a beastly cough."

He smiled faintly. "It's consumption," he said, "I found out to-day."

I stared at him stupidly.

"I don't mind," he said; "I'm dead sick of the whole business."

"How do you know it's consumption?" I asked at length.

"I went to three doctors to make sure; I tell you I don't care."

Little Penlow was listening now; before I could speak again he leaned over and took Caithness's hand affectionately.

"Brace up, old boy," he said, "go to California and get well."

"Of course," I cried, "you're a fool to stay in this cursed climate, Caithness!"

I spoke harshly for I was more affected than I cared to show.

"Chuck up your job! Let the Consolidated Press go to the devil!" urged Lynde.

"I have resigned," said Caithness quietly. A fit of coughing shook him, and he raised his napkin to his lips. He continued, "I thought I'd come around to-night and say good-bye."

The dog shifted his position under the bar and sighed again. One of the gas jets behind the bar blazed up suddenly; McManus turned it lower, cursing the gas company.

"Do you fellows know that I have scooped?" said Caithness abruptly.

"Not—not the fellow who shot Lil," faltered Penlow, who had thrown his whole soul into solving the mystery.

"Yes—the murderer of Lily White," said Caithness. In the silence I could hear McManus grinding his toothpick in his yellow teeth.

"I'm out of the Consolidated now," continued Caithness calmly,—"the scoop is yours if you want it, Penlow."

"But—but you"—began Penlow.

"I?" said Caithness fiercely, "what do I care for newspapers? What do I care who knows it now,—what paper prints it first?"

Lynde leaned over the table, his head in his hand; Penlow's pipe went out; he did not relight it.

"Did you never know," said Caithness with a touch of scorn in his voice, "that I also loved the girl? Do you think I am ashamed to confess it? Do you know what I have been through since she died? Hell? Oh, yes, that's what they say in books. It doesn't matter;—Penlow, when you are ready—"

Penlow started, then groped in his pocket for pencil and pad.

"I am ready, Jack," he said.

"This is the story," said Caithness, almost eagerly. "On the 13th of last November, Lily White, a girl living next door, was shot through the heart by a man who was jealous of her. He knew that she came into McManus's and gossiped with the newspaper men, and he knew that Wah-Wo had offered her all his money, which was a great deal. When she was chatting with us here, this man was not jealous,—have you got that, Penlow?"

"Yes," said Penlow, scratching away on his pad.

"He was not jealous when Lily chatted with us, but when he saw Wah-Wo talking to her one night under the electric light by the Joss-house, he watched the girl night and day. She said that she loved him—she laughed at him when he offered her marriage,—so he watched her. Have you got that, Penlow?"

"Yes."

"Then a day came when Lily was to go to the country to see her sister,—that is what she said,—to see her sister, and this man went with her to the train and saw her off on her journey. But something told him to watch the next in-coming train, and he did. And Lily was on it.

"He followed her. She came straight to Doyers Street, heavily veiled, and entered a house that you all know,—the house with the paper lanterns and red signs. Wah-Wo lives there. A week later she returned to the man who had followed her. He was waiting for her,—have you written that?"

"Yes, Jack."

"He was waiting in her room,—alone with that dog there. He accused her, and she denied it. She called Heaven to witness her innocence. He offered her marriage again; she laughed at him. Then he shot her through the heart."

Penlow ceased writing and looked up expectantly.

"The murderer's name? Have patience," said Caithness grimly smiling. "The man called to the dog,—her dog there, and, because he was the only living soul who knew the brute's name, the dog answered and followed him out into the street.

"All day long he wandered about the city, and at night he went back to look upon the dead. He did not care who saw him,—he courted discovery, but no one paid him any attention, and, as it now appears, nobody even saw him. About midnight he went away, leaving the dog crouched at the dead girl's feet, and since then he has moved like a living death among the people of the city, unsuspected, unnoticed by any,—except me." He paused and looked at us. Tears had quenched the pale flame in his eyes, and the hair clung to his damp forehead.

"That man killed the woman I loved," he said, "and now I am going to give him up!" Then he rose trembling. The sleeping dog sighed heavily; his hind legs quivered.

Caithness bent and touched the massive head, muttering, "Come!"

At his touch the dog raised its head and looked at him with grave eyes.

Then, moving toward the door, he whispered again, *calling the dog by name*; and the great brute rose stiffly, yawned, and slowly followed him out into the night.

The iron door slammed behind them; the damp odour of fog came from the black street. Lynde buried his head in his hands; McManus leaned heavily on the bar, pale as a corpse. Presently I heard the sound of rustling paper.

It was Penlow, tearing up his pad.

THE LITTLE MISERY

If you be dead also and are come hither to join us, I pity your lot, for you will be stunned with the noise of the dwarfs and the storks.

VATHEK.

I.

There was a river-driver beyond the Northwest Carry who respected neither moose nor man. Because he was the best river-driver on the West Branch they let him alone until he struck an Indian with a pick-pole.

The Indian's head was damaged and while he waited for it to heal, he selected his revenge. His revenge was simple and effective. He hunted up the moose-warden and told many lies. Deftly concealed among these lies, however, was a truth that infuriated the warden.

The river-driver, whose name was Skeene, sat on his haunches and sneered when the moose-warden glided into camp. But when he dug out a head and antlers behind a shanty, Skeene picked up his rifle, looked obliquely at the moose-warden, tied his blanket and fry-pan, hoisted his canoe onto his head, and walked away to the southward, still sneering. I don't know what they said about it in Foxcroft, but Hale, who owned the timber, and who thought he owned Skeene, hunted him up and sent him to work on the new cut-off, hoping the affair might blow over in time for Skeene to drive logs again. But Skeene turned lazy and lined the dead water with traps and set-lines, and when Hale remonstrated, Skeene laughed. Then Hale threatened him and hinted about moose-wardens, and $500 fines, but Skeene thrashed Hale before the whole camp, packed his kit and canoe, and paddled serenely away down the West Branch.

That really began the trouble, for Hale never forgave him. When Skeene started to guide for Henderson on the upper Portage, Hale heard of it and ran him out. That, of course, marked him among the guides in the lake-country, and Skeene perhaps felt the ostracism, for he quietly went to work for Colby on the new sluice that ran from the carry-pond to the lake. Possibly, if they had let him alone, he might have turned out as tame as a moose-bird,—he was only twenty-three,—but Hale remembered, and the Indian remembered, and one day a man came in to the Carry Camp with a 44 bullet in his wrist and an unserved warrant in his pocket. The man was a moose-warden, and the warrant was for Skeene.

When the news spread that Skeene had shot a warden, the guides from Portage to Lily-Bay condemned him. Down at Greenville a sheriff and posse boarded the "Katandin," and spent several weeks cruising about at public expense. The lake steamboat was comfortable, the food good, and the sheriff and posse were in no hurry to quit. Possibly they expected Skeene to come down to the shore and sit on the rocks; perhaps they fancied he might paddle across their bows in his sleep. Naturally he did neither. When at length somebody suggested that the sheriff and posse take to their canoes, that official steamed back to the foot of the lake in a huff, and presently the rumours of Skeene's misdoings became scarcely more definite than campfire gossip.

Perhaps even then, if they had given him a chance, he might have surrendered and taken his punishment, but they didn't give him the chance. A warden saw him building a lean-to, on the island that divides the West Branch. The warden waited until dark, crawled in outside the fire, and caught Skeene asleep. That is all the warden recollects, merely that he caught Skeene asleep. What Skeene did to the warden when he awoke, the official cannot remember distinctly.

Three weeks after that, Skeene walked into Kineo store, handling his rifle in a most alarming fashion. He suggested that they place certain provisions and ammunition in his canoe, which lay on the beach below. The three clerks complied with an enthusiasm borne of fright. Twenty minutes later Skeene, in his canoe, was seen making for Moose River. Two guides, just from Lily Bay, refused to fire at him, arguing it was not right to drown a man for stealing pork and powder. The hotel had not yet opened, and the people at the annex objected to a man-hunting trip, so they only notified the sheriff again and secretly wished Skeene in hell.

Of course, at the hotels they denied the very existence of Skeene; but the Bangor "News" printed the story, and people fought shy of Moose River and the lake beyond which is called Red Lake. In vain the guides declared the region safe. It was safe as far as they were concerned. It is not the nature of a guide—that is, a white guide—to inform on or interfere with any man. Skeene let them alone. The Indians, too, paddled about Red Lake when they wanted to. The Indian log-driver, however, stayed away after Skeene had shot a hole in his canoe. The canoe being bark, it was through Providence and a patch of gum that the log-driving half-breed ever paddled out of the mouth of Moose River.

Now if they had not started to hunt Skeene from the Lakes, he would never have troubled anybody, except possibly Hale and the half-breed. He went to Canada for a year, worked at anything that came along, and sent money to Kineo store to pay for his pork and powder. That, of course, won him the guides again. So when home-sickness drove him back to Red

Lake, he expected to be let alone. Hale, sluicing at the Northwest Carry, heard he had returned, and started for Red Lake with the log-driving half-breed and six men. Two days later they returned; Hale had a bullet in his leg above the knee and the half-breed carried a similar gift in his forearm.

This incident, while relieving the conversational monotony at camp and landing, bothered the sheriff cruelly. He went to Foxcroft where they said unpleasant things to him; he went back to the Landing and they made fun of him.

There was a captain on the lake named Snow,—a white-bearded, mild-eyed giant. When the local paper wanted an item it filled in with, "Extraordinary weather on the Lake in July! Steamboat 'Red-Deer' in port with six feet two inches of Snow in her pilot house!"

The sheriff went to see Snow, and, after a long confab, summoned his posse, boarded the Red-Deer, and left Greenville, as the local paper expressed it, "under sealed orders, bound for Moose River." Naturally, half a dozen canoes were aboard, some lying bottom upward on the superstructure, some lashed to the rail. The posse carried Winchesters, although no game was in season.

Off the Grey Gull, an island, the little steamboat slowed down and stopped, the canoes were hoisted over the rail and dropped; the posse embarked. The sheriff said good-bye in a voice made loud by nervousness, and the Red-Deer swung about and steamed back to the foot of the lake with six feet two inches of Snow in her pilot-house.

At the mouth of Moose River two more canoes were waiting; Hale sat in one, paddle glistening in the pale spring sunshine; in the other sat the Indian log-driver, nursing the hammer of a rifle.

Below the long ridge the water is nearly dead, although a canoe might drift to the point in twenty-four hours. It was paddling for a mile to the first wing-dam, and there, the sheriff, who led, flung his stern-paddle into the bottom of the canoe, flourished the setting-pole, and stood up. At the same moment a jet of flame leaped from the edge of the wing-dam and a bullet passed through the sheriff's hat. The amazed official promptly fell overboard, sank, rose, grasped the edge of the canoe, and swamped it, turning the bow-paddler into the river. The swift current landed them on a shoal before the sheriff could shriek more than twice, and they crawled up on a rock, sleek and wet as half drowned flies in a sap-pan.

The other canoes had halted; some of the posse waved their rifles, but nobody fired at the wing-dam except Hale. He banged away as fast as he could pump the breach-lever, and Billy Sebato, the Indian, took to the bushes and lay patiently waiting for a mark, purring with eagerness.

"Jim Skeene, you darned thief!" shouted Hale, "come out from them stones! Jest you come out on to that there wing-dam once!"

Above the rush and gurgle of the river they heard Skeene's voice: "You let me be or I'll shoot to kill!"

"Thief! Thief!" yelled Hale, dancing in his seat with anger, until the canoe heeled and almost swamped.

"I ain't no more thief than you be, Josh Hale!" bawled Skeene, "I paid for them rations and ca'tridges and you know damn well I did!" Before he could add anything, the Indian, Sebato, fired twice.

"If that nigger Sebato don't quit shootin' I'll let loose on all o' ye!" called Skeene, shaking his rifle above the wing-dam edge. "Git back to your dreen, Josh Hale, I tell you."

Hale had reloaded his magazine, and now, swinging his setting-pole with one hand, started to push his canoe among the rocks where he could hold it and fire under cover. Skeene evidently saw him for he slid suddenly to the corner of the wing-dam and fired three shots through the canoe, cutting a swale lengthwise at the water's edge.

"Oh, you sneaky bob-cat!" yelled Hale, white with rage. In another moment he was working cup and sponge to bail his canoe, which swung away on the current and drifted broadside across the sandbar below, where it settled in two feet of limpid water.

"Now'll you let me be?" called Skeene. "I hain't done nothin' to you. If that there moose-warden wants me let him come and get me. Ain't you ashamed to go huntin' a man like a Lucivee? I tell ye I'll shoot to kill, b' God I will, at the next man that fires!"

"You dasn't," shouted the sheriff from behind his rock; "you ain't half a man, Jim Skeene!"

"I be," said Skeene calmly, "but I don't want no fuss. You keep off'n this river, and you keep off'n this here wing-dam. And you stop sneakin' along the woods there, Billy Sebato! Git back there! Git back, or I'll shoot to kill!"

"You'll hang if you do!" bawled the sheriff.

"Then tell that nigger Indian to git back! Tell him quick! I see him—I—"

Sebato's rifle cracked, and the shot was repeated by Hale, wading out on the shoal. Then a forked flame flashed from the wing-dam, there came a crash and crackle of dry twigs, and the Indian pitched heavily over the bank into the swirling river.

The echoes of the shots died out among the trees; for a minute the gurgle of the river ripple alone troubled the stillness. A kingfisher wheeled up stream, the sun flashing on his blue wings; a fish soused in a calm pool below the dam. Presently the changed voice of the sheriff broke the silence:

"Jim Skeene, God help you, you'll swing for this."

Skeene's pale face appeared above the dam, but nobody shot at him.

"You drove me to it;" said Skeene. He spoke huskily. "I told him to git back,—I warned him to quit sneakin' up on me."

"Come down off'n that wing-dam," commanded Hale.

"Not for you, Josh Hale," replied Skeene, "nor not for any man o' ye! An' I won't be took neither. I'm goin' away to live quiet if they let me."

He crouched and watched them as they pushed their canoes out into the main channel. The sheriff and Hale advanced to the pool where Sebato lay.

A slender fillet of blood, a mere thread hung in the water just below the surface, and stretched out, following the current, floating like a red string.

"Bring them settin'-poles," said the sheriff soberly, "paddles won't stand the heft, an' he's hefty." Hale suddenly turned, snarling at the wing-dam; "Jim Skeene, you sneakin' muskrat!—" he said; but Skeene was gone when Hale's bullet stung the rock above.

II.

They gave Skeene little peace for two months. Week after week a string of canoes passed the swift water under the first and second wing-dams, poled to the point-trail, and, disembarking a file of riflemen, poled on again to the discharge at Red Lake. Week after week the distant flash of a paddle startled the deer at sunrise among the lily-pads. At evening, too, silent canoes stealing through the sedge-grass, roused the great blue herons from their heavenward contemplation and sent the sheldrake scuttling and splashing across shoal water with a noise like a churning twinscrew.

But they did not catch Skeene.

Once they saw him for a moment standing in the stern of his canoe. The canoe lay at the mouth of the Little Misery, that dead stretch of water and dead-fall, winding through the bog to the southward. They gave chase, trailing Skeene's canoe by the wake bubbles until they ran plump into quick water. But the Little Misery is a strange stream draining a strange land, and there, in that maze of cuts and channels, of "logans" and quick water, of swamp, shoal, sedge, and spectral ranks of dead trees, towering above swale and deadwood, they stood no more chance of flushing Skeene than a caribou has of raising three fawns in a season.

What he did with his canoe nobody might know. Certainly he left the main channel. Did he himself hide in the bog or dead-falls? Where do young sandpipers vanish on a shingle beach? Oh there were sounds in the swamp as the sheriff's posse steered through the even with silent paddle,— sounds that stir only in lonely places, faint splashes, a sound of a swirl in still water, the breeze in the swale-grass.

And so they hunted Skeene at twilight, at dusk of morning, at high noon, from the Northeast Carry to the Northwest Carry, from the West-Branch to Seboomook, from Portage to Lily Bay, and through a hundred miles of lake and stream, up and down, up and down. But Moose River bore no tales on its placid breast, and the wing-dams towered silent as twin Sphinxes, and the sounds that startled the silence where the Little Misery coils through the strange country, are mysteries even to those who interpret them.

It was in May that the ice went out, in company with Skeene; it was in July that they felt the bite of his bullets below the wing-dam; it was in August that they gave up the chase.

That evening, Skeene stood on a wind-fall in the depths of the Little Misery and watched three canoes file out of the discharge and glide into the swift water of Moose River. The next morning he started a lean-to on the ridge back of the Little Misery, and the sharp crack and thwack of his axe rang out over Red Lake. At sunrise a moose-cow heard it and ploughed hastily shoreward through the lily-pads with an ouf! woof! ouf! as she struck the pebbles on the beach. One by one the great blue herons flapped up from the dead pines, circled, sailed, and turned over to pitch head downwards into the sedge with dull cries.

At noon the echoes of axe-strokes died away and the hut was thatched with balsam, blue side skyward. By three o'clock a spike buck, a yearling, lay across a log on the ridge, and at four o'clock Skeene had satisfied his hunger.

He sat on the shore under the ridge, pensively picking his white teeth with the enjoyment of the abandoned. Across the lake the mountains turned to sapphire and ashes; a pale sky deepened into flame colour; the sun hung a globe of crimson in gilded mist.

One by one the last sunbeams reddened the trunks of the trees to the eastward, the foliage burned, the shore line glimmered. Like changing hues on a bubble, the colours deepened, and played over the placid lake. A single snowy bank of cloud, piled up in the east, glowed where the sun stained its edges. The midges danced above the sedge; the lake-wash rocked the swales, to and fro, to and fro. A trout broke in shallow water, flapped up and splashed again, and the red sky crimsoned the widening rings, spreading slowly shoreward.

In the days that followed, Skeene learned to talk to himself. When he did this he forgot that he had killed Sebato; after a while he forgot it altogether.

When the August afternoons were ablaze with brazen sunlight and the lake glistened like a sheet of steel, Skeene sprawled on a log in the shade and watched the great blue herons. When they "drove stakes" he mocked them with the same note until they answered "Ke-whack! Ke-whack! Ke-whack!" The red squirrel's thin treble he imitated; he called the chipmunks with a tsip! tsip! and laughed until his white teeth glistened when a carrion-jay alighted on his knee for a shin-joint half hacked. The great belted-kingfishers knew him, the sheldrake, stringing along the creek at evening, turned their bright eyes to his, the osprey who lived above the ledge, wheeled above him for hours, knowing that he also was a savage thing and hunted when hungry.

He was hungry several times between sunrise and sunset. The swift water of the Little Misery gave him a trout to every set-line; the deeper pools by the sedge gave him pleasure.

On the Little Misery deer swarm at evening, and he had meat for the price of a cartridge.

The white nights of August brought that vague unrest that all forest creatures feel. The deer girdled the roots of the ash-trees and the spike bucks grew bolder; the great blue herons danced their contre-dance, evening after evening, at first solemnly, advancing, retreating in stately quadrilles, lifting their slim shins high in the sedge; but, as the month ended, the contre-dance lost dignity and gained in abandon, until the lone loon out on the lake shook the silence with his demon's laughter. As the moon waned, the forest world stirred; its attitude was expectant; it waited. The cow-moose began to cast evil oblique glances on her calves, now turned darker; and the little bull moose-calf, frisked until his tiny bell swung like the wattle on a turkey.

An impatience, almost a sadness fell upon Skeene. And with sadness came fear. He covered his lean-to and built a smoke-hole through which blue haze rose in the calm morning air. But, like wild things in winter, he was wary, and the steam-hole of a beaver's house might be more easily located than the chimney of Skeene's hut.

When September came a hush fell over the forest; land and water were silent; the trout no longer broke water or leaped full length in the after-glow; the deer picked a silent path along the shore; the herons stood all day, heads stretched heavenward; the loon's maniac laughter was stilled. Silent and more silent the woods grew as the new moon, a faint tracery above the hills, rose in the evening sky. At its first quarter the silence deepened, at its half, the stillness was intense. Then one black night the Full Moon of September flashed in the sky, and before the last shore ripple had caught its glitter, a gigantic black shadow waded out into the lake and a roar shook the hills.

The first bull-moose had bellowed, and the rutting season had begun.

Instantly the forest, the lake, the shore, the stream were alive; the meat-birds cried from every cedar; the deer barked from the sedge; a lynx howled and miauled in the second growth. Everywhere plumage and fur were growing glossy and gay. Even Skeene sewed porcupine quills into his boot-moccasins, and sang fragments of a song he had heard in Quebec.

III.

Now there is a season for all things; in the fall the black moose grows blacker and sleeker; in the fall the red buck rubs the tattered velvet from every prong; in the spring the mewing cat-bird whistles dreamily as a spotted thrush; in the spring the snowbird changes its feathers, chameleon like, as the snow drifts or melts; and the dry chirring of the red squirrel grows sweeter.

"Each after its kind," says the quaint Book, and so the spruce-grouse drums in the long summer days, and the crested wood-duck ruffles its rainbow plumes, and the painted trout hang over the gravel beds in September, and the antlered moose barks at the September moon.

As for Skeene, he sewed porcupine quills in a semicircle over the instep of his moccasins, laced a string of scarlet trout-flies across his slouch hat, and listened to the bull-moose, bellowing out on the moonlit ridge.

At times he sang his Quebec song, at times he sighed. Twice he spared a yearling buck,—he could not tell why. He caught a big red sable, bigger than the coon-cat at the Carry House. It scratched and bit him, but he was very good to it. A lazy beaver, driven from the colony by his industrious relatives, bored a hole in the bank under Skeene's shanty. Beaver-tail and hindquarters are good, cold boiled, but Skeene let him live in peace and even piled enough poplar saplings at his door to last any lazy beaver a year. And all this time he was sorry he killed Sebato at the wing-dam; he wished he had shot him a year before in the bog-country,—it was a good chance and nobody would have been the wiser.

When the September moon waxed full and the water lapped softly along the lake ledge, Skeene's heart grew full, and the blood in his neck and cheeks ebbed and surged like moon-tides. So, on the second night, he took his rifle and dragged the canoe to the beach. But his heart failed him and he feared the Carry House, and he went back to his camp and rolled and grunted through a sleepless night. On the third evening he started on foot, but he hesitated when the lamp in the Carry House broke out, a red beam in the night. He stood, wretched, wistful, undecided, fingering his rifle butt, and his heart beat to suffocation. Something near him stirred and moaned among the rocks,—a miserable gluttonous fisher-cat, its head bristling with porcupine quills. And Skeene, sick with self-compassion, trailed the wounded creature to the water's edge and killed it,—pitying it as he pitied himself. Then, worn out with the fever in his veins, he slept openly where he lay, wondering if he should wake on Red Lake shore or on the shores of a redder lake.

On the fourth night of the full of the moon, he went swiftly across the ridge, unarmed, and the miles of woodland and shore sped away like mist, so eagerly he ran. On that night he heard the moose-cows calling the barking bull, and the whoof! of the dun doe in the sedge. Far on the shore the red beam of the Carry lamp signalled him and his blood flamed the answer in his face. And, as he strode up to the house, he saw a woman on the shore looking out into the night across the spectral lake. It was Lois, servant at South Carry. He had danced with her two years ago at Foxcroft Landing, he had sent her six otter pelts a month before he shot Sebato.

She was the girl he had come for.

Is it possible she expected him? The restlessness of September had drawn her to the lake and something had led him to her.

The moon, a silver lamp, traced a shining trail across the shadowy waters; his canoe grated softly on the shoal, a string of bubbles followed the paddle sweep, the foam whispered secrets to the clustered sedge-grass.

And so, together, they glided away on a trail of silver water to the strange country, drained by strange streams, stirred by strange winds. The red spark of the Carry lamp died out in the night, the little grey stars twinkled over the dead waters, pale sparks from phantom nuptial torches flaring in the north.

At dawn the sky crimsoned the Little Misery. They slept. At sunrise a moose roared a salute to the coming day.

They awoke and kissed each other.

IV.

When the public-spirited citizens of Foxcroft offered $500 reward for the capture of Skeene, Placide L'Hommedieu scratched his greasy chin, licked his lips, and went out to buy cartridges. Placide had trapped in the Province and thought he could trap as well in Maine.

"Monsieur L'Hommedieu what will you do with $500?" asked the Mayor of Foxcroft.

"Le Hommydoo won't need it," observed a grizzled portage guide who had once shot a match with Skeene. And he was right for they found L'Hommedieu a week later peacefully floating down Moose River in his canoe, with a bullet in his brain.

When Skeene paddled away with Lois, there was trouble in Foxcroft. Hale left sluice, drain, and chain, and wired the Sheriff at the Landing to meet him at Moosehead Inn. The Mayor went also, and next morning the reward was doubled for "James Skeene, Murderer, dead or alive."

Hale had never forgiven the blow at the cut-off, but a busy man would scarcely have left his sluice to hunt another man to death for that alone. No, Hale had other reasons, and they concerned neither Billy Sebato nor

Placide L'Hommedieu. They concerned Lois, servant at South Carry; for when she left with Jim Skeene she took Hale's betrothal ring with her.

After Skeene had set Placide L'Hommedieu afloat, with mud on his face and a bullet in his skull, he shoved the canoe into swift water at Moose River, broke both paddles, splintered the setting-pole, and solemnly watched the canoe out of sight.

Lois, waiting for him when he poled into the Little Misery, looked at his knife in the scolloped leather sheath, then at his rifle, and finally into his sombre eyes.

"I heard,—only one shot. Was it a deer?"

He nodded muttering that he had missed; but that night she caressed him, taking his curly head into her arms, and wept over him till daybreak crimsoned the world.

After that they were almost gay. He notched logs and built a hut and rammed moss into the cracks. Lois brought clay from the sweet water, and cut balsam until her little hands were stained to the palm. Twice he passed the three carrys to the C. P. R. and hung to a freight as far as Sainte Croix. They knew nothing and cared less in the Dominion, and he bought salt and pork and flour and cartridges with the proceeds of Hale's ring. The third trip he walked on the C. P. fearing the train, and he got his price for ten pelts, including musk-rat.

They knew that happiness that is bred in haunting fear, that fierce, that intense love whose roots are imbedded in terror. Lois had been to school and these were the things she knew;—that two and two make four, that Moose calves are born in May, that bark peels best in June, that Moose-calves are weaned in September. She knew also how to use Skeene's knife, and when he found beaver above swift water and told her so in the evening, she cut saplings and whittled trip-sticks and notched chokers while he hewed out the bed-pieces for the traps, and sharpened enough young ash to build the fences for winter traps. Mink traps, too, were no mystery to Lois, and they talked long and wisely concerning standards and cubbies and spindles while the embers died under the simmering tins and the deer whistled on the windy ridge.

Snow came, a phantom flurry through the pale sunshine, and Skeene lugged more deer hides into his hut. A hot week followed, sending the trout to the bottom-sands and the deer to the shallows; then came the ice; at first a brittle, glittering skin, encasing stem and reed, and wrinkling hidden stagnant pools. The wind in the grasses grew harsher, the reeds rattled at evening; vast flocks of little birds circled high in the sky for the winds of the South called them, and the geese were drifting overhead.

One day the snow came again, and at evening it had not ceased falling. A week later the lake froze and Skeene dragged his canoe into the hut and daubed it with white-lead, while Lois crept close to his side and strung snowshoes. At times she sang. He listened, lying beside the canoe. When she had sung the same song until evening he taught her the song he had learned in Quebec;

> "Mossieu Meenoose
> Mossieu Meenoose
> Mon dieu que to as
> Un villain chat la."

And she sang it and sewed scarlet braid across her moccasins.

During these weeks Hale was busy in Foxcroft. When the smaller lakes froze he leered sideways at the Sheriff and ordered a dozen pairs of snow-shoes. Once or twice he went back to his sluice and cursed, but the River Drivers regarded him with evil eyes, and the sluicers drove their props sullenly until he went away leaving a string of oaths in his wake. There were men of the stamp he wanted on the Province side of the C. P. R.; there was Achille Verdier, one-eyed and idle; there was greasy little Armand Fleury, dirtier for his fox-skin cap, dingier for the red braid on the tail. There also resided Wyombo, pigeon-toed, furtive, aboriginal. Much could be done with these gentlemen and $1000. The value of Hale's ring was $150, therefore the people of Foxcroft gossiped.

Snow fell on the frozen lake; the Little Misery was mantled, the carrys choked. All day long the meat-birds whined in the fir-trees and at night the sleet pelted the frozen snow. The deer yarded on the ridge, the moose on the slope above; the black bear buried his feeble nose in his stomach and dreamed, and the otters frisked over their slide. As for Lois, she was learning things; she learned that the fur on the belly of a young panther is wavy, she learned that men are brutes, and that Skeene was all the world to her; she learned that she also had her value, for she saw him swim the swift water of the Little Misery when she screamed affrighted by an impudent lynx. She learned that he sometimes preferred solitude to company, that he sometimes preferred sleep to caresses. She learned that he went hungry that she might eat, that he shivered while she slept under skin and blanket.

Sometimes they played together, Skeene and this slender girl, like young foxes in the snow. She would often hide, too, in the hollow of a great swamp-oak, and when he came home she would call: "Jim! Jim! find me!"

But God lives, and the world spins, and the hare turns white in winter, and the routine of the beginning and the end never varies.

And so it came about that Skeene, laughing up at Lois in the hollow swamp-oak, glanced over his shoulder and saw six black dots clustered upon the frozen lake to the southward. He said nothing but looked into the north. There were more dots there, more also on the ice in the west. For a moment he thought the east was still open; after a while he heard the scrape of a snow-shoe very near. Lois also heard and her face was like death as she reached down and took the rifle from Skeene's hand.

When he had climbed up into the hollow tree beside her and looked out from the hole above the great branch, he saw Hale peering at him from a dead-fall.

"Come down," said Hale.

Skeene clapped his rifle to his cheek and fired.

"Come down," repeated Hale from behind his dead-fall. Lois, trembling at Skeene's feet, shrank at the sombre voice from the woods. Skeene bent and kissed her and caressed her, muttering things she could not understand, but she caught his hand in hers and tore off the fur mitten and pressed it to her hot lips, moaning and-sobbing.

"Come down for the last time, Jim Skeene," said Hale slowly. Suddenly a rifle shot rang through the frozen forest. The hand that Lois held tightened against her lips, quivered, relaxed. Something outside fell clinking and clattering to the ground at the foot of the tree. It was Skeene's rifle; and Skeene sank forward, hanging half out of the hole in the tree, head downward, like a dead squirrel.

And beside him, the other wild thing sobbed and whimpered and moaned among the branches while below the swift axes bit into the tree from which the dead game hung, head downward.

"Look in the hut for the woman!" bawled Hale.

The tree swayed and crackled and fell crashing into the snow.

"Where's that woman?" shouted Hale from the hut;—"G—d d—n her!"—

But when at last he found her he changed his mind and let her stay with Skeene there in the snow.

ENTER THE QUEEN

"Votre amour me ferait dieu.
M'aimez-vous, mademoiselle?
Soupirez un mois, dit-elle.
Un mois! C'est la mort! Adieu!"

Souvenir cher à mes pensees!
Grâce à la fraîcheur qu 'il leur rend,
Je souris aux heures passées,
Je m'arrange du jour mourant.
                    BERANGER.

I.

The middle of the studio was occupied by a rug. The middle of the rug was occupied by Clifford. He sat on the floor playing a dirge on a brass cornet. Around him lay bureau drawers, empty trunks and satchels, flanked by cabinets and chests littered with palettes, underclothes, colour-tubes, pipes, and paint-rags.

When Elliott came in, an hour later, he found Clifford still performing on the cornet. He played "Hark! from the Tomb," and "Death and The Maiden"; and while he played he winked ominously at Elliott.

Now, when Clifford played on his cornet, something was amiss. Elliott knew this and watched him sideways, sullenly removing overcoat and gloves. Every dismal bleat of the brass prophesied calamity. The hollow studio echoed with forebodings of disaster.

"Stop that," said Elliott, flinging his hat on a chair; "what's the matter with you?"

"O Commander of the Faithful," said Clifford, "behold the end of the world! J'ai beau cherchai—je n'en trouve point—"

"Money?" asked Elliott, sitting down; "stop blowing into that cornet."

"I know of no other way to raise the wind," said Clifford,—"get your cornet and we'll play duets."

"You mean we are actually without means?"

Clifford threaded his way through an abatis of easels, canvasses, books, and bird-cages to the Japanese tea-table.

"Have some tea?" he inquired.

"No, I won't," snapped Elliott, "and you can tell me where our funds have gone."

Clifford poured himself a cup of tea, raised his eyes piously, sipped it, and looked at Elliott over the edge of the cup.

"Where's our money?" repeated Elliott; "you had charge of the common account for the last three months—"

Clifford sighed, unrolled a sheet of paper, shoved it toward his confrère, and offered himself more tea. Elliott examined the figures anxiously.

"You hopeless ass!" he blurted out. "Why didn't you draw the purse strings?"

"I can deny you nothing, my son," protested Clifford, casting furtive glances toward his cornet again.

"But we're ruined!" bawled Elliott in sudden fright.

"Utterly," admitted Clifford pleasantly.

Through the broad glass roof the pale winter sunlight fell over piles of rugs and weapons on the floor; in the garden the sparrows chirped unceasingly around the frozen fountain. Elliott sat motionless, hypnotised by the column of figures before him. Clifford regarded his canary birds with vague reproach.

At last Elliott broke the silence:

"We had enough,—more than enough to live on decently; we threw our money away! Ass that I am, I didn't realise I was such an ass."

"I didn't either," said Clifford.

"Oh, you didn't?" sneered Elliott; "who was it that spent five hundred francs on those idiot birds?"

They frowned at the two dozen canaries. The birds hopped aimlessly from pole to perch and from perch to pole.

"I didn't buy a coupé for a lady," retorted Clifford.

"No, but you gave garden parties with fireworks and Chinese lanterns, and the company broke windows and set the curtains ablaze, and the police fined us for shooting rockets without a permit—"

"Accidents," observed Clifford; "our social position in the Latin Quarter required us to entertain."

"Our social position on this planet will also require us to eat,—occasionally."

"There's the furniture."

"I won't! I won't! You hear me, Clifford! I'll not sell a chair. Isn't there any money in any of those bureau drawers?"

"No,—look for yourself," replied Clifford cheerfully.

"Now I'll not mortgage our furniture," said Elliott; "so you needn't finger my carved chairs. We must pull through,—I don't know how,—but we must pull through. I shall cut down my tobacco, I shall drink cheap wine, I shall see Colette at once—"

"Do you think she can stand the blow?" inquired Clifford.

"Your wit is unseasonable," said Elliott haughtily; "how much can you get for your canaries?"

Clifford flatly refused to sell the birds and played a dirge on his cornet. Then the horror of poverty laid hold of Elliott and drove him out into the Luxembourg where he sat in the fading sunshine until the drums boomed from the southern terrace and the challenge of the sentinels, droning, monotonous, sounded and resounded across the windy park.

There was a hint of snow in the air as he passed out into the Place de Medici. He clinked the few gold pieces in his pocket as he walked. This appalled him, and he stepped more quickly.

On the Boulevard, a slim white-browed girl, exquisitely gowned, called to him from a coupé. When he motioned the coachman to stop and stepped to the curb, she buried her nose in a bunch of violets and laughed.

"Colette," said Elliott gloomily, "Mr. Clifford and I are compelled to retire for the space of three months. Therefore, most charming and most wise Colette,—therefore—"

He raised one hand and opened his fingers as though releasing a butterfly.

II.

All that week Clifford roamed about the studio blowing melancholy blasts from his cornet. Elliott sold a picture to Solomon Moritz for twenty francs, regretted it, tried to get it back, beat Mr. Moritz with a mahl-stick and resisted an officer. To his horror the French Government insisted on entertaining him for a week at Mazas, whither Clifford visited his comrade daily until Saturday and freedom arrived.

"This is a hell of a country," observed Elliott as he shook the dust of Mazas from his heels in company with Clifford. "It's no place for the breadwinner; the Jews have the country by the throat."

"They said," observed Clifford, "that you had Moritz by the throat."

"I did; the ruffian refused me thirty francs for my 'Judgment of Solomon.'"

"Dear me!" exclaimed Clifford with an impudent gesture, "wasn't it worth it?"

"You will refrain," said Elliott furiously, "from poking me in the ribs,— now and hereafter."

Half an hour later they entered the studio and sat down opposite each other in silence. The canaries filled the room with their imbecile twittering, and hopped and hopped until Elliott jumped up and seized his hat.

"Is this studio a bird-cage?" he demanded bitterly.

Clifford said something about jail-birds and picked up his cornet. For an hour he played "'Tite Femme" and "Place aux Gosses." But when he attacked "The Emperor's Funeral March," Elliott seized him.

"Let go," said Clifford sullenly.

"No. See here, Clifford, let's be friends and let's try to be practical. We've got to make our living for the next three months. Let's stop squabbling and hold a conference. Will you?"

"Yes," replied Clifford amiably.

"Then where do we dine?"

"We haven't lunched yet."

"This is awful," muttered Elliott, staring at the canaries; "do you suppose we could eat those birds?"

In the silence that ensued a piano began in the studio above, and a voice sang:

> "Et qu'elle est folle dans sa joie,
> Lorsq'elle chante le matin,—
> Lorsqu'en tirant son bas de soie,
> Elle fait; sur son flanc qui ploie,
> Craquer son corset de satin!"

The piano ceased; there came a laugh, a double roll on a Tambour-Basque, and the clicking of castanets.

"Who's that?" said Elliott morosely. Then with a sneer he paraphrased the last line of the song. Clifford pricked up his ears but shook his head.

"Hear her laugh! I suppose she's dined," continued Elliott with a vicious eye on the birds.

"Well, are we going to eat those cursed canaries?"

"I never heard you swear like that," protested Clifford. "Has poverty weakened your intellect?"

"Yes," said Elliott savagely.

"If we eat 'em our meal will cost five hundred francs."

"Then you've got to sell them. They are no good,—yellow birds are always feeble-minded. Canaries are ridiculous."

The castanets began again, and the voice took up the Spanish measure:

> My Picador! My Picador!
> Thy Spanish customs I adore,
> Thou garlic loving,
> Cattle shoving,
> Spick-and-spangled Picador!

> I hear the mottled heifer roar,
> > My Picador!
> The people pounding on the floor,
> > My Picador!
> The ring is clear!
> The cow is here!
> They've had to haul her by the ear;
> The Banderillos linger near!
> Oh, Picador! My Picador!"

"She's very gay," observed Clifford, after another silence broken only by the distant click! click! click! of the castanets. "Hm! I—er—I suppose we ought to call—"

"Call," repeated Elliott; "when I'm hollow!"

"If we call," said Clifford briskly, "we may be invited to dinner." He smiled, whistled a bar or two, and poked the fire."

"Don't," said the other, "you waste fuel."

The wind showered the sleet across the great windows; in the twilight a chill crept in over the rugs; a distant shutter banged, rattled, and banged again.

Elliott jumped up and paced the floor.

"We've got to do something," he said, "and do it now. Where's your watch?"

"You ought to know," said Clifford reproachfully. "Yours is there too."

After a moment he continued; "I've got those cuff-buttons you gave me—" He went into his bedroom and returned with the cuff-buttons. Elliott took them, jerked on his overcoat, nodded, and opened the door.

"I'll be back in half an hour,—wait for me," he said, and slammed the door behind him.

III.

"Now, what the mischief am I to do for half an hour," mused Clifford, staring out of the blank window, both hands in his pockets, an empty pipe between his teeth. There was a vacancy in his stomach that bothered him, and the more he thought about it, the more it hurt. The canary birds were revelling in bird-seed; he eyed them enviously for a while, then walked up and down whistling. Every time he passed the big gilded cage he could hear the birds cracking and splitting the seeds, and the noise of the feast irritated him.

His neighbour on the floor above was singing away with heart and soul about bull-rings and toreadors, banging joyously upon the Basque drum or snapping and clicking the castanets.

"Dear! Dear!" he thought, "my neighbour is really very gay. She must have moved in to-day. I—I wonder what she's like!"

He listened, sitting close to his dying fire. After a moment he heard her cross the room and open the piano again.

"Dear! Dear!" he said to himself, "what a musical young lady! Probably an embryo actress from the Conservatoire;—or—or—"

The piano began; it was scales this time. For an hour he sat huddled before the cold ashes, listening to the five-fingered acrobatic exercises, alternately yawning with hunger and cursing Elliott. When six o'clock struck from the concierge's lodge he stood up, gazing dismally out into the night.

Suddenly he heard the scrape of feet outside, and he hurried to his door and opened it.

Through the lighted hallway a figure shuffled, carrying a large tray covered with a white napkin. It was a waiter from the Café Rose-Croix and Clifford knew him.

"Bon soir, Monsieur Clifford," he said doubtfully.

"Good evening, Placide, Placide,—er—is that little banquet for me? Oh, it's all right! I suppose Monsieur Elliott paid for it—"

"But, Monsieur," said the waiter, "this dinner is for a lady."

"What's that?" said Clifford sharply. Then he buttonholed Placide and hauled him inside the studio.

"Who is the lady? The one upstairs?"

"Yes—Mademoiselle Plessis—she awaits her dinner—let me go, Monsieur Clifford," pleaded Placide.

"Oh, I'm not going to play tricks on you," said Clifford, "here! hold on!—if you move I'll tip the tray. Now all I want you to do is—is—er—dear me!"

The odour of a nicely browned fowl disturbed his thoughts; his mind wandered with his eyes. Placide gaped at him. He knew Clifford and he dreaded him. "Here you!" said that young gentleman, removing his eyes from the fowl with an effort, "do you think that because I do you the honour of conversing with you that I wish to rob you? Do I look like a man to interfere with a lady's dinner? Placide, you know me?"

"I do, Monsieur," replied the waiter despondently.

"Then listen! I am going to make you my confidant! Think of that, Placide!"

The waiter looked at him obliquely and did not appear to appreciate the honour in store.

"Placide!"

"Monsieur!"

"I am in love!"

"Doubtless—if it is Monsieur's pleasure—"

"Silence! Idiot! I am about to bestow gifts; I am about to—"

"The chicken, Monsieur, is becoming cold—"

"I am," repeated Clifford majestically, "about to offer two dozen—twenty-four—canary birds to my adored. You may ask; what is that to you—"

"I do," began Placide.

"Silence! Pig! These twenty-four canaries are to be carried to her by—think of it, Placide!—by you!"

Placide rolled his eyes, big with anguish. The chicken exhaled a delicious aroma.

Clifford drew in a long breath of the fragrance. Then he lifted the enormous gilt cage, and placed it in Placide's hands. "Go up-stairs and take these cursed birds with the compliments of Foxhall Clifford, artist, American, 70 rue Bara, first floor, door on the right."

"But—but my tray—"

"Imbecile! Do you think I'm going to eat your tray? Come back for it and—tell me what the lady says."

Placide shuffled sullenly to the door; Clifford opened it.

"My tray—" began the unwilling waiter.

"Placide," said Clifford, "I have not dined—er—re—cently and my temper is uncertain. You are discreet. I wish to dine. Do you understand?"

Placide smirked.

"Then use your wits—and when I have ten francs—well—hasten, my good Placide."

When the waiter had gone, Clifford tiptoed over to the tray and sniffed at the napkin.

"Dear! Dear! he said, "what a wonderful congregation of perfumes. Now if she doesn't shut the door on Placide's nose—I—I hope—I delicately hope that I may receive my reward."

He paced to and fro, whistling, but never taking his eyes from the tray. After a few minutes he heard Placide's slippered tread on the stairs, and hastened to admit him.

"The young lady says," began Placide, lifting the tray, "—the young lady says that Monsieur is too amiable—"

Clifford's heart sank.

"And," pursued Placide with dreary deliberation, edging toward the staircase, "the young lady says that she hopes to see you"—

"When?" blurted out Clifford.

"Some day," grinned Placide, and escaped up the stairway, sneering, triumphant.

The blow staggered Clifford for a moment—but only for a moment. Before Placide had descended again, Clifford was changing his clothes; before Placide had passed the lodge-gate, Clifford had fastened a white neck-tie under a spotless collar. Then he tied a bit of crimson silk tightly around his forehead, inserted two feathers from a duster in the fillet where they waved like the plumes of a Sioux War-chief; and ten minutes later, radiant, patent-leathered, but starved, he rang gaily at the door of the studio overhead.

When Claire Plessis opened the door, Clifford bowed profoundly and skipped in, introducing himself with joyous abandon.

"It is the custom," he said, bowing again and again with something of an Oriental salaam, "it is the custom in America—in far distant, sunny America,—to call at once upon distinguished strangers who come to lodge in the building. Therefore, Mademoiselle,"—and although he spoke French flawlessly he brutalised it now to suit his purpose,—"therefore, Mademoiselle,"—He salaamed again, rapidly and said:

"How! How! How!"

"Monsieur," faltered the girl, not knowing whether to laugh or call for assistance,—"Monsieur, I am honoured—pray be—be seated."

"Mademoiselle—it is too much honour!"

"Monsieur—"

They bowed again, and Clifford sank into a chair, his duster plumes nodding on his head.

The girl regarded him with undisguised amazement. She saw his eyes rolling toward the white-covered table and thought, "Oh dear, what shall I do with this foreign savage who sends me canary birds by the gross and who skips like a dancing dervish?"

"Monsieur," she stammered.

"How! How! How!" grunted Clifford absently, sniffing the tablecloth.

"Nothing—nothing, Monsieur," she said hastily; "I wish to thank you for the birds—"

"We eat them in America," he said, and chattered his teeth.

"Like—like chickens?"

"What are chickens?"

She laughed and looked at the uncarved fowl on the table.

"Is that a chicken?" asked Clifford in his most awful French. "Is it good to eat?"

"If you would do me the honour to accept my hospitality, Monsieur, you could prove it for yourself," she said laughing, and a little more at ease. "I have not yet dined,—I am quite alone—"

Clifford accepted, rising with oriental languor, and bowed magnificently. He led her to her place, seated her, drew up a chair opposite, and smiled upon her. His feathers bobbed with every movement.

"Now of course, I must carve," she said, striving hard to repress an hysterical laugh; for Clifford, desiring to play his part of a foreign savage to perfection, was doing impossible things with his knife and fork.

"If she finds me out," he was thinking, "it will not be very gay for me." So he showed his teeth and muttered and salaamed occasionally, while the girl bowed to him over her slender glass of claret and helped him to more and more and more until the suffocating desire to laugh brought tears to her eyes.

"In America it is etiquette to eat until there is nothing left—at least I have read that in books," she ventured.

"It is," said Clifford, uncorking another bottle.

"You seem to like chicken," she said.

"Ah," he replied, "wait until you try my canary birds!"

"But," she cried, "I am not going to eat them!"

Their eyes met across the table. He felt that he was going to laugh; he looked into her big grey eyes. Her dark-fringed lashes were trembling too; on each cheek a dimple deepened; between her scarlet lips the white teeth parted; then she sank back, her hands flung helplessly into her lap, and, looking into each other's eyes, they burst into ringing peals of laughter.

Three times she dried the tears in her eyes, and, leaning forward, attempted to speak, but when her eyes met his again, she threw back her pretty head and laughed until the colour deepened to her throat. And so they sat there, trying to speak, but shrieking with laughter, until the glasses and bottles clinked and vibrated and the window panes sang again.

At last she murmured, "For shame, Monsieur! I—I ought to be very angry,—but I laugh—oh dear! oh! dear! I laugh and I should be furious! Fie! You play the foreigner—the—the untutored one who never saw chicken—oh dear! oh dear!—"

She rose, drying her eyes again on a dainty pocket handkerchief.

"Shame on you! How dared you come to my room and—oh dear—and tell me you eat canary birds—and walk like a dancing dervish, and do such things with your knife, and—what is your name?— mine is Claire."

When, three hours later, he rose to go, he had told her all,—the whole wretched truth, and she had watched him with curious grey eyes, now brimming with laughter, now exquisite in their sympathy. She forgave him—not easily—but when he removed the feathers from his headdress and said he was sorry, she held out her hand to him with brilliant eyes and grave lips.

"So—you are forgiven,—not because you deserve it. Here in the Quarter we are like the leaves in the Luxembourg; we bud with the promise of summer,—we unfold, we nestle and whisper together,—we grow gorgeous and brilliant,—then we fall. Let us live in friendship while we may,—we of the Latin Quarter. I forgive you, mon ami."

IV.

When Clifford reached his own door on the floor below, he heard voices in the studio. A hard world had driven some caution into his head and he listened for a moment to assure himself that the voices were not the voices of creditors.

"It's Elliott and Colette," he murmured, knocking discreetly. Elliott opened the door; on the piano-stool sat Colette demurely twisting the fur of her boa. Clifford bent over the extended hand, then looked at Elliott. The latter felt in his pocket, produced the cuff buttons, and tossed them on the table.

"You can keep your jewellery," he said, "I've got a better scheme; Colette proposed it—"

"You wouldn't listen to the other plan," she said shyly, "I don't want that coupé—"

"You mustn't say such things," interposed Clifford gravely; then, turning to Elliott, "what are we going to do?"

"Let me tell," cried Colette, fanning her flushed face with the end of the boa; "sit down and be very still,—you also, Monsieur Clifford,—there! Now listen! I, Colette, have a very beautiful plan."

"How to become a millionaire in a week,—by Mademoiselle Colette," began Clifford, and was beaten with the fur boa.

"Very well!" she cried; "then I shall not trouble myself,—oh! you had better say you are sorry! Now listen! It is my plan,—mine, Co-lette!"

She settled herself on the piano-stool, whirled around until her pointed shoes rested on the rug, smiled, buried her nose in the point of her boa, and said; "To begin, you are poor!—don't interrupt! It is well to begin at the beginning. Then, you are poor. You have nothing to live on—you improvident ones,—for three more months. Comment faire! Paint and sell pictures? No. Why? Because you have not yet learned enough at the Ecole des Beaux Arts! But yet you must live. How? Ah, Dick, if you would only let me return you that old coupé—there! I didn't mean it! Now let us begin again!—You are poor—"

"We're back where we started," began Clifford but was snubbed.

"So,—you are poor. You must earn *something*. How? Why, with your cornets!"

"Eh?" stammered Clifford.

"Exactly!" cried Colette; "you shall play every evening in Bobinot's or-chestra and gain many many francs, industrious ones! Voila!"

Clifford stared at her. She nodded her head at him and smiled.

"It's an idea," said Elliott; "Boissy told Colette that Bobinot's two cornet players had gone, and old Bobinot is looking for two new ones. It's a chance,—we need only play in the evenings—it will keep soul and body together—won't it? Why don't you say something?"

"It's an idea,—isn't it?" repeated Colette solemnly.

"What!" faltered Clifford, "play a cornet in that cheap Montparnasse Theatre,—Bobinot's! Suppose they hear of it in New York?"

"Suppose we have to go to the American Consul and ask him to ship us home," retorted Elliott. Bobinot's, the students' theatre on Montparnasse, was not the Théâtre Français perhaps, but the acting was good,—indeed it was better than that seen in most New York Theatres. Clifford had spent joyous evenings at this "Quarter" theatre; it was often better than the "Cluny"—even "Antonio, père et fils," admitted that.

"Still," he said, "the Quarter will never stop laughing—er—Colette in her coupé and you in the orchestra—"

"I shall not drive in my coupé until Dick wishes it!" cried Colette, crimson and white by turns. "For your bad taste I—I pardon you."

Too utterly snubbed to have a mind of his own, Clifford meekly made his peace with Colette and opened the door for her and Elliott.

"Are you sure we can get the place?" he asked. "Perhaps Bobinot won't want us."

"Bobinot must!" said Colette; "I shall call upon Claire Plessis who is to sing the première rôles there. She is sweet; she is also from Tours. That is my country. And I love her very much."

"Where does she live?" inquired Clifford with a guilty start.

"Upstairs. I shall call upon her to-morrow. Dick, are you coming? Then good-night, wicked one! Come, Dick, dear! To your evil conscience I leave you, Monsieur Clifford"— and she laughed and gave him her gloved hand.

Clifford closed the door gently behind them. For a moment he stood staring at the panels, then raised his eyes to the ceiling.

"I wonder," he thought, "I—I wonder whether Claire will tell Colette?"

He shivered. The Quarter is pitiless in ridicule.

Elliott came back late that night, but he was cheerful and he whistled as he shook the snow from hat and coat and stamped around the studio.

"We'll see Bobinot tomorrow," he said; "I tell you it's not a bad idea—all Colette's, too!"

"I thought you and Colette had agreed to disagree," observed Clifford.

The other reddened a little. "We have," he said—"for three months."

Before he was ready for bed he missed the canary birds and questioned Clifford, but the latter told him to mind his business. This Elliott cheerfully complied with and went to bed.

"By the way, did you dine to-night?" he called out before he closed his door.

"Yes," snapped Clifford.

V.

Thanks to Colette and Claire, through the medium of Boissy, the little snare-drummer, who lived on the top floor, Monsieur Bobinot consented to give Elliott and Clifford a trial.

Boissy presented them to Monsieur Bobinot as two eminent American virtuosi, but Bobinot sneered openly.

"Don't try to stuff me," he said; "they're two students on their uppers. What do I care as long as they can play?"

"They—they are very eminent"—pleaded Boissy—"their—hm!—technique is so original, Monsieur Bobinot—"

Bobinot turned a pair of hard bright eyes on Clifford.

"En effet, Monsieur Bobinot, we are students," said Clifford with magnificent condescension; "but we can blow harmony out of a broken bottle;—Elliott, kindly play 'The Battle of Buena Vista' for Monsieur Bobinot."

Elliott drew his cornet from beneath his overcoat and gravely performed the stirring war march with hideous variations, while Clifford imitated a drum with his knuckles on the window pane.

"Cannon," said Clifford, banging on a sheet of tin which lay on the floor.

"Let my properties alone!" shouted Bobinot.

"Drums,—the Mexicans retreating," continued Clifford serenely, returning to the window.

"Humph!" snorted Bobinot.

"Cries of the wounded!" observed Clifford, and emitted a series of piercing screams while Elliott continued his variations.

"Ow! Ow! Ow!" wailed Clifford, winking at Boissy who had sunk helpless on a chair, weak with laughter.

"Stop!" thundered Bobinot.

Elliott finished his variations and looked expectantly at the manager of the "Theatre Bobinot."

"It's d—n fine," said Monsieur Bobinot, "but I could manage to exist and earn an honest living without your artistic collaboration. I say I could dispense with your musical services, but I cannot, Messieurs, afford to lose from my personnel, two such splendid examples of human impudence. Consider yourselves engaged. Boissy, I'll pay you for this!"

"Then," said Clifford artlessly, "let's cement the contract with a bottle!"

"Bottle of what?" demanded Elliott; "we haven't any money! You mortify me!"

Clifford smiled blandly. "Come, Monsieur Bobinot, no hard feelings you know! What shall it be?"

"Whatever you like, Messieurs," said Bobinot grimly; "I'll take it out of your salary."

But Monsieur Bobinot was better than his word. He saw at a glance that the young fellows were in earnest, and he not only acted the host very decently, but, as Boissy dragged the two young men away, he handed them each a week's salary in advance.

"It's for your infernal cheek!" he said; "come to rehearsal at ten!"

The first week passed without a hitch. Elliott played the orchestrated scores for Clifford, and the latter, being quick and instinctively musical, learned his part by heart, to the utter demoralisation of the tenants on the upper floors. Mademoiselle Plessis stood it as long as she possibly could and then sent for Clifford.

"Monsieur Clifford," she said seriously, "this must stop."

"If it stops *I* stop," said Clifford; "I can't live on air."

"No," she said, "you are neither a chameleon nor an angel."

"Not an angel yet, but on the floor below," he said humbly.

Mademoiselle Plessis tapped her foot against the fender and brushed the leaves of her rôle with the tip of one white finger.

"Mon ami," she said, "I cannot learn my rôle if you toot all day on that cornet."

"What am I to do?" inquired Clifford miserably.

"You must have certain hours to practise. Monsieur Boissy plays on his drum from two until four; Monsieur Castro chooses that time for trombone exercise; why can *you* not play your cornet during those hours?"

"I will," said Clifford craftily, "but what shall I do from four until six?" He looked at her with eyes that appealed and languished.

"Do?"

"Ah, yes! It will be lonely up there on the floor above—won't it?" Mademoiselle Plessis raised her clear eyes to the ceiling.

"Is it so very lonely down there? It is not,—up here."

"Very. I think of you all day."

"Of me? How foolish!"

"Yes; I wish I were able to aid you to learn your parts."

"But you can't—"

"I could if you'd let me read your cues—"

—"I don't need that—"

—"Don't refuse—"

—"I must—"

—"Don't—"

—"But I do! And you are very silly.—"

So it was arranged that Clifford should bleat on his cornet from two until four, during which time Claire would go out for a walk; and from four to six, when Claire was at home, he might aid her by his presence and advice and judiciously regulated sympathy.

"The idea!" she said, with a pretty gesture of disdain; "you will only bother me. You had much better write me a little play."

"A 'lever de rideau!'" exclaimed Clifford; "by Jove, I'll do it!"

"Can you write French well enough, mon pauvre ami?"

"No, but you can supply all the localisms and wit. Will you?"

"We might try," she said with a doubtful smile. She was very much interested, however, and when, a few days later, he brought her a rough sketch of the "Queen of Siam," she read it with serious interest.

"It is a pretty idea," she said, flushing with pleasure. Then, resting her chin on her hand, she invited him to sit beside her.

"You know," she said thoughtfully, "if we are really going to collaborate, we must be very grave and serious for *you* are not working for pleasure and *I* am earning my bread—"

—"And honey,—oh! you'll have woodcock on toast and champagne too if this play goes!"

"Then let us make it go," she exclaimed enthusiastically.

"Let's!" he cried with equal fervour.

There was a pause.

"The play won't go if you don't take your pen in hand," she said.

—"But I will—"

"Then hadn't you better release my hand?"

And so the afternoons wore away while with heads together over the manuscript they chattered about exits and entries, scenarios, cues and "pan coupé's" and Clifford rose to the occasion, displaying a wit which matched her dainty cleverness and struck the quick warm spark of sympathy between them.

"Delicious!" she would laugh at some hastily pencilled bit of dialogue, and then, bending over the tablet "Don't you think that we might shorten the King's lines just here? See, I only strike out these three words—ah! see how much better it reads!"

"Much better!—very much better!"

"Very much; it flows smoothly now—oh! oh! how funny to make the Queen threaten them! How did you ever think of that?"

"Why, it follows naturally—you see she is all in armour, and the spurs trip up the archbishop—" And so the afternoons wore away.

This was all very pleasant, but it had its drawbacks and one winter evening toward six o'clock Clifford jumped up and stared at the clock horrified:

"Good heavens!" he muttered, "they are giving 'Pomme d'Api,' to-night and I haven't practised the music! What the deuce shall I do!"

"And you can't read music at sight? Oh, what a shame! It is all my fault, mon ami," she cried in contrition.

"No it isn't—only the afternoon flew, and I never thought. Bobinot will sack me for this!"

"You must get a substitute," she said," it's often done."

"Where can I find one?"

"Ask Boissy, he knows lots of people who do that sort of thing,—there's his drum now! go down and see him—hurry—go quickly, mon ami,—Oh! you mustn't!—you mustn't! There! my gown is all in wrinkles. I do not wish you ever to return,—no, never,—go quickly now or Boissy will be gone!—hasten!—ah well—then I will try to forgive you, mon ami."

As he galloped down the stairs and out into the street he felt as though he were treading on clouds—rosy clouds.

"Nevertheless," he said to himself, "I must never kiss her again."

VI.

The substitute cornet player was a success but was also very expensive. Clifford paid him thankfully, but it made a large hole in his meagre weekly salary, and he decided to do without substitutes in future. He explained to Elliott how it was, and the latter young gentleman, who viewed Clifford's infatuation for Claire with alarm, shook his head and sighed.

"You can't afford it, my son. Suppose you hadn't been able to get a cornet player? Bobinot would have bounced you."

"Now I am not so sure of that," said Clifford, who had been consulting Claire. "I understand that the leader of the orchestra—what's his name—"

—"Bock—"

—"Bock,—I understand that he's generally drunk and can't tell whether one or two cornets are playing."

"But he would see your empty place."

"I could get any ordinary man to sit there,—Selby would do it for the lark. If he pretended to play, Bock wouldn't know the difference. I had to pay that substitute of mine twenty francs. Kid Selby would do it to oblige me."

"And he could stuff the cornet with cotton," suggested Elliott.

"Exactly—Bock would never know. So any time we want a vacation we'll call on Selby, stuff his cornet with cotton, and let him blow his cheeks out while the other man does the playing? Where are you going?"

"I'm going to get Kid Selby—it's my turn for a vacation to-night," replied

Elliott laughing, and walked out, slamming the great doors.

Clifford opened his desk, took out a pile of manuscript, and, thrusting them into his pocket, hurried up-stairs to begin his daily collaboration with his fair neighbour. Time flew for them, but the "Queen of Siam" was slowly taking the shape of a curtain-raiser whose fate would soon be determined. The lyrics were fortunately few, and of course Claire rhymed them, for poetry in French was beyond Clifford's ken. And she rhymed them charmingly, setting them to the music of quaint old songs that all France knows. Clifford hung breathlessly over the piano, gaping with admiration.

Monsieur Bobinot had read the piece and had found it suitable,—so suitable in fact, that for a long time he refused to believe that Clifford could be the author.

"Voyons, confess he hashed it up from some old vaudeville!" he repeated to Mademoiselle Plessis, until at last he was constrained to accept it as original. Of course he cast Claire for the "Queen"; she refused to stir a step unless he did; and the other parts were given to Mesdames Paule Nevers, Bonelly, Mario-Widmer, and to Messieurs Max, Bourdielle, Deberg, Bayard, Brunet, and Simon. Naturally Max was cast for the Archbishop of Ept, and Bayard for the King, while Bourdeille's character, "Syleuse," was written entirely with the view that he should create the rôle.

Bobinot grumbled. It seemed to him that he had nothing to say about anything in his own theatre, but Mademoiselle Plessis had her way and the property man and costumer were already at work on the designs that Elliott furnished gratis. Deberg orchestrated the score.

"It would cost me," shouted Bobinot in a fury, as he blue-pencilled Elliott's voluminous directions on each drawing,—"it would cost me more than my theatre is worth to make these costumes according to Monsieur Elliott's advice. He can save himself literary work, and me several sous worth of blue pencil by sticking to his designing and leaving the execution to a man who wears a head in the proper place!"

The Théâtre Bobinot was flourishing. The "Serment d'Amour," "Princess des Canaries," "Mignapour," "Le Jour et la Nuit," followed successively "Le Panache," and "Pomme d'Api" of Offenbach; and already in the programme of "Les Domestiques," the comedy by Grangé and Deslandes, appeared the announcement of the preparations for "The Queen of Siam." "A comedy in three acts by M. Foxhall Clifford and Mlle. Claire Plessis"; for, at Bobinot's demand, the "lever de rideau," had been expanded into a three act musical comedy.

Bobinot said very little in praise of it either to Clifford or to Claire, but he bragged about it to everybody else in the Latin Quarter as well as in the Montparnasse Quarter. He refused to pay any cash for it, but signed a contract for a generous royalty, and Clifford and Claire were more than satisfied. The former promised princely sums to Elliott for his costume designs as soon as the money began to pour in. Elliott was grateful and redoubled his pages of instructions for Bobinot, whose curses rang loud and deep as he slashed through them with his blue pencil.

Clifford took a good many days off from the orchestra, and, finding that a cotton-stuffed cornet in the hands of the untutored and unmusical Selby was perfectly satisfactory, took more days off. Selby for his part, liked the fun and became the envy of the Quarter. At times, however, Clifford had slight clashes with Elliott when they both wanted the same night off.

"Come, come," Clifford would urge, "Claire isn't on to-night you know, and I've promised to dine with her at Thirion's."

"And I've promised Colette to meet her at the Vachette."

"But you can meet her there to-morrow and I can't meet Claire because she takes Nevers' place in 'Pomme d' Api.'"

Then Elliott would mutter; "the deuce take you and Claire!" But he always gave in and tootled away in the orchestra, while Selby, the delighted substitute beside him, puffed and perspired over a noiseless cotton-stuffed cornet. Bock, the besotted, never doubted that both cornets were playing.

"Thank goodness this won't last," thought Elliott; "our three months' poverty is up on Monday and then!—then this cursed orchestra can go to the devil!"

Rat-tat-tat—! rattled Bock's baton as he glanced at Elliott.

"Oh you old ass!" grumbled Elliott, toot! toot!—"go to Guinea!"—toot—toot—tootle—too-o-ot."

VII.

The humiliating part of it was that neither Clifford nor Elliott could attend the rehearsals of "the Queen of Siam" except in the orchestra. Bobinot was omnipresent, and they were obliged to occupy their places.

Now the orchestra was sunk in a pit so far below the footlights that although the musicians were visible to the audience, nothing on the stage could be seen by the musicians themselves.

When Clifford was not obliged to blow his cornet, he could hear Claire's sweet voice:

> "Oh, papa dear I much prefer
>   My helmet and my steel-ringed shirt,
> My jewelled hilt, my gilded spur,
>   Targe, Casque, Tassett and Bassinet

> So take away my waist and skirt!
>> Oh, take away
>> Oh, take away
> Oh-h! take away my maiden's skirt!"

Then he would stretch and crane his neck to see, but Bock always caught him with the angry rat-tat-tat!—"hé! la bas!" and he would clutch his cornet and breathe music and anathemas. "It's a pretty state of affairs if I can't see my own play," he grumbled to Elliott, "I'll fix that ass, Bock—just wait!"

When Claire and Georges Max held the stage, and the repartee made even the prompter chuckle, Clifford's curiosity almost crazed him, and he cursed impartially, Bobinot, Bock, the orchestra and himself.

Claire was delicious, Max irresistible.

Clifford squirmed and listened:

Claire; "L'archeveque!"

Max; "Mais non, il faut"—

Claire (excited); "Qu'i-1 vienne! Qu'il vienne! J'y suis, J'y reste!—Et quil fait attention à mes éperons!"

Max; "Mais—mais—c'est moi l'Archiveque—"

Claire (much disturbed); "Té! je le savais bien, Monseigneur!"

"That's going to take like wildfire," whispered Elliott lowering his cornet; "I wish I could see the expression on Max's face—"

"And on Claire's! Hear the prompter laugh!"

"Look out—here comes the flourish—ready—now! Enter the Queen, you know!"

"Tara—ta-ta-tata!" wheezed the cornets for the entry of the Queen, while Boissy's snare drum rattled the salute,

Clifford was sulky and spoke no more that morning, but the next day he went to see Selby.

"I'm d—d if I miss the first night of my own opera," he muttered.

VIII.

Clifford was determined to see the first night's performance but he decided not to tell Elliott, as that youth might also wish to see it. No, he would not mention it to Elliott; he would quietly arrange it for Selby to play the dummy and blow a cotton-stuffed cornet beside Elliott. True, the flourish of trumpets that was to announce the entrance of the Queen would be, strictly speaking, a flourish of one cornet, but Bock could never know and the audience wouldn't either for that matter. So he spoke to Selby and gave him his stuffed cornet.

"There's no cornet in the overture, you know—it's that stringed affair of Lalo's. You are to watch Elliott and pretend to toot when he does. The first flourish is when the Queen comes in," he explained to Selby.

Then he went to bed, chuckling, for he had covertly secured the last seat but one in a prominent box, and he chuckled again as he thought of Elliott's fury on beholding him among the spectators.

All the next day he chuckled too, watching Elliott furtively. The latter seemed very unsuspicious; he did not even mention a wish to view the performance. And at last the impatiently expected night arrived.

The Théâtre Bobinot was ablaze; banners waved from the mansard; posters flamed under the gas jets outside,—big yellow posters announcing "THE QUEEN OF SIAM!"

Inside the theatre the orchestra was assembling.

IX.

Selby pretended to fuss over the leaves of the score; he fiddled with his cornet a moment, then he sat down and looked up at the house.

The audience was not what is termed "brilliant," but the house was jammed with the good people of the Montparnasse Quarter, sandwiched in between hordes of Latin Quarter students, actresses, grisettes and vivacious young persons who preside over the counters of the Bon Marché and Grands Magazines of the Louvre. A first night always filled the little theatre, box, pit, and gallery, and the announcement of the "Queen of Siam," with Mlle. Claire Plessis, Mlle. Nevers and Max and Bourdeille, had stirred the Quarter profoundly.

Selby polished the mouthpiece of his cornet and called to Boissy, who left his snare drum and came over.

"Where is Elliott?" he asked.

"Hasn't come yet. Oh, you're here to give Clifford a chance? It's a good house, isn't it?"

"Great," said Selby pensively, "I bet Clifford makes a lot out of this. Here comes old Bock now."

The leader of the orchestra, vinous as usual, emerged from below, wiping his moustache, and walked straight to his seat.

"I wish Elliott would hurry," said Selby nervously. "There's no overture,—Bock cut it out because the play's long enough."

"I know—I know, but there he is taking a last look at the gallery and Elliott isn't here. The thing begins with a flourish of trumpets to the Queen."

As he spoke, a figure came out of the little door under the stage, holding a cornet.

"Thank goodness," said Selby, "here he is now,—no! by jingo, it's a new cornettist!"

The stranger sat down in Elliott's seat, picked pensively at some cotton in his cornet, and smiled at Selby.

"Where's Elliott?" said Selby hoarsely.

"In that box,—see him? He wants to witness the first act. He says"— But Selby sprang to his feet, pallid with fright.

"Can you play a cornet?" he almost shrieked.

"No,—can't you?" stammered the new arrival.

Before the wretched Selby could reply, Bock rapped for attention; there came three heavy knocks on the stage floor behind the curtain, and, as the violins began the "Air of the Petticoat," the curtain twitched, trembled, and began to ascend, exposing a brilliant stage and dozens of glittering limbs.

Clifford in his box, gazed at the chorus in rapture. Then, as the chorus began to sing, he felt a violent tug at his coat, and, looking round, beheld Elliott.

"You!" faltered Clifford, "what are you doing here?"

Elliott's face was shrunken with fright.

"Heavens!" he gasped, "they'll miss the flourish! Those fellows can't play! I—I didn't know you had engaged Selby so I hired a man in the street"—Clifford was rooted to the spot; his eyes fixed on the miserable substitutes below. Then his hair slowly rose as Max cried joyously:

"The Queen! The Queen! Hark—hark to the trumpets' shrill welcome!"

A dismal silence ensued. All eyes were turned on the orchestra where Selby sat frozen stiff with horror, while his companion, scarlet in the face, cheeks puffed out and eyes starting from their sockets, blew madly into his cotton-stuffed cornet from which no sound proceeded.

"Hark! The trumpets ring again!" cried Max, looking anxiously at Bock, who, speechless and furious, waved his wand toward Selby.

"Idiots! Play!" he roared at last.

"We can't!" gasped Selby. The audience screamed.

Claire coolly walked to the footlights, but the sight of Selby's face sent her into wild uncontrollable laughter.

Claire's laughter saved the piece. The house stood by her from that moment, and the "Queen of Siam" went merrily on to the sound of a cornet-less orchestra. For Clifford and Elliott and Selby had fled;—fled away into the snowy night, far, far from the haunts of men.

This is a story of the Quarter, truer than it ought to be. You have, doubtless, heard it before. It is not original with me. I myself have heard it told in London.

Ah! when shall we be wise, Madame?—When shall we learn wisdom—

we of the Quartier Montparnasse?

I could tell you how Clifford returned and was forgiven by Claire and Bobinot,—but I won't. I could tell you how Clifford presented his royalty rights to Claire on the occasion of her marriage to Monsieur Bobin—but there!—I nearly told you a stage secret! So I shall answer no more questions—unless you care to know about Colette and Elliott and Selby.

Do you?

> *"Ah! d'une ardeur sincere*
> *Le temps ne pent distraire,*
> *Et nos plus doux plaisirs*
> *Sont dans nos souvenirs.*
> *On pense, on pense encore*
> *A celle qu'on adore,*
> *Et l'on revient toujours*
> *A ses premiers amours."*

ANOTHER GOOD MAN

Une conscience sans Dieu est un tribunal sans juge.
                                        LAMARTINE.

I.

When Fradley came to Paris he renounced literature as a means of live-lihood, for, although his success as a writer in "Brooklyn Babyhood," had been pecuniarily satisfying, it occurred to him that painting might be less fatiguing than poetry, and he decided to adopt it as his profession.

His illustrations to his own rhymes had been, up to the present time, of archaic simplicity, and were limited to pen and ink productions representing infants afflicted with exaggerated eyes and eyelashes.

Young mothers hovered over the pages of "Brooklyn Babyhood" spelling out his rhymes to crowing infancy. In these jingles, children were told that they were "arch" and "cute," they were assured of their importance, their every action was applauded, solid pages of baby-talk were administered, and baby-ridden Brooklyn writhed with delight.

There were some people, however, who revolted,—some who even declared that Fradley was a public nuisance and that his rhymes inculcated self-consciousness; but these people were probably unnatural parents.

When he wrote his immortal poem, "How many toes has the Baby?" the Brooklyn "Banner" published the poem in full with a portrait of and a peon to "Brooklyn's Brilliant Son."

This was all very well but it couldn't last. A rival poet from Flatbush got hold of the Brooklyn "Star" and began a series of poems, the baby talk of which made Fradley's most earnest efforts fall flat. In vain he demanded to know the exact number of fingers and toes which the baby possessed; in vain he cooed and gurgled and bleated! The Flatbush poet was a woman, and she knew her business. When Fradley cooed, she cooed; when Fradley gurgled and bleated, she gurgled and bleated, backed up by the entire staff of the Brooklyn "Star." In vain Fradley called for a counting of toes; she extended her researches into distant sections of baby's anatomy, and Fradley was doomed. The last blow fell when the Flatbush poet produced

"BABY'S ICKLE TOOFY,"

which, translated freely, means "baby's little tooth." That settled it. Fickle

Brooklyn fell down and worshipped the Flatbush lady, and Fradley sullenly packed his bag and sailed for France.

When Fradley took up his abode in the Latin Quarter, he expected that his arrival would create something of a stir. It did not. He waited a month for appreciation and finally asked Garland what he thought of his illustrations.

"I haven't seen any," replied Garland.

"I didn't know you illustrated," added Carrington, but noticing the mortification on Fradley's face, said good-naturedly, "You know we don't see much over here except the Paris papers; what do you illustrate for?"

Fradley was speechless.

"What paper are they in?" asked Garland, yawning innocently.

"In 'Brooklyn Babyhood,'" snarled Fradley and left the café.

Carrington, a modest young Englishman with a high colour and blond moustache, looked troubled. Garland was irritated.

"You know," he said to Carrington, "if he shows that sort of temper the older men will be down on him."

"It's very annoying," said Carrington.

"Very. We new men have got to keep pretty quiet just now or the old men will make it hot for us. This man Fradley is enough to turn the whole studio against us. Did you make the fire this morning?"

"Oh, yes, of course. Clifford was very decent to me."

"He's all right, but there are some of the older men in Julian's who are spoiling to discipline us. Did you notice it to-day?"

"I fancy I did," replied Carrington, swallowing his beer.

"This man Fradley," continued Garland, "is enough to queer the whole batch of this year's men. Confound him, he's effeminate."

"Oh, I don't know," said Carrington pleasantly.

"Well, I do. His room is opposite mine, you know, and he's trotting in and bothering me all the time about the decorations of his boudoir. Whew! Why, Carrington, he has tied ribbons all over his furniture, and he has tidies and things about so that you are afraid to sit down. I don't want to misjudge the man, for we new men must hang together, but I draw the line at embroidered night shirts stuck all over with lace and ribbon."

"So do I," said Carrington, "does he do that sort of thing?"

"I suppose so. He brought one in to show me."

"Maybe it wasn't his," suggested Carrington.

"Possibly not. It would have been more appropriate for the Queen of Sheba."

II.

"Don't," said Clifford, "pat me on the back and tell me to keep my shirt on!"

"Nonsense!" said Elliott, "you are making a mountain out of a mole-hill!"

"And your language," said Selby, "is not exactly—"

"Oh, isn't it! Now you listen to me; the Café des Écoles is no boudoir, and if a man can't express his views here then I'm a fossil."

Rowden looked vaguely uneasy and Braith studied Clifford over his pipe.

"The Quarter," continued Clifford, "is going to the devil; do you deny it?"

"Yes," said Elliott cheerfully.

"That makes no difference—keep cool, Elliott, I know you only said it for argument, but it isn't so—"

"Messieurs, you must make less noise," said the proprietor, hurrying over from the desk.

"Stop pounding on the table and yelling," said Clifford to Carroll.

"If you don't," observed Elliott, "the sergot will come back and take our names again—"

"For the last time too, and Elliott's already got three, so he'll go to the cooler and devil a sou will I go bail," growled Clifford; "now listen to me, you fellows, if you want to know why the Quarter is going to the bow-wows. Just look at the crop of this year's men! Are we going to put up with McCloud. He threw the proprietor of the Café des Arts out of doors and ran the Café himself at ruinous rates until the proprietor came back with the police. I paid his fine."

"Well," said Elliott, "McCloud is certainly cocky for a nouveau!"

"Cocky? Well rather. Because he's a sort of infant Hercules and has played on the Australian team is no reason why he should split all the tables with his fist and do cheap feats of strength, and grab a cab by the hind wheels and hold it with the cabby yelling like a demon and everybody laughing at me—"

"You!"

"I was in the cab; it was on the Boulevard Montparnasse—"

"And you were going—" began Elliott.

"Never mind where I was going," said Clifford with dignity, "the fact remains that I was inside. It was lucky for McCloud that I was, for when a policeman nipped his budding humour my bail came in very handy."

"And is that," inquired Braith suavely, "the ground for your assertion that the Quarter is doomed?"

"Isn't it enough?" demanded Clifford;—"a nouveau taking liberties,—

making me ridiculous before the whole Montparnasse Quarter,—who know me—every one of them,—and to crown all, being with a lady—"

"Oh!" said Elliott tenderly. Osborne smirked and whistled the devil's quadrille, Elliott and Thaxton played phantom trombones with enervating effect and Carroll beat madly upon a bottle.

Clifford became redder and redder. His unrequited affection for that wonderful little creature, the new Bullier star, was a topic for mirth and gentle jest throughout the Latin Quarter. They had recently parted, friends,—it being understood that she liked him, but hardly cared to pin her affections to a man who sat helpless in a cab while somebody held the hind wheels and the boulevard laughed. It was putting it plainly perhaps, but it did no harm, and Clifford was very careful to keep it to himself.

"You fellows," observed Clifford scornfully, "had better stop those monkey shines. Put down that bottle, Carroll, or I'll take it away. You'll be trying to stuff it in your mouth next. Bite on the cork, it's better for teething."

This cruel thrust at the very recent advent of Carroll to full-fledged honours in the studio had its effect.

"I know," continued Clifford, "that you all think I'm blighted, but you're all mistaken. I'm sure you will see that I am right about these new men when I tell you what happened at the studio this morning. I sat down in a front place and waited for the roll call, and, before my name was called, a thing—a nouveau took the place himself."

"What!" cried the others incredulously.

"It's true," continued Clifford, "this baby—this nouveau violated all precedent, and, because his name came before mine on the list, he actually had the impudence to throw me down!"

The others looked thoughtful.

"That is going too far," observed Elliott gravely, "we must discipline these young gentlemen."

"There are two or three," said Thaxton, "who seem worse than the rest, for instance, young Garland—"

"Seems to me that was the creature's name who took my place," interrupted Clifford.

"It couldn't be—he's a decent fellow and makes the fire when he's told to," said Selby.

"Perhaps he didn't know you were an old man," suggested Elliott.

"Probably not," said Carroll, who was still smarting from the teething taunt, "Clifford hasn't been twice in the studio since the nouveaux came."

Elliott took out a note-book and wrote down Garland's name.

"I'll keep an eye on him," he said, "but there is another little wretch who ought to have an example made of him at once."

"Who?" asked Clifford.

"I believe his name is Fradley," replied Elliott lighting a cigar.

"Then we'll fix Fradley," muttered Clifford. "Who cares for a game of billiards?"

III.

The roll call was over at Julian's and every place had been marked in white chalk on the floor. The model in the first studio had profited by the confusion attendant on the distribution of bread, colours and canvasses, and, shuffling into his trousers and slippers, strolled into the second studio of Boulanger and Lefevre to investigate the cause of the uproar which had arisen and which continued with increasing violence.

The studio was packed with yelling students, some mounted on tabourets, some on the old dust-chest by the door, others on the stove and model stand. From Doucet's two studios a delegation had arrived, all of the Sculptors and most of Bouguereau's men were there, and the noise was terrific. A big blond fellow wearing the uniform of a cuirassier seemed to be directing things, and his bellows shook the windows and rattled the bones on "Pierre," the battered studio skeleton.

The clerk came in and remonstrated, but Clifford put him out and locked the glass door, leaving him gesticulating and taking names as fast as he could write. Then Jules peeped in, smiled sadly and beckoned to Boissy, the cuirassier massier. Boissy opened the door and explained that they were only "organising." That was sufficient, and Jules and the clerk withdrew.

When the classic halls of Julian's echoed with demoniac screams, catcalls, and howls—when voices were uplifted in every language except German, and the thickets of easels were mowed down in rows by some playful boot-heel, it was generally an indication that the students were "organising." They had a passion for organising, and they seldom failed to indulge it. Just now they were organising under the leadership of that strange creature, Sara, also known as "La Rousse," who was generally the root of all mischief in the Quarter. She stood on the model stand beside Boissy, her fiery red hair coiled along her neck, her wonderful white skin glistening, her mysterious face bathed in the sunshine which streamed down from the glass roof above.

With an inscrutable smile she studied the massed faces below her. Occasionally her eyes rested on some new man, who never failed to feel uncomfortable and look at the floor until the grayish-green eyes swept in another direction. Sara was haughty at best. In her sunniest smiles lurked the lightning of scorn, and in all her brief "affairs," the caprice of passion never disturbed her astounding egotism, never lowered the imperious head, never drove the shadow of irony from her scarlet lips.

Boissy shouted for silence, and banged on the floor with his spurred heels, but nobody paid attention until the girl took a step forward and held up both pink palms as if to shield her ears from the pandemonium. That was sufficient.

Then with a nod to Boissy, who straightened his epaulettes and looked fierce, she began very quietly.

"Messieurs il s'agit—" when an unlucky nouveau fell off a stool and crashed to the floor carrying several easels with him. He was mobbed at once amid cries of "Silence, cochon! Down with the Nouveau! Vive Sara!"

"C'est épatant," observed Sara with superb scorn, "fiche moi cet nouveau au clou!"

No sooner said than the unlucky youth was seized and hustled toward the dust-chest amid cries of "au clou! au clou!"

Elliott opened the lid of the dust-chest and looked at Boissy.

"What's his name," growled Boissy.

"Freddie Fradley," replied Elliott, "shall he go in?"

Fradley screamed and struggled, but at a sign from Sara they shoved him in, and, inserting some mahl-sticks under the lid to give him air, requested "Fatty" Carriere to sit on the top, which he did with alacrity. Sara tossed her glittering hair and continued, undeterred by the faint screams from the chest:

"Messieurs, you all know that on the night of the Mi-Carême, it is the custom of our studio to go en masse, to the Bullier. Messieurs, the massiers of all the studios have decided to honour me with an escort, but—" laughing proudly, "that is the difficulty! All of you wish to go with me, which you know very well is impossible. Are there not other girls in the Quarter?"

"No!" shouted the students in a spasm of gallantry.

She opened her arms with a peculiarly graceful motion. "You know that I adore you all,—all the Julian men, and I do not wish to show favouritism—"

"Vive Sara! Vive la Rousse!" came thundering from the students and was echoed by stifled yells from the dust-chest.

"Fatty" Carriere banged on the lid and uttered awful threats against Fradley's health unless he ceased. Sara smiled. "No, no favouritism," she said—"mais—mais comment faire?"

"Take us all as escorts!" cried Clifford, and the Frenchmen understood and took up the cry—"en choisisez pas! *nous voulons aller tous!*"

The girl's eyes sparkled, and she shook her head at Clifford. "Monsieur the incorrigible!"

Clifford waved his hat and cried,—"C'est entendu alors! Vive Sara!"

"Mais non, mon petit Clifford," smiled the girl, "c'est impossible—"

"Not at all," exclaimed Boissy with a reckless laugh, "Clifford and I—

we will arrange that!"

"Of course," replied Clifford, "we'll fix the police."

Then bedlam broke loose, and impromptu quadrilles began, and "Fatty" Carriere, unwilling to lose his share of the dance, hastily locked the chest, punched some air holes in the lid, oblivious of the danger which Fradley would run if anybody sat down on them, and went lumbering and gyrating about until his elephantine gambols shook the building.

Shortly afterward, the fatherly Monsieur Julian appeared, softly suggesting that work should begin, and ten minutes later the seats were full, the models posed in the various rooms, and the scrape of charcoal and palette knife alone broke the quiet of the studio.

Clifford, who had missed the morning roll-call, roamed about looking for a place. There appeared to be none. The lines of easels radiating in circles from the model-stand were all occupied. He glared at the nouveaux.

"This is disgusting," he observed to Elliott! "fancy a four-year man hunting a place and those fool nouveaux squatting on the tabourets!"

"Come in time,—it's the only way now," replied Elliott.

"Here is a place, Mr. Clifford," said Garland who was sitting in the front row. Clifford threaded his way among the easels to his side.

"It's very good of you," he said; "whose name is that on the floor?"

"Fradley's," said Garland. Clifford rubbed it out and substituted his own signature.

"This begins Fradley's discipline," he muttered, and called to Ciceri to bring him his portfolio. Then he looked at Garland and was prepossessed in his favor.

"You're a nouveau, are you not?" he asked amiably; "what is your name?"

"Garland."

"Mine is Clifford."

"Oh, we all know that," laughed Garland.

"Oh, you do!" said Clifford, "and how the devil do you know it?"

Garland did not think it prudent to mention the cab incident, and Clifford picked up his charcoal and squinted at the model.

"I hear," said Garland, "that you older men are going to discipline us."

"We are," said Clifford calmly.

"Why?"

"Well, you see, we usually receive a certain amount of respect and deference from new men, and before you fellows came nobody ever heard of a nouveau turning an old man out of his seat."

Carrington looked up from his easel. "I am a nouveau," he said, "and I think, Mr. Clifford, you will find that the nouveaux respect the traditions of the studio."

"I think so, too," insisted Garland.

Clifford looked at him coldly. "Didn't you turn me out last week?" he demanded.

"I," cried Garland, "never!"

"Fradley did," said Cary, "and I noticed it at the time and wondered why you didn't spank him, Clifford."

"Well, by Jove!" exclaimed Clifford, "I thought it was you, Garland."

"I know you did," replied Garland indignantly, "and a pretty life I've led with Rowden and Elliott and all the contour men making it hot for me. I respect the traditions and always will."

"Then I beg your pardon," said Clifford cordially, "come and see me at my studio."

All the nouveaux knew what that meant. It indicated that Garland would soon be released from menial work, and would find himself in the charmed circle of the powers that be.

"By the way," said Clifford, "there is that fellow Fradley in the dust chest. Hadn't I better let him out?"

"Has he enough air?" asked Selby.

"Plenty. I bored some more holes just now and asked him how he felt. He said I was no gentleman."

"He says," said Rowden, "that it's a disgrace to his family and a blot on his honour. He's an excitable customer and screams like a cat when addressed through the air-holes in the lid."

"Oh, let him out," said Clifford.

"No, he must be taught decency. He's been here three months, and that's long enough for the studio to size him up."

"Why did you put him in?" asked Garland.

"Because," replied Elliott, "he made a racket trying to go out when Sara was speaking."

"He couldn't help it, he fell off the stool; let him out," said Clifford.

"No, he must understand that this studio won't tolerate a sneak. Did you know that he went to old Julian with tales of our doings and said that for his part he never met such a rude and vulgar set of men before? He said he had not come to Paris to listen to models make speeches, but had expected to find a refined and elevating art atmosphere. He insisted that he could not draw if the studio was noisy, and he asked old Julian to stop the racket. Fancy the expression on Julian's face!"

Clifford's face was a study. "What impudence," he said, "what did Julian do?"

"He? Oh, he told him that he was not obliged to stay; that there were other schools in Paris." Clifford turned to his drawing and shrugged his shoulders. "Let him sit in the box then," he muttered, steadying his plumb line with the end of his pencil; "dust-chest discipline won't hurt him!"

Clifford was a clever draughtsman. The nouveaux watched him in respectful admiration as he constructed his study, indicated a shadow here and there, and then, dusting the paper, rapidly sketched in the essential outlines and began to model the head with a vigour and dash which did not at all detract from its value as a serious academic study.

Mid-day struck, and there was a scramble for hats and a rush for the stairs. Bouguereau's men came trampling out of their atelier with the studio band at their head and the studio mascot, a pale-eyed goat named "Tapage," bringing up the rear. Following Bouguereau's atelier came Doucet's two rooms and behind them Chapu's sculptors. The stairs were jammed, and as Clifford was in a hurry to get his luncheon, he persuaded "Tapage" to butt the passage clear, which the goat was only too glad to do, for he smelled the appetising odour of brown paper and cabbage leaves in the court below.

When Clifford had reached the restaurant on the corner of the boulevard he remembered that Fradley was still in the dust-bin. "The deuce!" he muttered, "I've got to go back and let the beggar out!"

Sara, who had been posing in the second studio for the concour men had also forgotten Fradley, and it was only when she had finished dressing and stood alone in the studio twisting up her burnished tresses, that a rustling in the dust-chest behind her recalled Fradley's existence to her mind.

"B'en vrai!" she exclaimed, "I forgot you, my friend!" and she stooped and drawing the bolt, lifted the heavy lid. Fradley was squatting in a corner of the chest.

"Ah! mais ça—c'est trop fort!" she cried in self-reproach; "I am so sorry."

Fradley snarled.

The girl looked at him curiously for a moment and then began to laugh. "To think that we all should have forgotten you, my poor friend! I shall scold Boissy and Clifford—oh—they shall catch it! Do you know you are very dusty?"

Fradley arose and surveyed his cuffs. Then he turned to the mirror and grew giddy with rage. His long, artistically arranged hair was full of straws, and his thin egotistical features bore little resemblance to Byron's at twenty, which he was confident they did when not smeared with soot.

"The rude, ungentlemanly creatures! The horrid brutes?" he cried. "I will complain to Julian, I will have them dismissed—"

"Comment?" said the girl.

Then Fradley plunged into the French language.

"Vooly voo Bonny moi—er—a—rest, or vooly voo pas! Je swee tray fachy,—er—er—tray, tray fachy!"

"You are angry ? Mais mon petit, to as raison!"

Fradley eyed her with animosity. "C'est votre faut!" he said; "Je dirais Musseer Julian toot sweet!"

"Comment?" inquired Sara.

"Wee! Wee!" he said with a venomous glance at her, "vooz avvy mis moi dans cette boite!" She did not understand his accusation, but she laughed wickedly and marched straight up to him. Before he knew what she was about she had deliberately thrown her arms about his neck and kissed him.

"There," she said calmly, "we must not be enemies, mon petit; now I forgive you for making a racket when I was trying to speak, and you may tell the whole atelier that Sara has kissed you." Then with an imperious nod she marched out of the studio leaving Fradley petrified.

A few moments later Clifford came in and found him still motionless, gaping vacantly.

"Oh, you're out, eh?" said Clifford. Fradley paid no attention to this salute, but stared at the door through which Sara had disappeared.

Clifford eyed him for a moment and then sat down on the chest.

"Fradley," he said, "you listen to me and I'll give you a pointer or two concerning this studio. Be manly and you'll get along. Don't kick against tradition. Better men than either of us have conformed to the customs here and filled the stove and searched for the 'grand reflecteur' on dark days."

He looked hard at Fradley. "You had better conform to custom or go somewhere else. We seldom haze here,—we never haze a manly man, and if you know anything about the École des Beaux Arts you will appreciate what I say."

Fradley was looking at him, but something in his eyes told Clifford he was not listening.

Then Clifford rose, disgusted, and swung out through the hall and down the stairs, leaving Fradley in an imbecile trance.

IV.

Fradley had delicate tastes. His rooms were hung with pale green draperies, tidies lay on every divan, and his initials were embroidered on his pillow shams. He worked very little at the studio.

"It is not necessary," he told Garland; "mere painting doesn't make an artist,—it's experience; an artist must be broad!" So Fradley began the process of broadening by going to theatres, concerts, exhibitions and museums. He also presented letters of introduction to families who maintained nourishing tables. There was one thing about him that Garland could not understand. Fradley was thin, very thin, but he ate ravenously, and Garland, eyeing him from his meagre face to his spindle shanks, wondered why he did not grow stouter.

"It's most extraordinary," he said to Carrington, "the fellow eats like a pig and grows thin on it. It's very disagreeable to me. I wish he'd stop coming in here every evening."

"You're too severe on him," said Carrington.

"I am? Well just wait until he begins visiting you with a roll of manuscript poems to read. By Jove, he nearly drives me idiotic!"

"Oh, he's a very decent fellow," said Carrington; "he's a man of splendid morals—"

"—According to himself," said Garland. "Since he arrived in the Quarter he has not missed an evening in telling us how he scorns the immoral students of this immoral Quarter, and how innocent and pure he is himself. I take no stock in that sort of thing. You and I are morally decent, but we don't sound trumpets on that account."

Carrington was silent for a moment, then he said diffidently; "I'm rather sorry for him; he isn't popular, you know. I think we ought to be friendly to him."

"It's his own fault that he is unpopular."

"Perhaps so; anyway I might as well tell you that he asked us to come to see him to-night. I accepted."

"Good heavens," groaned Garland, "he's sure to read us a poem."

"What of it?"

"Oh, I can stand it if you can. I'm tired and cross, but if you have accepted that settles it."

"It's nine o'clock," said Carrington, glancing at his watch, "we might as well go now and get away early. I'm dead tired myself. Come on, old chap, and face the music. We nouveaux should stick together!"

"You're d—n democratic for an aristocrat," laughed Garland, following him across the hallway to Fradley's door. They found Fradley sitting before the piano. He could not play the piano, but he had an enervating habit of striking single notes with one finger which filled Garland with murderous inclinations.

"Ah!" said Fradley in affected surprise, "Garland?—and Lord Ronald Carrington—"

"How are you, Fradley," said Carrington hastily, "trot out your verses, for Garland and I are going to sport our oak directly—we're dead beat from the studio concour."

Carrington had worked modestly in the Quarter for months, living under his name of Carrington with no prefix, for he hated notoriety and fuss, and was perfectly aware that a fuss would be made over him if people discovered him to be identical with the young Lord Carrington who led his company so gallantly in Burmah. He had resigned from the service to study art, and he worked hard and faithfully to make up for lack of ability. It took Fradley to discover his title and identity and, much to Carrington's chagrin, he spread the glad news and fell down and worshipped.

"Come," said Garland, "let's hear your verses. Got anything to smoke?"

"You may smoke," murmured Fradley, in a trance before Carrington, "for Lord Carrington smokes—"

"For goodness, sake call me Carrington," said Ronald, "and give us some tobacco will you?"

Fradley produced his tobacco and then began to glide about the room tidying things, arranging knick-knacks, dusting albums, until Garland shuddered.

"Come, Fradley," he said, as amiably as he could, "trot out your grog and poetry and let's get to bed. You know we only have to-morrow on the concour and we must get up early."

Fradley tripped over to the piano, found his manuscript, tripped back again to the fireplace, sat down, throwing one lank leg over the other, and coughed gently.

"It's only a trifle—a little thing I finished tonight. Let me read it to you."

Garland, aghast at the bulky manuscript, lighted a cigar and gave himself up to gloom. Carrington settled back in his chair and determined to enjoy it.

"It is entitled, 'The Kiss of Sin,'" observed Fradley.

"Oh, fin-de-siècle?" inquired Carrington.

"I thought you were opposed to immorality," said Garland.

"This is moral!" gasped Fradley, "do you think I would—"

"No—no! go on, old fellow," said Carrington.

"For Heaven's sake," muttered Garland.

Then with a smile the poet began:

> "Her burnished hair is red as flame,
>   Her red lips burn like fire,
> And she has pressed the kiss of shame,
> Upon my lips. Am I to blame?
> Away, bold siren! Learn to tame
>   Thy culpable desire!"

"Now is that immoral?" asked Fradley.

Ronald was dozing, eyes wide open.

"No," said Garland, "that's harmless; go on," and he curled himself up in the armchair and thought of Sara La Rousse. The poem was in cantos and they were numerous. Some cantos were tearful, some tempestuous. Many paid beautiful tribute to temperance, such as the verse beginning:

"Away! away! with the rose-wreathed cup!"

A little further along, Fradley's morals tottered, for the lines,

"Oh, never shall lips of mine be pressed
To thy wicked mouth or thy sinful breast!"

were almost immediately followed by:

"Beautiful creature, fly with me!
I'll build thee a house 'neath the hawthorn tree."

"I thought you said you gave her the shake!" interrupted Garland querulously. Carrington woke up at the same moment and looked terribly ashamed of himself.

"Very charming," he murmured, "it's about Sara, isn't it?"

Fradley blushed. "Oh, no—er—it's only a poetic fancy."

"Any red-headed girl—eh?" said Garland rising; "well, I am awfully obliged to you,—we'll have the rest of it soon I hope—come along, Ronald."

Fradley accompanied them to the door.

"Are you going to that—that orgie at the Bal Bullier on Mi-Carême?" he asked.

"I am," said Garland.

"Are you?" he asked of Carrington.

"Oh, yes, I suppose so; everybody else is going."

"And do you think it right?"

"No—it's not decent; you would not enjoy it," said Garland with a malicious smile. "Don't go."

"I don't know—I don't know," murmured Fradley; "an artist must be broad—"

"Especially when he's abroad—"

"Oh, come on!" grumbled Carrington,—"good night, Fradley, awfully obliged you know."

The poet entered his boudoir and lighting a wax candle looked at himself in the mirror. He smoothed his love-locks, touched his lips with glycerine, and crawling into an embroidered night-shirt sank languidly upon the bed, pulling the silken coverlet over his ears. Then he began to think of Sara.

V.

From the Seine to the Bullier, the Boulevard St. Michel lay glistening under the frosty stars. On the fountain in the Place St. Michel, the iron griffins which spat water all summer into the basin below, sat grim and helpless, jaws and claws bound in chains of ice. Above them victorious St. Michel lifted the flat of his sword to spank a prostrate Satan whose nether limbs were now mercifully padded with snow.

The Boulevard, packed from gutter to gutter, echoed with the fanfare of Carnival. Cabs crowded along five deep; tram-cars and omnibuses wheezed and tooted and ploughed their way through the constantly increasing throngs.

With mask and horn and mirliton the crowd swept through the boulevard, while from the terraces and windows of every café, students sprawled, and shouted and chanted strange anthems to celebrate the Mi-Carême.

The Café Vachette was festooned with gas jets, the Café de la Source glowed under clusters of electric globes, the Cafés d'Harcourt and Rouge were ablaze with lanterns and electricity, and the ice-covered fountain in the Place de Medici flashed back from its crystalline basin a million sparkling rays of blue and gold. On top of the hill the Bullier rose terraced with coloured lamps, bathed in a flood of electric light, which traced a trembling network of shadows over the asphalt among the trees of the Avenue de L'Observatoire. And among the shadows which the branches flung across the parkway, partly concealed by the terrace of the café which forms the angle of the avenue, a figure, enveloped in a sealskin overcoat, shivered and peered across the square to where the frivolous and godless were pouring along the sidewalk to the Bullier. On they swept, with horn and song and the rattle of canes on bench and shutter; and past them dashed cab after cab, halting for an instant at the entrance, while visions of light draperies and lighter feet sped across the foyer to the cloak-room. Now a band of architects arrived, chanting the slogan of Lalou, now a masked company of artists in blouse and béret, locking arms with a dozen of the gentler sex. At times the throng closed about some favourite who immediately mounted a boulevard bench to harangue them on the evil of being serious.

The figure in the sealskin overcoat appeared to be interested, and ventured a little way along the square, but was almost immediately frightened back by the voice of a compatriot, inebriated but melodious;

<blockquote>
"He didn't come back no more.

N—o!"

He didn't come more.
</blockquote>

"N—n she sat by the fire—hic!"

It was Arizona.

"N—n she sat by the fire—"

here memory proved treacherous, and, after several attempts to recall the fate of the abandoned one, Arizona jerked a large felt hat over one eye, squared his shoulders, advanced his lower jaw and began to yell. "Come an' pick up the dead—aw! Come an' rescue the dyin'! It's my night to howl, an' a souvenir goes with each an' every corpse!"

Across the square somebody in the crowd shouted: "Arizona, shut up!"

"W'as that?" demanded Arizona indignantly; and, encircling a tree with one arm, he started the other in a rapid rotary motion increasing in velocity until it looked like an extinct Catherine-wheel.

"What's the matter, Arizona?" asked Garland who came running across the street; "you know you mustn't yell like that in English."

"A souvenir goes with each corpse," said Arizona sullenly, "I'm a pitiless wolf—"

"You're a pitiful ass," said Clifford, coming up, "whom are you scrapping with now?"

"If I find him I'll jump on to his neck," said Arizona sulkily.

"He means Fradley," said Elliott to Clifford, "he's jealous because Sara forbade him to assault Fradley."

The figure in the sealskin coat shuddered behind his tree.

"Arizona, my son," said Clifford, "you're a nouveau yet, and you'd better not make yourself too conspicuous. You're drunk too, and if I catch you trying to get into the Bullier I'll settle with you in a way you'll remember. Give me that six-shooter—quick. Now don't try any of your cheap cowboy humor in the Latin Quarter. Go home."

"Look yere, Clifford," said Arizona, "I'm a noovo but I ain't no slouch, an' you fellows never have to tell me to be less fresh. Now I—hic!—I objec' to Fradley chasin' Sara—"

"You have no claims on Sara," said Elliott laughing.

"All right, then I hain't, but I objec' to that fool-hen Fradley scratchin' alkali in my sage-bush. Mebbe Sara ain't my business; but I'm doin' dooty about thet there public claim, an' I'm death on jumpers like him!"

At that moment the uproar on the boulevard was redoubled. A battalion of singing students, each clad in evening dress over which was draped a white blouse, was advancing from the Boulevard Montparnasse.

"Come on, Garland,—Arizona, go home!" said Clifford, and he hurried across the square to join the procession, followed by Elliott and Garland.

In the middle of the procession, enthroned upon the roof of a cab sat Sara. She was engaged in exploding squibs while Boissy held the terrified horse down to a sideway prance. Behind the cab marched Julian's young hopefuls, singing "*Le Bal à l'Hôtel de Ville*." Sara fired a whole bunch of squibs as the cab came to a halt before the statue of Marshal Ney, then, as it moved on into the flare of light, a mighty shout arose; Vive Sara!" to which that young person politely replied, "Vive l'atelier Julien!"

A moment later Sara and her cohorts were engulfed in the throng passing through the foyer of the Bal Bullier.

Half an hour later, Arizona appeared at the box office and charged in with a whoop which raised the hair under the silver helmet of the cavalryman on guard. It was, however, nearly twelve o'clock when Fradley, his eyes bulging with fright, sidled into the lobby, bought his ticket and sought the den of the female harpies who take checks for wraps. He slipped the sealskin overcoat from his meagre frame, and a harpy grabbed it. He hurriedly thrust the zinc check into his pocket, smoothed his love-locks and tripped timidly to the head of the stairs which leads down to the floor of the ballroom. Here a coarse red-necked man relieved him of his ticket, and he stood face to face with the gilded demon—*Vice!* For a moment he thought of flight; then something on the floor below made him blush violently.

"Get out of the way! You're blocking the stairs!" shouted the red-necked man, but Fradley did not hear him in the din. Then a brutal cavalryman seized Fradley and hustled him down the stairs.

"Stop!" screamed the poet, but somebody in the crowd below caught him by the leg. It was a fearful struggle. The red-necked man vociferated, the soldier pushed and the masked figure below hauled away at his feet. Fradley felt he was losing consciousness; the scene swam before him. For one awful moment he saw, in the gaudy surging masses below, the glittering pit of hell—his ears were stunned by the crash of demoniac music,— then something gave way, the soldier snickered, and Fradley found himself jerked headlong into the gulf, only to be caught in the arms of a stalwart personage wearing a false nose and a tin crown over one ear.

"Welcome to Pandemonium!" yelled the crowned personage, as he banged Fradley over the head with a bladder; "and may I ask, Monsieur, if you generally come into a Royal Presence on your head?"

Before Fradley could reply, a Nautch Girl caught him around the neck and swung him into the crush of dancers. He struggled violently.

"What! you won't dance?" she cried, with a stamp of her bangled sandals.

"No, I won't!" cried Fradley, perspiring with terror.

"You shall!" she insisted.

Then a clown with his face all white, came squealing and tumbling along, neatly floored him in an unexpected flip-flap, picked him up, and laying his chalky face on his shoulder, shrieked and sobbed, "oh, mon frère! mon frère!" This was the last straw. With a wrench and a twist he freed himself and fled to the gallery, where he found a vacant table and sat down to collect his thoughts. Little by little his fright gave way to anger. A waiter dusted the chalk from his coat and told him that there was a mirror behind the musicians' box. Here he smoothed his hair and rebuttoned his collar, keeping a suspicious eye on two young ladies of the ballet who were practising strange steps before an adjoining mirror.

"Monsieur," said one of them, "have the goodness to tell me whether I do the "grand écart," as well as "La Goulu."

"What is the 'grand écart'?" asked Fradley stiffly. He was instructed, and he withdrew in haste to his table in the gallery.

A quadrille was in progress below. He stood on his chair to see and then sat down again, not to see. This manoeuvre he repeated at intervals and ended by remaining on his chair. "For," he argued, "it's life,—and an artist must be broad."

Before the quadrille ended, he was playfully toppled from his chair by a Spanish dancer, who took his place and offered to reward him with a kiss which he refused. After a while the dancer skipped off with an Arab, and a feeling akin to loneliness took possession of Fradley.

The dull red and blue woodwork of the Bullier was hung with the banners of all nations. In the musicians' gallery, Conor and his orchestra banged away at the "March into Hell," and the tables trembled with the crash of the brass. The floor was crowded to suffocation. Imbecile shrieking clowns in ruffles and powder, went madly bounding about, Turks footed it with Russian peasant girls, gendarmes wearing false noses and enormous moustaches locked arms with "ces messieurs" of the Vilette who wore the charming costume of that quarter including "favoris" and "rouflaquettes." Students in evening-dress galloped about playing circus, and a pretty Cupid, mounted on one young gentleman's shoulders, challenged a shepherdess, mounted on another, to a race, so away they went, crying "Allons! houp! houp!" From a near corner a monotonous chanting arose, where some thirty students were squatting in a ring beating upon drums with their hands. It was the rhythmic air of an Egyptian dance which was being executed in the middle by a willowy white-veiled girl who swung two gilded scimitars. Like sheet lightning the broad blades of the swords flashed above the silver-flecked veil, as her slender, supple figure swayed to the music.

"Brava! Bis! Bis!" they cried, and the girl, with eyes like stars above her veil, whirled the scimitars into circles of flame. Suddenly she stood rigid, there came a clash of steel, the swords lay crossed before her, and, as the minor air swelled out, she whipped off her veil and sent it floating and billowing above her head while her little feet began to move to and fro among the swords, blade upward on the floor. The applause was deafening as she tossed back her head and said with the merriest laugh, "Je veux bien boire un bock!"

Clifford jumped up from the floor and picking up the swords presented them on one knee.

"Tiens! c'est toi, mon ami?"

"Yes. Forgive me the cab, Cécile," he murmured, drawing her half resisting arm through his.

"I can't forgive you. It was too ridiculous to sit there,—and somebody holding the hind wheels."

"Oh, Cécile—"

"No—no!"

"Ma petite Cécile—"

"By Jove, she's going to forgive him," said Elliott to Rowden who was dancing attendance on the pretty Cupid.

"Mr. Rowden, I insist," pouted the Cupid, shaking her curls.

"But I don't enjoy playing circus," pleaded Rowden, as Boissy pranced proudly by, his epaulettes over his ears, bearing Sara as Diana, who prodded him on with a silver-gilt arrow.

Then Cupid became petulant and signified her intention of seeking another steed, and presently Elliott became the pleased spectator of his friend careering about in company with similarly burdened youths.

"I'm not in it," sighed Elliott, until he spied Margot, who stamped her foot and called for a steed. Shortly afterwards he joined the rest in feats of the haut-école.

To say that Fradley was enjoying himself is not strictly true. Once every ten minutes he subdued some bound of a tortured conscience with the thought; "artists must be broad;" but except for these encounters with his doubts he found it all secretly thrilling and pleasant. He was lonely, in a way, yet he hardly knew what he would want of company. As for speaking to any of those bright-eyed young persons who now and then slapped his face with a rose or rattled a tambourine over his hat,—that was out of the question. No, indeed! He would look on, "because an artist must be broad," but he had no desire to contaminate himself with a word or a smile from such as they. No, indeed! No! No! There seemed to be some need of repeating this frequently to himself, but curiously enough it did not assuage his loneliness. Once a black-eyed Mephistopheles poked her pointed red feather into his eyes and then begged pardon with an irresistible smile which, fortunately for history, came several centuries too late for St. Anthony.

What Fradley might have done had not the girl been carried off by Garland, nobody can tell. He felt a thump in his throat and a murderous feeling toward Garland, and yet he was sure that he had been about to wither temptation with a frown. Carrington spoke in his ear.

"Look at Sara! Magnificent!" Fradley turned.

Seated upon a table in the gallery with the air of an Empress, Sara received the homage of the Quarter. Behind her Cécile and Clifford waved gaudy fans and imbibed champagne in tall goblets. The curly-headed Cupid and the black-eyed Mephistopheles were endangering their silken hose by sliding down the balustrade, aided and applauded by a Japanese maid and three fairies.

Fradley had eyes for Sara only. "Vulgar," he said.

"Yes," said Carrington doubtfully. A great wave of loneliness swept over Fradley.

"Shameless!" he gasped.

Then Sara's strange grey eyes met his across the whirl of the carnival; he saw her throw up her haughty head and send to him a wonderful smile,—a smile that scorched and yet healed, and in an agony of doubt he opened his lips to cry again to Carrington—to the world, "shameless!" but his lips were dry, and his voice died in his throat with a click.

The music clashed; Cécile dropped her glass and clasped Clifford's hand; Sara sprang into Boissy's arms,—there was a rush, a tempest of cheers, and Fradley, jostled and hustled clung to a pillar,—clung a moment only, then was swept away, into the throng.

"Dance!" cried a breathless voice behind him, and, "dance!" cried another voice beside him. He tried to stem the tide,—he shut his eyes, but soft arms were around his neck and a puff of perfume smote him like a blow in the face, and "dance! dance!" cried a voice in his ear. He knew the voice, his eyes flew open and he cried out, but "dance! dance! dance!" she panted, and her burnished hair flew in his face. He saw the crescent on her brow, he saw the strange grey eyes below it. Each separate hair in the fiery mane flashed like a perfumed flame, and he reeled and steadied himself with a soft hand that sought his own, while the orchestra thundered and the rosy ring of faces floated away, away, into an endless rosy chain.

When it was that he drank something, he could not remember. He was very thirsty, and iced champagne was but a temporary relief.

"Good!" cried Boissy with a stare, "so you're going in for it!"

Fradley looked at him, but Sara dropped her hand on his arm saying, "Toi, to sais bien danser," and turning scornfully to Boissy, "go away. You dance like a gendarme!"

The music began again, and with the music bedlam broke loose. There was no pretence of sets. After a couple had danced themselves into exhaustion, they climbed over the balcony and watched the others. Cécile tossed her veil into the human whirlpool below, laughing delightedly as the silver stars were rent from it and sent scaling into the air. Rowden howled through the din for Clifford to pledge him, and smashed glass after glass in a vain effort to make him hear, while the black-eyed Mephistopheles, perched on Garland's shoulders, poured out goblet after goblet of gold-dust and flung it over the throng until heads and shoulders glittered with the golden scales. Elliott had climbed into the orchestra with a bottle of champagne, and while the grateful musicians were quenching their thirst, he pounded on the spare cymbals until the handles came off and Monsieur Conor ejected him.

Then in the height of the delirium, Arizona shook the walls with his war-cry. "Aw! I'm bad! b-b-a-a-d! Me teeth is choke-bored an' a hair-trigger works both feet!" Fradley heard that cry and trembled. It came nearer and nearer.

"Pick up the dead! Pick up the dyin', an' git the souvenir!"

Sara cried: "Arizona, va t 'en!" but it was too late. With a howl from Arizona and a scream from Fradley, they clinched and fell, Arizona on top. He remembered that he punched Arizona and in turn received a tap on the ear which made him forget that he was alive. Garland picked him up, and when consciousness returned he saw Sara, furious, withering Arizona with her scorn.

"Go!" she cried, pointing to the door.

Arizona, humbled and dishevelled, went.

It needed much cooling liquid to put Fradley back where he had been prior to Arizona's assault, and that condition was far from normal. He proffered menaces, he attempted to divest himself of his coat, but Sara, very pale, and paler still after each goblet in which she pledged the exalted Fradley, took possession of him with all the blindness of sudden caprice.

Fradley felt that his hour,—the hour of the truly great, had struck. Dimly he recalled that other Fradley, the normal one, timid as a rabbit, dreading battle, loathing brute force. Vaguely he remembered that other and normal Fradley, moral, temperate in all but feeding. And he scorned him! Buried forever let him be, that *other* recreant Fradley! And all the while he went on talking with the others, capering when they capered, drinking when they drank, returning gibe for gibe, defending his own, claiming and pushing his claim with threats—warlike threats, and all the time, dimly, dully commiserating, scorning that other,—that normal Fradley.

Later he revived enough to have a pang of fright as the cold air of the boulevard blew in his face, but the cab was warm and cosey and he sank back to the cushions with a sigh of content. As in a dream he heard the rattle of wheels and the cries of the driver. Other cabs passed—endless lines of them. It seemed centuries before his cab stopped and when it did he objected to leaving it, but Sara had her way, alas now as hazy as his own, and the porter who opened the door for them at the Café Sylvain, winked solemnly at the ancient cabby, who only shook his white head and drove slowly away.

ENVOI.

The rock-ribbed Planet drifts across the Sun,
    Swarming with creatures creeping on the crust,
    Freighted with fears, and tears, and human dust,
Speaking the blank star-beacons, one by one.

Tossed on the ocean of Ten Million Nights,
    The Moon a battered battle-lantern swings;
    A Meteor a battle-pennant flings,
Lost in the ocean of Ten Million Lights.

Down to the Sea in Ships! Who knows?—Who knows
    What Unseen Thing shall climb the mist-hung shrouds
    And set the spread of splendid crowding clouds,
And light the signals set in starry rows?

Deep in the Black Crypt of the Universe
    A feeble thing stood sobbing on a star;
    "I live! I live! 'Tis mine to make or mar!"
And Silence was the Answer and the Curse.

Bee-haunted blossoms bud and bloom at Noon;
    Bird-haunted meadows belt the Seven Zones;
    And under all lie bedded human bones,
    And over all still swings the tarnished moon.

On Men and Haunts of Men—if all Light dies,
    And, where a million stars hang tenantless
    Whence the last ray is fled,—yet—none the less
A Million Lamps are trimmed for other Skies.

Believe it, O my soul! Arise and go
    Forth among Men and seek the Haunts of Men;—
    Nor shalt thou, O my soul, return again
To tell thou knowest naught; We know! We know!

R. W. C.
April, 1896.

FROM THE KING IN YELLOW

ROBERT W. CHAMBERS

THE STREET OF THE FIRST SHELL

Be of Good Cheer, the Sullen Month will die,
And a young Moon requite us by and by:
Look how the Old one, meagre, bent, and wan
With age and Fast, is fainting from the sky.

I.

The room was already dark. The high roofs opposite cut off what little remained of the December daylight. The girl drew her chair nearer the window, and choosing a large needle, threaded it, knotting the thread over her fingers. Then she smoothed the baby garment across her knees, and bending, bit off the thread and drew the smaller needle from where it rested in the hem. When she had brushed away the stray threads and bits of lace, she laid it again over her knees caressingly. Then she slipped the threaded needle from her corsage and passed it through a button, but as the button spun down the thread, her hand faltered, the thread snapped, and the button rolled across the floor. She raised her head. Her eyes were fixed on a strip of waning light above the chimneys. From somewhere in the city came sounds like the distant beating of drums, and beyond, far beyond, a vague muttering, now growing, swelling, rumbling in the distance like the pounding of surf upon the rocks, now like the surf again, receding, growling, menacing. The cold had become intense, a bitter piercing cold which strained and snapped at joist and beam and turned the slush of yesterday to flint. From the street below every sound broke sharp and metallic—the clatter of sabots, the rattle of shutters or the rare sound of a human voice. The air was heavy, weighted with the black cold as with a pall. To breathe was painful, to move an effort.

In the desolate sky there was something that wearied, in the brooding clouds, something that saddened. It penetrated the freezing city cut by the freezing river, the splendid city with its towers and domes, its quays and bridges and its thousand spires. It entered the squares, it seized the avenues and the palaces, stole across bridges and crept among the narrow streets of the Latin Quarter, grey under the grey of the December sky. Sadness, utter sadness. A fine icy sleet was falling, powdering the pavement with a tiny crystalline dust. It sifted against the window-panes and drifted in heaps along the sill. The light at the window had nearly failed, and the girl bent low over her work. Presently she raised her head, brushing the curls from her eyes.

"Jack?"

"Dearest?"

"Don't forget to clean your palette."

He said, "All right," and picking up the palette, sat down upon the floor in front of the stove. His head and shoulders were in the shadow, but the firelight fell across his knees and glimmered red on the blade of the palette-knife. Full in the firelight beside him stood a color-box. On the lid was carved,

J. TRENT
École des Beaux Arts
1870

This inscription was ornamented with an American and a French flag.

The sleet blew against the window-panes, covering them with stars and diamonds, then, melting from the warmer air within, ran down and froze again in fern-like traceries.

A dog whined and the patter of small paws sounded on the zinc behind the stove.

"Jack, dear, do you think Hercules is hungry?"

The patter of paws was redoubled behind the stove.

"He's whining," she continued nervously, "and if it isn't because he's hungry it is because—"

Her voice faltered. A loud humming filled the air, the windows vibrated.

"Oh, Jack," she cried, "another—" but her voice was drowned in the scream of a shell tearing through the clouds overhead.

"That is the nearest yet," she murmured.

"Oh, no," he answered cheerfully, "it probably fell way over by Montmartre," and as she did not answer, he said again with exaggerated unconcern, "They wouldn't take the trouble to fire at the Latin Quarter; anyway they haven't a battery that can hurt it."

After a while she spoke up brightly: "Jack, dear, when are you going to take me to see Monsieur West's statues?"

"I will bet," he said, throwing down his palette and walking over to the window beside her, "that Colette has been here today."

"Why?" she asked, opening her eyes very wide. Then, "Oh, it's too bad!—really, men are tiresome when they think they know everything! And I warn you that if Monsieur West is vain enough to imagine that Colette—"

From the north another shell came whistling and quavering through the sky, passing above them with long-drawn screech which left the windows singing.

"That," he blurted out, "was too near for comfort."

They were silent for a while, then he spoke again gaily: "Go on, Sylvia, and wither poor West;" but she only sighed, "Oh, dear, I can never seem to get used to the shells."

He sat down on the arm of the chair beside her.

Her scissors fell jingling to the floor; she tossed the unfinished frock after them, and putting both arms about his neck drew him down into her lap.

"Don't go out tonight, Jack."

He kissed her uplifted face; "You know I must; don't make it hard for me."

"But when I hear the shells and—and know you are out in the city—"

"But they all fall in Montmartre—"

"They may all fall in the Beaux Arts; you said yourself that two struck the Quai d'Orsay—"

"Mere accident—"

"Jack, have pity on me! Take me with you!"

"And who will there be to get dinner?"

She rose and flung herself on the bed.

"Oh, I can't get used to it, and I know you must go, but I beg you not to be late to dinner. If you knew what I suffer! I—I—cannot help it, and you must be patient with me, dear."

He said, "It is as safe there as it is in our own house."

She watched him fill for her the alcohol lamp, and when he had lighted it and had taken his hat to go, she jumped up and clung to him in silence. After a moment he said: "Now, Sylvia, remember my courage is sustained by yours. Come, I must go!" She did not move, and he repeated: "I must go." Then she stepped back and he thought she was going to speak and waited, but she only looked at him, and, a little impatiently, he kissed her again, saying: "Don't worry, dearest."

When he had reached the last flight of stairs on his way to the street a woman hobbled out of the house-keeper's lodge waving a letter and calling: "Monsieur Jack! Monsieur Jack! this was left by Monsieur Fallowby!"

He took the letter, and leaning on the threshold of the lodge, read it:

> "DEAR JACK
> "I believe Braith is dead broke and I'm sure Fallowby is. Braith swears he isn't, and Fallowby swears he is, so you can draw your own conclusions. I've got a scheme for a dinner, and if it

works, I will let you fellows in.

"Yours faithfully,
"WEST"

"P.S.—Fallowby has shaken Hartman and his gang, thank the Lord! There is something rotten there—or it may be he's only a miser.

"P.P.S.—I'm more desperately in love than ever, but I'm sure she does not care a straw for me."

"All right," said Trent, with a smile, to the concierge; "but tell me, how is Papa Cottard?"

The old woman shook her head and pointed to the curtained bed in the lodge.

"*Père* Cottard!" he cried cheerily, "how goes the wound today?" He walked over to the bed and drew the curtains. An old man was lying among the tumbled sheets.

"Better?" smiled Trent.

"Better," repeated the man wearily; and, after a pause, "Have you any news, Monsieur Jack?"

"I haven't been out today. I will bring you any rumor I may hear, though goodness knows I've got enough of rumors," he muttered to himself. Then aloud: "Cheer up; you're looking better."

"And the sortie?"

"Oh, the sortie, that's for this week. General Trochu sent orders last night."

"It will be terrible."

"It will be sickening," thought Trent as he went out into the street and turned the corner toward the rue de Seine; "slaughter, slaughter, phew! I'm glad I'm not going."

The street was almost deserted. A few women muffled in tattered military capes crept along the frozen pavement, and a wretchedly clad gamin hovered over the sewer-hole on the corner of the Boulevard. A rope around his waist held his rags together. From the rope hung a rat, still warm and bleeding.

"There's another in there," he yelled at Trent; "I hit him but he got away."

Trent crossed the street and asked: "How much?"

"Two francs for a quarter of a fat one; that's what they give at the St. Germain Market."

A violent fit of coughing interrupted him, but he wiped his face with the palm of his hand and looked cunningly at Trent.

"Last week you could buy a rat for six francs, but," and here he swore vilely, "the rats have quit the rue de Seine and they kill them now over by the new hospital. I'll let you have this for seven francs; I can sell it for ten in the Isle St. Louis."

"You lie," said Trent, "and let me tell you that if you try to swindle anybody in this quarter the people will make short work of you and your rats."

He stood a moment eyeing the gamin, who pretended to snivel. Then he tossed him a franc, laughing. The child caught it, and thrusting it into his mouth wheeled about to the sewer-hole. For a second he crouched, motionless, alert, his eyes on the bars of the drain, then leaping forward he hurled a stone into the gutter, and Trent left him to finish a fierce grey rat that writhed squealing at the mouth of the sewer.

"Suppose Braith should come to that," he thought; "poor little chap;" and hurrying, he turned in the dirty passage des Beaux Arts and entered the third house to the left.

"Monsieur is at home," quavered the old concierge.

Home? A garret absolutely bare, save for the iron bedstead in the corner and the iron basin and pitcher on the floor.

West appeared at the door, winking with much mystery, and motioned Trent to enter. Braith, who was painting in bed to keep warm, looked up, laughed, and shook hands.

"Any news?"

The perfunctory question was answered as usual by: "Nothing but the cannon."

Trent sat down on the bed.

"Where on earth did you get that?" he demanded, pointing to a half-finished chicken nestling in a wash-basin.

West grinned.

"Are you millionaires, you two? Out with it."

Braith, looking a little ashamed, began, "Oh, it's one of West's exploits," but was cut short by West, who said he would tell the story himself.

"You see, before the siege, I had a letter of introduction to a '*type*' here, a fat banker, German-American variety. You know the species, see. Well, of course I forgot to present the letter, but this morning, judging it to be a favorable opportunity, I called on him.

"The villain lives in comfort—fires, my boy!—fires in the anterooms! The Buttons finally condescends to carry my letter and card up, leaving me standing in the hallway, which I did not like, so I entered the first room I saw and nearly fainted at the sight of a banquet on a table by the fire. Down comes Buttons, very insolent. No, oh, no, his master, 'is not at home, and in fact is too busy to receive letters of introduction just now; the siege, and many business difficulties—'

"I deliver a kick to Buttons, pick up this chicken from the table, toss my card on to the empty plate, and addressing Buttons as a species of Prussian pig, march out with the honors of war."

Trent shook his head.

"I forgot to say that Hartman often dines there, and I draw my own conclusions," continued West. "Now about this chicken, half of it is for Braith and myself, and half for Colette, but of course you will help me eat my part because I'm not hungry."

"Neither am I," began Braith, but Trent, with a smile at the pinched faces before him, shook his head saying, "What nonsense! You know I'm never hungry!"

West hesitated, reddened, and then slicing off Braith's portion, but not eating any himself, said good-night, and hurried away to number 470 rue Serpente, where lived a pretty girl named Colette, orphan after Sedan, and Heaven alone knew where she got the roses in her cheeks, for the siege came hard on the poor.

"That chicken will delight her, but I really believe she's in love with West," said Trent. Then walking over to the bed: "See here, old man, no dodging, you know, how much have you left?"

The other hesitated and flushed.

"Come, old chap," insisted Trent.

Braith drew a purse from beneath his bolster, and handed it to his friend with a simplicity that touched him.

"Seven sous," he counted; "you make me tired! Why on earth don't you come to me? I take it d—d ill, Braith! How many times must I go over the same thing and explain to you that because I have money it is my duty to share it, and your duty and the duty of every American to share it with me? You can't get a cent, the city's blockaded, and the American Minister has his hands full with all the German riff-raff and deuce knows what! Why don't you act sensibly?"

"I—I will, Trent, but it's an obligation that perhaps I can never even in part repay. I'm poor and—"

"Of course you'll pay me! If I were a usurer I would take your talent for security. When you are rich and famous—"

"Don't, Trent—"

"All right, only no more monkey business."

He slipped a dozen gold pieces into the purse, and tucking it again under the mattress smiled at Braith.

"How old are you?" he demanded.

"Sixteen."

Trent laid his hand lightly on his friend's shoulder. "I'm twenty-two, and

I have the rights of a grandfather as far as you are concerned. You'll do as I say until you're twenty-one."

"The siege will be over then, I hope," said Braith, trying to laugh, but the prayer in their hearts: "How long, O Lord, how long!" was answered by the swift scream of a shell soaring among the storm-clouds of that December night.

II.

West, standing in the doorway of a house in the rue Serpentine, was speaking angrily. He said he didn't care whether Hartman liked it or not; he was telling him, not arguing with him.

"You call yourself an American!" he sneered; "Berlin and hell are full of that kind of American. You come loafing about Colette with your pockets stuffed with white bread and beef, and a bottle of wine at thirty francs and you can't really afford to give a dollar to the American Ambulance and Public Assistance, which Braith does, and he's half starved!"

Hartman retreated to the curbstone, but West followed him, his face like a thunder-cloud. "Don't you dare to call yourself a countryman of mine," he growled—"no—nor an artist either! Artists don't worm themselves into the service of the Public Defense where they do nothing but feed like rats on the people's food! And I'll tell you now," he continued dropping his voice, for Hartman had started as though stung, "you might better keep away from that Alsatian Brasserie and the smug-faced thieves who haunt it. You know what they do with suspects!"

"You lie, you hound!" screamed Hartman, and flung the bottle in his hand straight at West's face. West had him by the throat in a second, and forcing him against the dead wall shook him wickedly.

"Now you listen to me," he muttered, through his clenched teeth. "You are already a suspect and—I swear—I believe you are a paid spy! It isn't my business to detect such vermin, and I don't intend to denounce you, but understand this! Colette don't like you and I can't stand you, and if I catch you in this street again I'll make it somewhat unpleasant. Get out, you sleek Prussian!"

Hartman had managed to drag a knife from his pocket, but West tore it from him and hurled him into the gutter. A gamin who had seen this burst into a peal of laughter, which rattled harshly in the silent street. Then everywhere windows were raised and rows of haggard faces appeared demanding to know why people should laugh in the starving city.

"Is it a victory?" murmured one.

"Look at that," cried West as Hartman picked himself up from the pavement, "look! you miser! look at those faces!" But Hartman gave *him* a look which he never forgot, and walked away without a word. Trent, who suddenly appeared at the corner, glanced curiously at West, who merely nodded toward his door saying, "Come in; Fallowby's upstairs."

"What are you doing with that knife?" demanded Fallowby, as he and Trent entered the studio.

West looked at his wounded hand, which still clutched the knife, but saying, "Cut myself by accident," tossed it into a corner and washed the blood from his fingers.

Fallowby, fat and lazy, watched him without comment, but Trent, half divining how things had turned, walked over to Fallowby smiling.

"I've a bone to pick with you!" he said.

"Where is it? I'm hungry," replied Fallowby with affected eagerness, but Trent, frowning, told him to listen.

"How much did I advance you a week ago?"

"Three hundred and eighty francs," replied the other, with a squirm of contrition.

"Where is it?"

Fallowby began a series of intricate explanations, which were soon cut short by Trent.

"I know; you blew it in—you always blow it in. I don't care a rap what you did before the siege: I know you are rich and have a right to dispose of your money as you wish to, and I also know that, generally speaking, it is none of my business. But *now* it is my business, as I have to supply the funds until you get some more, which you won't until the siege is ended one way or another. I wish to share what I have, but I won't see it thrown out of the window. Oh, yes, of course I know you will reimburse me, but that isn't the question; and, anyway, it's the opinion of your friends, old man, that you will not be worse off for a little abstinence from fleshly pleasures. You are positively a freak in this famine-cursed city of skeletons!"

"I *am* rather stout," he admitted.

"Is it true you are out of money?" demanded Trent.

"Yes, I am," sighed the other.

"That roast sucking pig on the rue St. Honoré—is it there yet?" continued Trent.

"Wh-at?" stammered the feeble one.

"Ah—I thought so! I caught you in ecstasy before that sucking pig at least a dozen times!"

Then laughing, he presented Fallowby with a roll of twenty franc pieces saying: "If these go for luxuries you must live on your own flesh," and went over to aid West, who sat beside the wash-basin binding up his hand.

West suffered him to tie the knot, and then said: "You remember, yesterday, when I left you and Braith to take the chicken to Colette."

"Chicken! Good heavens!" moaned Fallowby.

"Chicken," repeated West, enjoying Fallowby's grief—"I—that is, I must explain that things are changed. Colette and I—are to be married—"

"What—what about the chicken?" groaned Fallowby.

"Shut up!" laughed Trent, and slipping his arm through West's, walked to the stairway.

"The poor little thing," said West, "just think, not a splinter of firewood for a week and wouldn't tell me because she thought I needed it for my clay figure. Whew! When I heard it I smashed that smirking clay nymph to pieces, and the rest can freeze and be hanged!" After a moment he added timidly: "Won't you call on your way down and say *bon soir?* It's No. 17."

"Yes," said Trent, and he went out softly, closing the door behind. He stopped on the third landing, lighted a match, scanned the numbers over the row of dingy doors, and knocked at No. 17. "C'est toi, Georges?" The door opened.

"Oh, pardon, Monsieur Jack, I thought it was Monsieur West," then blushing furiously, "Oh, I see you have heard! Oh, thank you so much for your wishes, and I'm sure we love each other very much—and I'm dying to see Sylvia and tell her and—"

"And what?" laughed Trent.

"I am very happy," she sighed.

"He's pure gold," returned Trent, and then gaily: "I want you and George to come and dine with us tonight. It's a little treat—you see tomorrow is Sylvia's fête. She will be nineteen. I have written to Thorne, and the Guernalecs will come with their cousin Odile. Fallowby has engaged not to bring anybody but himself."

The girl accepted shyly, charging him with loads of loving messages to Sylvia, and he said good-night.

He started up the street, walking swiftly, for it was bitter cold, and cutting across the rue de la Lune he entered the rue de Seine. The early winter night had fallen, almost without warning, but the sky was clear and myriads of stars glittered in the heavens. The bombardment had become furious—a steady rolling thunder from the Prussian cannon punctuated by the heavy shocks from Mont Valérien.

The shells streamed across the sky leaving trails like shooting stars, and now, as he turned to look back, rockets blue and red flared above the horizon from the Fort of Issy, and the Fortress of the North flamed like a bonfire.

"Good news!" a man shouted over by the Boulevard St. Germain. As if by magic the streets were filled with people—shivering, chattering people with shrunken eyes.

"Jacques!" cried one. "The Army of the Loire!"

"Eh! *mon vieux*, it has come then at last! I told thee! I told thee! Tomorrow—tonight—who knows?"

"Is it true? Is it a sortie?"

Someone said: "Oh, God—a sortie—and my son?" Another cried: "to the Seine? They say one can see the signals of the Army of the Loire from the Pont Neuf."

There was a child standing near Trent who kept repeating: "Mamma, Mamma, then tomorrow we may eat white bread?" and beside him, an old man swaying, stumbling, his shriveled hands crushed to his breast, muttering as if insane.

"Could it be true? Who has heard the news? The shoemaker on the rue de Buci had it from a mobile who had heard a Franc-tireur repeat it to a captain of the National Guard."

Trent followed the throng surging through the rue de Seine to the river.

Rocket after rocket clove the sky, and now, from Montmartre, the cannon clanged, and the batteries on Montparnasse joined in with a crash. The bridge was packed with people.

Trent asked: "Who has seen the signals of the Army of the Loire?"

"We are waiting for them," was the reply.

He looked toward the north. Suddenly the huge silhouette of the Arc de Triomphe sprang into black relief against the flash of a cannon. The boom of the gun rolled along the quay and the old bridge vibrated.

Again over by the Point du Jour a flash and heavy explosion shook the bridge, and then the whole eastern bastion of the fortifications blazed and crackled, sending a red flame into the sky.

"Has anyone seen the signals yet?" he asked again.

"We are waiting," was the reply.

"Yes, waiting," murmured a man behind him, "waiting, sick, starved, freezing, but waiting. Is it a sortie? They go gladly. Is it to starve? They starve. They have no time to think of surrender. Are they heroes—these Parisians? Answer me, Trent!"

The American Ambulance surgeon turned about and scanned the parapets of the bridge.

"Any news, Doctor?" asked Trent mechanically.

"News?" said the doctor; "I don't know any—I haven't time to know any. What are these people after?"

"They say that the Army of the Loire has signaled Mont Valérien."

"Poor devils." The doctor glanced about him for an instant, and then: "I'm so harried and worried that I don't know what to do. After the last sortie we had the work of fifty ambulances on our poor little corps. Tomorrow there's another sortie, and I wish you fellows could come over to headquarters. We may need volunteers. How is madame?" he added abruptly.

"Well," replied Trent, "but she seems to grow more nervous every day. I ought to be with her now."

"Take care of her," said the doctor, then with a sharp look at the people: "I can't stop now—goodnight!" and he hurried away muttering, "Poor devils!"

Trent leaned over the parapet and blinked at the black river surging through the arches. Dark objects, carried swiftly on the breast of the current, struck with a grinding tearing noise against the stone piers, spun around for an instant, and hurried away into the darkness. The ice from the Marne.

As he stood staring into the water, a hand was laid on his shoulder. "Hello, Southwark!" he cried, turning around; "this is a queer place or you!"

"Trent, I have something to tell you. Don't stay here—don't believe in the Army of the Loire:" and the *attaché* of the American Legation slipped his arm through Trent's and drew him toward the Louvre.

"Then it's another lie!" said Trent bitterly.

"Worse—we know at the Legation—I can't speak of it. But that's not what I have to say. Something happened this afternoon. The Alsatian Brasserie was visited and an American named Hartman has been arrested. Do you know him?"

"I know a German who calls himself an American—his name is Hartman."

"Well, he was arrested about two hours ago. They mean to shoot him."

"What!"

"Of course we at the Legation can't allow them to shoot him offhand, but the evidence seems conclusive."

"Is he a spy?"

"Well, the papers seized in his rooms are pretty damning proofs, and besides he was caught, they say, swindling the Public Food Committee. He drew rations for fifty, how, I don't know. He claims to be an American artist here, and we have been obliged to take notice of it at the Legation. It's a nasty affair."

"To cheat the people at such a time is worse than robbing the poor-box," cried Trent angrily. "Let them shoot him!"

"He's an American citizen."

"Yes, oh yes," said the other with bitterness. "American citizenship is a precious privilege when every goggle-eyed German—" His anger choked him.

Southwark shook hands with him warmly. "It can't be helped, we must own the carrion. I am afraid you may be called upon to identify him as an American artist," he said with a ghost of a smile on his deep-lined face; and walked away through the Cours la Rein.

Trent swore silently for a moment and then drew out his watch. Seven o'clock. "Sylvia will be anxious," he thought, and hurried back to the river. The crowd still huddled shivering on the bridge, a sombre pitiful congregation, peering out into the night for the signals of the Army of the Loire: and their hearts beat time to the pounding of the guns, their eyes lighted with each flash from the bastions, and hope rose with the drifting rockets.

A black cloud hung over the fortifications. From horizon to horizon the cannon smoke stretched in wavering bands, now capping the spires and domes with cloud, now blowing in streamers and shreds along the streets, now descending from the housetops, enveloping quays, bridges, and river, in a sulphurous mist. And through the smoke pall the lightning of the cannon played, while from time to time a rift above showed a fathomless black vault set with stars.

He turned again into the rue de Seine, that sad abandoned street, with its rows of closed shutters and desolate ranks of unlighted lamps. He was a little nervous and wished once or twice for a revolver, but the slinking forms which passed him in the darkness were too weak with hunger to be dangerous, he thought, and he passed on unmolested to his doorway. But there somebody sprang at his throat. Over and over the icy pavement he rolled with his assailant, tearing at the noose about his neck, and then with a wrench sprang to his feet.

"Get up," he cried to the other.

Slowly and with great deliberation, a small gamin picked himself out of the gutter and surveyed Trent with disgust.

"That's a nice clean trick," said Trent; "a whelp of your age! You'll finish against a dead wall! Give me that cord!"

The urchin handed him the noose without a word.

Trent struck a match and looked at his assailant. It was the rat-killer of the day before.

"H'm! I thought so," he muttered.

"Tiens, c'est toi?" said the gamin tranquilly.

The impudence, the overpowering audacity of the ragamuffin took Trent's breath away.

"Do you know, you young strangler," he gasped, "that they shoot thieves of your age?"

The child turned a passionless face to Trent. "Shoot, then."

That was too much, and he turned on his heel and entered his hotel.

Groping up the unlighted stairway, he at last reached his own landing and felt about in the darkness for the door. From his studio came the sound of voices, West's hearty laugh and Fallowby's chuckle, and at last he found the knob and, pushing back the door, stood a moment confused by the light.

"Hello, Jack!" cried West, "you're a pleasant creature, inviting people to dine and letting them wait. Here's Fallowby weeping with hunger—"

"Shut up," observed the latter, "perhaps he's been out to buy a turkey."

"He's been out garroting, look at his noose!" laughed Guernalec. "So now we know where you get your cash!" added West; "vive le coup du Père Francois!"

Trent shook hands with everybody and laughed at Sylvia's pale face.

"I didn't mean to be late; I stopped on the bridge a moment to watch the bombardment. Were you anxious, Sylvia?"

She smiled and murmured, "Oh, no!" but her hand dropped into his and tightened convulsively.

"To the table!" shouted Fallowby, and uttered a joyous whoop. "Take it easy," observed Thorne, with a remnant of manners; "you are not the host, you know."

Marie Guernalec, who had been chattering with Colette, jumped up and took Thorne's arm and Monsieur Guernalec drew Odile's arm through his.

Trent, bowing gravely, offered his own arm to Colette, West took in Sylvia, and Fallowby hovered anxiously in the rear.

"You march around the table three times singing the Marseillaise," explained Sylvia, "and Monsieur Fallowby pounds on the table and beats time."

Fallowby suggested that they could sing after dinner, but his protest was drowned in the ringing chorus—

> Aux armes!
> Formez vos bataillons!

Around the room they marched singing,

> Marchons! Marchons!

with all their might, while Fallowby with very bad grace, hammered on the table, consoling himself a little with the hope that the exercise would increase his appetite. Hercules, the black and tan, fled under the bed, from which retreat he yapped and whined until dragged out by Guernalec and placed in Odile's lap.

"And now," said Trent gravely, when everybody was seated, "listen!" and he read the menu.

Beef Soup à la Siège de Paris.

Fish.
Sardines a la père Lachaise.
(White Wine)

Ròti (Red Wine).
Fresh Beef à la sortie.

Vegetables.
Canned Beans à la chasse-pot,
Canned Peas Gravelotte,
Potatoes Irlandaises,
Miscellaneous.

Cold Corned Beef à la Thiers,
Stewed Prunes à la Garibaldi.

Dessert.
Dried prunes – White bread,
Currant Jelly,
Tea – Café,
Liqueurs,
Pipes and Cigarettes.

Fallowby applauded frantically, and Sylvia served the soup. "Isn't it delicious?" sighed Odile.

Marie Guernalec sipped her soup in rapture.

"Not at all like horse, and I don't care what they say, horse doesn't taste like beef," whispered Colette to West. Fallowby, who had finished, began to caress his chin and eye the tureen.

"Have some more, old chap?" enquired Trent.

"Monsieur Fallowby cannot have any more," announced Sylvia; "I am saving this for the concierge." Fallowby transferred his eyes to the fish.

The sardines, hot from the grille, were a great success. While the others were eating Sylvia ran downstairs with the soup for the old concierge and her husband, and when she hurried back, flushed and breathless, and had slipped into her chair with a happy smile at Trent, that young man arose, and silence fell over the table. For an instant he looked at Sylvia and thought he had never seen her so beautiful.

"You all know," he began, "that today is my wife's nineteenth birthday—"

Fallowby, bubbling with enthusiasm, waved his glass in circles about his head to the terror of Odile and Colette, his neighbors; and Thorne, West and Guernalec refilled their glasses three times before the storm of applause which the toast of Sylvia had provoked, subsided.

Three times the glasses were filled and emptied to Sylvia, and again to Trent, who protested.

"This is irregular," he cried, "the next toast is to the twin Republics, France and America!"

"To the Republics! To the Republics!" they cried, and the toast was drunk amid shouts of Vive la France! Vive l'Amerique! Vive la Nation!"

Then Trent, with a smile at West, offered the toast, "To a Happy Pair!" and everybody understood, and Sylvia leaned over and kissed Colette, while Trent bowed to West.

The beef was eaten in comparative calm, but when it was finished and a portion of it set aside for the old people below, Trent cried: "Drink to Paris! May she rise from her ruins and crush the invader!" and the cheers rang out, drowning for a moment the monotonous thunder of the Prussian guns.

Pipes and cigarettes were lighted, and Trent listened an instant to the animated chatter around him, broken by ripples of laughter from the girls or the mellow chuckle of Fallowby. Then he turned to West.

"There is going to be a sortie tonight," he said. "I saw the American Ambulance surgeon just before I came in and he asked me to speak to you fellows. Any aid we can give him will not come amiss."

Then dropping his voice and speaking in English, "As for me, I shall go out with the ambulance tomorrow morning. There is of course no danger, but it's just as well to keep it from Sylvia."

West nodded. Thorne and Guernalec, who had heard, broke in and offered assistance, and Fallowby volunteered with a groan.

"All right," said Trent rapidly—"no more now, but meet me at Ambulance headquarters tomorrow morning at eight."

Sylvia and Colette, who were becoming uneasy at the conversation in English, now demanded to know what they were talking about.

"What does a sculptor usually talk about?" cried West, with a laugh.

Odile glanced reproachfully at Thorne, her fiancé.

"You are not French, you know, and it is none of your business, this war," said Odile with much dignity.

Thorne looked meek, but West assumed an air of outraged virtue. "It seems," he said to Fallowby, "that a fellow cannot discuss the beauties of Greek sculpture in his mother tongue, without being openly suspected."

Colette placed her hand over his mouth and turning to Sylvia, murmured, "They are horridly untruthful, these men."

"I believe the word for ambulance is the same in both languages," said Marie Guernalec saucily; "Sylvia, don't trust Monsieur Trent."

"Jack," whispered Sylvia, "promise me —"

A knock at the studio door interrupted her.

"Come in!" cried Fallowby, but Trent sprang up, and opening the door, looked out. Then with a hasty excuse to the rest, he stepped into the hallway and closed the door.

When he returned he was grumbling.

"What is it, Jack?" cried West.

"What is it?" repeated Trent savagely; "I'll tell you what it is. I have received a dispatch from the American Minister to go at once and identify and claim, as a fellow-countryman and a brother artist, a rascally thief and a German spy!"

"Don't go," suggested Fallowby.

"If I don't they'll shoot him at once."

"Let them," growled Thorne.

"Do you fellows know who it is?"

"Hartman!" shouted West, inspired.

Sylvia sprang up deathly white, but Odile slipped her arm around her and supported her to a chair, saying calmly, "Sylvia has fainted—it's the hot room—bring some water."

Trent brought it at once.

Sylvia opened her eyes, and after a moment rose, and supported by Marie Guernalec and Trent, passed into the bedroom.

It was the signal for breaking up, and everybody came and shook hands with Trent, saying they hoped Sylvia would sleep it off and that it would be nothing.

When Marie Guernalec took leave of him, she avoided his eyes, but he spoke to her cordially and thanked her for her aid.

"Anything I can do, Jack?" enquired West, lingering, and then hurried downstairs to catch up with the rest.

Trent leaned over the banisters, listening to their footsteps and chatter, and then the lower door banged and the house was silent. He lingered, staring down into the blackness, biting his lips; then with an impatient movement, "I am crazy!" he muttered, and lighting a candle, went into the bedroom. Sylvia was lying on the bed. He bent over her, smoothing the curly hair on her forehead.

"Are you better, dear Sylvia?"

She did not answer, but raised her eyes to his. For an instant he met her gaze, but what he read there sent a chill to his heart and he sat down covering his face with his hands.

At last she spoke in a voice, changed and strained—a voice which he had never heard, and he dropped his hands and listened, bolt upright in his chair.

"Jack, it has come at last. I have feared it and trembled—ah! how often have I lain awake at night with this on my heart and prayed that I might die before you should ever know of it! For I love you, Jack, and if you go away I cannot live. I have deceived you—it happened before I knew you, but since that first day when you found me weeping in the Luxembourg and spoke to me, Jack, I have been faithful to you in every thought and deed. I loved you from the first and did not dare to tell you this—fearing that you would go away; and since then my love has grown—grown—and oh! I suffered!—but I dared not tell you. And now you know, but you do not know the worst. For him—now—what do I care? He was cruel—oh, so cruel!"

She hid her face in her arms.

"Must I go on? Must I tell you—can you not imagine, oh! Jack—"

He did not stir; his eyes seemed dead.

"I—I was so young, I knew nothing, and he said — said that he loved me—"

Trent rose and struck the candle with his clenched fist, and the room was dark.

The bells of St. Sulpice tolled the hour, and she started up, speaking with feverish haste—"I must finish! When you told me you loved me you—you asked me nothing; but then, even then, it was too late, and *that other life* which binds me to him, must stand for ever between you and me! For there *is another* whom he has claimed, and is good to. He must not die—they cannot shoot him, for that *other's* sake!"

Trent sat motionless, but his thoughts ran on in an interminable whirl.

Sylvia, little Sylvia, who shared with him his student life—who bore with him the dreary desolation of the siege without complaint—this slender blue-eyed girl whom he was so quietly fond of, whom he teased or caressed as the whim suited, who sometimes made him the least bit impatient with her passionate devotion to him—could this be the same Sylvia who lay weeping there in the darkness?

Then he clenched his teeth. "Let him die! Let him die!"—but then—for Sylvia's sake, and—for that *other's* sake—Yes, he would go—he *must* go—his duty was plain before him. But Sylvia—he could not be what he had been to her, and yet a vague terror seized him, now all was said. Trembling, he struck a light.

She lay there, her curly hair tumbled about her face, her small white hands pressed to her breast.

He could not leave her, and he could not stay. He never knew before that he loved her. She had been a mere comrade, this girl wife of his. Ah! he loved her now with all his heart and soul, and he knew it, only when it was too late. Too late? Why? Then he thought of that *other* one, binding her, linking her forever to the creature, who stood in danger of his life. With an oath he sprang to the door, but the door would not open—or was it that he pressed it back—locked it—and flung himself on his knees beside the bed, knowing that he dared not for his life's sake leave what was his all in life.

III.

It was four in the morning when he came out of the Prison of the Condemned with the Secretary of the American Legation. A knot of people had gathered around the American Minister's carriage, which stood in front of the prison, the horses stamping and pawing in the icy street, the coachman huddled on the box, wrapped in furs. Southwark helped the Secretary into the carriage, and shook hands with Trent, thanking him for coming.

"How the scoundrel did stare," he said; "your evidence was worse than a kick, but it saved his skin for the moment at least—and prevented complications."

The Secretary sighed. "We have done our part. Now let them prove him a spy and we wash our hands of him. Jump in, Captain! Come along, Trent!"

"I have a word to say to Captain Southwark, I won't detain him," said Trent hastily, and dropping his voice, "Southwark, help me now. You know the story from the blackguard. You know the—the child is at his rooms. Get it, and take it to my own apartment, and if he is shot, I will provide a home for it."

"I understand," said the Captain gravely.

"Will you do this at once?"

"At once," he replied.

Their hands met in a warm clasp, and then Captain Southwark climbed into the carriage, motioning Trent to follow; but he shook his head saying, "Goodbye!" and the carriage rolled away. He watched the carriage to the end of the street, then started toward his own quarter, but after a step or two hesitated, stopped, and finally turned away in the opposite direction. Something—perhaps it was the sight of the prisoner he had so recently confronted, nauseated him. He felt the need of solitude and quiet to collect his thoughts. The events of the evening had shaken him terribly, but he would walk it off, forget, bury everything, and then go back to Sylvia. He started on swiftly, and for a time the bitter thoughts seemed to fade, but when he paused at last, breathless, under the Arc de Triomphe, the bitterness and the wretchedness of the whole thing—yes, of his whole misspent life came back with a pang. Then the face of the prisoner, stamped with the horrible grimace of fear, grew in the shadows before his eyes.

Sick at heart he wandered up and down under the great Arc, striving to occupy his mind, peering up at the sculptured cornices to read the names of the heroes and battles which he knew were engraved there, but always the ashen face of Hartman followed him, grinning with terror!—or was it terror?—was it not triumph?—At the thought he leaped like a man who feels a knife at his throat, but after a savage tramp around the square, came back again and sat down to battle with his misery.

The air was cold, but his cheeks were burning with angry shame. Shame? Why? Was it because he had married a girl whom chance had made a mother? *Did* he love her? Was this miserable bohemian existence, then, his end and aim in life? He turned his eyes upon the secrets of his heart, and read an evil story—the story of the past, and he covered his face for shame, while, keeping time to the dull pain throbbing in his head, his heart beat out the story for the future. Shame and disgrace.

Roused at last from a lethargy which had begun to numb the bitterness of his thoughts, he raised his head and looked about. A sudden fog had settled in the streets; the arches of the Arc were choked with it. He would go home. A great horror of being alone seized him. *But he was not alone.* The fog was peopled with phantoms. All around him in the mist they moved, drifting through the arches in lengthening lines, and vanished, while from the fog others rose up, swept past and were engulfed. He was not alone, for even at his side they crowded, touched him, swarmed before him, beside him, behind him, pressed him back, seized, and bore him with them through the mist. Down a dim avenue, through lanes and alleys white with fog, they moved, and if they spoke their voices were dull as the vapour which shrouded them. At last in front, a bank of masonry and earth cut by a massive iron barred gate towered up in the fog. Slowly and more slowly they glided, shoulder to shoulder and thigh to thigh. Then all movement ceased. A sudden breeze stirred the fog. It wavered and eddied. Objects became more distinct. A pallor crept above the horizon, touching the edges of the watery clouds, and drew dull sparks from a thousand bayonets. Bayonets—they were everywhere, cleaving the fog or flowing beneath it in rivers of steel. High on the wall of masonry and earth a great gun loomed, and around it figures moved in silhouettes. Below, a broad torrent of bayonets swept through the iron barred gateway, out into the shadowy plain. It became lighter. Faces grew more distinct among the marching masses and he recognized one.

"You, Philippe!"

The figure turned its head.

Trent cried, "Is there room for me?" but the other only waved his arm in a vague adieu and was gone with the rest. Presently the cavalry began to pass, squadron on squadron, crowding out into the darkness; then many cannon, then an ambulance, then again the endless lines of bayonets. Beside him a cuirassier sat on his steaming horse, and in front, among a group of mounted officers he saw a general, with the astrakhan collar of his dolman turned up about his bloodless face.

Some women were weeping near him and one was struggling to force a loaf of black bread into a soldier's haversack. The soldier tried to aid her, but the sack was fastened, and his rifle bothered him, so Trent held it, while the woman unbuttoned the sack and forced in the bread, now all wet with her tears. The rifle was not heavy. Trent found it wonderfully manageable. Was the bayonet sharp? He tried it. Then a sudden longing, a fierce, imperative desire took possession of him.

"*Chouette!*" cried a gamin, clinging to the barred gate, "*encore toi mon vieux?*"

Trent looked up, and the rat-killer laughed in his face. But when the soldier had taken the rifle again, and thanking him, ran hard to catch his battalion, he plunged into the throng about the gateway.

"Are you going?" he cried to a marine who sat in the gutter bandaging his foot.

"Yes."

Then a girl—a mere child—caught him by the hand and led him into the café which faced the gate. The room was crowded with soldiers, some, white and silent, sitting on the floor, others groaning on the leather-covered settees. The air was sour and suffocating.

"Choose!" said the girl with a little gesture of pity; "they can't go!"

In a heap of clothing on the floor he found a capote and képi.

She helped him buckle his knapsack, cartridge-box, and belt, and showed him how to load the chassepot rifle, holding it on her knees.

When he thanked her she started to her feet.

"You are a foreigner!"

"American," he said, moving toward the door, but the child barred his way.

"I am a Bretonne. My father is up there with the cannon of the marine. He will shoot you if you are a spy."

They faced each other for a moment. Then sighing, he bent over and kissed the child. "Pray for France, little one," he murmured, and she repeated with a pale smile: "For France and you, beau Monsieur."

He ran across the street and through the gateway. Once outside, he edged into line and shouldered his way along the road. A corporal passed, looked at him, repassed, and finally called an officer. "You belong to the 60th," growled the corporal looking at the number on his képi.

"We have no use for Franc-tireurs," added the officer, catching sight of his black trousers.

"I wish to volunteer in place of a comrade," said Trent, and the officer shrugged his shoulders and passed on.

Nobody paid much attention to him, one or two merely glancing at his trousers. The road was deep with slush and mud-ploughed and torn by wheels and hoofs. A soldier in front of him wrenched his foot in an icy rut and dragged himself to the edge of the embankment groaning. The plain on either side of them was grey with melting snow. Here and there behind dismantled hedge-rows stood wagons, bearing white flags with red crosses. Sometimes the driver was a priest in rusty hat and gown, sometimes a crippled mobile. Once they passed a wagon driven by a Sister of Charity. Silent empty houses with great rents in their walls, and every window blank, huddled along the road. Further on, within the zone of danger, nothing of human habitation remained except here and there a pile of frozen bricks or a blackened cellar choked with snow.

For some time Trent had been annoyed by the man behind him, who kept treading on his heels. Convinced at last that it was intentional, he turned to remonstrate and found himself face to face with a fellow-student from the Beaux Arts. Trent stared.

"I thought you were in the hospital!"

The other shook his head, pointing to his bandaged jaw.

"I see, you can't speak. Can I do anything?"

The wounded man rummaged in his haversack and produced a crust of black bread.

"He can't eat it, his jaw is smashed, and he wants you to chew it for him," said the soldier next to him.

Trent took the crust, and grinding it in his teeth morsel by morsel, passed it back to the starving man.

From time to time mounted orderlies sped to the front, covering them with slush. It was a chilly, silent march through sodden meadows wreathed in fog. Along the railroad embankment across the ditch, another column moved parallel to their own. Trent watched it, a sombre mass, now distinct, now vague, now blotted out in a puff of fog. Once for half-an-hour he lost it, but when again it came into view, he noticed a thin line detach itself from the flank, and, bellying in the middle, swing rapidly to the west. At the same moment a prolonged crackling broke out in the fog in front. Other lines began to slough off from the column, swinging east and west, and the crackling became continuous. A battery passed at full gallop, and he drew back with his comrades to give it way. It went into action a little to the right of his battalion, and as the shot from the first rifled piece boomed through the mist, the cannon from the fortifications opened with a mighty roar. An officer galloped by shouting something which Trent did not catch, but he saw the ranks in front suddenly part company with his own, and disappear in the twilight. More officers rode up and stood beside him peering into the fog. Away in front the crackling had become one prolonged crash. It was dreary waiting. Trent chewed some bread for the man behind, who tried to swallow it, and after a while shook his head, motioning Trent to eat the rest himself. A corporal offered him a little brandy and he drank it, but when he turned around to return the flask, the corporal was lying on the ground. Alarmed, he looked at the soldier next to him, who shrugged his shoulders and opened his mouth to speak, but something struck him and he rolled over and over into the ditch below. At that moment the horse of one of the officers gave a bound and backed into the battalion, lashing out with his heels. One man was ridden down; another was kicked in the chest and hurled through the ranks. The officer sank his spurs into the horse and forced him to the front again, where he stood trembling. The cannonade seemed to draw nearer. A staff-officer, riding slowly up and down the battalion, suddenly collapsed in his saddle and clung to his horse's mane. One of his boots dangled, crimsoned and dripping, from the stirrup. Then out of the mist in front men came running. The roads, the fields, the ditches were full of them, and many of them fell. For an instant he imagined he saw horsemen riding about like ghosts in the vapours beyond, and a man behind him cursed horribly, declaring he too had seen them, and that they were Uhlans; but the battalion stood inactive, and the mist fell again over the meadows.

The colonel sat heavily upon his horse, his bullet-shaped head buried in the astrakhan collar of his dolman, his fat legs sticking straight out in the stirrups.

The buglers clustered about him with bugles poised, and behind him a staff-officer in a pale blue jacket smoked a cigarette and chatted with a captain of hussars. From the road in front came the sound of furious galloping and an orderly reined up beside the colonel, who motioned him to the rear without turning his head. Then on the left a confused murmur arose which ended in a shout. A hussar passed like the wind, followed by another and another, and then squadron after squadron whirled by them into the sheeted mists. At that instant the colonel reared in his saddle, the bugles clanged, and the whole battalion scrambled down the embankment, over the ditch and started across the soggy meadow. Almost at once Trent lost his cap. Something snatched it from his head, he thought it was a tree branch. A good many of his comrades rolled over in the slush and ice, and he imagined that they had slipped. One pitched right across his path and he stopped to help him up, but the man screamed when he touched him and an officer shouted, "Forward! Forward!" so he ran on again. It was a long jog through the mist, and he was often obliged to shift his rifle.

When at last they lay panting behind the railroad embankment, he looked about him. He had felt the need of action, of a desperate physical struggle, of killing and crushing. He had been seized with a desire to fling himself among masses and tear right and left. He longed to fire, to use the thin sharp bayonet on his chassepot. He had not expected this. He wished to become exhausted, to struggle and cut until incapable of lifting his arm. Then he had intended to go home. He heard a man say that half the battalion had gone down in the charge, and he saw another examining a corpse under the embankment. The body, still warm, was clothed in a strange uniform, but even when he noticed the spiked helmet lying a few inches further away, he did not realize what had happened.

The colonel sat on his horse a few feet to the left, his eyes sparkling under the crimson képi. Trent heard him reply to an officer: "I can hold it, but another charge, and I won't have enough men left to sound a bugle."

"Were the Prussians here?" Trent asked of a soldier who sat wiping the blood trickling from his hair.

"Yes. The hussars cleaned them out. We caught their crossfire."

"We are supporting a battery on the embankment," said another.

Then the battalion crawled over the embankment and moved along the lines of twisted rails. Trent rolled up his trousers and tucked them into his woollen socks: but they halted again, and some of the men sat down on the dismantled railroad track. Trent looked for his wounded comrade from the Beaux Arts. He was standing in his place, very pale. The cannonade had become terrific. For a moment the mist lifted. He caught a glimpse of the first battalion motionless on the railroad track in front, of regiments on either flank, and then, as the fog settled again, the drums beat and the music of the bugles began away on the extreme left. A restless movement passed among the troops, the colonel threw up his arm, the drums rolled, and the battalion moved off through the fog. They were near the front now, for the battalion was firing as it advanced. Ambulances galloped along the base of the embankment to the rear, and the hussars passed and repassed like phantoms. They were in the front at last, for all about them was movement and turmoil, while from the fog, close at hand, came cries and groans and crashing volleys. Shells fell everywhere, bursting along the embankment, splashing them with frozen slush. Trent was frightened. He began to dread the unknown, which lay there crackling and flaming in obscurity. The shock of the cannon sickened him. He could even see the fog light up with a dull orange as the thunder shook the earth. It was near, he felt certain, for the colonel shouted "Forward!" and the first battalion was hastening into it. He felt its breath, he trembled, but hurried on. A fearful discharge in front terrified him. Somewhere in the fog men were cheering, and the colonel's horse, streaming with blood plunged about in the smoke.

Another blast and shock, right in his face, almost stunned him, and he faltered. All the men to the right were down. His head swam; the fog and smoke stupefied him. He put out his hand for a support and caught something. It was the wheel of a gun-carriage, and a man sprang from behind it, aiming a blow at his head with a rammer, but stumbled back shrieking with a bayonet through his neck, and Trent knew that he had killed. Mechanically he stooped to pick up his rifle, but the bayonet was still in the man, who lay, beating with red hands against the sod. It sickened him and he leaned on the cannon. Men were fighting all around him now, and the air was foul with smoke and sweat. Somebody seized him from behind and another in front, but others in turn seized them or struck them solid blows. The click! click! click! of bayonets infuriated him, and he grasped the rammer and struck out blindly until it was shivered to pieces.

A man threw his arm around his neck and bore him to the ground, but he throttled him and raised himself on his knees. He saw a comrade seize the cannon, and fall across it with his skull crushed in; he saw the colonel tumble clean out of his saddle into the mud; then consciousness fled.

When he came to himself, he was lying on the embankment among the twisted rails. On every side huddled men who cried out and cursed and fled away into the fog, and he staggered to his feet and followed them. Once he stopped to help a comrade with a bandaged jaw, who could not speak but clung to his arm for a time and then fell dead in the freezing mire; and again he aided another, who groaned: "Trent, c'est moi—Philippe," until a sudden volley in the midst relieved him of his charge.

An icy wind swept down from the heights, cutting the fog into shreds. For an instant, with an evil leer the sun peered through the naked woods of Vincennes, sank like a blood-clot in the battery smoke, lower, lower, into the blood-soaked plain.

IV.

When midnight sounded from the belfry of St. Sulpice the gates of Paris were still choked with fragments of what had once been an army.

They entered with the night, a sullen horde, spattered with slime, faint with hunger and exhaustion. There was little disorder at first, and the throng at the gates parted silently as the troops tramped along the freezing streets. Confusion came as the hours passed. Swiftly and more swiftly, crowding squadron after squadron and battery on battery, horses plunging and caissons jolting, the remnants from the front surged through the gates, a chaos of cavalry and artillery struggling for the right of way. Close upon them stumbled the infantry; here a skeleton of a regiment marching with a desperate attempt at order, there a riotous mob of Mobiles crushing their way to the streets, then a turmoil of horsemen, cannon, troops without officers, officers without men, then again a line of ambulances, the wheels groaning under their heavy loads.

Dumb with misery the crowd looked on.

All through the day the ambulances had been arriving, and all day long the ragged throng whimpered and shivered by the barriers. At noon the crowd was increased ten-fold, filling the squares about the gates, and swarming over the inner fortifications.

At four o'clock in the afternoon the German batteries suddenly wreathed themselves in smoke, and the shells fell fast on Montparnasse. At twenty minutes after four two projectiles struck a house in the rue de Bac, and a moment later the first shell fell in the Latin Quarter.

Braith was painting in bed when West came in very much scared.

"I wish you would come down; our house has been knocked into a cocked hat, and I'm afraid that some of the pillagers may take it into their heads to pay us a visit tonight."

Braith jumped out of bed and bundled himself into a garment which had once been an overcoat.

"Anybody hurt?" he enquired, struggling with a sleeve full of dilapidated lining.

"No. Colette is barricaded in the cellar, and the concierge ran away to the fortifications. There will be a rough gang there if the bombardment keeps up. You might help us—"

"Of course," said Braith; but it was not until they had reached the rue Serpente and had turned in the passage which led to West's cellar, that the latter cried: "Have you seen Jack Trent today?"

"No," replied Braith, looking troubled, "he was not at Ambulance Headquarters."

"He stayed to take care of Sylvia, I suppose."

A bomb came crashing through the roof of a house at the end of the alley and burst in the basement, showering the street with slate and plaster. A second struck a chimney and plunged into the garden, followed by an avalanche of bricks, and another exploded with a deafening report in the next street.

They hurried along the passage to the steps which led to the cellar. Here again Braith stopped.

"Don't you think I had better run up to see if Jack and Sylvia are well entrenched? I can get back before dark."

"No. Go in and find Colette, and I'll go."

"No, no, let me go, there's no danger."

"I know it," replied West calmly; and, dragging Braith into the alley, pointed to the cellar steps. The iron door was barred.

"Colette! Colette!" he called. The door swung inward, and the girl sprang up the stairs to meet them. At that instant, Braith, glancing behind him, gave a startled cry, and pushing the two before him into the cellar, jumped down after them and slammed the iron door. A few seconds later a heavy jar from the outside shook the hinges.

"They are here," muttered West, very pale.

"That door," observed Colette calmly, "will hold for ever."

Braith examined the low iron structure, now trembling with the blows rained on it from without. West glanced anxiously at Colette, who displayed no agitation, and this comforted him.

"I don't believe they will spend much time here," said Braith; "they only rummage in cellars for spirits, I imagine."

"Unless they hear that valuables are buried there."

"But surely nothing is buried here?" exclaimed Braith uneasily. "Unfortunately there is," growled West. "That miserly landlord of mine—"

A crash from the outside, followed by a yell, cut him short; then blow after blow shook the doors, until there came a sharp snap, a clinking of metal and a triangular bit of iron fell inwards, leaving a hole through which struggled a ray of light.

Instantly West knelt, and shoving his revolver through the aperture fired every cartridge. For a moment the alley resounded with the racket of the revolver, then absolute silence followed.

Presently a single questioning blow fell upon the door, and a moment later another and another, and then a sudden crack zigzagged across the iron plate.

"Here," said West, seizing Colette by the wrist, "you follow me, Braith!" and he ran swiftly toward a circular spot of light at the further end of the cellar. The spot of light came from a barred manhole above. West motioned Braith to mount on his shoulders.

"Push it over. You *must!*"

With little effort Braith lifted the barred cover, scrambled out on his stomach, and easily raised Colette from West's shoulders. "Quick, old chap!" cried the latter.

Braith twisted his legs around a fence-chain and leaned down again. The cellar was flooded with a yellow light, and the air reeked with the stench of petroleum torches. The iron door still held, but a whole plate of metal was gone, and now as they looked a figure came creeping through, holding a torch.

"Quick!" whispered Braith. "Jump!" and West hung dangling until Colette grasped him by the collar, and he was dragged out. Then her nerves gave way and she wept hysterically, but West threw his arm around her and led her across the gardens into the next street, where Braith, after replacing the man-hole cover and piling some stone slabs from the wall over it, rejoined them. It was almost dark. They hurried through the street, now only lighted by burning buildings, or the swift glare of the shells. They gave wide berth to the fires, but at a distance saw the flitting forms of pillagers among the debris. Sometimes they passed a female fury crazed with drink shrieking anathemas upon the world, or some slouching lout whose blackened face and hands betrayed his share in the work of destruction. At last they reached the Seine and passed the bridge, and then Braith said: "I must go back. I am not sure of Jack and Sylvia." As he spoke, he made way for a crowd which came trampling across the bridge, and along the river wall by the d'Orsay barracks. In the midst of it West caught the measured tread of a platoon. A lantern passed, a file of bayonets, then another lantern which glimmered on a deathly face behind, and Colette gasped, "Hartman!" and he was gone. They peered fearfully across the embankment, holding their breath. There was a shuffle of feet on the quay, and the gate of the barracks slammed. A lantern shone for a moment at the postern, the crowd pressed to the grille, then came the clang of the volley from the stone parade.

One by one the petroleum torches flared up along the embankment, and now the whole square was in motion. Down from the Champs Elysées and across the Place de la Concorde straggled the fragments of the battle, a company here, and a mob there. They poured in from every street, followed by women and children, and a great murmur, borne on the icy wind, swept through the Arc de Triomphe and down the dark avenue—"Perdus! perdus!"

A ragged end of a battalion was pressing past, the spectre of annihilation. West groaned. Then a figure sprang from the shadowy ranks and called West's name, and when he saw it was Trent he cried out. Trent seized him, white with terror.

"Sylvia?"

West stared speechless, but Colette moaned, "Oh, Sylvia! Sylvia!—and they are shelling the Quarter!"

"Trent!" shouted Braith; but he was gone, and they could not overtake him.

The bombardment ceased as Trent crossed the Boulevard St. Germain, but the entrance to the rue de Seine was blocked by a heap of smoking bricks. Everywhere the shells had torn great holes in the pavement. The café was a wreck of splinters and glass, the bookstore tottered, ripped from roof to basement, and the little bakery, long since closed, bulged outward above a mass of slate and tin.

He climbed over the steaming bricks and hurried into the rue de Tournon. On the corner a fire blazed, lighting up his own street, and on the blank wall, beneath a shattered gas lamp, a child was writing with a bit of cinder,

"HERE FELL THE FIRST SHELL"

The letters stared him in the face. The rat-killer finished and stepped back to view his work, but catching sight of Trent's bayonet, screamed and fled, and as Trent staggered across the shattered street, from holes and crannies in the ruins fierce women fled from their work of pillage, cursing him.

At first he could not find his house, for the tears blinded him, but he felt along the wall and reached the door. A lantern burned in the concierge's lodge and the old man lay dead beside it. Faint with fright he leaned a moment on his rifle, then, snatching the lantern, sprang up the stairs. He tried to call, but his tongue hardly moved. On the second floor he saw plaster on the stairway, and on the third the floor was torn and the concierge lay in a pool of blood across the landing. The next floor was his, *theirs*. The door hung from its hinges, the walls gaped. He crept in and sank down by the bed, and there two arms were flung around his neck, and a tear-stained face sought his own.

"Sylvia!"

"O Jack! Jack! Jack!"

From the tumbled pillow beside them a child wailed.

"They brought it; it is mine," she sobbed.

"Ours," he whispered, with his arms around them both.

Then from the stairs below came Braith's anxious voice.

"Trent! Is all well?"

THE STREET OF OUR LADY OF THE FIELDS

Et tous les jours passés dans la tristesse
Nous sont comptés comme des jours heureux!

I.

The street is not fashionable, neither is it shabby. It is a pariah among streets—a street without a Quarter. It is generally understood to lie outside the pale of the aristocratic Avenue de l'Observatoire. The students of the Montparnasse Quarter consider it swell and will have none of it. The Latin Quarter, from the Luxembourg, its northern frontier, sneers at its respectability and regards with disfavor the correctly costumed students who haunt it. Few strangers go into it. At times, however, the Latin Quarter students use it as a thoroughfare between the rue de Rennes and the Bullier, but except for that and the weekly afternoon visits of parents and guardians to the Convent near the rue Vavin, the street of Our Lady of the Fields is as quiet as a Passy boulevard. Perhaps the most respectable portion lies between the rue de la Grande Chaumière and the rue Vavin, at least this was the conclusion arrived at by the Reverend Joel Byram, as he rambled through it with Hastings in charge. To Hastings the street looked pleasant in the bright June weather, and he had begun to hope for its selection when the Reverend Byram shied violently at the cross on the Convent opposite.

"Jesuits," he muttered.

"Well," said Hastings wearily, "I imagine we won't find anything better. You say yourself that vice is triumphant in Paris, and it seems to me that in every street we find Jesuits or something worse."

After a moment he repeated, "Or something worse, which of course I would not notice except for your kindness in warning me."

Dr. Byram sucked in his lips and looked about him. He was impressed by the evident respectability of the surroundings. Then, frowning at the Convent he took Hastings's arm and shuffled across the street to an iron gateway which bore the number 201 *bis* painted in white on a blue ground. Below this was a notice printed in English.

1. For Porter please oppress once.
2. For Servant please oppress twice.
3. For Parlor please oppress thrice.

Hastings touched the electric button three times, and they were ushered through the garden and into the parlor by a trim maid. The dining-room door, just beyond, was open, and from the table in plain view a stout woman hastily arose and came toward them. Hastings caught a glimpse of a young man with a big head and several snuffy old gentlemen at breakfast, before the door closed and the stout woman waddled into the room, bringing with her an aroma of coffee and a black poodle.

"It ees a plaisir to you receive!" she cried. "Monsieur is Anglish? No? Americain? Off course. My pension it ees for Americains surtout. Here all spik Angleesh, c'est à dire, ze personnel; ze sairvants do spik, plus ou moins, a little. I am happy to have you comme pensionnaires—"

"Madame," began Dr. Byram, but was cut short again.

"Ah, yess, I know. Ah! mon Dieu! you do not spik Frainch but you have come to lairne! My husband does spik Frainch wiss ze pensionnaires. We have at ze moment a family Americaine who learn of my husband Frainch—"

Here the poodle growled at Dr. Byram and was promptly cuffed by his mistress.

"Veux tu!" she cried, with a slap, "veux tu! Oh! le vilain, oh! le vilain!"

"Mais, madame," said Hastings, smiling, "il n'a pas l'air tres féroce."

The poodle fled, and his mistress cried, "Ah, ze accent charming! He does spik already Frainch like a Parisien young gentleman!"

Then Dr. Byram managed to get in a word or two and gathered more or less information with regard to prices.

"It ees a pension sérieux; my clientèle ees of ze best, indeed a pension de famille where one ees at 'ome."

Then they went upstairs to examine Hastings's future quarters, test the bed-springs and arrange for the weekly towel allowance. Dr. Byram appeared satisfied.

Madame Marotte accompanied them to the door and rang for the maid, but as Hastings stepped out into the gravel walk, his guide and mentor paused a moment and fixed Madame with his watery eyes.

"You understand," he said, "that he is a youth of most careful bringing up, and his character and morals are without a stain. He is young and has never been abroad, never even seen a large city, and his parents have requested me, as an old family friend living in Paris, to see that he is placed under good influences. He is to study art, but on no account would his parents wish him to live in the Latin Quarter if they knew of the immorality which is rife there."

A sound like the click of a latch interrupted him and he raised his eyes, but not in time to see the maid slap the big-headed young man behind the parlor-door.

Madame coughed, cast a deadly glance behind her and then beamed on Dr. Byram.

"It ees well zat he come here. The pension more serious, il n'en existe pas, eet ees not any!" she announced with conviction.

So, as there was nothing more to add, Dr. Byram joined Hastings at the gate.

"I trust," he said, eyeing the Convent, "that you will make no acquaintances among Jesuits!"

Hastings looked at the Convent until a pretty girl passed before the gray façade, and then he looked at her. A young fellow with a paint-box and canvas came swinging along, stopped before the pretty girl, said something during a brief but vigorous handshake at which they both laughed, and he went his way, calling back, "À demain Valentine!" as in the same breath she cried, "À demain!"

"Valentine," thought Hastings, "what a quaint name;" and he started to follow the Reverend Joel Byram, who was shuffling towards the nearest tramway station.

II.

"An' you are pleas wiz Paris, Monsieur 'Astang?" demanded Madame Marotte the next morning as Hastings came into the breakfast-room of the pension, rosy from his plunge in the limited bath above.

"I am sure I shall like it," he replied, wondering at his own depression of spirits.

The maid brought him coffee and rolls. He returned the vacant glance of the big-headed young man and acknowledged diffidently the salutes of the snuffy old gentlemen. He did not try to finish his coffee, and sat crumbling a roll, unconscious of the sympathetic glances of Madame Marotte, who had tact enough not to bother him.

Presently a maid entered with a tray on which were balanced two bowls of chocolate, and the snuffy old gentlemen leered at her ankles. The maid deposited the chocolate at a table near the window and smiled at Hastings. Then a thin young lady, followed by her counterpart in all except years, marched into the room and took the table near the window. They were evidently American, but Hastings, if he expected any sign of recognition, was disappointed. To be ignored by compatriots intensified his depression. He fumbled with his knife and looked at his plate.

The thin young lady was talkative enough. She was quite aware of Hastings's presence, ready to be flattered if he looked at her, but on the other hand she felt her superiority, for she had been three weeks in Paris and he, it was easy to see, had not yet unpacked his steamer-trunk.

Her conversation was complacent. She argued with her mother upon the relative merits of the Louvre and the Bon Marché, but her mother's part of the discussion was mostly confined to the observation, "Why, Susie!"

The snuffy old gentlemen had left the room in a body, outwardly polite and inwardly raging. They could not endure the Americans, who filled the room with their chatter.

The big-headed young man looked after them with a knowing cough, murmuring, "Gay old birds!"

"They look like bad old men, Mr. Bladen," said the girl.

To this Mr. Bladen smiled and said, "They've had their day," in a tone which implied that he was now having his.

"And that's why they all have baggy eyes," cried the girl. "I think it's a shame for young gentlemen—"

"Why, Susie!" said the mother, and the conversation lagged.

After a while Mr. Bladen threw down the *Petit Journal*, which he daily studied at the expense of the house, and turning to Hastings, started to make himself agreeable. He began by saying, "I see you are American."

To this brilliant and original opening, Hastings, deadly homesick, replied gratefully, and the conversation was judiciously nourished by observations from Miss Susie Byng distinctly addressed to Mr. Bladen. In the course of events, Miss Susie forgetting to address herself exclusively to Mr. Bladen, and Hastings replying to her general question, the entente cordiale was established, and Susie and her mother extended a protectorate over what was clearly neutral territory.

"Mr. Hastings, you must not desert the pension every evening as Mr. Bladen does. Paris is an awful place for young gentlemen, and Mr. Bladen is a horrid cynic."

Mr. Bladen looked gratified.

Hastings answered, "I shall be at the studio all day, and I imagine I shall be glad enough to come back at night."

Mr. Bladen, who, at a salary of fifteen dollars a week, acted as agent for the Pewly Manufacturing Company of Troy, N.Y., smiled a skeptical smile and withdrew to keep an appointment with a customer on the Boulevard Magenta.

Hastings walked into the garden with Mrs. Byng and Susie, and, at their invitation, sat down in the shade before the iron gate. The chestnut trees still bore their fragrant spikes of pink and white, and the bees hummed among the roses, trellised on the white-walled house.

A faint freshness was in the air. The watering carts moved up and down the street, and a clear stream bubbled over the spotless gutters of the rue de la Grande Chaumière. The sparrows were merry along the curb-stones, taking bath after bath in the water and ruffling their feathers with delight.

In a walled garden across the street a pair of blackbirds whistled among the almond trees.

Hastings swallowed the lump in his throat, for the song of the birds and the ripple of water in a Paris gutter brought back to him the sunny meadows of Millbrook.

"That's a blackbird," observed Miss Byng; "see him there on the bush with pink blossoms. He's all black except his bill, and that looks as if it had been dipped in an omelet, as some Frenchman says—"

"Why, Susie!" said Mrs. Byng.

"That garden belongs to a studio inhabited by two Americans," continued the girl serenely, "and I often see them pass. They seem to need a great many models, mostly young and feminine—"

"Why, Susie!"

"Perhaps they prefer painting that kind, but I don't see why they should invite five, with three more young gentlemen, and all get into two cabs and drive away singing. This street," she continued, "is dull. There is nothing to see except the garden and a glimpse of the Boulevard Montparnasse through the rue de la Grande Chaumière. No one ever passes except a policeman. There is a convent on the corner."

"I thought it was a Jesuit College," began Hastings, but was at once overwhelmed with a Baedecker description of the place, ending with, "On one side stand the palatial hotels of Jean Paul Laurens and Guillaume Bouguereau, and opposite, in the little Passage Stanislas, Carolus Duran paints the masterpieces which charm the world."

The blackbird burst into a ripple of golden throaty notes, and from some distant green spot in the city an unknown wild bird answered with a frenzy of liquid trills until the sparrows paused in their ablutions to look up with restless chirps.

Then a butterfly came and sat on a cluster of heliotrope and waved his crimson-banded wings in the hot sunshine. Hastings knew him for a friend, and before his eyes there came a vision of tall mullins and scented milkweed alive with painted wings, a vision of a white house and woodbine-covered piazza—a glimpse of a man reading and a woman leaning over the pansy bed—and his heart was full. He was startled a moment later by Miss Byng.

"I believe you are homesick!" Hastings blushed. Miss Byng looked at him with a sympathetic sigh and continued: "Whenever I felt homesick at first I used to go with mamma and walk in the Luxembourg Gardens. I don't know why it is, but those old-fashioned gardens seemed to bring me nearer home than anything in this artificial city."

"But they are full of marble statues," said Mrs. Byng mildly; "I don't see the resemblance myself."

"Where is the Luxembourg?" enquired Hastings after a silence.

"Come with me to the gate," said Miss Byng. He rose and followed her, and she pointed out the rue Vavin at the foot of the street.

"You pass by the convent to the right," she smiled; and Hastings went.

III.

The Luxembourg was a blaze of flowers.

He walked slowly through the long avenues of trees, past mossy marbles and old-time columns, and threading the grove by the bronze lion, came upon the tree-crowned terrace above the fountain. Below lay the basin shining in the sunlight. Flowering almonds encircled the terrace, and, in a greater spiral, groves of chestnuts wound in and out and down among the moist thickets by the western palace wing. At one end of the avenue of trees the Observatory rose, its white domes piled up like an eastern mosque; at the other end stood the heavy palace, with every window-pane ablaze in the fierce sun of June.

Around the fountain, children and white-capped nurses armed with bamboo poles were pushing toy boats, whose sails hung limp in the sunshine. A dark policeman, wearing red epaulettes and a dress sword, watched them for a while and then went away to remonstrate with a young man who had unchained his dog. The dog was pleasantly occupied in rubbing grass and dirt into his back while his legs waved into the air.

The policeman pointed at the dog. He was speechless with indignation.

"Well, Captain," smiled the young fellow.

"Well, Monsieur Student," growled the policeman.

"What do you come and complain to me for?"

"If you don't chain him I'll take him," shouted the policeman.

"What's that to me, mon capitaine?"

"Wha-t! Isn't that bulldog yours?"

"If it was, don't you suppose I'd chain him?"

The officer glared for a moment in silence, then deciding that as he was a student he was wicked, grabbed at the dog, who promptly dodged. Around and around the flower-beds they raced, and when the officer came too near for comfort, the bulldog cut across a flower-bed, which perhaps was not playing fair.

The young man was amused, and the dog also seemed to enjoy the exercise.

The policeman noticed this and decided to strike at the fountainhead of the evil. He stormed up to the student and said, "As the owner of this public nuisance I arrest you!"

"But," objected the other, "I disclaim the dog."

That was a poser. It was useless to attempt to catch the dog until three gardeners lent a hand, but then the dog simply ran away and disappeared in the rue de Medici.

The policeman shambled off to find consolation among the white-capped nurses, and the student, looking at his watch, stood up yawning. Then catching sight of Hastings, he smiled and bowed. Hastings walked over to the marble, laughing.

"Why, Clifford," he said, "I didn't recognize you."

"It's my moustache," sighed the other. "I sacrificed it to humor a whim of—of—a friend. What do you think of my dog?"

"Then he is yours?" cried Hastings.

"Of course. It's a pleasant change for him, this playing tag with police-men, but he is known now and I'll have to stop it. He's gone home. He always does when the gardeners take a hand. It's a pity; he's fond of rolling on lawns." Then they chatted for a moment of Hastings's prospects, and Clifford politely offered to stand his sponsor at the studio.

"You see, old tabby, I mean Dr. Byram, told me about you before I met you," explained Clifford, "and Elliott and I will be glad to do anything we can." Then looking at his watch again, he muttered, "I have just ten minutes to catch the Versailles train; au revoir," and started to go, but catching sight of a girl advancing by the fountain, took off his hat with a confused smile.

"Why are you not at Versailles?" she said, with an almost imperceptible acknowledgment of Hastings's presence.

"I—I'm going," murmured Clifford.

For a moment they faced each other, and then Clifford, very red, stam-mered, "With your permission I have the honor of presenting to you my friend, Monsieur Hastings."

Hastings bowed low. She smiled very sweetly, but there was something of malice in the quiet inclination of her small Parisienne head.

"I could have wished," she said, "that Monsieur Clifford might spare me more time when he brings with him so charming an American."

"Must—must I go, Valentine?" began Clifford.

"Certainly," she replied.

Clifford took his leave with very bad grace, wincing, when she added, "And give my dearest love to Cecile!" As he disappeared in the rue d'As-sas, the girl turned as if to go, but then suddenly remembering Hastings, looked at him and shook her head.

"Monsieur Clifford is so perfectly harebrained," she smiled, "it is em-barrassing sometimes. You have heard, of course, all about his success at the Salon?"

He looked puzzled and she noticed it.

"You have been to the Salon, of course?"

"Why, no," he answered, "I only arrived in Paris three days ago."

She seemed to pay little heed to his explanation, but continued: "Nobody imagined he had the energy to do anything good, but on varnishing day the Salon was astonished by the entrance of Monsieur Clifford, who strolled about as bland as you please with an orchid in his buttonhole, and a beautiful picture on the line."

She smiled to herself at the reminiscence, and looked at the fountain.

"Monsieur Bouguereau told me that Monsieur Julian was so astonished that he only shook hands with Monsieur Clifford in a dazed manner, and actually forgot to pat him on the back! Fancy," she continued with much merriment, "fancy papa Julian forgetting to pat one on the back."

Hastings, wondering at her acquaintance with the great Bouguereau, looked at her with respect. "May I ask," he said diffidently, "whether you are a pupil of Bouguereau?"

"I?" she said in some surprise. Then she looked at him curiously. Was he permitting himself the liberty of joking on such short acquaintance?

His pleasant serious face questioned hers.

"Tiens," she thought, "what a droll man!"

"You surely study art?" he said.

She leaned back on the crooked stick of her parasol, and looked at him. "Why do you think so?"

"Because you speak as if you did."

"You are making fun of me," she said, "and it is not good taste."

She stopped, confused, as he colored to the roots of his hair.

"How long have you been in Paris?" she said at length.

"Three days," he replied gravely.

"But—but—surely you are not a nouveau! You speak French too well!"

Then after a pause, "Really, are you a nouveau?"

"I am," he said.

She sat down on the marble bench lately occupied by Clifford, and tilting her parasol over her small head looked at him.

"I don't believe it."

He felt the compliment, and for a moment hesitated to declare himself one of the despised. Then mustering up his courage, he told her how new and green he was, and all with a frankness which made her blue eyes open very wide and her lips part in the sweetest of smiles.

"You have never seen a studio?"

"Never."

"Nor a model?"

"No."

"How funny," she said solemnly. Then they both laughed.

"And you," he said, "have seen studios?"

"Hundreds."

"And models?"

"Millions."

"And you know Bouguereau?"

"Yes, and Henner, and Constant and Laurens, and Puvis de Chavannes and Dagnan and Courtois, and – and all the rest of them!"

"And yet you say you are not an artist."

"Pardon," she said gravely, "did I say I was not?"

"Won't you tell me?" he hesitated.

At first she looked at him, shaking her head and smiling, then of a sudden her eyes fell and she began tracing figures with her parasol in the gravel at her feet. Hastings had taken a place on the seat, and now, with his elbows on his knees, sat watching the spray drifting above the fountain jet. A small boy, dressed as a sailor, stood poking his yacht and crying, "I won't go home! I won't go home!" His nurse raised her hands to Heaven.

"Just like a little American boy," thought Hastings, and a pang of homesickness shot through him.

Presently the nurse captured the boat, and the small boy stood at bay.

"Monsieur René, when you decide to come here you may have your boat."

The boy backed away scowling.

"Give me my boat, I say," he cried, "and don't call me René, for my name's Randall and you know it!"

"Hello!" said Hastings—"Randall?—that's English."

"I am American," announced the boy in perfectly good English, turning to look at Hastings, "and she's such a fool she calls me René because mamma calls me Ranny—"

Here he dodged the exasperated nurse and took up his station behind Hastings, who laughed, and catching him around the waist lifted him into his lap.

"One of my countrymen," he said to the girl beside him. He smiled while he spoke, but there was a queer feeling in his throat.

"Don't you see the stars and stripes on my yacht?" demanded Randall. Sure enough, the American colors hung limply under the nurse's arm.

"Oh," cried the girl, "he is charming," and impulsively stooped to kiss him, but the infant Randall wriggled out of Hastings's arms, and his nurse pounced upon him with an angry glance at the girl.

She reddened and then bit her lips as the nurse, with eyes still fixed on her, dragged the child away and ostentatiously wiped his lips with her handkerchief.

Then she stole a look at Hastings and bit her lip again.

"What an ill-tempered woman!" he said. "In America, most nurses are flattered when people kiss their children."

For an instant she tipped the parasol to hide her face, then closed it with a snap and looked at him defiantly.

"Do you think it strange that she objected?"

"Why not?" he said in surprise.

Again she looked at him with quick searching eyes.

His eyes were clear and bright, and he smiled back, repeating, "Why not?"

"You *are* droll," she murmured, bending her head.

"Why?"

But she made no answer, and sat silent, tracing curves and circles in the dust with her parasol. After a while he said—"I am glad to see that young people have so much liberty here. I understood that the French were not at all like us. You know in America—or at least where I live in Millbrook, girls have every liberty—go out alone and receive their friends alone, and I was afraid I should miss it here. But I see how it is now, and I am glad I was mistaken."

She raised her eyes to his and kept them there.

He continued pleasantly—"Since I have sat here I have seen a lot of pretty girls walking alone on the terrace there—and then *you* are alone too. Tell me, for I do not know French customs—do you have the liberty of going to the theatre without a chaperone?"

For a long time she studied his face, and then with a trembling smile said, "Why do you ask me?"

"Because you must know, of course," he said gaily.

"Yes," she replied indifferently, "I know."

He waited for an answer, but getting none, decided that perhaps she had misunderstood him.

"I hope you don't think I mean to presume on our short acquaintance," he began—"in fact it is very odd but I don't know your name. When Mr. Clifford presented me he only mentioned mine. Is that the custom in France?"

"It is the custom in the Latin Quarter," she said with a queer light in her eyes. Then suddenly she began talking almost feverishly.

"You must know, Monsieur Hastings, that we are all un peu sans gêne here in the Latin Quarter. We are very Bohemian, and etiquette and ceremony are out of place. It was for that Monsieur Clifford presented you to me with small ceremony, and left us together with less—only for that, and I am his friend, and I have many friends in the Latin Quarter, and we all know each other very well—and I am not studying art, but — but —"

"But what?" he said, bewildered.

"I shall not tell you—it is a secret," she said with an uncertain smile. On both cheeks a pink spot was burning, and her eyes were very bright.

Then in a moment her face fell. "Do you know Monsieur Clifford very intimately?"

"Not very."

After a while she turned to him, grave and a little pale.

"My name is Valentine—Valentine Tissot. Might—might I ask a service of you on such very short acquaintance?"

"Oh," he cried, "I should be honored."

"It is only this," she said gently, "it is not much. Promise me not to speak to Monsieur Clifford about me. Promise me that you will speak to no one about me."

"I promise," he said, greatly puzzled.

She laughed nervously. "I wish to remain a mystery. It is a caprice."

"But," he began, "I had wished, I had hoped that you might give Monsieur Clifford permission to bring me, to present me at your house."

"My—my house!" she repeated.

"I mean, where you live, in fact, to present me to your family."

The change in the girl's face shocked him.

"I beg your pardon," he cried, "I have hurt you."

And as quick as a flash she understood him because she was a woman.

"My parents are dead," she said.

Presently he began again, very gently.

"Would it displease you if I beg you to receive me? It is the custom?"

"I cannot," she answered. Then glancing up at him, "I am sorry; I should like to; but believe me, I cannot."

He bowed seriously and looked vaguely uneasy.

"It isn't because I don't wish to. I—I like you; you are very kind to me."

"Kind?" he cried, surprised and puzzled.

"I like you," she said slowly, "and we will see each other sometimes if you will."

"At friends' houses."

"No, not at friends' houses."

"Where?"

"Here," she said with defiant eyes.

"Why," he cried, "in Paris you are much more liberal in your views than we are."

She looked at him curiously.

"Yes, we are very Bohemian."

"I think it is charming," he declared.

"You see, we shall be in the best of society," she ventured timidly, with a pretty gesture toward the statues of the dead queens, ranged in stately ranks above the terrace.

He looked at her, delighted, and she brightened at the success of her innocent little pleasantry.

"Indeed," she smiled, "I shall be well chaperoned, because you see we are under the protection of the gods themselves; look, there are Apollo, and Juno, and Venus, on their pedestals," counting them on her small gloved fingers, "and Ceres, Hercules, and—but I can't make out—"

Hastings turned to look up at the winged god under whose shadow they were seated.

"Why, it's Love," he said.

IV.

"There is a nouveau here," drawled Laffat, leaning around his easel and addressing his friend Bowles, "there is a nouveau here who is so tender and green and appetising that Heaven help him if he should fall into a salad bowl."

"Hayseed?" enquired Bowles, plastering in a background with a broken palette-knife and squinting at the effect with approval.

"Yes, Squeedunk or Oshkosh, and how he ever grew up among the daisies and escaped the cows, Heaven alone knows!"

Bowles rubbed his thumb across the outlines of his study to "throw in a little atmosphere," as he said, glared at the model, pulled at his pipe and finding it out struck a match on his neighbor's back to relight it.

"His name," continued Laffat, hurling a bit of bread at the hat-rack, "his name is Hastings. He *is* a berry. He knows no more about the world"—and here Mr. Laffat's face spoke volumes for his own knowledge of that planet—"than a maiden cat on its first moonlight stroll."

Bowles now having succeeded in lighting his pipe, repeated the thumb touch on the other edge of the study and said, "Ah!"

"Yes," continued his friend, "and would you imagine it, he seems to think that everything here goes on as it does in his d—d little backwoods ranch at home; talks about the pretty girls who walk alone in the street; says how sensible it is; and how French parents are misrepresented in America; says that for his part he finds French girls—and he confessed to only knowing one—as jolly as American girls. I tried to set him right, tried to give him a pointer as to what sort of ladies walk about alone or with students, and he was either too stupid or too innocent to catch on. Then I gave it to him straight, and he said I was a vile-minded fool and marched off."

"Did you assist him with your shoe?" enquired Bowles, languidly interested.

"Well, no."

"He called you a vile-minded fool."

"He was correct," said Clifford from his easel in front.

"What—what do you mean?" demanded Laffat, turning red.

"*That*," replied Clifford.

"Who spoke to you? Is this your business?" sneered Bowles, but nearly lost his balance as Clifford swung about and eyed him.

"Yes," he said slowly, "it's my business."

No one spoke for some time.

Then Clifford sang out, "I say, Hastings!"

And when Hastings left his easel and came around, he nodded toward the astonished Laffat.

"This man has been disagreeable to you, and I want to tell you that any time you feel inclined to kick him, why, I will hold the other creature."

Hastings, embarrassed, said, "Why no, I don't agree with his ideas, nothing more."

Clifford said "Naturally," and slipping his arm through Hastings's, strolled about with him, and introduced him to several of his own friends, at which all the nouveaux opened their eyes with envy, and the studio were given to understand that Hastings, although prepared to do menial work as the latest nouveau, was already within the charmed circle of the old, respected and feared, the truly great.

The rest finished, the model resumed his place, and work went on in a chorus of songs and yells and every ear-splitting noise which the art student utters when studying the beautiful.

Five o'clock struck—the model yawned, stretched and climbed into his trousers, and the noisy contents of six studios crowded through the hall and down into the street. Ten minutes later, Hastings found himself on top of a Montrouge tram, and shortly afterward was joined by Clifford.

They climbed down at the rue Gay-Lussac.

"I always stop here," observed Clifford, "I like the walk through the Luxembourg."

"By the way," said Hastings, "how can I call on you when I don't know where you live?"

"Why, I live opposite you."

"What—the studio in the garden where the almond trees are and the blackbirds—"

"Exactly," said Clifford. "I'm with my friend Elliott."

Hastings thought of the description of the two American artists which he had heard from Miss Susie Byng, and looked blank.

Clifford continued, "Perhaps you had better let me know when you think of coming so—so that I will be sure to—to be there," he ended rather lamely.

"I shouldn't care to meet any of your model friends there," said Hastings, smiling. "You know—my ideas are rather straitlaced—I suppose you would say, puritanical. I shouldn't enjoy it and wouldn't know how to behave."

"Oh, I understand," said Clifford, but added with great cordiality—"I'm sure we'll be friends although you may not approve of me and my set, but you will like Severn and Selby because—because, well, they are like yourself, old chap."

After a moment he continued, "There is something I want to speak about. You see, when I introduced you, last week, in the Luxembourg, to Valentine—"

"Not a word!" cried Hastings, smiling; "you must not tell me a word of her!"

"Why—"

"No—not a word!" he said gaily. "I insist—promise me upon your honor you will not speak of her until I give you permission; promise!"

"I promise," said Clifford, amazed.

"She is a charming girl—we had such a delightful chat after you left, and I thank you for presenting me, but not another word about her until I give you permission."

"Oh," murmured Clifford.

"Remember your promise," he smiled, as he turned into his gateway.

Clifford strolled across the street and, traversing the ivy-covered alley, entered his garden.

He felt for his studio key, muttering, "I wonder—I wonder—but of course he doesn't!"

He entered the hallway, and fitting the key into the door, stood staring at the two cards tacked over the panels.

FOXHALL CLIFFORD

RICHARD OSBORNE ELLIOTT

"Why the devil doesn't he want me to speak of her?"

He opened the door, and, discouraging the caresses of two brindle bulldogs, sank down on the sofa.

Elliott sat smoking and sketching with a piece of charcoal by the window.

"Hello," he said without looking around.

Clifford gazed absently at the back of his head, murmuring, "I'm afraid, I'm afraid that man is too innocent. I say, Elliott," he said at last, "Hastings—you know the chap that old Tabby Byram came around here to tell us about—the day you had to hide Colette in the armoire—"

"Yes, what's up?"

"Oh, nothing. He's a brick."

"Yes," said Elliott, without enthusiasm.

"Don't you think so?" demanded Clifford.

"Why yes, but he is going to have a tough time when some of his illusions are dispelled."

"More shame to those who dispel 'em!"

"Yes—wait until he comes to pay his call on us, unexpectedly, of course—"

Clifford looked virtuous and lighted a cigar.

"I was just going to say," he observed, "that I have asked him not to come without letting us know, so I can postpone any orgie you may have intended—"

"Ah!" cried Elliott indignantly, "I suppose you put it to him in that way."

"Not exactly," grinned Clifford. Then more seriously, "I don't want anything to occur here to bother him. He's a brick, and it's a pity we can't be more like him."

"I am," observed Elliott complacently, "only living with you—"

"Listen!" cried the other. "I have managed to put my foot in it in great style. Do you know what I've done? Well—the first time I met him in the street—or rather, it was in the Luxembourg, I introduced him to Valentine!"

"Did he object?"

"Believe me," said Clifford, solemnly, "this rustic Hastings has no more idea that Valentine is—is—in fact is Valentine, than he has that he himself is a beautiful example of moral decency in a Quarter where morals are as rare as elephants. I heard enough in a conversation between that blackguard Laffat and the little immoral eruption, Bowles, to open my eyes. I tell you Hastings is a trump! He's a healthy, clean-minded young fellow, bred in a small country village, brought up with the idea that saloons are way-stations to hell—and as for women—"

"Well" demanded Elliott

"Well," said Clifford, "his idea of the dangerous woman is probably a painted Jezabel."

"Probably," replied the other.

"He's a trump!" said Clifford, "and if he swears the world is as good and pure as his own heart, I'll swear he's right."

Elliott rubbed his charcoal on his file to get a point and turned to his sketch saying, "He will never hear any pessimism from Richard Osborne E."

"He's a lesson to me," said Clifford. Then he unfolded a small perfumed note, written on rose-colored paper, which had been lying on the table before him.

He read it, smiled, whistled a bar or two from "Miss Helyett," and sat down to answer it on his best cream-laid note-paper. When it was written and sealed, he picked up his stick and marched up and down the studio two or three times, whistling.

"Going out?" enquired the other, without turning.

"Yes," he said, but lingered a moment over Elliott's shoulder, watching him pick out the lights in his sketch with a bit of bread.

"Tomorrow is Sunday," he observed after a moment's silence.

"Well?" enquired Elliott.

"Have you seen Colette?"

"No, I will tonight. She and Rowden and Jacqueline are coming to Boulant's. I suppose you and Cécile will be there?"

"Well, no," replied Clifford. "Cécile dines at home tonight, and I—I had an idea of going to Mignon's."

Elliott looked at him with disapproval.

"You can make all the arrangements for La Roche without me," he continued, avoiding Elliott's eyes.

"What are you up to now?"

"Nothing," protested Clifford.

"Don't tell me," replied his chum, with scorn; "fellows don't rush off to Mignon's when the set dine at Boulant's. Who is it now?—but no, I won't ask that—what's the use!" Then he lifted up his voice in complaint and beat upon the table with his pipe. "What's the use of ever trying to keep track of you? What will Cécile say—oh, yes, what will she say? It's a pity you can't be constant two months, yes, by Jove! and the Quarter is indulgent, but you abuse its good nature and mine too!"

Presently he arose, and jamming his hat on his head, marched to the door.

"Heaven alone knows why anyone puts up with your antics, but they all do and so do I. If I were Cécile or any of the other pretty fools after whom you have toddled and will, in all human probabilities, continue to toddle, I say, if I were Cécile I'd spank you! Now I'm going to Boulant's, and as usual I shall make excuses for you and arrange the affair, and I don't care a continental where you are going, but, by the skull of the studio skeleton! if you don't turn up tomorrow with your sketching-kit under one arm and Cécile under the other—if you don't turn up in good shape, I'm done with you, and the rest can think what they please. Good-night."

Clifford said good-night with as pleasant a smile as he could muster, and then sat down with his eyes on the door. He took out his watch and gave Elliott ten minutes to vanish, then rang the concierge's call, murmuring, "Oh dear, oh dear, why the devil do I do it?"

"Alfred," he said, as that gimlet-eyed person answered the call, "make yourself clean and proper, Alfred, and replace your sabots with a pair of shoes. Then put on your best hat and take this letter to the big white house in the Rue de Dragon. There is no answer, *mon petit* Alfred."

The concierge departed with a snort in which unwillingness for the errand and affection for M. Clifford were blended. Then with great care the young fellow arrayed himself in all the beauties of his and Elliott's wardrobe. He took his time about it, and occasionally interrupted his toilet to play his banjo or make pleasing diversion for the bulldogs by gambling about on all fours. "I've got two hours before me," he thought, and borrowed a pair of Elliott's silken footgear, with which he and the dogs played ball until he decided to put them on. Then he lighted a cigarette and inspected his dress-coat. When he had emptied it of four handkerchiefs, a fan, and a pair of crumpled gloves as long as his arm, he decided it was not suited to add *éclat* to his charms and cast about in his mind for a substitute. Elliott was too thin, and, anyway, his coats were now under lock and key. Rowden probably was as badly off as himself. Hastings! Hastings was the man! But when he threw on a smoking-jacket and sauntered over to Hastings's house, he was informed that he had been gone over an hour.

"Now, where in the name of all that's reasonable could he have gone!" muttered Clifford, looking down the street.

The maid didn't know, so he bestowed upon her a fascinating smile and lounged back to the studio.

Hastings was not far away. The Luxembourg is within five minutes' walk of the rue Notre Dame des Champs, and there he sat under the shadow of a winged god, and there he had sat for an hour, poking holes in the dust and watching the steps which lead from the northern terrace to the fountain. The sun hung, a purple globe, above the misty hills of Meudon. Long streamers of clouds touched with rose swept low on the western sky, and the dome of the distant Invalides burned like an opal through the haze. Behind the Palace the smoke from a high chimney mounted straight into the air, purple until it crossed the sun, where it changed to a bar of smoldering fire. High above the darkening foliage of the chestnuts the twin towers of St. Sulpice rose, an ever-deepening silhouette.

A sleepy blackbird was caroling in some near thicket, and pigeons passed and repassed with the whisper of soft winds in their wings. The light on the Palace windows had died away, and the dome of the Pantheon swam aglow above the northern terrace, a fiery Valhalla in the sky; while below in grim array, along the terrace ranged, the marble ranks of queens looked out into the west.

From the end of the long walk by the northern façade of the Palace came the noise of omnibuses and the cries of the street. Hastings looked at the

Palace clock. Six, and as his own watch agreed with it, he fell to poking holes in the gravel again. A constant stream of people passed between the Odéon and the fountain. Priests in black, with silver-buckled shoes; line soldiers, slouchy and rakish; neat girls without hats bearing milliners' boxes; students with black portfolios and high hats; students with berets and big canes; nervous, quickstepping officers, symphonies in turquoise and silver; ponderous jangling cavalrymen all over dust; pastry cooks' boys skipping along with utter disregard for the safety of the basket balanced on the impish head; and then the lean outcast, the shambling Paris tramp, slouching with shoulders bent and little eye furtively scanning the ground for smokers' refuse—all these moved in a steady stream across the fountain circle and out into the city by the Odéon, whose long arcades were now beginning to flicker with gas-jets. The melancholy bells of St. Sulpice struck the hour and the clock-tower of the Palace lighted up. Then hurried steps sounded across the gravel and Hastings raised his head.

"How late you are," he said, but his voice was hoarse and only his flushed face told how long had seemed the waiting.

She said, "I was kept—indeed, I was so much annoyed—and—and I may only stay a moment."

She sat down beside him, casting a furtive glance over her shoulder at the god upon his pedestal.

"What a nuisance, that intruding cupid still there?"

"Wings and arrows too," said Hastings, unheeding her motion to be seated.

"Wings," she murmured, "oh, yes—to fly away with when he's tired of his play. Of course it was a man who conceived the idea of wings, otherwise Cupid would have been insupportable."

"Do you think so?"

"*Ma foi*, it's what men think."

"And women?"

"Oh," she said, with a toss of her small head, "I really forget what we were speaking of."

"We were speaking of love," said Hastings.

"*I* was not," said the girl. Then looking up at the marble god, "I don't care for this one at all. I don't believe he knows how to shoot his arrows—no, indeed, he is a coward—he creeps up like an assassin in the twilight. I don't approve of cowardice," she announced, and turned her back on the statue.

"I think," said Hastings quietly, "that he does shoot fairly—yes, and even gives one warning."

"Is it your experience, Monsieur Hastings?"

He looked straight into her eyes and said, "He is warning me."

"Heed the warning then," she cried, with a nervous laugh. As she spoke she stripped off her gloves, and then carefully proceeded to draw them on again. When this was accomplished she glanced at the Palace clock, saying, "Oh dear, how late it is!" furled her umbrella, then unfurled it, and finally looked at him.

"No," he said, "I shall not heed his warning."

"Oh dear," she sighed again, "still talking about that tiresome statue!" Then stealing a glance at his face, "I suppose—I suppose you are in love."

"I don't know," he muttered, "I suppose I am."

She raised her head with a quick gesture. "You seem delighted at the idea," she said, but bit her lip and trembled as his eyes met hers. Then sudden fear came over her and she sprang up, staring into the gathering shadows.

"Are you cold?" he said.

But she only answered, "Oh dear, oh dear, it is late—so late! I must go—good-night."

She gave him her gloved hand a moment and then withdrew it with a start.

"What is it?" he insisted. "Are you frightened?"

She looked at him strangely.

"No—no—not frightened—you are very good to me—"

"By Jove!" he burst out, "what do you mean by saying I'm good to you? That's at least the third time, and I don't understand!"

The sound of a drum from the guard-house at the palace cut him short. "Listen," she whispered, "they are going to close. It's late, oh, so late!"

The rolling of the drum came nearer and nearer, and then the silhouette of the drummer cut the sky above the eastern terrace. The fading light lingered a moment on his belt and bayonet, then he passed into the shadows, drumming the echoes awake. The roll became fainter along the eastern terrace, then grew and grew and rattled with increasing sharpness when he passed the avenue by the bronze lion and turned down the western terrace walk. Louder and louder the drum sounded, and the echoes struck back the notes from the grey palace wall; and now the drummer loomed up before them—his red trousers a dull spot in the gathering gloom, the brass of his drum and bayonet touched with a pale spark, his epaulettes tossing on his shoulders. He passed leaving the crash of the drum in their ears, and far into the alley of trees they saw his little tin cup shining on his haversack. Then the sentinels began the monotonous cry: "On ferme! On fe-rme!" and the bugle blew from the barracks in the rue de Tournon.

"On ferme! On ferme!"

"Good-night," she whispered, "I must return alone tonight."

He watched her until she reached the northern terrace, and then sat down on the marble seat until a hand on his shoulder and a glimmer of bayonets warned him away.

She passed on through the grove, and turning into the rue de Medici, traversed it to the Boulevard. At the corner she bought a bunch of violets and walked on along the Boulevard to the rue des Écoles. A cab was drawn up before Boulant's, and a pretty girl aided by Elliott jumped out.

"Valentine!" cried the girl, "come with us!"

"I can't," she said, stopping a moment—"I have a rendezvous at Mignon's."

"Not Victor?" cried the girl, laughing, but she passed with a little shiver, nodding good-night, then turning into the Boulevard St. Germain, she walked a little faster to escape a gay party sitting before the Café Cluny who called to her to join them. At the door of the Restaurant Mignon stood a coal-black negro in buttons. He took off his peaked cap as she mounted the carpeted stairs.

"Send Eugène to me," she said at the office, and passing through the hallway to the right of the dining-room stopped before a row of panelled doors. A waiter passed and she repeated her demand for Eugène, who presently appeared, noiselessly skipping, and bowed murmuring, "Madame."

"Who is here?"

"No one in the cabinets, madame; in the half Madame Madelon and Monsieur Gay, Monsieur de Clamart, Monsieur Clisson, Madame Marie and their set." Then he looked around and bowing again murmured, "Monsieur awaits madame since half an hour," and he knocked at one of the panelled doors bearing the number six.

Clifford opened the door and the girl entered.

The garçon bowed her in, and whispering, "Will Monsieur have the goodness to ring?" vanished.

He helped her off with her jacket and took her hat and umbrella.

When she was seated at the little table with Clifford opposite she smiled and leaned forward on both elbows looking him in the face.

"What are you doing here?" she demanded.

"Waiting," he replied, in accents of adoration.

For an instant she turned and examined herself in the glass. The wide blue eyes, the curling hair, the straight nose and short curled lip flashed in the mirror an instant only, and then its depths reflected her pretty neck and back. "Thus do I turn my back on vanity," she said, and then leaning forward again, "What are you doing here?"

"Waiting for you," repeated Clifford, slightly troubled.

"And Cécile."

"Now don't, Valentine—"

"Do you know," she said calmly, "I dislike your conduct?"

He was a little disconcerted, and rang for Eugène to cover his confusion.

The soup was bisque, and the wine Pommery, and the courses followed each other with the usual regularity until Eugène brought coffee, and there was nothing left on the table but a small silver lamp.

"Valentine," said Clifford, after having obtained permission to smoke, "is it the Vaudeville or the Eldorado—or both, or the Nouveau Cirque, or—"

"It is here," said Valentine.

"Well," he said, greatly flattered, "I'm afraid I couldn't amuse you—"

"Oh, yes, you are funnier than the Eldorado."

"Now see here, don't guy me, Valentine. You always do, and, and—you know what they say—a good laugh kills—"

"What?"

"Er— er—love and all that."

She laughed until her eyes were moist with tears. "Tiens," she cried, "he is dead, then!"

Clifford eyed her with growing alarm.

"Do you know why I came?" she said.

"No," he replied uneasily, "I don't."

"How long have you made love to me?"

"Well," he admitted, somewhat startled—"I should say—for about a year."

"It is a year, I think. Are you not tired?"

He did not answer.

"Don't you know that I like you too well to—to ever fall in love with you?" she said. "Don't you know that we are too good comrades—too old friends for that? And were we not—do you think that I do not know your history, Monsieur Clifford?"

"Don't be—don't be so sarcastic," he urged; "don't be unkind, Valentine."

"I'm not. I'm kind. I'm very kind—to you and to Cécile."

"Cécile is tired of me."

"I hope she is," said the girl, "for she deserves a better fate. Tiens, do you know your reputation in the Quarter? Of the inconstant, the most inconstant—utterly incorrigible and no more serious than a gnat on a summer night. Poor Cécile!"

Clifford looked so uncomfortable that she spoke more kindly.

"I like you. You know that. Everybody does. You are a spoiled child here. Everything is permitted you and everyone makes allowance, but everyone cannot be a victim to caprice."

"Caprice!" he cried. "By Jove, if the girls of the Latin Quarter are not capricious—"

"Never mind—never mind about that! You must not sit in judgment—you of all men. Why are you here tonight? Oh," she cried, "I will tell you why! Monsieur receives a little note; he sends a little answer; he dresses in his conquering raiment—"

"I don't," said Clifford, very red.

"You do, and it becomes you," she retorted with a faint smile. Then again, very quietly, "I am in your power, but I know I am in the power of a friend. I have come to acknowledge it to you here—and it is because of that that I am here to beg of you—a—a favor."

Clifford opened his eyes, but said nothing.

"I am in—great distress of mind. It is Monsieur Hastings."

"Well?" said Clifford, in some astonishment.

"I want to ask you," she continued in a low voice, "I want to ask you to—to—in case you should speak of me before him—not to say—not to say—"

"I shall not speak of you to him," he said quietly.

"Can—can you prevent others?"

"I might if I was present. May I ask why?"

"That is not fair," she murmured; "you know how—how he considers me—as he considers every woman. You know how different he is from you and the rest. I have never seen a man—such a man as Monsieur Hastings."

He let his cigarette go out unnoticed.

"I am almost afraid of him—afraid he should know—what we all are in the Quarter. Oh, I do not wish him to know! I do not wish him to—to turn from me—to cease from speaking to me as he does! You—you and the rest cannot know what it has been to me. I could not believe him—I could not believe he was so good and—and noble. I do not wish him to know—so soon. He will find out—sooner or later, he will find out for himself, and then he will turn away from me. Why!" she cried passionately, "why should he turn from me and not from *you?*"

Clifford, much embarrassed, eyed his cigarette.

The girl rose, very white. "He is your friend—you have a right to warn him."

"He is my friend," he said at length.

They looked at each other in silence.

Then she cried, "By all that I hold to me most sacred, you need not warn him!"

"I shall trust your word," he said pleasantly.

V.

The month passed quickly for Hastings, and left few definite impressions after it. It did leave some, however. One was a painful impression of meeting Mr. Bladen on the Boulevard des Capucines in company with a very pronounced young person whose laugh dismayed him, and when at last he escaped from the café where Mr. Bladen had hauled him to join them in a bock he felt as if the whole boulevard was looking at him, and judging him by his company. Later, an instinctive conviction regarding the young person with Mr. Bladen sent the hot blood into his cheek, and he returned to the pension in such a miserable state of mind that Miss Byng was alarmed and advised him to conquer his homesickness at once.

Another impression was equally vivid. One Saturday morning, feeling lonely, his wanderings about the city brought him to the Gare St. Lazare. It was early for breakfast, but he entered the Hotel Terminus and took a table near the window. As he wheeled about to give his order, a man passing rapidly along the aisle collided with his head, and looking up to receive the expected apology, he was met instead by a slap on the shoulder and a hearty, "What the deuce are you doing here, old chap?" It was Rowden, who seized him and told him to come along. So, mildly protesting, he was ushered into a private dining-room where Clifford, rather red, jumped up from the table and welcomed him with a startled air which was softened by the unaffected glee of Rowden and the extreme courtesy of Elliott. The latter presented him to three bewitching girls who welcomed him so charmingly and seconded Rowden in his demand that Hastings should make one of the party, that he consented at once. While Elliott briefly outlined the projected excursion to La Roche, Hastings delightedly ate his omelet, and returned the smiles of encouragement from Cécile and Colette and Jacqueline. Meantime Clifford in a bland whisper was telling Rowden what an ass he was. Poor Rowden looked miserable until Elliott, divining how affairs were turning, frowned on Clifford and found a moment to let Rowden know that they were all going to make the best of it.

"You shut up," he observed to Clifford, "it's fate, and that settles it."

"It's Rowden, and that settles it," murmured Clifford, concealing a grin. For after all he was not Hastings's wet nurse. So it came about that the train which left the Gare St. Lazare at 9:15 a.m. stopped a moment in its career towards Havre and deposited at the red-roofed station of La Roche a merry party, armed with sunshades, trout-rods, and one cane, carried by the non-combatant, Hastings. Then, when they had established their camp in a grove of sycamores which bordered the little river Ept, Clifford, the acknowledged master of all that pertained to sportsmanship, took command.

"You, Rowden," he said, "divide your flies with Elliott and keep an eye on him or else he'll be trying to put on a float and sinker. Prevent him by force from grubbing about for worms."

Elliott protested, but was forced to smile in the general laugh.

"You make me ill," he asserted; "do you think this is my first trout?"

"I shall be delighted to see your first trout," said Clifford, and dodging a fly hook, hurled with intent to hit, proceeded to sort and equip three slender rods destined to bring joy and fish to Cécile, Colette, and Jacqueline. With perfect gravity he ornamented each line with four split shot, a small hook, and a brilliant quill float.

"*I* shall never touch the worms," announced Cécile with a shudder.

Jacqueline and Colette hastened to sustain her, and Hastings pleasantly offered to act in the capacity of general baiter and taker-off of fish. But Cécile, doubtless fascinated by the gaudy flies in Clifford's book, decided to accept lessons from him in the true art, and presently disappeared up the Ept with Clifford in tow.

Elliott looked doubtfully at Colette.

"I prefer gudgeons," said that damsel with decision, "and you and Monsieur Rowden may go away when you please; may they not, Jacqueline?"

"Certainly," responded Jacqueline.

Elliott, undecided, examined his rod and reel.

"You've got your reel on wrong side up," observed Rowden.

Elliott wavered, and stole a glance at Colette.

"I—I—have almost decided to— er—not to flip the flies about just now," he began. "There's the pole that Cécile left—"

"Don't call it a pole," corrected Rowden.

"*Rod*, then," continued Elliott, and started off in the wake of the two girls, but was promptly collared by Rowden.

"No, you don't! Fancy a man fishing with a float and sinker when he has a fly rod in his hand! You come along!"

Where the placid little Ept flows down between its thickets to the Seine, a grassy bank shadows the haunt of the gudgeon, and on this bank sat Colette and Jacqueline and chattered and laughed and watched the swerving of the scarlet quills, while Hastings, his hat over his eyes, his head on a bank of moss, listened to their soft voices and gallantly unhooked the small and indignant gudgeon when a flash of a rod and a half-suppressed scream announced a catch. The sunlight filtered through the leafy thickets awaking to song the forest birds. Magpies in spotless black and white flirted past, alighting nearby with a hop and bound and twitch of the tail. Blue and white jays with rosy breasts shrieked through the trees, and a low-sailing hawk wheeled among the fields of ripening wheat, putting to flight flocks of twittering hedge birds.

Across the Seine a gull dropped on the water like a plume. The air was pure and still. Scarcely a leaf moved. Sounds from a distant farm came faintly, the shrill cock-crow and dull baying. Now and then a steam-tug with big raking smoke-pipe, bearing the name "Guêpe 27," ploughed up the river dragging its interminable train of barges, or a sailboat dropped down with the current toward sleepy Rouen.

A faint fresh odour of earth and water hung in the air, and through the sunlight, orange-tipped butterflies danced above the marsh grass, soft velvety butterflies flapped through the mossy woods.

Hastings was thinking of Valentine. It was two o'clock when Elliott strolled back, and frankly admitting that he had eluded Rowden, sat down beside Colette and prepared to doze with satisfaction.

"Where are your trout?" said Colette severely.

"They still live," murmured Elliott, and went fast asleep.

Rowden returned shortly after, and casting a scornful glance at the slumbering one, displayed three crimson-flecked trout.

"And that," smiled Hastings lazily, "that is the holy end to which the faithful plod—the slaughter of these small fish with a bit of silk and feather."

Rowden disdained to answer him. Colette caught another gudgeon and awoke Elliott, who protested and gazed about for the lunch baskets, as Clifford and Cécile came up demanding instant refreshment. Cécile's skirts were soaked, and her gloves torn, but she was happy, and Clifford, dragging out a two-pound trout, stood still to receive the applause of the company.

"Where the deuce did you get that?" demanded Elliott.

Cécile, wet and enthusiastic, recounted the battle, and then Clifford eulogized her powers with the fly, and, in proof, produced from his creel a defunct chub, which, he observed, just missed being a trout.

They were all very happy at luncheon, and Hastings was voted "charming". He enjoyed it immensely—only it seemed to him at moments that flirtation went further in France than in Millbrook, Connecticut, and he thought that Cécile might be a little less enthusiastic about Clifford, that perhaps it would be quite as well if Jacqueline sat further away from Rowden, and that possibly Colette could have, for a moment at least, taken her eyes from Elliott's face. Still he enjoyed it—except when his thoughts drifted to Valentine, and then he felt that he was very far away from her. La Roche is at least an hour and a half from Paris. It is also true that he felt a happiness, a quick heart-beat when, at eight o'clock that night the train which bore them from La Roche rolled into the Gare St. Lazare and he was once more in the city of Valentine.

"Good-night," they said, pressing around him. "You must come with us next time!"

He promised, and watched them, two by two, drift into the darkening city, and stood so long that, when again he raised his eyes, the vast Boulevard was twinkling with gas-jets through which the electric lights stared like moons.

VI.

It was with another quick heart-beat that he awoke next morning, for his first thought was of Valentine.

The sun already gilded the towers of Notre Dame, the clatter of workmen's sabots awoke sharp echoes in the street below, and across the way a blackbird in a pink almond tree was going into an ecstasy of trills.

He determined to awake Clifford for a brisk walk in the country, hoping later to beguile that gentleman into the American church for his soul's sake. He found Alfred the gimlet-eyed washing the asphalt walk which led to the studio.

"Monsieur Elliott?" he replied to the perfunctory enquiry, "*je ne sais pas.*"

"And Monsieur Clifford," began Hastings, somewhat astonished.

"Monsieur Clifford," said the concierge with fine irony, "will be pleased to see you, as he retired early; in fact he has just come in."

Hastings hesitated while the concierge pronounced a fine eulogy on people who never stayed out all night and then came battering at the lodge gate during hours which even a gendarme held sacred to sleep. He also discoursed eloquently upon the beauties of temperance, and took an ostentatious draught from the fountain in the court.

"I do not think I will come in," said Hastings.

"Pardon, monsieur," growled the concierge, "perhaps it would be well to see Monsieur Clifford. He possibly needs aid. Me he drives forth with hair-brushes and boots. It is a mercy if he has not set fire to something with his candle."

Hastings hesitated for an instant, but swallowing his dislike of such a mission, walked slowly through the ivy-covered alley and across the inner garden to the studio. He knocked. Perfect silence. Then he knocked again, and this time something struck the door from within with a crash.

"That," said the concierge, "was a boot." He fitted his duplicate key into the lock and ushered Hastings in. Clifford, in disordered evening dress, sat on the rug in the middle of the room. He held in his hand a shoe, and did not appear astonished to see Hastings.

"Good-morning, do you use Pears' soap?" he enquired with a vague wave of his hand and a vaguer smile.

Hastings's heart sank. "For Heaven's sake," he said, "Clifford, go to bed."

"Not while that—that Alfred pokes his shaggy head in here an' I have a shoe left."

Hastings blew out the candle, picked up Clifford's hat and cane, and said, with an emotion he could not conceal, "This is terrible, Clifford—I—never knew you did this sort of thing."

"Well, I do," said Clifford.

"Where is Elliott?"

"Ole chap," returned Clifford, becoming maudlin, "Providence which feeds—feeds—er—sparrows an' that sort of thing watcheth over the intemperate wanderer—"

"Where is Elliott?"

But Clifford only wagged his head and waved his arm about. "He's out there—somewhere about." Then suddenly feeling a desire to see his missing chum, lifted up his voice and howled for him.

Hastings, thoroughly shocked, sat down on the lounge without a word. Presently, after shedding several scalding tears, Clifford brightened up and rose with great precaution.

"Ole chap," he observed, "do you want to see er—er miracle? Well, here goes. I'm goin' to begin."

He paused, beaming at vacancy.

"Er miracle," he repeated.

Hastings supposed he was alluding to the miracle of his keeping his balance, and said nothing.

"I'm goin' to bed," he announced, "poor ole Clifford's goin' to bed, an' that's er miracle!"

And he did with a nice calculation of distance and equilibrium which would have rung enthusiastic yells of applause from Elliott had he been there to assist *en connaisseur*. But he was not. He had not yet reached the studio. He was on his way, however, and smiled with magnificent condescension on Hastings, who, half an hour later, found him reclining upon a bench in the Luxembourg. He permitted himself to be aroused, dusted and escorted to the gate. Here, however, he refused all further assistance, and bestowing a patronizing bow upon Hastings, steered a tolerably true course for the rue Vavin.

Hastings watched him out of sight, and then slowly retraced his steps toward the fountain. At first he felt gloomy and depressed, but gradually the clear air of the morning lifted the pressure from his heart, and he sat down on the marble seat under the shadow of the winged god.

The air was fresh and sweet with perfume from the orange flowers. Everywhere pigeons were bathing, dashing the water over their iris-hued breasts, flashing in and out of the spray or nestling almost to the neck along the polished basin. The sparrows, too, were abroad in force, soaking their dust-colored feathers in the limpid pool and chirping with might and main. Under the sycamores which surrounded the duck-pond opposite the fountain of Marie de Medici, the water-fowl cropped the herbage, or waddled in rows down the bank to embark on some solemn aimless cruise.

Butterflies, somewhat lame from a chilly night's repose under the lilac leaves, crawled over and over the white phlox, or took a rheumatic flight toward some sun-warmed shrub. The bees were already busy among the heliotrope, and one or two grey flies with brick-colored eyes sat in a spot of sunlight beside the marble seat, or chased each other about, only to return again to the spot of sunshine and rub their fore-legs, exulting.

The sentries paced briskly before the painted boxes, pausing at times to look toward the guard-house for their relief.

They came at last, with a shuffle of feet and click of bayonets, the word was passed, the relief fell out, and away they went, crunch, crunch, across the gravel.

A mellow chime floated from the clock-tower of the palace, the deep bell of St. Sulpice echoed the stroke. Hastings sat dreaming in the shadow of the god, and while he mused somebody came and sat down beside him. At first he did not raise his head. It was only when she spoke that he sprang up.

"You! At this hour?"

"I was restless, I could not sleep." Then in a low, happy voice—"And *you!* at this hour?"

"I—I slept, but the sun awoke me."

"*I* could not sleep," she said, and her eyes seemed, for a moment, touched with an indefinable shadow. Then, smiling, "I am so glad—I seemed to know you were coming. Don't laugh, I believe in dreams."

"Did you really dream of —of my being here?"

"I think I was awake when I dreamed it," she admitted. Then for a time they were mute, acknowledging by silence the happiness of being together. And after all their silence was eloquent, for faint smiles, and glances born of their thoughts, crossed and recrossed, until lips moved and words were formed, which seemed almost superfluous. What they said was not very profound. Perhaps the most valuable jewel that fell from Hastings's lips bore direct reference to breakfast.

"I have not yet had my chocolate," she confessed, "but what a material man you are."

"Valentine," he said impulsively, "I wish—I do wish that you would— just for this once—give me the whole day—just for this once."

"Oh dear," she smiled, "not only material, but selfish!"

"Not selfish, hungry," he said, looking at her.

"A cannibal too; oh dear!"

"Will you, Valentine?"

"But my chocolate—"

"Take it with me."

"But déjeuner—"

"Together, at St. Cloud."

"But I can't—"

"Together—all day—all day long; will you, Valentine?"

She was silent.

"Only for this once."

Again that indefinable shadow fell across her eyes, and when it was gone she sighed. "Yes—together, only for this once."

"All day?" he said, doubting his happiness.

"All day," she smiled; "and oh, I am so hungry!"

He laughed, enchanted.

"What a material young lady it is."

On the Boulevard St. Michel there is a crémerie painted white and blue outside, and neat and clean as a whistle inside. The auburn-haired young woman who speaks French like a native, and rejoices in the name of Murphy, smiled at them as they entered, and tossing a fresh napkin over the zinc *tête-à-tête* table, whisked before them two cups of chocolate and a basket full of crisp, fresh croissants.

The primrose-colored pats of butter, each stamped with a shamrock in relief, seemed saturated with the fragrance of Normandy pastures.

"How delicious!" they said in the same breath, and then laughed at the coincidence.

"With but a single thought," he began.

"How absurd!" she cried with cheeks all rosy. "I'm thinking I'd like a croissant."

"So am I," he replied triumphant, "that proves it."

Then they had a quarrel; she accusing him of behavior unworthy of a child in arms, and he denying it, and bringing counter-charges, until Mademoiselle Murphy laughed in sympathy, and the last croissant was eaten under a flag of truce. Then they rose, and she took his arm with a bright nod to Mlle Murphy, who cried them a merry: "*Bonjour, madame! Bonjour, monsieur!*" and watched them hail a passing cab and drive away. "*Dieu! qu'il est beau,*" she sighed, adding after a moment, "Do they be married, I dunno—*ma foi ils ont bien l'air.*"

The cab swung around the rue de Medici, turned into the rue de Vaugirard, followed it to where it crosses the rue de Rennes, and taking that noisy thoroughfare, drew up before the Gare Montparnasse. They were just in time for a train and scampered up the stairway and out to the cars as the last note from the starting-gong rang through the arched station.

The guard slammed the door of their compartment, a whistle sounded, answered by a screech from the locomotive, and the long train glided from the station, faster, faster, and sped out into the morning sunshine. The summer wind blew in their faces from the open window, and sent the soft hair dancing on the girl's forehead.

"We have the compartment to ourselves," said Hastings.

She leaned against the cushioned window-seat, her eyes bright and wide open, her lips parted. The wind lifted her hat, and fluttered the ribbons under her chin. With a quick movement she untied them, and, drawing a long hat-pin from her hat, laid it down on the seat beside her. The train was flying.

The color surged in her cheeks, and, with each quick-drawn breath, her breath rose and fell under the cluster of lilies at her throat. Trees, houses, ponds, danced past, cut by a mist of telegraph poles.

"Faster! faster!" she cried.

His eyes never left her, but hers, wide open, and blue as the summer sky, seemed fixed on something far ahead—something which came no nearer, but fled before them as they fled.

Was it the horizon, cut now by the grim fortress on the hill, now by the cross of a country chapel? Was it the summer moon, ghostlike, slipping through the vaguer blue above?

"Faster! faster!" she cried.

Her parted lips burned scarlet.

The car shook and shivered, and the fields streamed by like an emerald torrent. He caught the excitement, and his faced glowed.

"Oh," she cried, and with an unconscious movement caught his hand, drawing him to the window beside her. "Look! lean out with me!"

He only saw her lips move; her voice was drowned in the roar of a trestle, but his hand closed in hers and he clung to the sill. The wind whistled in their ears. "Not so far out, Valentine, take care!" he gasped.

Below, through the ties of the trestle, a broad river flashed into view and out again, as the train thundered along a tunnel, and away once more through the freshest of green fields. The wind roared about them. The girl was leaning far out from the window, and he caught her by the waist, crying, "Not too far!" but she only murmured, "Faster! faster! Away out of the city, out of the land, faster, faster! Away out of the world!"

"What are you saying all to yourself?" he said, but his voice was broken, and the wind whirled it back into his throat.

She heard him, and, turning from the window looked down at his arm about her. Then she raised her eyes to his. The car shook and the windows rattled. They were dashing through a forest now, and the sun swept the dewy branches with running flashes of fire. He looked into her troubled eyes; he drew her to him and kissed the half-parted lips, and she cried out, a bitter, hopeless cry, "Not that—not that!"

But he held her close and strong, whispering words of honest love and passion, and when she sobbed—"Not that—not that—I have promised! You must—you must know—I am—not—worthy—" In the purity of his own heart her words were, to him, meaningless then, meaningless for ever after. Presently her voice ceased, and her head rested on his breast. He leaned against the window, his ears swept by the furious wind, his heart in a joyous tumult. The forest was passed, and the sun slipped from behind the trees, flooding the earth again with brightness. She raised her eyes and looked out into the world from the window. Then she began to speak, but her voice was faint, and he bent his head close to hers and listened. "I cannot turn from you; I am too weak. You were long ago my master—master of my heart and soul. I have broken my word to one who trusted me, but I have told you all—what matters the rest?" He smiled at her innocence and she worshipped his. She spoke again: "Take me or cast me away—what matters it? Now with a word you can kill me, and it might be easier to die than to look upon happiness as great as mine."

He took her in his arms, "Hush, what are you saying? Look—look out at the sunlight, the meadows and the streams. We shall be very happy in so bright a world."

She turned to the sunlight. From the window, the world below seemed very fair to her.

Trembling with happiness, she sighed: "Is this the world? Then I have never known it."

"Nor have I, God forgive me," he murmured.

Perhaps it was our gentle Lady of the Fields who forgave them both.

RUE BARRÉE

For let Philosopher and Doctor preach
Of what they will and what they will not—each
Is but one link in an eternal chain
That none can slip nor break nor over-reach.

Crimson nor yellow roses nor
The savour of the mounting sea
Are worth the perfume I adore
That clings to thee.

The languid-headed lilies tire,
The changeless waters weary me;
I ache with passionate desire
Of thine and thee.

There are but these things in the world—
Thy mouth of fire,
Thy breasts, thy hands, thy hair upcurled
And my desire.

I.

One morning at Julian's, a student said to Selby, "That is Foxhall Clifford," pointing with his brushes at a young man who sat before an easel, doing nothing.

Selby, shy and nervous, walked over and began: "My name is Selby—I have just arrived in Paris, and bring a letter of introduction—" His voice was lost in the crash of a falling easel, the owner of which promptly assaulted his neighbor, and for a time the noise of battle rolled through the studios of MM. Boulanger and Lefebvre, presently subsiding into a scuffle on the stairs outside. Selby, apprehensive as to his own reception in the studio, looked at Clifford, who sat serenely watching the fight.

"It's a little noisy here," said Clifford, "but you will like the fellows when you know them." His unaffected manner delighted Selby. Then with a simplicity that won his heart, he presented him to half a dozen students of as many nationalities. Some were cordial, all were polite. Even the majestic creature who held the position of massier, unbent enough to say: "My friend, when a man speaks French as well as you do, and is also a friend of Monsieur Clifford, he will have no trouble in this studio. You expect, of course, to fill the stove until the next new man comes?"

"Of course."

"And you don't mind chaff?"

"No," replied Selby, who hated it.

Clifford, much amused, put on his hat, saying, "You must expect lots of it at first."

Selby placed his own hat on his head and followed him to the door. As they passed the model stand there was a furious cry of "Chapeau! Chapeau!" and a student sprang from his easel menacing Selby, who reddened but looked at Clifford.

"Take off your hat for them," said the latter, laughing.

A little embarrassed, he turned and saluted the studio.

"Et moi?" cried the model.

"You are charming," replied Selby, astonished at his own audacity, but the studio rose as one man, shouting: "He has done well! he's all right!" while the model, laughing, kissed her hand to him and cried: "À demain, beau jeune homme!"

All that week Selby worked at the studio unmolested. The French students christened him "l'Enfant Prodigue," which was freely translated, "The Prodigious Infant," "The Kid," "Kid Selby," and "Kidby." But the disease soon ran its course from "Kidby" to "Kidney," and then naturally to "Tidbits," where it was arrested by Clifford's authority and ultimately relapsed to "Kid."

Wednesday came, and with it M. Boulanger. For three hours the students writhed under his biting sarcasms—among the others Clifford, who was informed that he knew even less about a work of art than he did about the art of work. Selby was more fortunate. The professor examined his drawing in silence, looked at him sharply, and passed on with a non-committal gesture. He presently departed arm in arm with Bouguereau, to the relief of Clifford, who was then at liberty to jam his hat on his head and depart.

The next day he did not appear, and Selby, who had counted on seeing him at the studio, a thing which he learned later it was vanity to count on, wandered back to the Latin Quarter alone.

Paris was still strange and new to him. He was vaguely troubled by its splendor. No tender memories stirred his American bosom at the Place du Châtelet, nor even by Notre Dame. The Palais de Justice with its clock and turrets and stalking sentinels in blue and vermilion, the Place St. Michel with its jumble of omnibuses and ugly water-spitting griffins, the hill of the Boulevard St. Michel, the tooting trams, the policemen dawdling two by two, and the table-lined terraces of the Café Vachette were nothing to him, as yet, nor did he even know, when he stepped from the stones of the Place St. Michel to the asphalt of the Boulevard, that he had crossed the frontier and entered the student zone—the famous Latin Quarter.

A cabman hailed him as "bourgeois," and urged the superiority of driving over walking. A gamin, with an appearance of great concern, requested the latest telegraphic news from London, and then, standing on his head, invited Selby to feats of strength. A pretty girl gave him a glance from a pair of violet eyes. He did not see her, but she, catching her own reflection in a window, wondered at the color burning in her cheeks. Turning to resume her course, she met Foxhall Clifford, and hurried on. Clifford, open-mouthed, followed her with his eyes; then he looked after Selby, who had turned into the Boulevard St. Germain toward the rue de Seine. Then he examined himself in the shop window. The result seemed to be unsatisfactory.

"I'm not a beauty," he mused, "but neither am I a hobgoblin. What does she mean by blushing at Selby? I never before saw her look at a fellow in my life—neither has anyone in the Quarter. Anyway, I can swear she never looks at me, and goodness knows I have done all that respectful adoration can do."

He sighed, and murmuring a prophecy concerning the salvation of his immortal soul swung into that graceful lounge which at all times characterized Clifford. With no apparent exertion, he overtook Selby at the corner, and together they crossed the sunlit Boulevard and sat down under the awning of the Café du Cercle. Clifford bowed to everybody on the terrace, saying, "You shall meet them all later, but now let me present you to two of the sights of Paris, Mr. Richard Elliott and Mr. Stanley Rowden."

The "sights" looked amiable, and took vermouth.

"You cut the studio today," said Elliott, suddenly turning on Clifford, who avoided his eyes.

"To commune with nature?" observed Rowden.

"What's her name this time?" asked Elliott, and Rowden answered promptly, "Name, Yvette; nationality, Breton—"

"Wrong," replied Clifford blandly, "it's Rue Barrée."

The subject changed instantly, and Selby listened in surprise to names which were new to him, and eulogies on the latest Prix de Rome winner. He was delighted to hear opinions boldly expressed and points honestly debated, although the vehicle was mostly slang, both English and French. He longed for the time when he too should be plunged into the strife for fame.

The bells of St. Sulpice struck the hour, and the Palace of the Luxembourg answered chime on chime. With a glance at the sun, dipping low in the golden dust behind the Palais Bourbon, they rose, and turning to the east, crossed the Boulevard St. Germain and sauntered toward the École de Medecine. At the corner a girl passed them, walking hurriedly. Clifford smirked, Elliot and Rowden were agitated, but they all bowed, and, without raising her eyes, she returned their salute. But Selby, who had lagged behind, fascinated by some gay shop window, looked up to meet two of the bluest eyes he had ever seen. The eyes were dropped in an instant, and the young fellow hastened to overtake the others.

"By Jove," he said, "do you fellows know I have just seen the prettiest girl—" An exclamation broke from the trio, gloomy, foreboding, like the chorus in a Greek play.

"Rue Barrée!"

"What!" cried Selby, bewildered.

The only answer was a vague gesture from Clifford.

Two hours later, during dinner, Clifford turned to Selby and said, "You want to ask me something; I can tell by the way you fidget about."

"Yes, I do," he said, innocently enough; "it's about that girl. Who is she?"

In Rowden's smile there was pity, in Elliott's bitterness.

"Her name," said Clifford solemnly, "is unknown to anyone; at least," he added with much conscientiousness, "as far as I can learn. Every fellow in the Quarter bows to her and she returns the salute gravely, but no man has ever been known to obtain more than that. Her profession, judging from her music-roll, is that of a pianist. Her residence is in a small and humble street which is kept in a perpetual process of repair by the city authorities, and from the black letters painted on the barrier which defends the street from traffic, she has taken the name by which we know her—Rue Barrée. Mr. Rowden, in his imperfect knowledge of the French tongue, called our attention to it as Roo Barry—"

"I didn't," said Rowden hotly.

"And Roo Barry, or Rue Barrée, is today an object of adoration to every rapin in the Quarter—"

"We are not rapins," corrected Elliott.

"*I* am not," returned Clifford, "and I beg to call to your attention, Selby, that these two gentlemen have at various and apparently unfortunate moments, offered to lay down life and limb at the feet of Rue Barrée. The lady possesses a chilling smile which she uses on such occasions and," here he became gloomily impressive, "I have been forced to believe that neither the scholarly grace of my friend Elliott nor the buxom beauty of my friend Rowden have touched that heart of ice."

Elliott and Rowden, boiling with indignation, cried out, "And you!"

"I," said Clifford blandly, "do fear to tread where you rush in."

II.

Twenty-four hours later Selby had completely forgotten Rue Barrée. During the week he worked with might and main at the studio, and Saturday night found him so tired that he went to bed before dinner and had a nightmare about a river of yellow ochre in which he was drowning. Sunday morning, apropos of nothing at all, he thought of Rue Barrée, and ten seconds afterwards he saw her. It was at the flower-market on the marble bridge. She was examining a pot of pansies. The gardener had evidently thrown heart and soul into the transaction, but Rue Barrée shook her head.

It is a question whether Selby would have stopped then and there to inspect a cabbage-rose had not Clifford unwound for him the yarn of the previous Tuesday. It is possible that his curiosity was piqued, for with the exception of a hen-turkey, a boy of nineteen is the most openly curious biped alive. From twenty until death he tries to conceal it. But, to be fair to Selby, it is also true that the market was attractive. Under a cloudless sky the flowers were packed and heaped along the marble bridge to the parapet. The air was soft, the sun spun a shadowy lacework among the palms and glowed in the hearts of a thousand roses. Spring had come—was in full tide. The watering carts and sprinklers spread freshness over the Boulevard, the sparrows had become vulgarly obtrusive, and the credulous Seine angler anxiously followed his gaudy quill floating among the soapsuds of the lavoirs. The white-spiked chestnuts clad in tender green vibrated with the hum of bees. Shoddy butterflies flaunted their winter rags among the heliotrope. There was a smell of fresh earth in the air, an echo of the woodland brook in the ripple of the Seine, and swallows soared and skimmed among the anchored river craft. Somewhere in a window a caged bird was singing its heart out to the sky.

Selby looked at the cabbage-rose and then at the sky. Something in the song of the caged bird may have moved him, or perhaps it was that dangerous sweetness in the air of May.

At first he was hardly conscious that he had stopped, then he was scarcely conscious why he had stopped, then he thought he would move on, then he thought he wouldn't, then he looked at Rue Barrée.

The gardener said, "Mademoiselle, this is undoubtedly a fine pot of pansies."

Rue Barrée shook her head.

The gardener smiled. She evidently did not want the pansies. She had bought many pots of pansies there, two or three every spring, and never argued. What did she want then? The pansies were evidently a feeler toward a more important transaction. The gardener rubbed his hands and gazed about him.

"These tulips are magnificent," he observed, "and these hyacinths—" He fell into a trance at the mere sight of the scented thickets.

"That," murmured Rue, pointing to a splendid rose-bush with her furled parasol, but in spite of her, her voice trembled a little. Selby noticed it, more shame to him that he was listening, and the gardener noticed it, and, burying his nose in the roses, scented a bargain. Still, to do him justice, he did not add a centime to the honest value of the plant, for after all, Rue was probably poor, and anyone could see she was charming.

"Fifty francs, Mademoiselle."

The gardener's tone was grave. Rue felt that argument would be wasted. They both stood silent for a moment. The gardener did not eulogise his prize—the rose-tree was gorgeous and anyone could see it.

"I will take the pansies," said the girl, and drew two francs from a worn purse. Then she looked up. A tear-drop stood in the way refracting the light like a diamond, but as it rolled into a little corner by her nose a vision of Selby replaced it, and when a brush of the handkerchief had cleared the startled blue eyes, Selby himself appeared, very much embarrassed. He instantly looked up into the sky, apparently devoured with a thirst for astronomical research, and as he continued his investigations for fully five minutes, the gardener looked up too, and so did a policeman. Then Selby looked at the tips of his boots, the gardener looked at him and the police-man slouched on. Rue Barrée had been gone some time.

"What," said the gardener, "may I offer Monsieur?"

Selby never knew why, but he suddenly began to buy flowers. The gardener was electrified. Never before had he sold so many flowers, never at such satisfying prices, and never, never with such absolute unanimity of opinion with a customer. But he missed the bargaining, the arguing, the calling of Heaven to witness. The transaction lacked spice.

"These tulips are magnificent!"

"They are!" cried Selby warmly.

"But alas, they are dear."

"I will take them."

"Dieu!" murmured the gardener in a perspiration, "he's madder than most Englishmen."

"This cactus—"

"Is gorgeous!"

"Alas—"

"Send it with the rest."

The gardener braced himself against the river wall.

"That splendid rose-bush," he began faintly.

"That is a beauty. I believe it is fifty francs—"

He stopped, very red. The gardener relished his confusion. Then a sudden cool self-possession took the place of his momentary confusion and he held the gardener with his eye, and bullied him.

"I'll take that bush. Why did not the young lady buy it?"

"Mademoiselle is not wealthy."

"How do you know?"

"*Dame*, I sell her many pansies; pansies are not expensive."

"Those are the pansies she bought?"

"These, Monsieur, the blue and gold."

"Then you intend to send them to her?"

"At mid-day after the market."

"Take this rose-bush with them, and"—here he glared at the gardener—"don't you dare say from whom they came." The gardener's eyes were like saucers, but Selby, calm and victorious, said: "Send the others to the Hôtel du Sénat, 7 rue de Tournon. I will leave directions with the concierge."

Then he buttoned his glove with much dignity and stalked off, but when well around the corner and hidden from the gardener's view, the conviction that he was an idiot came home to him in a furious blush. Ten minutes later he sat in his room in the Hôtel du Sénat repeating with an imbecile smile: "What an ass I am, what an ass!"

An hour later found him in the same chair, in the same position, his hat and gloves still on, his stick in his hand, but he was silent, apparently lost in contemplation of his boot toes, and his smile was less imbecile and even a bit retrospective.

III.

About five o'clock that afternoon, the little sad-eyed woman who fills the position of concierge at the Hôtel du Sénat held up her hands in amazement to see a wagon-load of flower-bearing shrubs draw up before the doorway. She called Joseph, the intemperate garçon, who, while calculating the value of the flowers in *petits verres*, gloomily disclaimed any knowledge as to their destination.

"*Voyons*," said the little concierge, "*cherchons la femme!*"

"You?" he suggested.

The little woman stood a moment pensive and then sighed. Joseph caressed his nose, a nose which for gaudiness could vie with any floral display.

Then the gardener came in, hat in hand, and a few minutes later Selby stood in the middle of his room, his coat off, his shirt-sleeves rolled up. The chamber originally contained, besides the furniture, about two square feet of walking room, and now this was occupied by a cactus. The bed groaned under crates of pansies, lilies and heliotrope, the lounge was covered with hyacinths and tulips, and the washstand supported a species of young tree warranted to bear flowers at some time or other.

Clifford came in a little later, fell over a box of sweet peas, swore a little, apologized, and then, as the full splendor of the floral *fête* burst upon him, sat down in astonishment upon a geranium. The geranium was a wreck, but Selby said, "Don't mind," and glared at the cactus.

"Are you going to give a ball?" demanded Clifford.

"N—no—I'm very fond of flowers," said Selby, but the statement lacked enthusiasm.

"I should imagine so." Then, after a silence, "That's a fine cactus."

Selby contemplated the cactus, touched it with the air of a connoisseur, and pricked his thumb.

Clifford poked a pansy with his stick. Then Joseph came in with the bill, announcing the sum total in a loud voice, partly to impress Clifford, partly to intimidate Selby into disgorging a *pourboire* which he would share, if he chose, with the gardener. Clifford tried to pretend that he had not heard, while Selby paid bill and tribute without a murmur. Then he lounged back into the room with an attempt at indifference which failed entirely when he tore his trousers on the cactus.

Clifford made some commonplace remark, lighted a cigarette and looked out of the window to give Selby a chance. Selby tried to take it, but getting as far as—"Yes, spring is here at last," froze solid. He looked at the back of Clifford's head. It expressed volumes. Those little perked-up ears seemed tingling with suppressed glee. He made a desperate effort to master the situation, and jumped up to reach for some Russian cigarettes as an incentive to conversation, but was foiled by the cactus, to whom again he fell a prey. The last straw was added.

"Damn the cactus." This observation was wrung from Selby against his will—against his own instinct of self-preservation, but the thorns on the cactus were long and sharp, and at their repeated prick his pent-up wrath escaped. It was too late now; it was done, and Clifford had wheeled around.

"See here, Selby, why the deuce did you buy those flowers?"

"I'm fond of them," said Selby.

"What are you going to do with them? You can't sleep here."

"I could, if you'd help me take the pansies off the bed."

"Where can you put them?"

"Couldn't I give them to the concierge?"

As soon as he said it he regretted it. What in Heaven's name would Clifford think of him! He had heard the amount of the bill. Would he believe that he had invested in these luxuries as a timid declaration to his concierge? And would the Latin Quarter comment upon it in their own brutal fashion? He dreaded ridicule and he knew Clifford's reputation.

Then somebody knocked.

Selby looked at Clifford with a hunted expression which touched that young man's heart. It was a confession and at the same time a supplication. Clifford jumped up, threaded his way through the floral labyrinth, and putting an eye to the crack of the door, said, "Who the devil is it?"

This graceful style of reception is indigenous to the Quarter.

"It's Elliott," he said, looking back, "and Rowden too, and their bulldogs." Then he addressed them through the crack.

"Sit down on the stairs; Selby and I are coming out directly."

Discretion is a virtue. The Latin Quarter possesses few, and discretion seldom figures on the list. They sat down and began to whistle.

Presently Rowden called out, "I smell flowers. They feast within!"

"You ought to know Selby better than that," growled Clifford behind the door, while the other hurriedly exchanged his torn trousers for others.

"*We* know Selby," said Elliott with emphasis.

"Yes," said Rowden, "he gives receptions with floral decorations and invites Clifford, while we sit on the stairs."

"Yes, while the youth and beauty of the Quarter revel," suggested Rowden; then, with sudden misgiving, "Is Odette there?"

"See here," demanded Elliott, "is Colette there?"

Then he raised his voice in a plaintive howl, "Are you there, Colette, while I'm kicking my heels on these tiles?"

"Clifford is capable of anything," said Rowden; "his nature is soured since Rue Barrée sat on him."

Elliott raised his voice: "I say, you fellows, we saw some flowers carried into Rue Barrée's house at noon."

"Posies and roses," specified Rowden.

"Probably for her," added Elliott, caressing his bulldog.

Clifford turned with sudden suspicion upon Selby. The latter hummed a tune, selected a pair of gloves and, choosing a dozen cigarettes, placed them in a case. Then walking over to the cactus, he deliberately detached a blossom, drew it through his buttonhole, and picking up hat and stick, smiled upon Clifford, at which the latter was mightily troubled.

IV.

Monday morning at Julian's, students fought for places; students with prior claims drove away others who had been anxiously squatting on coveted tabourets since the door was opened in hopes of appropriating them at roll-call; students squabbled over palettes, brushes, portfolios, or rent the air with demands for Ciceri and bread. The former, a dirty ex-model, who had in palmier days posed as Judas, now dispensed stale bread at one sou and made enough to keep himself in cigarettes. Monsieur Julian walked in, smiled a fatherly smile and walked out. His disappearance was followed by the apparition of the clerk, a foxy creature who flitted through the battling hordes in search of prey.

Three men who had not paid dues were caught and summoned. A fourth was scented, followed, outflanked, his retreat towards the door cut off, and finally captured behind the stove. About that time, the revolution assuming an acute form, howls rose for "Jules!"

Jules came, umpired two fights with a sad resignation in his big brown eyes, shook hands with everybody and melted away in the throng, leaving an atmosphere of peace and good-will. The lions sat down with the lambs, the massiers marked the best places for themselves and friends, and, mounting the model stands, opened the roll-calls.

The word was passed, "They begin with C this week."

They did.

"Clisson!"

Clisson jumped like a flash and marked his name on the floor in chalk before a front seat.

"Caron!"

Caron galloped away to secure his place. Bang! went an easel. "*Nom de Dieu!*" in French—"Where in h—l are you goin'!" in English. Crash! a paintbox fell with brushes and all on board. "*Dieu de Dieu de —*" spat! A blow, a short rush, a clinch and scuffle, and the voice of the massier, stern and reproachful: "Cochon!"

Then the roll-call was resumed.

"Clifford!"

The massier paused and looked up, one finger between the leaves of the ledger.

"Clifford!"

Clifford was not there. He was about three miles away in a direct line and every instant increased the distance. Not that he was walking fast—on the contrary, he was strolling with that leisurely gait peculiar to himself. Elliott was beside him and two bulldogs covered the rear. Elliott was reading the "Gil Blas," from which he seemed to extract amusement, but deeming boisterous mirth unsuitable to Clifford's state of mind, subdued his amusement to a series of discreet smiles. The latter, moodily aware of this, said nothing, but leading the way into the Luxembourg Gardens installed himself upon a bench by the northern terrace and surveyed the landscape with disfavor. Elliott, according to the Luxembourg regulations, tied the two dogs and then, with an interrogative glance toward his friend, resumed the "Gil Blas" and the discreet smiles.

The day was perfect. The sun hung over Notre Dame, setting the city in a glitter. The tender foliage of the chestnuts cast a shadow over the terrace and flecked the paths and walks with tracery so blue that Clifford might here have found encouragement for his violent "impressions" had he but looked; but as usual in this period of his career, his thoughts were anywhere except in his profession. Around about, the sparrows quarreled and chattered their courtship songs, the big rosy pigeons sailed from tree to tree, the flies whirled in the sunbeams and the flowers exhaled a thousand perfumes which stirred Clifford with languorous wistfulness. Under this influence he spoke.

"Elliott, you are a true friend—"

"You make me ill," replied the latter, folding his paper. "It's just as I thought—you are tagging after some new petticoat again. And," he continued wrathfully, "if this is what you've kept me away from Julian's for— if it's to fill me up with the perfections of some little idiot—"

"Not idiot," remonstrated Clifford gently.

"See here," cried Elliott, "have you the nerve to try to tell me that you are in love again?"

"Again?"

"Yes, again and again and again and—by George, have you?"

"This," observed Clifford sadly, "is serious."

For a moment Elliott would have laid hands on him, then he laughed from sheer helplessness. "Oh, go on, go on; let's see, there's Clémence and Marie Tellec and Cosette and Fifine, Colette, Marie Verdier—"

"All of whom are charming, most charming, but I never was serious—"

"So help me, Moses," said Elliott, solemnly, "each and every one of those named have separately and in turn torn your heart with anguish and have also made me lose my place at Julian's in this same manner; each and every one, separately and in turn. Do you deny it?"

"What you say may be founded on facts—in a way—but give me the credit of being faithful to one at a time—"

"Until the next came along."

"But this—this is really very different. Elliott, believe me, I am all broken up."

Then, there being nothing else to do, Elliott gnashed his teeth and listened.

"It's—it's Rue Barrée."

"Well," observed Elliott, with scorn, "if you are moping and moaning over *that* girl—the girl who has given you and myself every reason to wish that the ground would open and engulf us—well, go on!"

"I'm going on—I don't care; timidity has fled—"

"Yes, your native timidity."

"I'm desperate, Elliott. Am I in love? Never, never did I feel so d—n miserable. I can't sleep; honestly, I'm incapable of eating properly."

"Same symptoms noticed in the case of Colette."

"Listen, will you?"

"Hold on a moment, I know the rest by heart. Now let me ask you something. Is it your belief that Rue Barrée is a pure girl?"

"Yes," said Clifford, turning red.

"Do you love her—not as you dangle and tiptoe after every pretty inanity—I mean, do you honestly love her?"

"Yes," said the other doggedly, "I would—"

"Hold on a moment; would you marry her?"

Clifford turned scarlet. "Yes," he muttered.

"Pleasant news for your family," growled Elliott in suppressed fury. "'Dear father, I have just married a charming grisette whom I'm sure you'll welcome with open arms, in company with her mother, a most estimable and cleanly washlady.' Good heavens! This seems to have gone a little further than the rest. Thank your stars, young man, that my head is level enough for us both. Still, in this case, I have no fear. Rue Barrée sat on your aspirations in a manner unmistakably final."

"Rue Barrée," began Clifford, drawing himself up, but he suddenly ceased, for there where the dappled sunlight glowed in spots of gold, along the sun-flecked path, tripped Rue Barrée. Her gown was spotless, and her big straw hat, tipped a little from the white forehead, threw a shadow across her eyes.

Elliott stood up and bowed. Clifford removed his head-covering with an air so plaintive, so appealing, so utterly humble that Rue Barrée smiled.

The smile was delicious and when Clifford, incapable of sustaining himself on his legs from sheer astonishment, toppled slightly, she smiled again in spite of herself. A few moments later she took a chair on the terrace and drawing a book from her music-roll, turned the pages, found the place, and then placing it open downwards in her lap, sighed a little, smiled a little, and looked out over the city. She had entirely forgotten Foxhall Clifford.

After a while she took up her book again, but instead of reading began to adjust a rose in her corsage. The rose was big and red. It glowed like fire there over her heart, and like fire it warmed her heart, now fluttering under the silken petals. Rue Barrée sighed again. She was very happy. The sky was so blue, the air so soft and perfumed, the sunshine so caressing, and her heart sang within her, sang to the rose in her breast. This is what it sang: "Out of the throng of passers-by, out of the world of yesterday, out of the millions passing, one has turned aside to me."

So her heart sang under his rose on her breast. Then two big mouse-colored pigeons came whistling by and alighted on the terrace, where they bowed and strutted and bobbed and turned until Rue Barrée laughed in delight, and looking up beheld Clifford before her. His hat was in his hand and his face was wreathed in a series of appealing smiles which would have touched the heart of a Bengal tiger.

For an instant Rue Barrée frowned, then she looked curiously at Clifford, then when she saw the resemblance between his bows and the bobbing pigeons, in spite of herself, her lips parted in the most bewitching laugh. Was this Rue Barrée? So changed, so changed that she did not know herself; but oh! that song in her heart which drowned all else, which trembled on her lips, struggling for utterance, which rippled forth in a laugh at nothing—at a strutting pigeon—and Mr. Clifford.

"And you think, because I return the salute of the students in the Quarter, that you may be received in particular as a friend? I do not know you, Monsieur, but vanity is man's other name—be content, Monsieur Vanity, I shall be punctilious—oh, most punctilious in returning your salute."

"But I beg—I implore you to let me render you that homage which has so long—"

"Oh dear; I don't care for homage."

"Let me only be permitted to speak to you now and then—occasionally—very occasionally."

"And if *you*, why not another?"

"Not at all–I will be discretion itself."

"Discretion–why?"

Her eyes were very clear, and Clifford winced for a moment, but only for a moment. Then the devil of recklessness seizing him, he sat down and offered himself, soul and body, goods and chattels. And all the time he knew he was a fool and that infatuation is not love, and that each word he uttered bound him in honor from which there was no escape. And all the time Elliott was scowling down on the fountain plaza and savagely checking both bulldogs from their desire to rush to Clifford's rescue—for even they felt there was something wrong, as Elliott stormed within himself and growled maledictions.

When Clifford finished, he finished in a glow of excitement, but Rue Barrée's response was long in coming and his ardor cooled while the situation slowly assumed its just proportions. Then regret began to creep in, but he put that aside and broke out again in protestations. At the first word Rue Barrée checked him.

"I thank you," she said, speaking very gravely. "No man has ever before offered me marriage." She turned and looked out over the city. After a while she spoke again. "You offer me a great deal. I am alone, I have nothing, I am nothing." She turned again and looked at Paris, brilliant, fair, in the sunshine of a perfect day. He followed her eyes.

"Oh," she murmured, "it is hard—hard to work always—always alone with never a friend you can have in honor, and the love that is offered means the streets, the boulevard—when passion is dead. I know it—*we* know it—we others who have nothing—have no one, and who give ourselves, unquestioning—when we love—yes, unquestioning—heart and soul, knowing the end."

She touched the rose at her breast. For a moment she seemed to forget him, then quietly—"I thank you, I am very grateful." She opened the book and, plucking a petal from the rose, dropped it between the leaves. Then looking up she said gently, "I cannot accept."

V.

It took Clifford a month to entirely recover, although at the end of the first week he was pronounced convalescent by Elliott, who was an authority, and his convalescence was aided by the cordiality with which Rue Barrée acknowledged his solemn salutes. Forty times a day he blessed Rue Barrée for her refusal, and thanked his lucky stars, and at the same time, oh, wondrous heart of ours!—he suffered the tortures of the blighted.

Elliott was annoyed, partly by Clifford's reticence, partly by the unexplainable thaw in the frigidity of Rue Barrée. At their frequent encounters, when she, tripping along the rue de Seine, with music-roll and big straw hat would pass Clifford and his familiars steering an easterly course to the Café Vachette, and at the respectful uncovering of the band would color and smile at Clifford, Elliott's slumbering suspicions awoke. But he never found out anything, and finally gave it up as beyond his comprehension, merely qualifying Clifford as an idiot and reserving his opinion of Rue Barrée. And all this time Selby was jealous. At first he refused to acknowledge it to himself, and cut the studio for a day in the country, but the woods and fields of course aggravated his case, and the brooks babbled of Rue Barrée and the mowers calling to each other across the meadow ended in a quavering "Rue Bar-rée-e!" That day spent in the country made him angry for a week, and he worked sulkily at Julian's, all the time tormented by a desire to know where Clifford was and what he might be doing. This culminated in an erratic stroll on Sunday which ended at the flower-market on the Pont au Change, began again, was gloomily extended to the morgue, and again ended at the marble bridge. It would never do, and Selby felt it, so he went to see Clifford, who was convalescing on mint juleps in his garden.

They sat down together and discussed morals and human happiness, and each found the other most entertaining, only Selby failed to pump Clifford, to the other's unfeigned amusement. But the juleps spread balm on the sting of jealousy, and trickled hope to the blighted, and when Selby said he must go, Clifford went too, and when Selby, not to be outdone, insisted on accompanying Clifford back to his door, Clifford determined to see Selby back half way, and then finding it hard to part, they decided to dine together and "flit." To flit, a verb applied to Clifford's nocturnal prowls, expressed, perhaps, as well as anything, the gaiety proposed. Dinner was ordered at Mignon's, and while Selby interviewed the chef, Clifford kept a fatherly eye on the butler. The dinner was a success, or was of the sort generally termed a success. Toward the dessert Selby heard someone say as at a great distance, "Kid Selby, drunk as a lord."

A group of men passed near them; it seemed to him that he shook hands and laughed a great deal, and that everybody was very witty. There was Clifford opposite swearing undying confidence in his chum Selby, and there seemed to be others there, either seated beside them or continually passing with the swish of skirts on the polished floor. The perfume of roses, the rustle of fans, the touch of rounded arms and the laughter grew vaguer and vaguer. The room seemed enveloped in mist. Then, all in a moment each object stood out painfully distinct, only forms and visages were distorted and voices piercing. He drew himself up, calm, grave, for the moment master of himself, but very drunk. He knew he was drunk, and was as guarded and alert, as keenly suspicious of himself as he would have been of a thief at his elbow. His self-command enabled Clifford to hold his head safely under some running water, and repair to the street considerably the worse for wear, but never suspecting that his companion was drunk. For a time he kept his self-command. His face was only a bit paler, a bit tighter than usual; he was only a trifle slower and more fastidious in his speech. It was midnight when he left Clifford peacefully slumbering in somebody's armchair, with a long suede glove dangling in his hand and a plumy boa twisted about his neck to protect his throat from drafts. He walked through the hall and down the stairs, and found himself on the sidewalk in a quarter he did not know. Mechanically he looked up at the name of the street. The name was not familiar. He turned and steered his course toward some lights clustered at the end of the street. They proved farther away than he had anticipated, and after a long quest he came to the conclusion that his eyes had been mysteriously removed from their proper places and had been reset on either side of his head like those of a bird. It grieved him to think of the inconvenience this transformation might occasion him, and he attempted to cock up his head, hen-like, to test the mobility of his neck. Then an immense despair stole over him—tears gathered in the tear-ducts, his heart melted, and he collided with a tree.

This shocked him into comprehension; he stifled the violent tenderness in his breast, picked up his hat and moved on more briskly. His mouth was white and drawn, his teeth tightly clinched. He held his course pretty well and strayed but little, and after an apparently interminable length of time found himself passing a line of cabs. The brilliant lamps, red, yellow, and green annoyed him, and he felt it might be pleasant to demolish them with his cane, but mastering this impulse he passed on. Later an idea struck him that it would save fatigue to take a cab, and he started back with that intention, but the cabs seemed already so far away and the lanterns were so bright and confusing that he gave it up, and pulling himself together looked around.

A shadow, a mass, huge, undefined, rose to his right. He recognized the Arc de Triomphe and gravely shook his cane at it. Its size annoyed him. He felt it was too big. Then he heard something fall clattering to the pavement and thought probably it was his cane but it didn't much matter. When he had mastered himself and regained control of his right leg, which betrayed symptoms of insubordination, he found himself traversing the Place de la Concorde at a pace which threatened to land him at the Madeleine. This would never do. He turned sharply to the right and crossing the bridge passed the Palais Bourbon at a trot and wheeled into the Boulevard St. Germain. He got on well enough although the size of the War Office struck him as a personal insult, and he missed his cane, which it would have been pleasant to drag along the iron railings as he passed. It occurred to him, however, to substitute his hat, but when he found it he forgot what he wanted it for and replaced it upon his head with gravity. Then he was obliged to battle with a violent inclination to sit down and weep. This lasted until he came to the rue de Rennes, but there he became absorbed in contemplating the dragon on the balcony overhanging the Cour du Dragon, and time slipped away until he remembered vaguely that he had no business there, and marched off again. It was slow work. The inclination to sit down and weep had given place to a desire for solitary and deep reflection. Here his right leg forgot its obedience and attacking the left, outflanked it and brought him up against a wooden board which seemed to bar his path. He tried to walk around it, but found the street closed. He tried to push it over, and found he couldn't. Then he noticed a red lantern standing on a pile of paving-stones inside the barrier. This was pleasant. How was he to get home if the boulevard was blocked? But he was not on the boulevard. His treacherous right leg had beguiled him into a detour, for there, behind him lay the boulevard with its endless line of lamps—and here, what was this narrow dilapidated street piled up with earth and mortar and heaps of stone? He looked up. Written in staring black letters on the barrier was

RUE BARRÉE

He sat down. Two policemen whom he knew came by and advised him to get up, but he argued the question from a standpoint of personal taste, and they passed on, laughing. For he was at that moment absorbed in a problem. It was, how to see Rue Barrée. She was somewhere or other in that big house with the iron balconies, and the door was locked, but what of that? The simple idea struck him to shout until she came. This idea was replaced by another equally lucid—to hammer on the door until she came; but finally rejecting both of these as too uncertain, he decided to climb into the balcony, and opening a window politely enquire for Rue Barrée. There was but one lighted window in the house that he could see. It was on the second floor, and toward this he cast his eyes. Then mounting the wooden barrier and clambering over the piles of stones, he reached the sidewalk and looked up at the façade for a foothold. It seemed impossible. But a sudden fury seized him, a blind, drunken obstinacy, and the blood rushed to his head, leaping, beating in his ears like the dull thunder of an ocean. He set his teeth, and springing at a window-sill, dragged himself up and hung to the iron bars. Then reason fled; there surged in his brain the sound of many voices, his heart leaped up beating a mad tattoo, and gripping at cornice and ledge he worked his way along the facade, clung to pipes and shutters, and dragged himself up, over and into the balcony by the lighted window. His hat fell off and rolled against the pane. For a moment he leaned breathless against the railing—then the window was slowly opened from within.

They stared at each other for some time. Presently the girl took two un-steady steps back into the room. He saw her face—all crimsoned now—he saw her sink into a chair by the lamplit table, and without a word he followed her into the room, closing the big door-like panes behind him. Then they looked at each other in silence.

The room was small and white; everything was white about it—the curtained bed, the little wash-stand in the corner, the bare walls, the china lamp, and his own face—had he known it—but the face and neck of Rue were surging in the color that dyed the blossoming rose-tree there on the hearth beside her. It did not occur to him to speak. She seemed not to expect it. His mind was struggling with the impressions of the room. The whiteness, the extreme purity of everything occupied him—began to trouble him. As his eye became accustomed to the light, other objects grew from the surroundings and took their places in the circle of lamplight. There was a piano and a coal-scuttle and a little iron trunk and a bath-tub. Then there was a row of wooden pegs against the door, with a white chintz curtain covering the clothes underneath. On the bed lay an umbrella and a big straw hat, and on the table, a music-roll unfurled, an inkstand, and sheets of ruled paper. Behind him stood a wardrobe faced with a mirror, but somehow he did not care to see his own face just then. He was sobering.

The girl sat looking at him without a word. Her face was expressionless, yet the lips at times trembled almost imperceptibly. Her eyes, so wonderfully blue in the daylight, seemed dark and soft as velvet, and the color on her neck deepened and whitened with every breath. She seemed smaller and more slender than when he had seen her in the street, and there was now something in the curve of her cheek almost infantine. When at last he turned and caught his own reflection in the mirror behind him, a shock passed through him as though he had seen a shameful thing, and his clouded mind and his clouded thoughts grew clearer. For a moment their eyes met, then his sought the floor, his lips tightened, and the struggle within him bowed his head and strained every nerve to the breaking. And now it was over, for the voice within had spoken. He listened, dully interested but already knowing the end—indeed it little mattered—the end would always be the same for him—he understood now—always the same for him, and he listened, dully interested, to a voice which grew within him. After a while he stood up, and she rose at once, one small hand resting on the table. Presently he opened the window, picked up his hat, and shut it again. Then he went over to the rosebush and touched the blossoms with his face. One was standing in a glass of water on the table and mechanically the girl drew it out, pressed it with her lips and laid it on the table beside him. He took it without a word and crossing the room, opened the door. The landing was dark and silent, but the girl lifted the lamp and gliding past him slipped down the polished stairs to the hallway. Then unchaining the bolts, she drew open the iron wicket.

Through this he passed with his rose.

FROM
THE MAKER OF MOONS

ROBERT W. CHAMBERS

IN THE NAME OF THE MOST HIGH

I.

"Il n'est pas nécessaire qu'il y ait de l'amour dans un livre pour nous charmer, mais il est nécessaire qu'il y ait beaucoup de tendresse."

J. JOUBERT.

On the third day toward noon the fire slackened; the smoke from the four batteries on the bluff across the north fork of the river slowly lifted, drifting to the east. The Texas riflemen kept up a pattering fusilade until one o'clock, then their bugles rang "Cease firing," and the echoes of the last sulky shot died out against the cliffs.

Keenan, crouching behind one of his hot guns, could see the Texas sharp-shooters retiring to the bluff, little grey shadows in the scrub-oak thicket gliding, flitting like wild hedge-birds toward the nest of cannon above.

"Don't let 'em get away like that!" shouted Douglas, "give it to them in the name of God!"

And Keenan smiled, and sent the Texans a messenger in the name of God—a messenger which fell thundering from the sky above them, crushing the face of the iron-stained cliff and the lives of those who had clustered there to breathe a little.

"Amen," said Keenan, patting his gun.

Douglas crawled out of a hole in the rocks and drew himself up to the edge of the breastworks. Cleymore emerged from a shallow rifle-pit and walked slowly along the intrenchments, motioning his men back into their burrows.

"Because," he said, "a hole in the hill is worth two in your head—get into that ditch, Morris!—Cunningham, if you don't duck that red head of yours, I'll dock it!"

"Captain Cleymore," said Douglas, lowering his field-glass, "two batteries have limbered up, and are trotting toward the cemetery—"

"May they trot into it, and stay there!" said Keenan, examining the wreck of an ammunition chest in the ditch.

Cleymore studied the bluff with his marine glasses for a while, then called to Keenan: "How many guns have you now?"

"Four," shouted Keenan from the ditch; "all my horses are shot except two mules—" A burst of laughter cut him short—his own tattered artillerymen, to their credit, did not smile, but Douglas and Kellogg laughed and rows of grinning faces emerged from holes and pits along the ditch until Cleymore shouted, "Down!" and his infantry disappeared, chuckling. Keenan, red in the face, turned to his battery-men who were running the guns forward, and put his own ragged shoulder to the wheel. Cleymore sat down on a stone and watched a lank artilleryman splicing the dented staff of the battery guidon.

"I guess that'll dew, Capting," he drawled, holding the staff out to Cleymore, who took it and rubbed the polished wood with his sleeve.

"It will do, Pillsbury," he said, "where is O'Halloran?"

"Shot in the stummick," said the private, "and unable tew work."

"Dead?"

"I pre-sume likely he's daid, sir," returned Pillsbury through his nose.

"I've got a man for the guidon," called Keenan from the ditch, and a fat freckled cannoneer waddled forward and stood at attention.

"Look out!" sang out Douglas from his post on the breastworks, and "Down!" cried Cleymore, as a shell rose in the air over them and the boom of a gun rolled across the river from the bluff. The scream of the shell ceased; a white cloud shot with lightning appeared in the air above them, and a storm of shrapnel swept the breastworks. Cleymore sprang to his feet, but the fat cannoneer remained on the ground.

"Get up," said Cleymore, cautiously, "Pillsbury lift him; is he dead?"

"I guess," said Pillsbury, "he's sufferin' from a hereditary disease."

"Eh? What disease?" snapped Cleymore, stepping forward.

"I guess it's death," said Pillsbury, with an expressionless wink.

Cleymore stared at him through his eyeglasses, then turned on his heel.

"I wish," grumbled Keenan, "that the wounded would make less noise. Douglas, send them another bucket of water, will you? Is the surgeon dead?"

"Dying," said Kellogg,—"never mind, Douglas, I'll see to the water; keep your glass on their batteries; what are they doing now?"

"Nothing," replied Douglas, "wait a bit—ah! here come their sharpshooters again!"

"To hell with them!" muttered Keenan savagely, for his battery-men had been cruelly scourged by the sharpshooters, and he almost foamed with rage when he looked over into the ditch at the foot of the mound. The odour from the ditch had become frightful.

"Look down there, Captain," he called to Cleymore, his voice trembling with passion, but Cleymore only nodded sadly. He was watching something else. A figure in the uniform of a staff-officer, filthy with grime and sweat, had crawled through what was left of the covered bridge across the South Fork, and was wriggling his way toward the debris of Keenan's battery. Cleymore watched him with puckered eyes.

"What do you want, sonny?" he asked, as the staff officer crept past him,—"orders? Give 'em to me—keep to the ground, you fool," he added, as a flight of bullets swept overhead. The staff-officer lifted a flushed face, scratched and smeared with dust and sweat, and attempted a salute.

"Colonel Worth's compliments to Colonel Randal—" he began, but was interrupted by Cleymore: "Colonel Randal's in the ditch below with most of his regiment piled on top of him. What are your orders?—hold on to the bridge till hell freezes?—I thought so,—I'm Cleymore, Captain in the 10th New York Sharpshooters, yonder's what's left of us, and there's two dozen of Colonel Randal's Rhode Islanders among 'em, too. Major Wilcox has got a hole in his face, and can't speak—you see what's left of Keenan's battery—four guns, and few to serve 'em except my riflemen. Isn't General Hooker in sight?"

The staff-officer raised his blue eyes to the wreck of the battery, and then looked questioningly at Cleymore. The latter lay moodily twisting and untwisting the stained leather thong whipped about his sword hilt.

"I'm ranking officer here," he said, "the rest are dead. My compliments to General Kempner, and tell him his orders shall be obeyed. Both bridges are mined. Murphy is watching for Longstreet—What are you shivering for?"

"Ague," said the staff-officer in a low voice.

Cleymore spat out a mouthful of dust that a bullet had flung in his face, and wiped his glasses on his sleeve. "Who are you from, anyway?" he demanded. "I don't take orders from Colonel Worth."

"General Kempner is dead," said the staff-officer simply.

Keenan came up chewing a twig and whistling.

"Captain Cleymore," said the staff-officer, "my horse has been shot and Colonel Worth is waiting. Will you point out to me the quickest way back?"

"Back!" broke in Keenan, "you can't get back, my boy!"

"I must," said the youngster, without glancing at the artillery officer.

"Oh, if it's a case of must," said Cleymore indifferently, "come ahead," and he rose to his knees and peered across the swollen South Fork, now a vast torrent of mud.

Crack! Crack! rang the rifles from the opposite shore, and the little staff-officer's cap was jerked from his head and rolled down the embankment into the river. Keenan cursed.

"Come on, sonny," said Cleymore, scrambling down the embankment to the ditch. The ditch was choked with mangled bodies in blue, flung one over the other amid smashed gun-wheels, caissons, knapsacks, and rifles; and the staff-officer hesitated for an instant at the brink.

"Jump!" called Cleymore, "here! Get down behind this rock and keep your nose out of sight; those Texas gentlemen waste few bullets; are you hit?"

"No," said the little staff-officer.

"Bull luck; did you see Randal's men? The shells did it—look there."

He pointed the length of the ditch. The staff-officer turned pale. Everywhere corpses,—mere heaps of blue rags, stained yellow by dust and black with stiff blood, everywhere dented canteens, twisted muskets, unsavory scattered clothing, worn shoes, and shrunken blue caps. A big black horse, bloated and dusty lay with both hind legs stark in the air; under him were dead men, mostly Keenan's, by the red stripes on the faded trousers.

Cleymore pulled his short blond moustache and turned to the staff-officer.

"You see that slaughter pen," he said; "tell Colonel Worth."

The staff-officer felt for his cap, remembered it had been shot off his head, and looked gravely at Cleymore.

"I have four guns and two hundred and twenty odd men," said the latter; "if they bring back their batteries, an hour or two will see us all in the ditch below with Randal; if they don't we can hold on to the South Fork bridge I fancy. Do you know why they withdrew their batteries?"

"No,—unless it was to shell Colonel Worth's cavalry. His men are in the woods behind the railroad. If you can hold the bridge until night they will keep the line open. Colonel Worth is waiting. I must go back now, Captain."

Cleymore leaned along the edge of the protecting ledge and handed his field-glasses to the boy.

"Now," he said, "you can see the bend in the river. There are three pines on the bank above—see?"

"Yes."

"Take the foot-path by those pines until you come to a burnt barn. Follow the river after that and if the iron bridge isn't blown up yet you can get across; if it is blown up you can't join Colonel Worth."

"But—a—a boat—"

"A boat in that?"

They looked at the foaming torrent, thundering among the rocks. After a moment the staff-officer pointed to the shot-torn bridge below them.

"Oh," said Cleymore, "you came that way, didn't you? Well, miracles happen, and that was one of them, but if you try to get back that way, the performance won't be encored, and you can bet your curly head on that, my son."

"It's the shortest way," said the little staff-officer.

"Yes, the shortest way to Kingdom come," said Cleymore, disgusted; "if you're not shot, the Texans will catch you."

They were crouching on the hot dried grass, side by side. The sweat poured down Cleymore's forehead washing the powder grime into thick patches over his young face. He threw his blackened jacket open at the throat, rubbed his forehead with his sleeve and said, "Whew!"

"It's the shortest way," repeated the other, rising to his knees.

"You can't go," said Cleymore, sharply, "the bridge is mined and Murphy may blow it up any moment."

The youth handed back the field-glass with a smile. For a moment their eyes met, then Cleymore's flushed face turned a bright crimson and he caught his breath, murmuring "I'm blest!"

"Captain Cleymore," said the staff-officer coolly, "you are detaining me from my duty. Have I your permission to leave?"

They eyed each other steadily.

"You must not go," said Cleymore in a curious, husky voice, "let me send a man—"

"Have I your leave?"

"Come back," cried Cleymore, "I won't give it!"—but the youngster sprang to his feet, touched his curly head in quick salute, and started on a run toward the covered bridge, holding his sabre close to his thigh.

"Drop!" shouted Cleymore, and began to swear under his breath, but the youngster ran on, and to Cleymore's amazement, the rifles of the fierce Texans on the other side of the river were silent.

On and still on ran the boy, until, with a sigh of astonishment and relief, Cleymore saw him push in among the handful of blue-clad engineers at the end of the bridge; but he went no further, for they stopped him with levelled bayonets, shaking their heads and gesticulating, and suddenly Cleymore noticed that the bridge was afire at the further end.

"Murphy's fired the bridge!" he called out to Kellogg on the plateau above.

Kellogg's head appeared over a shattered gun limber. "Then Longstreet's coming, you bet!"

"I suppose so, can't you see anything? Call Douglas."

The Texas rifles cracked again. Kellogg did not answer. "Can't you see any movement near the woods?" demanded Cleymore from his rock. Then he looked carefully at Kellogg's head, appearing to rest between two bits of sod, and he saw, in the middle of the forehead, a round dark spot from which a darker line crept slowly down over the nose.

After a second or two he turned from the dead eyes staring fixedly at him, and looked across the river where the rifles were spitting death. The round white blotches of smoke hung along the river bank like shreds of cotton floating. Then he glanced toward the bridge again. There was a commotion there; a group of excited soldiers around a slender figure, bareheaded, gesticulating.

"What's that hop o' my thumb up to now?" he muttered excitedly, and raised his field-glass.

"By Jingo! Trying to cross the bridge, and it's afire!"

For a moment he knelt, his eye glued to the field-glasses, then with an angry exclamation he turned toward the floating rifle-smoke along the opposite bank. The chances were that he'd be hit, and he knew it, but he only muttered pettishly; "Young fool," and started, stooping low, toward the swaying knot of men at the bridge.

The chances were ten to one that he'd be hit, and he was, but he only straightened up and ran on. The minié-balls came whining about his head, the blood ran down into his boot, and filled it so that he slopped as he ran. And after all he was too late, for, as he panted up to the bridge, far down the covered way he saw the youngster speeding over the smoking rafters.

"Stop him!" he gasped.

A soldier raised his rifle, but Cleymore jerked it down.

"Not that way," he said, leaning back on his sword.

Along the dry timbered tunnel crept the boy, for the fire was all about him now. Once he fell but rose again.

"Has the mine been fired—the powder trail?" asked Cleymore, in a dull voice.

A soldier nodded and opened his mouth to speak, but a deafening roar drowned his voice and gave Cleymore his answer.

"Is that all?" asked Cleymore again, as the smoke rushed skyward, and the ground trembled and cracked beneath them.

"One more," said a sergeant curtly, as Captain Murphy hurried up. The whole further section of the bridge had crumbled into the torrent below. The smoke swept through the tunnel, and when it lifted Cleymore caught a glimpse of a figure dragging itself back from the gulf ahead. The soldiers saw it too.

"He *would* go," said one of them, as though speaking to himself.

Cleymore tore off his jacket and held it before his face.

"You can't do it!" cried Murphy, horrified.

"Let go—I must," said Cleymore quietly, "cut the match, if you can."

"The other mines are on fire! In the name of God, Cleymore!" urged the engineer officer, holding him back by both shoulders.

"Damn you, Murphy, let me go!" cried Cleymore fiercely; "let go, I say."

"I will not, Cleymore; we can't lose you for a fool of a boy—"

"But it's a woman!" roared Cleymore, wrenching himself free.

II.

As he ran through the smoke-choked bridge, bright little flames shot from the crackling timbers, and he felt the hot breath of the furnace underneath. And all the time he kept repeating as he ran, "I'm a fool, I'm a fool, it's all up now"; but he hurried on, shielding his face with his braided jacket, feeling his way through the flurries of smoke and sparks until a whirl of flame blocked his way; and on the edge of the burning depths he found what he was looking for.

She was very slender and light, in her ragged uniform, and he lifted her and wrapped his jacket about her head. Then he started back, increasing his speed as the black smoke rolled up from the planks under foot, but it was easier than he had dared dream of, for she revived, and when Murphy loomed up in the gloom, and steadied them with an arm, he laughed aloud from sheer nervousness. Then a terrific explosion threw him on his face, but Murphy helped him up, and he seized his burden again and staggered toward the hill where Keenan's guns were already thundering, and the crack—crack—crackle of rifles echoed and re-echoed from rock to cliff.

"You're hit," said Douglas, as he entered the entrenchment.

"I know it," said Cleymore, hastily scanning the rifle-pits, "keep the men under cover, Douglas—what's up? Wait, I'll be there in a second. Here, Pillsbury, take this wo—this officer to my burrow and stay there until I come!"

Douglas, lying close to the top of the breastworks, glasses levelled, began to speak in a monotonous voice: "The two batteries have returned and are unlimbering to the west; they seem to have cavalry too; a heavy column is moving parallel to the railroad—infantry and ammunition convoy; more infantry coming through the cemetery; I can see more on the hill beyond; the batteries have unlimbered—look out!"

"Down!" shouted Cleymore, but the shells sailed high overhead and plunged into the muddy torrent of the South Fork.

"Keenan," he called, "do you want volunteers?"

"Not yet—damn the Texans!" bawled Keenan through the increasing din.

Douglas began, "Cleymore, they are—" and fell over stone dead.

Cleymore heard the minié-balls' thud! thud! as they struck the dead body, half flung across the breastwork, and Keenan, maddened by the bullets which searched his dwindling files, bellowed hoarsely, as one by one his guns flashed and roared, "Now! In the name of God, lads, to hell with them!"

Like red devils in the pit the cannoneers worked at their guns, looming through the infernal smoke pall stripped to their waists. Keenan, soaked with sweat and black from eyes to ankle, raged like a fiend from squad to squad while his guns crashed and the whole hill vomited flame.

Thicker and blacker rolled the smoke from the battery emplacement, until it shrouded the hill. Then out of the darkness reeled Keenan howling for volunteers and weeping over the loss of another gun.

"Three left?" motioned Cleymore faintly with his lips.

"Three! Number four dismounted and all killed; send me some of your infantry!" and the artilleryman plunged into the blazing furnace again. Below them the grass and abatis caught fire and the smarting smoke of green wood almost blinded Cleymore. Murphy and his engineers were at work among the crackling logs, but after a while the dull blows of their axes died away and Cleymore knew they were dead.

"More men for the guns!" roared Keenan from the darkness, and a dozen Rhode Islanders tumbled out of their burrows and groped their way into the battery. In another moment Keenan came staggering out again, gasping like a fish and waving his arms blindly.

"They've got another gun, Cleymore,—only two now,—more men for the guns "

Cleymore, half fainting from the loss of blood, motioned to his men for volunteers; and they came, cheering for old New York, and vanished, engulfed in the battery smoke.

The hill was swept by fierce cyclones of lead; bullets flew in streams, whistling, hurtling among the rocks, rebounding into the rifle-pits, carrying death to those below. Great shells tore through the clouds, bursting and shattering the cliff overhead. A whirlwind of flame from the burning bridge swept over the hillside, hiding the river and the heights opposite, and the burning abatis belched smoke and torrents of sparks. Cleymore sat down near the burrow, and picked the bits of cloth from the long tear which the bullet had made in his flesh above the knee. The last of the engineer company came toiling up from the railroad bridge, and the lieutenant nodded to his question, "Yes, the bridge is blown out of the water. Where can I put my men in, Captain?"

Cleymore pointed to the pits, and they went into them, cheering shrilly. A moment later a shell fell into one of the crowded pits and exploded, throwing out a column of sand and bodies torn limb from limb. Only one gun was firing now from Keenan's battery, but from that one gun the lightning sped continuously, fed by a constantly renewed stream of volunteers. Cleymore, watching Keenan, thought that he had really gone mad. Perhaps he had, and perhaps that is why Heaven directed a bullet to his brain, before the loss of his last gun should kill him with grief. Then a shell smashed up the muzzle of the last gun, and the remnants of the servants dragged themselves away to lie panting like hounds on the scorched earth, or die inch by inch from some gaping wound.

"The jig is up," said Cleymore aloud to himself.

For a quarter of an hour the enemy's guns rained shells into the extinct crater—the tomb of Keenan and his cannon. Then, understanding that Keenan had been silenced forever, their fire died out, and Cleymore could hear bugles blowing clearly in the distance.

He staggered to his feet and called to his men, but of the 10th New York Rifles, only thirty came stumbling from the pits. Pillsbury also answered the call, sauntering unconcernedly from the burrow whither he had carried Cleymore's charge.

All around them the wounded were shrieking for water, and Cleymore aided his men to carry them to the spring which flowed sparkling from the rocks above. It was out of the question to remove them,—it was useless to think of burying the dead. The three days' struggle for the hill had ended, and now all the living would have to leave,—all except one.

"Pillsbury," said Cleymore, "take my men, and strike for the turnpike due north. I can't walk—I am too weak yet, but you have time to get out. March!"

The men refused, and Pillsbury called for a litter of rifles, but a volley whistled in among them and they reeled.

"Save thet there flag!" shouted Pillsbury, "I've got the guidon!"

Cleymore lay on the ground motionless, and when they lifted him his head fell back.

"Daid," said Pillsbury, soberly, "poor cuss!"

A rifleman threw his jacket over Cleymore's face, and started running down the hill to where the colour-guard was closing around a bundle of flags, black and almost dropping from the staffs.

"Save the colours!" they cried, and staggered on toward the north.

III.

It may have been thirst, it may have been the groans of the wounded that roused Cleymore. He was lying close by the rivulet that ran from the rock spring, and he plunged hands and head into it and soaked his fill.

The wound on his leg had stiffened, but to his surprise he found it neatly dressed and bandaged. Had aid arrived?

"Hello!" he called.

The deep sigh of a dying man was his only answer. He hardly dared to look around. The air was stifling with the scent of blood and powder and filthy clothing, and he rose painfully to his feet and tottered into the cool burrow among the rocks.

His blanket and flask lay there, but before he raised the flask to his lips he lifted the corner of the blanket nervously. Underneath stood a small oblong box, into which was screwed an electric button. Two insulated wires entered the ground directly in front of the box, which was marked in black letters, "Watson's Excelsior Soap."

Cleymore replaced the blanket, swallowed a mouthful of whiskey and lay down, utterly exhausted. It was late in the afternoon when he awoke from the pain in his leg, but somebody had bandaged it again while he slept, and he was able to move out into the intrenchments. Most of the wounded were dead—the rest were dying in silence. He did what he could for Cunningham who joked feebly and watched Morris with quiet eyes. Morris died first, and Cunningham, hearing the death-rattle in his comrade's throat, murmured: "Phin he lived he bate me, but oi'll give him a race to the Saints fur his money! Is Dick Morris dead now?"

"Dead," said Cleymore.

"Thin, good-bye, Captain dear," whispered Cunningham.

At first Cleymore thought he was sleeping.

The evening fell over the hilltop, and the last of the wounded shivered and died with drawn face upturned to the driving clouds. Cleymore covered the boy's face—he was scarcely sixteen—and sat down with his back against a rock.

The wreck of Keenan's battery rose before him in the twilight, stark and mute, silhouetted against the western horizon. Lights began to sparkle along the opposite river bank, and now, from the heights, torches swung in semi-circles signalling victory for the army of the South, death and disaster to the North. Far away over the wooded hills dull sounds came floating on the breeze, the distant rhythmic cadence of volley firing. There were fires too, faint flares of light on the horizon where Thomas was "standing like a rock." On a nearer slope a house and barn were burning, lighting up the stumps and rocks in the clearing, and casting strange shadows over the black woods. In the gathering twilight someone came down the cliffs at his back, treading carefully among the shellsplit fragments, and Cleymore saw it was the little staff-officer. She did not see him until he called her.

"I want to thank you for dressing that scratch of mine," he said, rising.

"You are very welcome," she said, "is it better?"

"Yes—and you?"

"You saved my life," she said.

"But are you burnt—you must have been—"

"No—only stifled. Are the wounded alive? I did what I could."

"They are dead," said Cleymore. She unhooked her sabre, and sat down beside him looking off over the valley.

After a silence he said: "I suppose you are one of our spies—I have heard of the women spies, and I once saw Belle Boyd. How did you happen to take the place of an aide-de-camp?"

"Am I to tell all my secrets to an infantry captain?" she said, with a trace of a smile in her blue eyes.

"Oh, I suppose not," he answered, and relapsed into silence.

Presently she drew a bit of bacon and hard-tack from her pouch and quietly divided it. They both drank from the rivulet after the meal was finished. She brushed the water from her lips with a sun-tanned hand, and looking straight at Cleymore, said: "The hill below the abatis is mined, is it not?"

"Now, really," said Cleymore, "am I to tell all my secrets to a girl spy?" She stared at him for a moment, and then smiled.

"I know it already," she said.

"Oh," said Cleymore, "and do you know where the wires are buttoned?"

"Wires?" she exclaimed.

"Of course. Be thankful that poor Murphy's mines at the bridge were old-fashioned. If there had been wires there, you would not be sitting here."

"And you have stayed to fire this mine?" she said at length.

"Yes."

"The bridges are gone, and the river is impassable. It will be days before Longstreet's men can cross."

"I know it," said Cleymore, "but when they come, I'll be here—and so will the mine."

The spy dropped her clasped hands into her lap.

"I'll blow them to hell!" said Cleymore savagely, glaring at the silent dead around him. Then he begged her pardon for forgetting himself, and leaned against the rock to adjust his eyeglasses.

"That would be useless butchery," said the girl, earnestly.

"That will do," said Cleymore, in a quiet voice.

The girl shrank away as though she had been struck. Cleymore noticed it, and said: "If you are a Government spy, you are subject to army regulations. I would rather treat you as a woman, but I cannot while you wear that uniform or hold a commission. How, in Heaven's name, did you come to enter the service? You can't be eighteen—you are of gentle breeding?"

"I am a spy!" she exclaimed, "and I thank God, and I hate the enemies of my country!"

"Amen," said Cleymore, wondering at her fierce outburst.

"Do you not hate the Confederates?" she demanded.

"No," he answered, gravely, "but I hate the rebellion."

"But you must hate your enemies; I do."

"I don't; it makes me sick to see them go down—splendid fellows,— Americans, and to think that such troops might have stood shoulder to shoulder with our own, under the same flag, against the world!—aye, against ten worlds! I hate the rebels? By Heaven, no! Think of Thomas and Grant and Lee and Jackson leading a united army against those thieving French in Mexico! Think of Sherman and Sheridan and Johnston and Stuart facing the fat-brained treachery of England! I tell you I respect the rebels. Look at that heap of dead! Look at those smashed guns! Look at me—the defeated commander, crouching in this slaughter pen, waiting to spring a mine—and die. The men who reduced me to this have my respect as soldiers and my love and admiration as Americans, but if I could blow them all to the four winds by one touch of an electric button, I'd do it, and bless the chance!" The girl trembled at his fervour.

"That is a strange creed," she murmured.

"Creed? The Union, in the Name of God—that's my creed!"

IV.

The next day it rained. The rebel batteries flung a dozen shells among Keenan's ruined guns, but, receiving no answer, ceased firing. Cleymore was stiff and ill, but he managed to reach the intrenchment and rest his field-glasses against a rock. The four batteries were in motion, filing along the river bank toward the cemetery where a flag drooped above a marquee, the headquarters of some general. The Texan Riflemen were moving about the scrub-oak, showing themselves fearlessly, and a battalion of engineers was hard at work on the smouldering piers of the bridge. Dark masses of troops appeared on the distant hillsides as far as the eye could reach, and along the railroad track cavalry were riding through the rain.

All day long Cleymore watched the rebel army, and at night he shared his hard-tack and bacon with the girl. They spoke very little to each other, but when Cleymore was looking at the rebels her eyes never left him. Once, when he crept into his cave to swallow a drop of brandy, she hurried from rifle-pit to rifle-pit, evidently searching for something, but when again he reappeared she was seated listlessly against the rocky wall, her blond head buried in her hands. And that night too, when he was tossing in feverish slumber, she passed like a shadow through the intrenchment, over rocks, down among the dead in the hollows, her lantern shining on distorted faces and clenched hands.

The next day the rain still fell; the engineers were steadily at work on the ruined bridge, but the river had swollen enormously, and Cleymore could not see that they had progressed. He went back to his cave and dropped on the blanket, the box marked "Watson's Excelsior Soap" at his side. The girl brought him a bit of hard-tack and a cup of water. It was the last crumb left in the camp, except three biscuits which she had in her own pockets. She did not tell him so.

Toward midnight he fell asleep, and when she saw that he slept, she bent over him and looked into his face, lighting a match. Then she softly raised the blanket and saw his arm encircling a box marked "Watson's Excelsior Soap." As she stooped to touch the wires he stirred in his sleep and smiled, and she shrank away, covering her eyes with her hands. The next day she brought Cleymore his biscuit and cup of water, for his strength was ebbing, and he could scarcely crawl to the breastworks. She ate nothing herself. The engineers were progressing a little, the sun shone on the wasted hills, and the music of a Confederate band came in gusts across the river from the cemetery.

"They are playing 'Dixie,'" said the girl; but Cleymore only sighed and pulled the dirty blanket over his face. The next day she brought him his biscuit, there was but one left now, and he, not knowing, asked for another, and she gave him the last.

About noon he called to her, and she helped him to the breastworks and held his field-glasses. The engineers had made alarming progress, for the river was falling rapidly.

"They'll be over to-morrow," he said.

When he was lying in his blanket once more, he beckoned her to come close beside him.

"Are you ill?" he asked.

She shook her head.

"You are so white and frail—I thought you might be ill."

"Oh, no," she said.

"Have you plenty to eat?"

"Plenty."

"When are you going?"

"Going?" she faltered.

"You must go, of course," he said, querulously, "they will be over the river to-morrow."

"And you?" said the girl.

"It's my business to stay here."

"And—fire the mine?"

"And fire the mine," he repeated.

"What is the use? They will enter all the same."

"Not all of them," said Cleymore, grimly.

"No—not all of them—a hundred half-starved young fellows will be mangled—a hundred mothers will be childless—but what matter, Captain Cleymore?"

"What matter," he repeated,—"my orders are to defend this hill until hell freezes over, and I am going to do it." Then, again, he wearily asked pardon for his words.

Toward evening she saw he was sleeping; his eye-glasses had fallen beside him on the blanket. Almost timidly she picked them up, held them a moment, then bent her head and touched them with her lips.

The morning broke in a burst of splendid sunlight. Over the river the rebel bands were playing when Cleymore's hot eyes unclosed, but he could not rise from his blanket.

The girl brought him a cup of water and held it while he drank.

"There are no more biscuits," she said.

"I shall not need them," he murmured, "what are the rebels doing?"

"They are massing to cross. The bridge is almost ready."

"And I'm ready," he said, "good-bye."

The girl knelt beside him and took both of his hands in hers. "I am not going," she said.

"I order you," he muttered.

"I refuse," she answered gently.

A hectic flush touched the hollows under his eyes and he raised his head. "I order you to leave these works," he said angrily.

"And I refuse," she repeated gently.

A burst of music from the river bank came up to them as their eyes met in mute conflict. Cleymore's hand instinctively felt for the button and the wires, then he gave a great cry and sat up among his rags, and the girl rose slowly to her feet beside him.

"Traitor!" he gasped, and pointed at her with shaking hands.

She turned perfectly white for a moment, then a wan smile touched her lips, and she quietly drew a revolver from her jacket.

"I am not a traitor," she said, "I am a Confederate spy, and I cut those wires last night. You are my prisoner, Captain Cleymore."

The silence was broken by the noise from the bands, now massing about the further end of the completed bridge. Cleymore bent silently over the ruined wires, touched the button, then, turning savagely, whipped his revolver to his head and pulled the trigger. The hammer struck an empty cylinder, and he flung it from him with a sob.

In an instant the girl was on her knees beside him, raised him in her arms, holding his head on her shoulder.

"Is it so hard to surrender to a woman?" she asked, "see, I give you my revolver—here—now shoot me down at your feet! I cut those wires! Shoot fearlessly—Ah, do you think I care for my life?"

Cleymore raised his head a little.

"I surrender," he sighed, and fainted.

Then there came a great sound of cheering from below, the drums rattled, and the music of the bugles swelled nearer and nearer, until a crash of eager feet sounded among the branches of the abatis and a figure clad in grey leaped upon the breastworks and drove the steel point of a standard into the gravel.

"In the name of God!" he shouted in a voice choked with emotion.

"Let him pray," muttered the dusty veterans of Longstreet's infantry as they wheeled into the parallels, "he's one of Jackson's men."

And all these things were done in the Name of the Most High.

THE BOY'S SISTER

"Le plus grand tort de la plupart des maris envers leurs femmes, c'est de les avoir épousées."

"Je ne me sens jamais plus seul que lorsque je livre mon coeur à quelque ami."

MAUPASSANT.

I.

Garland's profession took him to Ten Pin Corners. His profession was to collect butterflies for the Natural History Museum of New York. "Uncle Billy," who kept the Constitution Hotel at Ten Pin Corners, thought "bug huntin'" was a "dampoor bizness, even fur a dood,"—and perhaps it was—but that is none of your business or mine. Garland lived at the Constitution Hotel. The hotel did small honour to its name, in fact it would have ruined any other constitution. It was ruining Garland's by degrees, but a man of twenty-five doesn't notice such things. So Garland swallowed his saleratus biscuits and bolted pork and beans, and was very glad that he was alive.

He had met the male population of Ten Pin Corners over the bar at the Constitution Hotel,—it being a temperance state—and there he had listened to their views on all that makes life worth living.

He tried to love his fellow-countrymen. When Orrin Hayes spat upon the stove and denounced woman's suffrage—when Cy Pettingil, whose wife was obliged to sign his name for him, agreed profanely—when the Hon. Hanford Perkins, A. P. A., demonstrated the wickedness of Catholicism, and proffered vague menaces against Rome, Garland conscientiously repressed a shudder.

"They are my countrymen, God bless 'em," he thought, smiling upon the free-born.

Uncle Billy's felonious traffic in the "j'yfull juice," did not prevent his attendance at town meeting, nor his enthusiastic voice against local option.

"I ain't no dum fool," he observed to Garland, "let the wimmen hey their way."

"But don't you think," suggested Garland, "that a liberal law would be better?”

“Naw,” replied Uncle Billy.

“But don’t you think even a poor law should be observed until wise legislation can find a remedy?”

“Naw,” said Uncle Billy, and closed the subject.

Sometimes Uncle Billy would come out on the verandah where Garland was sitting in the sun, fussing over some captured caterpillar. His invariable salute was, “More bugs? Gosh!” Once he brought Garland a cockroach, and suggested the bar-room as a new and interesting collecting ground, but Garland explained that his business did not include such augean projects, and the thrifty old man was baffled.

“What’s them bugs good fur?” he demanded at length. Garland explained, but Uncle Billy never got over the impression that Garland’s real business was the advertising of Persian Powder. Most of the prominent citizens of Ten Pin Corners came to Garland to engage his services as potato-beetle exterminator, measuring-worm destroyer, and general annihilator of mosquitos, and to each in turn he carefully explained what his profession was.

They were skeptical—sometimes sarcastic. One thing, however, puzzled them; he had never been known to try to sell anybody Persian Powder, for, possessed with the idea that he was some new species of drummer, they found this difficult to reconcile with their suspicions.

“Bin a-buggin’, haint ye?” was the usual salute from the free-born whom he met in the fields; and when Garland smiled and nodded, the free-born would expectorate and chuckle, “Oh, yew air slick, Mister Garland, yew’re more ‘n a Yankee than I be.”

Ten Pin Corners was built along both sides of the road; the Constitution Hotel stood at one extremity of the main street, the Post Office at the other. Garland once asked why the place was called Ten Pin Corners, and Uncle Billy told him a lie about its having been named from his, Uncle Billy’s, palatial ten pin alley.

“Then why not Ten Pin Alley?” asked Garland.

“Cuz it ain’t no alley,” sniffed Uncle Billy.

“But,” persisted Garland, “why Corners?”

“Becuz there haint no corners,” said Uncle Billy evasively, and retired to his bar, thirsty and irritated. “Asks enough damfool que-estions t’ set a man crazy,” he confided to the Hon. Hanford Perkins; “I’ve hed drummers an’ drummers at the Constitooshun, but I h’aint seen nothin’ tew beat him.”

The Hon. Hanford Perkins looked at Uncle Billy and spat gravely upon the stove, and Uncle Billy spat also, to put himself on an equality with the Hon. Hanford Perkins.

Concerning the mendacity of Uncle Billy there could be no question. Ten Pin Corners had been originally Ten Pines Corners. Half a mile from the terminus of the main street stood a low stone house. It was included in the paternal government of Ten Pin Corners, and it was from this house, surrounded by ten gigantic pines, and from the four cross-roads behind it, now long disused and overgrown with grass and fireweed, that the village name degenerated from Ten Pines to Ten Pin.

Thither Garland was wont to go in the evenings, for the pines were the trysting places of moths—grey moths with pink and black under wings, brown moths with gaudy orange under wings, rusty red moths flecked with silver, nankeen yellow moths, the product of the measuring-worm, big fluffy moths, little busy moths, and moths that you and I know nothing about. The sap from the pines attracted some of these creatures, the lily garden in front of the stone house attracted others, and the whole combination attracted Garland. Also there lived in the stone house a boy's sister.

One afternoon when Uncle Billy's continued expectoration and Cy Pettingil's profanity had driven Garland from the hotel, he wandered down into a fragrant meadow, butterfly net in one hand, trout rod in the other, and pockets stuffed with cyanide jar, fly-book, sandwiches, and *Wilson on Hybrids*.

The stream was narrow and deep, for the most part flowing silently between level banks fragrant with mint and scented grass; but here and there a small moss-grown dam choked the current into a deeper pool below, into which poured musical waterfalls.

There were trout there, yellow, speckled, and greedy, but devious in their ways, and uncertain as April mornings. There were also frogs there, solemn green ones that snapped at the artificial flies and came out of the water with slim limbs outstretched and belly glistening.

"It's like pulling up some nude dwarf, when they grab the fly," wrote Garland to his chief in New York, "really they look so naked and indecent." Otherwise Garland was fond of frogs; he often sat for hours watching them half afloat along the bank or squatting majestically upon some mossy throne.

That afternoon he had put on a scarlet ibis fly, and the frogs plunged and lunged after it, flopping into the pools and frightening the lurking trout until Garland was obliged to substitute a yellow fly in self defence. But the trout were coy. One great fellow leaped for the fly, missed it, leaped again to see what was wrong, and finding out, fled into the depths, waving his square tail derisively. Garland walked slowly down the brook, casting ahead into the stream, sometimes catching his fly in the rank grass, sometimes deftly defeating the larcenous manoeuvres of some fat frog, and now and then landing a plump orange-bellied trout among the perfumed mint, where it flopped until a merciful tap on the nose sent its vital spark into Nirvana and its crimson flecked body into Garland's moss-lined creel.

Once or twice he dropped his rod in the grass to net some conceited butterfly that flaunted its charms before the serious-minded clover bees, but he seldom found anything worth keeping, and the butterfly was left to pursue its giddy interrupted flight.

As he passed, walking lightly on the flowering turf, the big black crickets sang to him, the katydids scraped for him, and the grasshoppers, big and little, brown, green, and yellow, hopped out of the verdure before him, a tiny escort of outriders.

It was nearly four o'clock in the afternoon when he came to the last pool, before the meadow brook flows silently into the woods where slim black trout lurk under submerged rocks and mosquitos swoop thankfully upon the wanderer.

On the bank of the pool sat a beautiful boy watching a cork floating with the current. "Hello," said Garland, "you ought to be in school, Tip."

The boy looked at Garland through gilded tangled curls. "Can't you see I 'm fishin'?" he said in a whisper.

"I see," said Garland, "but you know your sister wouldn't allow it. Why did you stay away from school, Tip?"

The angelic eyes were lowered a moment, then the boy carefully raised his pole, and, seeing the bait intact, dropped it into the water again.

"Bill Timerson biffed me," said the child.

"If Willy Timerson struck you, you should not stay away from school," he said; "did you—er—hit him back?"

"Did I?"

"Did you?" repeated Garland, repressing a smile.

"Heu! Why, Mister Garland, I slammed that d—n mug of his—"

"Tip!" said Garland.

The boy hung his head and looked at the cork. Garland sat down beside him and lighted his pipe. After a moment he said: "Tip, I thought you promised me not to swear."

The boy was silent.

"Did you?" said Garland.

"Yes," replied the boy, sullenly.

"Well?" persisted Garland.

"I lied," said the boy.

"You forgot," said Garland, quietly, "you don't lie, Tip."

The boy looked at him shyly, then turned to his cork again.

"Tip," said Garland, "what do you think of these?" he opened his creel and Tip looked in.

"Hell!" said the child softly.

"What!" interrupted Garland.

"There!" said Tip calmly, "I lied again; lam me one in the snoot, Mister Garland."

Garland touched the boy lightly on the forehead. "You will try," he said, trying to conceal the despair in his voice.

"Yes," cried the child fervently, "I will, Mr. Garland, so help me—I mean, cross my heart!" After a moment he added, "I—I brought you a green worm—here it is—"

"Hello! A Smerinthus, eh? Much obliged, Tip; where did you get it?"

"Sister found it on the piazza,—she said mebbe you'd want it," replied the child lifting his line again; "say, Mister Garland, Squire Perkins says you're loony."

"What," laughed Garland.

"Solemn," continued the child, "he says you was onct a book agent or a drummer, but you 're loony now and can't work."

"The Hon. Hanford Perkins, Tip?" asked Garland, laughing frankly.

"Yep, ole Perkins hisself."

"To whom did he eulogize me, Tip?"

"What, sir?"

"To whom did he say this?"

"To sister—an' Celia turned her back on him; I seen it. Are you loony?"

Garland was laughing but managed to say, no.

"That's what I said," said Tip, scowling at the water, "and I said you'd kick the hel—you'd kick the stuffins outen him if he said it much more. Will you, Mr. Garland?"

"I—I don't know," said Garland, trying to control his mirth, "you mustn't say that sort of thing, you know, Tip."

"I know it," said Tip, resignedly, "I hove 'n apple through his hat though,—last night."

Then Garland explained to Tip all about the deference due to age, but so pleasantly that the child listened to every word.

"All right," he said, "I'll let the ole man be,—I was plannin' to bust a window," he continued, with a trace of regret, "but I won't!" he cried in a climax of pious resignation.

Garland watched a distant butterfly critically for a moment, then picked up his rod and creel and shook the ashes from his pipe.

"Goin' to see Cis?" inquired Tip.

"Hem! Hum! I—er—may pass by that way," replied Garland.

"You won't tell her that I smashed Bill Timerson?"

"Of course not," said Garland, "that's for you to tell her."

"I won't," said the child doggedly.

"Very well," said Garland, walking away.

Tip watched him, but he did not turn, and the child's face became troubled.

"I will tell, Mr. Garland!" he called across the meadow.

"All right, Tip," answered Garland, cheerily.

II.

Before Garland came in sight of the low stone house he caught the fragrance of the lilies. The sun glittered low on the horizon, long luminous shadows stretched over meadow and pasture, and a thin blue haze floated high among the feathery tops of the pines about the house. A white nanny-goat of tender age, tethered on the velvet turf, cried "me—h! me—h!" watching him with soft silly eyes. Except for the kid, and a Maltese cat asleep on the porch, there was no sign of life about the house. Garland turned and looked out over the pastures. A spot of greyish-pink was moving down there. He watched it for a moment, quietly refilling his pipe, then dropped his rod and net upon the turf, and threw himself on the ground beside them. From time to time he raised his eyes from the pages of *Wilson on Hybrids* to note the progress of the pink spot in the distant pasture. Wilson was most interesting on hybrids. What Wilson had to say was this: "There can be no doubt that hybrid forms of these two splendid butterflies, Nymphalis Arthemis and Nymphalis Ephestion, exist in the localities frequented by these species. In the little village of Ten Pin Corners, Professor Wormly discovered an unknown hybrid, which, unfortunately, he was unable to capture or describe."

This was what Wilson had to say on hybrids. This was what Garland thought: "I'd give fifty dollars to capture one of these hybrids;—I wonder what Celia is doing in the pasture? It may not have been a hybrid; it may only have been a variety. Celia is milking the Alderney, that's what she's doing. Still Wormly ought to know what he's about. Celia has finished milking; now it's the Jersey's turn. I should like to see a hybrid of Arthemis and—hello! Celia has finished, I fancy." Then he laid down his book and carefully retied his necktie.

When Celia arrived and placed her milk pail on the porch, Garland jumped to his feet with hypocritical surprise.

"You are milking early," he said, "did you just come from the pasture?"

The girl looked at her pail and nodded. The sunlight gilded her arms, bare to the shoulder, and glittered in a fierce halo around her burnished hair. She had her brother's soft blue eyes, fringed with dark lashes, but the beauty of her mouth was indescribable. Garland, as usual, offered to take the milk pail, and she, as usual, firmly declined.

"You never let me," he said, "I wanted to bring it up from the pasture, but I knew what you'd say."

"Then you saw me in the pasture," she asked.

"Er—er—yes," he admitted.

"I saw you too," she said, and sat down in the red sunlight under the pines.

Garland sat down also, and made an idle pass at a white butterfly with his net.

"Have you caught any new butterflies today?" she asked, bending to tie her shoestring.

"No, nothing new," he answered. She straightened up, brushed a drop or two of milk from the hem of her pink skirt, passed a slim hand over her crumpled apron, and leaned back against the tree trunk, touching her hair lightly with her fingers.

"Last night," she said, "a great green miller-moth came around the lamp. I caught him for you."

"A Luna," he said, "thank you, Celia."

"Luna," she repeated gravely, "is he rare?"

She had picked up a few phrases from Garland and used them with pretty conscientiousness.

"No," said Garland, "not very rare—but I will keep this one."

"I caught some more, too," she continued, "a yellow miller—"

"Moth, Celia."

"Miller-moth—"

"No—a moth—"

"A yellow moth," she continued serenely, "that had eyes on its wings."

"Saturnia Io," said Garland.

"Io," repeated the girl, softly, "is it rare?"

"It is rare here. I will keep it."

The Maltese cat lifted its voice and rubbed its arched back against the milk pail. Its name was Julia and Garland called it to him.

"Julia has a saucer of milk on the porch; she is only teasing," said Celia.

But Julia's voice was sustained and piercing, and Garland rose laughing and poured a few drops of warm fresh milk into the half-filled saucer. Then Julia exposed the depth of her capriciousness; she sniffed at the milk, walked around it twice, touched the saucer playfully, patted a stray leaf with velvet paw, and then suddenly pretending that she was in danger of instant annihilation from some impending calamity, pranced into the middle of the lawn, crooked her tail, rushed half way up a tree-trunk, slid back, and finally charged on the tethered kid with swollen tail and ears flattened.

Garland went back to his seat on the turf. "It is the way of the world," he said gaily.

Celia picked up a pine cone and sniffed daintily at the dried apex.

"Julia was not hungry; she only wanted attention," he added.

"Some people are hungry for attention too,—and never get it," said Celia.

Garland knew what she meant. It was common gossip among the free-born who congregated about the saliva stricken stove at Uncle Billy's or sat on musty barrels in the Post Office store.

"But," said Garland, "you do not want *his* attention,—now."

"No," she said indifferently, "I do not want it now,—it is too late."

"Then don't let's think about it," said Garland quickly.

"Think! think!" she answered without impatience, "what else can I do?"

"And you think of him?" he asked.

"No, not of him, but of his injustice," she said quietly.

They had talked sometimes on the subject—he never knew just how it came about. Perhaps his interest in Tip had moved her to the confidence, if it could be called a confidence, for all the free-born were unbidden participants in the secret. The story was commonplace enough. When Celia was sixteen, four years back, she lived with an elect uncle in the manufacturing town of Highfield, forty miles down the river. One day a road company with more repertoire than cash, stranded at Bowles' Opera House and drifted back by highway and byway toward Boston. One member of the company, however, did not drift back. His name was Clarence Minster and he said he had found salvation, which was true in one sense, for Celia's elect uncle clawed him into the fold and having cleansed his soul, gave him a job to cleanse the stable at very few dollars a month. Celia was young and simple and pitiful. She also possessed five hundred dollars of her own. So Clarence Minster first ran away with her and then with most of her five hundred dollars. Unfortunately the marriage was legal, and the uncle implacable, so Celia took her brother Tip in one hand, and a thinned-out pocket-book in the other, and went to her dead parent's home, the stone house at Ten Pin Corners. She sometimes heard of Minster, never from him. He had struck the public taste as "Dick Willard," the hero of the lachrymose melodrama, "Honour," and his photographs were occasionally seen in Highfield store windows.

This was Celia's story—part of it. The other part began as she began to listen to Garland, and to bring him delicate winged moths that sought her chamber lamp as she bent over Tip's patched clothes. Something also was beginning for Garland; he felt it growing as he moved among the lilies in the dusk while Celia held the bullseye lantern, and the great sphinx moths hovered over the pinks. He felt it in the crystal clear mornings when sleepy butterflies clung to the late lilacs, and Celia moved far afield through raspberries and yellow buttercups. He felt it now, as he lay beside her among level shadows and gilt-tipped verdure—he felt it and wondered whether it was love. Perhaps Celia could have told him, I don't know, but it was plain enough to the tethered kid and the Maltese cat, to the drifting swallows, and the orioles in the linden tree besides the well-sweep. It was simple and self-evident to the Alderney, lowing at the bars, to the Jersey staring stolidly at Celia, to the robins, the hedge birds—yes, to the tireless crickets chirping from every tussock.

Now whether or not it was equally plain to Tip as he came trudging up the gravel walk, I do not know.

He said, "Hello, Cis," and came and kissed her—a thing he did not often do voluntarily. "I smashed Bill Timerson in the jaw," he continued, "and he told the teacher, and I dasn't go back." Then he glanced humbly at Garland.

Celia had tears in her eyes, and she also turned instinctively to Garland. "Speak to him, please," she said, "I can do nothing."

"Yes you can," said Tip—"you and Mr. Garland together. I've told him."

"Tip will go back to school to-morrow," said Garland, "and take his thrashing."

Tip looked doubtful.

"And," continued Garland, "as Bill Timerson is older and stronger than Tip, Tip will continue to punch him whenever assaulted."

"Oh—no!" pleaded Celia.

"Let him," said Garland, smiling. Tip threw his arms around his sister's neck and kissed her again, and she held him tightly to her milk-stained apron.

"Mr. Garland knows," she whispered, "my darling, try to be good."

III.

Garland leaned back in his chair in the dingy bar-room of the Constitution Hotel. His abstracted gaze wandered from Uncle Billy to a framed chromo on the wall, a faithful reproduction of some catchup bottles, a boiled lobster and a platter of uninviting oysters. The Hon. Hanford Perkins was speaking—he had been speaking for half an hour. For years, like Peffer, he had been telling the Government what to do, but his patience, unlike Peffer's, was exhausted, and now he had decided to let the country go to the devil. He wrote no more letters to the *Highfield Banner*, he sulked, and an ungrateful country never even knew it. At times, however, under the kindly stimulus of Uncle Billy's "j'yfull juice," he condescended to address the freeborn in the bar-room of the Constitution Hotel. He was doing it now. He had touched upon silver with the elephantine dexterity of a Populist, he had settled the tariff to the satisfaction of Ten Pin Corners, he spoke of the folly of maintaining a navy, and dismissed the army with a masterly sarcasm in which the phrase, "fuss 'n feathers" was dwelt upon. Uncle Billy, in the popular attitude of a cherub, elbows on the bar, gazed at him with undisguised admiration. Cy Pettingil, fearful that he was not on an equality with the drummer in the corner, spat upon the stove until he was. Then the drummer told an unclean story which was a success, but the Hon. Hanford Perkins, feeling slighted at the loss of attention, told a scandalous bit of gossip which threw the drummer's story into the shade.

Garland stirred restlessly, and opened *Wilson on Hybrids* again. He had been reading for a moment or two when a name caught his ear, and he closed his book and raised his eyes.

The Hon. Hanford Perkins was speaking, and Garland leaned over and touched his coat sleeve.

"You are speaking of a woman," he said, "that is not the tone to use nor is this the place to discuss any woman."

"Hey?" said the Hon. Hanford, with a laugh, and winked at Uncle Billy.

"I guess he can say what he dam pleases in my house," said Uncle Billy, expectorating; "the girl's not yourn."

"The girl," added Cy Pettingil, "is a damned little—"

Then Garland took Cy Pettingil by the throat, swung him around the room twice, and kicked him headlong into the billiard-table, under which Pettingil hastily scrambled.

"Now," said Garland to the Honourable Hanford Perkins, "do you want to follow Pettingil? If you do, just wag that bunch of whiskers on your chin again."

The drummer in the corner smiled uneasily, picked up his sample case and key, and said goodnight in an uncertain voice to Garland. Uncle Billy's eyes were fixed upon Garland with a fascinated stare, and his jaw slowly dropped. The Hon. Hanford Perkins cast one amazed glance at Pettingil, another at Uncle Billy, and waddled majestically out into the street.

When Garland had picked up his book and left the hotel, Cy Pettingil crawled from beneath the billiard-table and approached Uncle Billy. He expectorated and leaned on the bar, but no amount of ejected saliva could re-establish him in his own estimation—he felt this bitterly.

"I'll git the law on him," he said after a moist silence, and rubbed his red hand over his chin. "I'll hev the law onto him," he repeated; but Uncle Billy was non-committal.

"Gimme a little bug-juice," said Cy, after an uncomfortable silence, and tossed a quarter upon the bar, with ostentatious carelessness,—"I'm dry, Billy."

"Yew be?" said Uncle Billy, "wall, yew don't git no bug-juice nor nawthin' here."

"Hey!" said Pettingil.

"Naw," said Uncle Billy, scornfully, and retired to the depths of the bar.

Garland walked slowly down the road in the twilight, switching the grass with the bamboo staff of his butterfly-net, angry with himself and nauseated with the free-born. And as he walked he was aware of a light touch on his arm, and a lighter footstep by his side. It was Tip.

"I—I was in the hallway of the hotel," said Tip, eagerly, "'n' I seen what you done to Cy Pettingil—"

"What were you doing there?" said Garland sharply.

"Buyin' salt for Cis,—oh! I just love you, Mister Garland!" And before Garland could raise his eyes, Tip had flung himself into his arms sobbing: "I ain't big enough to lick all the loafers in town, but I lick all their sons, and Cis says I am growin' fast. Oh, you do love me and Cis, don't you, Mister Garland?"

"Yes," said Garland, gravely, and kissed his wet face. Then he took him by the hand and told him how low and mean a bar-room fight was, and that he must never tell Celia what had happened. He tried to explain to him what was necessary to resent, and what was not; he spoke sympathetically as he always did, and Tip absorbed every word.

"Now let us forget it," said Garland, "Tip, your grammar is very uncertain. Why do you not try to speak as your sister does?"

"The boys I play with don't speak that way," said Tip.

"Neither does Cy Pettingil,—he speaks as you do," said Garland.

Tip's hand trembled and clasped Garland's tighter. "Learn me what to say, Mister Garland," he said after a silence.

"I will," replied Garland, "how would you like to go to school in Boston?"

"When?"

"Next winter."

"Can Cis come too?"

"I—hadn't thought,—you can't leave her, can you, Tip?"

"No," said Tip.

"Well—we'll see—you need not speak of this to your sister; I will—er—discuss the question with her later," said Garland.

Celia was standing under the pines as they walked up the gravel path. She knew his footsteps and came up on the verandah to greet him.

"Why, you are all over white!" she said; "has Tip spilled the salt on you?"

"Tip and I hugged each other to the detriment of the salt," said Garland laughing and brushing the white grains from his coat.

"Tip, dear, have you been naughty?" asked Celia.

"Nope," said Tip so promptly that even Celia laughed, and Tip retired to bed, glowing with virtuous resolves. Celia went up to his room and waited until he had said his prayers. She was troubled by the fervency of his prayer for Garland, but joined faintly in the Amen, and covered Tip with the white sheets.

"Mr. Garland says he loves you, Cis," said Tip, holding up his lips to be kissed. Celia caught her breath and laid one hand on the bedpost.

"Tip," she faltered.

"Yep—an' me, too," said Tip, blissfully.

He fell asleep soon; Celia stood and watched him in the moonlight. She was thinking of Garland; Tip was dreaming of him.

When she came down, Garland was busy among the lilies with bulls-eye lantern and butterfly net, and she took a chair on the verandah and watched him. Two "Imperial" moths had fallen to his lot, perfect specimens, and he was happy, for had not Professor Wormly cautiously deplored the absence of this species in the whole country?

"One on Wormly," laughed Garland, dropping the great yellow and violet-brown moths from his cyanide-jar into her lap, "are they not pretty, Celia?"

Since Garland had come, Celia had seen beauty through his eyes wherever his eyes saw it; the shadows on the pasture, the long light over the hills, the massed pines red in the sunset, the morning meadow sheeted with cobwebs. For the first time in her innocent life she had turned to watch the colour in the evening sky, she had stooped to lift a clover-drunk butterfly and examine the rainbow span of its wings, she lingered at the bars, listening to the music of the meadow brook along the alders. So when he asked her if the moths were beautiful, she smiled and saw that they were; and when he asked her to hold his lantern among the lilies, she prettily consented.

Up and down they moved, to and fro through the lilies and clustered pinks, but the moonlight was too clear and the swift sphinx moths did not visit the garden that night.

He was standing still, looking at the lilies, and she was swinging the lantern idly. "About Tip," he said abruptly, "do you think the school here is good for him?"

"I know it is not," she said sadly.

"His English is alarming," said Garland.

"I know it—what can I do?"

"I don't know; if he goes to school he will play with those children, I suppose."

"He was such a well-bred child," said Celia, "before—before we came here. He talked when he was three. I seem to have little influence over him."

"You have a great deal—not in that way perhaps. Suppose you take Tip out of school, Celia."

"What would become of him?" exclaimed Celia in gentle alarm.

"It's better than leaving him there. I—er—I might help him a bit."

"But—it's very, very kind of you—but you will go away before winter—will you not?"

"I don't know," said Garland, and instinctively laid his hand on hers. At the contact, her cheeks flamed in the darkness.

"Celia," he said, "I do not want to go."

Her face was turned from him. After a moment his fingers unclosed and her impassive hand fell to her side. The swift touch left him silent and awkward. He tried to speak lightly again but could not. Finally he folded his net, extinguished the lantern and said good-night. Long after he had disappeared she stood among the lilies, her hands softly clasped to her breast.

IV.

"Heu!" sniffed Uncle Billy, as he poured out a glass of beer for himself behind the fly-soiled bar at the Constitution Hotel, "there hain't a man araound taown dass say a word abaout the Minster girl when Mister Garland 's a settin' here."

"Mister Garland's a skunk!" said Cy Pettingil, morosely.

"He ain't the skunk that yew be, Cy Pettingil," retorted Uncle Billy, wiping his mouth with the back of his hand.

Garland came in a moment later, satchel in hand, and laid a roll of bills on the bar. Uncle Billy moistened his thumb with his tongue, counted them, and shoved them into his waistcoat pocket. "C'rect," he said, shifting his quid, "what can I dew for yew, sir?"

"Send this satchel with my trunk," said Garland, "good-bye, Uncle Billy."

Uncle Billy emerged from the bar, wiped his right hand on his trousers and extended it.

"Good luck, an' many bugs to yew, Mister Garland. I'm real cut up that yew air goin', sir; ennything in the bug line thet I hev I'll send t' Noo York."

"Thank you, Uncle Billy," said Garland, and walked out of the hotel, gloves in one hand, cane in the other.

Cy Pettingil sneered when he was gone, but, receiving no sympathy from Uncle Billy, went home and nagged at his wife, a pale woman weighed down with trouble and American pastry—until she retorted. Then he struck her.

Garland walked on past the church and schoolhouse, through the sweet-briar lane by the Post Office, and, taking the path above the cemetery, followed it until he came in sight of the stone house among the pines. The Maltese cat trotted out to greet him, the tethered kid stared at him from the lawn, but Celia was invisible, and he stood hesitating under the woodbine on the porch. He had never entered Celia's house. She had never asked him in, and he knew that she was right. He sat down under the pines and looked off over the pastures where the Alderney and Jersey were feeding along the brookside.

Garland had come to say good-bye. There was nothing that he could do for Tip; Celia was not able to send him to a better school, nor could she have afforded to go with him. Even if she should accept an offer to send Tip to school, what would she do there alone in that scandal nest of the freeborn? So Garland sat poking pine cones with his stick and crumpling his gloves in his brown hand until a tangle of sun-warmed curls rose over the fence and Tip appeared, smoking a cigarette. When he saw Garland he dropped the cigarette and looked the other way, whistling.

"Come, Tip," said Garland, wearily, "let's have it out before Celia comes."

Tip went to him at once.

"Who gave you that cigarette?" asked Garland.

"No one, I made it."

"Tobacco?"

"No, sir, sweet-fern and corn silk."

"That is not much better. Tip, are you going to stop this?"

The child picked up a pine cone, examined it carefully, and tossed it toward the Maltese cat.

"Answer me," said Garland.

The child was silent.

"Very well," said Garland.

"I promise!" cried Tip,—"I won't never smoke nothing,—don't go away, Mr. Garland!"

"Is that your word of honour, Tip?"

"Yes, sir."

"All right," said Garland, smiling, "now you have promised me not to drink or smoke until you are twenty-one. I know I can trust you, and I am very happy. You need not tell Celia of this."

"I—I will if you want?" said Tip, humbly.

"No,—it will only worry her—and you have promised now. What did you do in school today?"

"I punched Jimmy Bro—"

"I did not ask for an account of your athletic victories," said Garland, "I merely wished to know in what particular branch of the applied sciences you excelled."

"Wh—a—at, sir?"

"Were you perfect in reading?"

"N—no, sir."

"In writing?"

"No—o—"

"In arithmetic?"

Tip stirred restlessly, and looked at the Maltese cat. Then he brightened and said, "A skunk got into the cellar while school was goin'. Teacher told us all about skunks an' anermals."

"Oh," said Garland, "an object lesson in natural history?"

"Yep. Skunk ain't its real name, its real name is Methodist Americanus—"

"What 's that?" exclaimed Garland.

"Methodist Americanus—"

"Mephetis Americanus, Tip," said Garland gravely.

"Oh! I thought the man what named it might have had a uncle like mine—"

"Tip!"

"Yes, sir?"

"That will do," said Garland seriously.

The child nodded contentedly and began an elaborate series of evolutions, the object of which was to capture the Maltese cat. The cat was perfectly aware of this; she allowed the boy to approach her until his hand was within an inch of her back; then she ran a few feet, cocked her ears, switched her tail, and pretended to forget him. After a while they disappeared behind the lilac bushes at the end of the verandah, and Garland leaned back against the tree and poked at pine cones again.

The sun sank lower and lower, flooding the pastures, tinging the calm meadow pools with the splendour of its fading glory. In the evening glow the turf burned like golden tapestry, the swallows twittered among the chimneys or drifted and rose high in the quiet air, and the chickens looked up with restless peeps to their roost in the lilac branches. An orange light, ever deepening, dyed the edges of the pools where the ripples of a rising fish or a low dipping gnat disturbed the surface reflection of the placid evening sky. From palest green to grey the horizon changed until, like a breath creeping over a window, a rosy flush stained the zenith. And the sun had set.

With sunset Celia came, walking slowly over the grass that shone in the shadows with a green almost metallic. She started slightly when Garland moved in the shade of the pines, but came to him, offering her hand.

"Then you are going," she said simply.

"Yes,—I am going. My train leaves at nine to-night. How did you know?"

She glanced at his gloves and stick and smiled gently.

"I am going," he said, "because they want me in New York. Some day I will come back—"

A ghost of a smile touched her lips again. He moved impatiently nearer, and she looked at his troubled eyes.

"Shall I come back?" he asked awkwardly.

"Yes—come; Tip will welcome you—"

"And you?"

"I,"—she said softly—"I don't know."

"What troubles you?" he said; but she turned her head toward the sunset. "What troubles you?" he said again;—"is—is *he* coming?"

She dropped her head.

"When?" asked Garland in a hard voice.

"To-night."

Something of the horror in her face as she turned it was reflected in his own. This, then, was the reward for her quiet struggle for life; this was the reward,—the return of this miserable actor whom she had learned to loathe—her husband! Whew! the stench of perfume and grease paint seemed to fill his nostrils; he could see the smooth fat face shaved blue, as he had seen it behind the footlights in the metropolis, the bull neck, the professional curly head!

Then he set his teeth and dug his stick into the turf at his feet. The girl moved a step from him.

"Celia," he said unsteadily, "have you ever thought of divorce?"

"Yes."

They were silent again. The whistle of a distant train startled Garland from his reverie and he picked up his gloves and buttoned his coat. It was the incoming train from New York. With a frightened glance at him she held out her hand, murmuring good-bye, and turned toward the house, but he stepped swiftly to her side and touched her arm.

Oh, the terror in the eyes that met his,—and the kiss,—as she clung to his breast in the twilight there—the kiss that solved all problems, that broke down barriers and made the way plain and clear,—the way that they should travel together through life and the life to come.

And so they went away into the world together, and Tip went with them, one dimpled hand in Garland's, one clasping the Maltese cat close to his breast.

THE CRIME

"'How,' says he, blessing himself, 'would I whip this
child …. if it were my child.'"

SAMUEL PEPYS.

"Heark! Oh, heark! you guilty trees,
In whose gloomy galleries
Was the cruellest murder done
That e're yet eclipst the suune."

I.

Now it happened one day in the early Springtime when the sky was
china blue and filmy clouds trailed like lace across the disk of a pale sun,
that I, Henry Stenhouse, nineteen years of age, well and sound in mind and
body, decided to commit a crime.

The crime which I contemplated was murder. For three years past I had
watched the object of my pursuit; I had peered at him at night as he lay
sleeping, I had crept stealthily to his home, evening after evening, waiting
for a chance to kill him. I had seen him moving about on his daily business,
growing fatter and sleeker, serene, sly, self-centred, absorbed in his own
affairs, yet keeping a keen, shrewd eye upon strangers. For he mistrusted
strangers; those who passed by him, not even noticing him, he mistrusted
less than he did others who came to him with smiles and outstretched
hands.

He never accepted anything from anybody. A strange step or the sound
of a strange voice made him shy and suspicious. But he was cold and selfish, cold-blooded as a fish—in fact he—but I had better tell you a little
more about him first. He was my enemy; I determined to kill him, and
perhaps he read it in my drawn face and sparkling eyes, for, as I stepped
toward him, the first time, he turned and fled—fled straight across the
Clovermead River.

And although I searched the river banks up and down and up and down
again, I saw no more of him that day.

When I went home, excited, furious, I made passionate preparations to
kill him. All night long I tossed feverishly in my tumbled bed, longing, ach-

ing for the morning. When the morning came I stole out of the house and bent my steps towards the river, for I had reason to believe that he lived somewhere in that neighbourhood. As I crept along, the early morning sun glittered on something that I clutched with nervous fingers. It was a weapon.

This happened three years ago; I did not find him that morning although I searched until the shadows fell over meadow and thicket. That night too found me on his trail, but the calm Spring moon rose over Clovermead village and its pale light fell on no scene of blood.

So for three years I trailed him and stalked him, always awaiting the moment to strike,—praying for an opportunity to slay; but he never gave me one. He was fierce and shifty, swift as lightning when aroused, but the battle that I offered he declined. Oh, he was deep,—deep and crafty, cold-blooded as a fish,—in fact, he was a fish, Mine Enemy, the Trout.

Do you imagine that the killing of Mine Enemy was a crime? No, my friend—that, properly done, was what is known as sport; improperly done, it is murder;—there, the murder's out! I was going to catch the trout with bait!

You, dear brethren of the angle, brave fly-fishermen, all, wet or dry, turn not from me with loathing! Hear my confession, the confession of one who was tempted, listened, fell, and fished for a trout with a worm!

Anyway, it's your own fault if you throw down this book and beat your breasts with cruel violence. I told you that my story was to be the story of a crime, and if you don't like to read about crimes, you had no business to begin this tale. There are worse crimes too,—some people habitually fish with bait; some net fish, and there exist a few degraded objects in human shape who snare trout with a wicked wire loop on the end of a sapling.

Now I don't propose to tell you about these things, I am no depraved realist, so thank your stars that the crime I contemplated was no worse than it was, and listen to the story of an erring brother. Mea culpa!

I was only nineteen, a student at the State School of Engineering, and in my senior year. What I did in engineering was barely sufficient to carry me through my examination; what I did in shooting and trout fishing might have furnished material for a sporting library. I had no particular aversion to my profession; my father before me had been a mining engineer. I was not entirely ignorant either; I knew mica-chist from malachite, and I could—but that's of no consequence now. It is true, however, that instead of applying myself to the studies of my profession I spent a great deal of time contributing to a New York sporting journal called the *Trigger*. I produced a couple of columns a week on such subjects as "German Trout *versus* Natives," "Do Automatic Reels Pay?" and "Experiments with the Amherst Pheasant." But my article entitled "The Enemies of the Spawning-Beds," won me recognition, and I became a regular contributor to the *Trigger*.

How I ever passed my examinations is one of those mysteries that had better remain uninvestigated. I don't remember that I studied or attended many lectures. I was too busy, shooting or fishing, or writing for the *Trigger*.

Also there existed a girls' boarding-school a mile away.

This school was run by two old maids, the Misses Timmins. It was the Timmins sisters' aim in life to prevent the members of their school from coming into contact with the engineers from Clovermead; therefore we knew them all.

The means of communication were varied and ingenious, for the little maidens at the boarding-school were quite as enthusiastic as we were. We never went through the formality of an introduction,—it was not expected; we spoke when we had the chance, and thanked fortune for the chance.

There was, however, one weird custom laid down by the boarding-school maidens, a tradition which had existed as long as the school; and this was well understood by the Clovermead Engineers. It was this: no youth could expect to spoon with any Timmins maiden unless he first declared his intentions by serenading her.

We were not all blessed with a high order of musical ability,—I played a harmonica,—but we were willing to try. I had tried several times. The results were very sweet,—I don't mean in a musical way.

So between the boarding-school and the *Trigger* I found little leisure, and the less leisure I had the less I felt inclined to occupy it with engineering problems. Besides, there was the big trout to think of, Mine Enemy, whom I had sworn to drag from the depths of that most delicious of streams, the Clovermead River.

During these three years while I persistently fished for Mine Enemy (and goodness knows I had never before beheld so lusty a trout!) every fly known to anglers, and many flies unknown to anybody but myself, I tried on that impassive fish.

And he grew fatter and fatter.

I remember well the day of the temptation. I was sitting at the foot of the big oak tree that spreads above the pool where Mine Enemy lurked. Wearied with casting, I had sought the shadow of the oak and had lighted a cigarette to change my luck. And as I sat on the cool turf, I was aware of an angle worm, travelling along at my feet on business of its own. Scarcely conscious of what I did, I picked up a twig and tossed the little worm over the bank.

Then, in a moment, I was sorry, for I never willingly bother little things. I watched the worm sinking slowly into the crystalline depths of the pool.

When at last the little worm struck the bottom I suppose it was both astonished and indignant for it began to twist and turn and shoot out like a telescope over the gravelly bottom.

I was sorry, as I say, and I hoped it might make its way to the bank again and bore into it.

Several inquisitive minnows, half as long as the angle worm, gathered around it staring and opening their diminutive mouths. Then, all at once, the minnows darted away, scattering in every direction, and a huge shadow fell upon the gravel, a trout, monstrous, lazy, slowly gliding out from the dark bank to where the worm wriggled, pushing its pink head among the pebbles.

Very deliberately the great fish opened his mouth—not very wide—and the little worm was gone. For five minutes the trout lay there, and I watched him, scarcely daring to breathe. After a while I cautiously reached for my rod, freed the line and leader, bent a little forward, and cast over the fish. Lightly as snowflakes falling on window panes, the flies drifted onto the placid surface of the pool. The trout did not stir.

It was at this moment that temptation overtook me; my sinful eyes roved over the turf where the angle worm had been, and, brethren; forgive me!—I lusted after bait!!

"It will be so easy," whispered the tempter, "no one will ever know!"

"Get behind me, Satan," said I.

"But it's so easy,—and the big trout will never touch artificial flies!"

"Avaunt Apollyon!" I groaned while the sweat stood in beads on my eyebrows.

So I overcame the devil, and went away to avoid further contention. And Heaven rewarded me with the sight of a pretty girl playing a guitar at her window.

She was so pretty that the fact alone was reward enough, but Heaven never does things by halves, Madame, and when for an instant I paused by the brier hedge to listen, the pretty girl gave me one of those swift, provoking sidelong glances, and then, touching her guitar, looked innocently up into the sky.

And this is what she sang:

> "Young am I, and yet unskilled
> How to make a lover yield;
> How to keep and how to gain,
> When to love and when to feign!"

> "Take me, take me some of you
> While I yet am young and true;
> He that has me first is blest,
> For I may deceive the rest."

And the guitar went *strum!* tum-tum! *strum!* tum-tum! tinkle-tinkle-tinkle-*strum!* tum-tum!

"The little innocent thing," I thought, and looked at her through the hedge.

She was not so very young; she might have been my own age. She was sitting in one of the windows of the dormitory which belonged to the Misses Timmins' Select Boarding-school for Young Ladies!

Evidently the Misses Timmins were not in the immediate neighbourhood.

"Dear little innocent thing," I repeated to myself.

I moved slightly. She looked at me with that dreamy confiding look that stirs the pulses of some people. I am one of those people.

"She is lonely," said I to myself, "it is the duty—nay, the precious privilege of the happy to sympathize with the lonely."

There was a bud of sweet-brier beside my cheek. I picked it, sniffed it pensively, and looked at the girl in the window.

She looked at me, glanced down at her guitar, thrummed a little, sighed a little, and ate a bonbon.

Ah, that sigh!—gentle, troubling, irresistible.

"She," thought I to myself, "shall be my goddess,—this humble dormitory shall be my temple, this window my shrine! Hither will I come to worship and bring burnt offerings,—almonds and bon-bons. This village will not be so dull after all," I thought to myself.

"What time," said I, speaking very gently, for I did not wish to disturb the Misses Timmins with my rude voice,—"what time, Mademoiselle, would it be advisable for an enamoured lover to serenade the delicious object of his adoration?"

"We retire at half-past nine, fair sir," said the maiden innocently.

I knew I was not mistaken. The poor child was lonely.

"Heavens!" said I,—"driven to retire at half past nine! Are—er—the—Misses Timmins—er —fierce?"

"They are deaf," said the maiden, with a childlike smile.

"Ah,—unhappy ladies! This is a fine old building, a noble façade. Are you fond of architecture?"

"My window is the one I am sitting in," said the maid with simple confidence, "I could let down a string in case you had matters of grave import or state despatches to communicate."

"Ahem!" said I, "have you a string there now?"

"Yes, fair sir."

So I slid through the hedge and stood under her window holding up my creel.

"I have," said I, "a few small brook trout here—nothing to boast of—but if you would accept—"

"Indeed you are too kind—"

"They may vary the monotony of prunes and weak tea for supper—"

"Fair sir, I see you have known other boarding-school maidens!"

"Foi de gentilhomme!" I protested.

"Which is not pronounced the way we pronounce French here," she said,—"let me see the trout."

I opened the creel.

"I will accept," said the girl graciously, and let down a string, to which I fastened my creel. "You are very daring—how do you know that the whole school are not watching?"

"Because," said I, "this is the afternoon when the whole school takes a solemn ramble into the country."

"I am not rambling," she said.

"All do not ramble on days of recreation," I replied significantly.

"You know a great deal about this boarding-school, fair sir. I suppose you also know I am confined to my room as a disciplinary precaution."

"Monstrous!" I cried, suppressing my satisfaction.

"I only made a cider cocktail," she said.

"Monstrous!" I repeated, "cider cocktails are no good."

By this time she had lowered the creel to me again and I slung it on my shoulders and picked up my rod from the lawn.

"I will bring offerings," I said, "do you like bon-bons, gentle maiden?"

"Yes, and pickles," she said gravely.

"And music?"

"Sometimes—not too classical—"

"I will serenade you!" I cried enthusiastically,—"you say the Misses Timmins are deaf?"

"Shame on you! you know they are. What do you play? I am not sure that I will accept a serenade."

"The banjo and the harmonica—not both at once. I play the harmonica best, but I can't sing to it at the same time, you know. Shall I come?"

"Y—es. Are you fond of pickled peaches? I can let some down to you."

I was on the point of accepting a pickled peach,—I would have accepted a pickled turnip from her,—when, out of the tail of my eye, I saw the tops of multi-coloured sunshades appearing above the crest of the hill, and I knew that the Misses Timmins were returning with their flock.

"You must go!" she whispered hurriedly, "go quickly!"

"Good-bye,—good-night," I said, "you are the loveliest, sweetest—"

"Quick,—what?"

"Angel,—divine, glorious, er—"

"Oh, hasten! What?"

"And I love you!"

"You mustn't say that;—must you? Oh, hurry and say it again—if you must—"

"Oh, I must!" I cried, heedless of all the Timminses on earth, "I really must—"

"My name is May Thorne—go quickly now."

"Mine is Harry Stenhouse—the deuce! they're at the gate!"

They were.

Scarcely had I slipped around the building before I heard the chatter and laughter of girls and the patter of feet on the gravel walk. I had heard it before under similar circumstances. But there was a back gate; and I went. Now see how virtue is its own reward! I had resisted the devil and—he gave me another chance.

II.

"Yes," said I to myself, remembering how I had piously ascribed my reward to Heaven,—"yes, I was mistaken. I should have said: 'The devil, Madame, never does things by halves.'"

I looked back at the dormitory door. One of the Misses Timmins was snipping roses from the porch trellis.

"To eke out the meagre evening meal," I thought; "poor little maid—poor little May! Only nanny-goats eat roses, and an empty stomach rejoiceth not in perfumes."

This sounded to me like an Eastern proverb. It smacked well, and I repeated it to myself luxuriously.

"Some day," thought I, "when I am famous, and people begin to write books to prove that I'm not, I'll marry May,—if I like her as well as I do now—and she likes me,—ahem!" I'd forgotten that part.

"There is something about this little maid," I mused, "that touches my better nature; something too subtle to analyze, and anyway, I'm not good at that sort of analysis. She is fond of eating trout, I'm fond of catching them. Clearly we were designed for each other,—if only for an hour or so."

By this time I had reached my own gate, and stood pensively regarding a pair of tiny chipping birds that were absorbed in the excitement of a violent Spring courtship.

"Certainly," said I to myself, "I am infatuated, and I'm proud of it. Any man would be—any man whose mind was not all mouse-coloured and neutral."

In the mellow evening light the pools of rain water glimmered like sheets of gold. Two swallows sat on a telegraph wire twittering to each other of the coming summer, two migrating blue-jays stopped in the apple tree by the porch to chatter scandal. A pair of belated white butterflies fluttered sleepily about the lower branches of the lilac bushes.

"They're probably married also," thought I, "and now they're going home to bed. Everything that runs or flies or hops seems to be mated—except me. True, I don't fly—unless from the Misses Timmins."

I opened my creel and looked moodily into it. Fishing, after all, was cold comfort compared to stealing an interview with a winsome maid who ate bon-bons to guitar accompaniment.

"May," said I to myself, softly, "May,—might,—May makes might and might makes right—pshaw! I'll not go bothering my conscience with every little incident that comes up." I had some consideration for my conscience; I knew how tired it was.

The rain water in the long road ruts glimmered with a deeper orange light. A bat fluttered around the darkening foliage of the maples; a cricket creaked from door-sill.

"The bat," thought I, "is looking for a little lady-bat; the cricket is serenading; I think that I'll follow their example. I wish I could play on my harmonica and sing at the same time."

About ten o'clock that night, the moon being well up, I went out onto the porch and looked at it until I felt sufficiently sentimental to sit on the damp grass under May's window and make music as I understood it. So I took my banjo under my arm, dropped my harmonica into my coat pocket, and tip-toed off down the road as many a better man had done before me, and would continue to do as long as that boarding-school existed.

O delicious night in early Spring! Lured by the balm in the soft night winds, all the little field creatures had come out of their holes in meadow and pasture, in orchard and thicket, and were scraping away on monotonous shrill melodies, accentuated by the treble of hundreds of tree toads. In every shadowy orchard Katydids performed countless encores to the bass "bravos!" of the great bull-frogs along the mill-brook's reedy banks. All living things did their part to celebrate the coming Summer, even a distant skunk added his mite to the spicy night. Personally I preferred the roadside lilacs, but it's all a matter of taste, and George the Fourth liked his oysters over-ripe.

"If these bull-frogs," thought I, "keep up their sonorous tom-toms, it will ruin my serenade—I know it, from experience."

By this time I had reached the dormitory hedge.

"A brassy cornet would be lost in this hubbub," I mused bitterly, looking up at the third window on the second floor.

I thumbed the bass string of my banjo doubtfully, paused, cleared my throat, included frogs, toads, katydids, and crickets in one general and comprehensive anathema, and sang this rehashed song:

> "Ye little loves that round her wait
> To bring me tidings of my fate,
> As May upon her pillow lies,
> Ah! gently whisper—Harry dies."

> "If this will not her pity move,
> And the proud fair disdains to love,
> Smile and say 'tis all a lie,
> And haughty Henry scorns to die!"

"Bother take it," I muttered, "I shouldn't have sung that last verse—it may offend her. That's the trouble about those old songs; you never can tell what you're singing until you've put your foot in it."

This mixed metaphor was probably due to the confusion in my mind, for what with the frogs and a lurking fear of the Misses Timmins, I was not as cool as I might have been.

While I was singing, two or three windows were softly raised, and now more were being raised, and I caught glimpses of shadowy white-draped figures leaning from sills or dodging behind curtains.

And now *her* window opened softly; I saw a shape between the curtains and the sweet notes of a guitar came throbbing out into the night.

"Miss Thorne," I whispered, "ask those young ladies to go in, please. They always come and bother."

Some of them took the hint. I did not care for the rest, for time was precious, and I feared the Timmins! So I told Miss Thorne in a hollow, passionate whisper that it was out of the question for me to try to live without her,—and a few other facts calculated to melt solid rocks into tears. But when I desired to be informed concerning her constancy, she interrupted me.

"What was that last verse you sang?" she asked.

"Oh, that was only one of those old songs, you know; I didn't intend—"

"One of those old songs? Very well. Listen to this one then, and be assured of my constancy."

> "The time that is to come, is not;
> How then can it be mine?

> The present moment's all my lot,
> And that, as fast as it is got,
> Harry, is only thine!
>
> Then talk not of inconstancy,
> False hearts and broken vows;
> If I, by miracle, can be
> This live-long minute true to thee,
> 'T is all that Heaven allows."

It was a pretty revenge for my parrot-like repetition of a verse that was out of place, but when, from a neighbouring window, another voice cried "Brava May! serves him right!" I was annoyed and protested in hoarse whispers.

Then all those little maids began to make fun of me. I thought I could distinguish May's silvery mocking laughter, and, hurt and angry, I shook the dew of the lawn from my shoes, and went away, nursing my wrath and my hurt pride.

"That's what one gets," I mused, "that's what a man gets by meddling with things that don't concern him! I was an ass to make eyes at her. I was doubly an ass to think that she would care for good music—I was a triple ass to sing that idiotic old song. It was a too-cock-sure-independent—well don't-if-you-don't-want-to! sort of song, and women don't like that. Women are all alike—it is only circumstances that change them. I wish I had sense enough to let 'em alone! The confounded song hurt her vanity—that's what's the matter!"

I sat down on a flat rock by the roadside and blew a dismal strain from my harmonica. It comforted me a little, so I played "Sir Daniel O'Donnel" and "Casey's Lament."

The weird strains of the latter wrung howls from a dog in a stable near by, so I changed to a pleasanter air to save his feelings. But my heart was heavy; I eyed the moon furtively and moped.

"Those feather-headed girls always come and listen every time a fellow tries to do a little wooing on his own account," I muttered; "Barclay had the same experience, so did Kendall and Gordon. I'll be hanged if I repeat this fiasco—it's cursedly silly, anyway, and I don't care whether it's customary and traditional. I'll not play circus for any woman on earth!"

I wiped my harmonica on my handkerchief and played "Bannigan's Barracks" in a minor key. The dog in the stable howled intermittently.

I could see the dark mass of the dormitory out of the corner of my eye. A candle flickered behind one of the windows, I could not tell which, from where I was sitting.

And, as I eyed it askance, tooting resignedly the while, I saw somebody appear at the great gate, open it, and move swiftly out and up the moonlit road toward me.

"Some of those girls have told a Timmins, and she's coming to do me!" I thought. "I don't care. Miss Thorne made me ridiculous, and I'll not see her again, and I'm on the public highway! Let the Misses Timmins advance!"

So I struck up a lively quickstep on my harmonica, and blinked innocently at the moon. The figure was close to me now, I saw it, but I tootled away, regardless.

"Mr. Stenhouse!"

I turned slowly.

"Oh, I know it is terribly imprudent, and if I 'm caught I'll be sent home, but I heard your harmonica—oh, such dismal strains!—and I thought if only I could see you for a second to tell you that it was not I that laughed, for I think your serenade was—was perfectly charming—there!"

We were standing face to face in the moonlight. At last I said: "I was a fool to sing that song; I'm sorry, Miss Thorne."

"Oh, it was not the song as much as it was that you said—you gave me to understand quite frankly that you had—had been to the school before. You said 'the girls always bothered—'"

"Did I say that?"

"Yes,—it was most humiliating for—for me."

"Oh, I'm a perfect idiot," I admitted.

She looked down at her slippers—they had been hurriedly and carelessly tied—and I noticed it and knelt to repair the oversight.

"I was in such haste," she said. "Is it true that you have serenaded the dormitory before?"

"Not the dormitory—"

"You know what I mean; have you?"

"All the fellows do," I said, vaguely.

She tapped her foot on the gravel.

"Those strings are sufficiently tied," she said, "tell me whom you serenaded?"

"I can't do that, Miss Thorne."

"Why? Then tell me when it was."

"When? Oh, last year, before I ever imagined such a girl as you existed. It's a silly custom, anyway—"

"It isn't,—it's charming—when the man has any tact. It's the tradition of the school that no girl shall spoon with a man who hasn't serenaded her, and I do not expect to break the traditions of my school—"

"Only the rules, Miss Thorne?"

"Only the rules—and a heart or two!"

"Or *two!*"

"Faith, sir," she said maliciously, "did you think you were the only one?"

"Yes," said I, "I did."

"And you tell me deliberately that you had serenaded other girls there before I came—I don't know how many, perhaps a dozen, twenty, fifty, the whole school!"

"What!" I cried, bewildered.

"Oh, I don't care," she said, "I only wished to show you what men are and what their selfishness requires of women,—to sacrifice everything while they sacrifice nothing."

"And you don't care?" I asked.

"No, Mr. Stenhouse."

"Then why did you risk everything to come and tell me?"

"W—what?" she stammered.

"Miss Thorne," said I, very gravely, "your school is noted for its escapades. It is known in the village, not as the 'Misses Timmins's Select Boarding-School for Young Ladies,' but as 'The Devil's Own.' We engineer students are a reckless lot, also. We are, to put it plainly, a godless crew, but this—this is somehow different. I am beginning to believe that our thoughtless folly—yours and mine, may leave one of us miserable for life."

"Me?"

"Who knows? I can only speak for myself,—I—I have changed already,—yes, in these few moments that we stood here face to face—"

"What do you mean?" she said mockingly.

"I mean that in another minute I shall love you—in another second!"

"Are you serious?" she demanded incredulously. Then, "Oh, I thought you jolly and clever, and you prove to be soft and silly! Master Harry, you bore me!"

"Do I?" I answered angrily. "Well, I'll never do it again, and I was a fool to believe you would understand anything but chocolate-creams and dormitory flirting!"

"Not only soft and silly, but a boor," she said. "Good-night. No, you need not walk to the gate with me—I never wish to set eyes on you again."

III.

On the first day of June I passed my final examinations at the great Engineering School at Clovermead, and was then ready to let myself loose on the mining regions of a deluded world.

The commencement exercises bored me; I went fishing most of the time, or else stayed in my rooms writing "Dry Fly Casting as a Fine Art" for the

Trigger. In the long fragrant evenings I took lonely walks by the river or sat under the oak playing minor airs on my harmonica.

At the end of the first week in June the commencement exercises were over, the visiting hordes from New York and Boston had flitted away to Newport or Bar Harbor, the Government officers went back to Washington and West Point, and the little village of Clovermead lay in the sunshine, white, sweet-scented, deserted.

The Misses Timmins's "Select Boarding-School for Young Ladies" had its commencement—a rainbow affair—and dissolved, leaving, as residue, an empty school-house and a dormitory dedicated to silence.

I didn't go to their commencement, not because I was not invited, for most of the fellows went anyway. No, since my last serenade, I had shunned the school and all it works.

It was true that I lingered in the village of Clovermead after my fellow-students had departed, not, as I frequently explained to myself, to catch a last glimpse of Miss Thorne, but to catch that veteran trout in the Clovermead River. "I shall never see Miss Thorne again," I said to myself, "and I 'm glad of it."

So on the day of her commencement I went fishing, very far off and I passed a miserable day. It rained, among other things.

The next morning the sun shone in at my window and I looked out into the village with a strange weight at my heart. I did not feel hungry, but went to breakfast, determined to let nothing disturb me or my appetite. As I touched the sugar-tongs to the sugar, a faint whistle came on the June wind from the distant railroad station.

"There go the young ladies from the boarding-school," said my landlady; "do take one of these shirred eggs, Mr. Stenhouse."

"Thank you," said I, with a queer sensation in my throat.

"May has gone," I was thinking. After a while I said aloud: "what of it!"

"I beg your pardon," said my landlady, smiling.

"I beg yours—it was nothing; I was only thinking that I was alone in the village."

"I hope you will stay," she said, fingering the black-edged handkerchief in her lap.

"You are very good," I replied; "I shall stay until I catch that big trout in the river."

"Then poor luck to you!" smiled the kindly old lady, "what time will you have your dinner, Mr. Stenhouse?"

I went back to my room and sat down by the window. A flowering branch of late apple blossoms scraped across the sash as I threw it open and leaned out.

For a long while I listened to the droning of bees among the half-opened buds, thinking that the warmth had fled from the sunshine and the scent was gone from mead and sedge.

And "why?" I repeated to myself again and again, until a sullen anger seized me and I tramped up and down my room, my hands buried in the canvas pockets of my shooting coat.

"Now," said I to myself, "this is d—d foolishness. I'll just go and try for that trout, and I'll catch him too," I added, gritting my teeth to dull the pain in my heart,—"I'll catch him by fair means or foul,—yes, by jingo! I'll use a worm!" No, I felt no horror for the deed I was about to commit. All that was base and depraved in my nature had risen with my better feelings to combat a depression, a sorrow, that was so sudden, so deep, that I hardly understood it.

Under such circumstances the truly good come out strong,—in novels; others do something wrong to occupy their minds. Wallowing dulls the capability of suffering,—for a time. It is much practised by weak and strong, contemporary fiction to the contrary.

So it happened one day in early June, when the sky was china blue and filmy clouds trailed like lace across the disk of a pale sun, that I, Henry Stenhouse, well and sound in mind and body, decided to commit a crime.

I started down the road, swinging my creel over my shoulder and whistling, buoyed up by that false exhilaration which always took possession of me when I felt myself on good terms with the devil. In my pocket nestled my luncheon, a small flask of Bordeaux, fly-book, harmonica, reel, and a *tin bait box*.

Imagine what it costs me to write this!

Well it's written,—and on I went, whistling "Sir Daniel O'Donnel," as though I had not a care in the world and love was but an old wive's tale.

Yet, whistle as I would, I could not close my eyes to the caustic criticism of the sunny world on my solitary condition. Robins hopped about the pastures in pairs, blue-birds flew from sapling to fence, in pairs, yellow butterflies whirled over the clover in dozens and dozens of pairs, and the very trees, the silver birches, the maples and elms, all seemed to grow in pairs. Two by two I counted oak and beach, nestling in each others shadows, two by two the twinkling silver aspens seemed to wink at me with every leaf.

I alone was alone.

"Because," said I to myself, "I've got brains"; but the boast fell only on the idle unbelieving ears of the corn, too young to understand or sympathize.

A great tenderness was in my heart, but I crushed it out, and turned into the fields, treading my way through rustling corn where June breezes lingered, whispering.

When I struck the hazel patch I felt better, and I whistled "Sir Daniel O'Donnel" again.

A wood-thrush, striving to imitate me, produced an unconscious masterpiece; a cat-bird mewed unceasingly from the deeper growth. Both had mates.

I took the hidden path through the beech-woods until I came to a big pine. Here, following a trail, known to myself, I entered the denser woods, crossed the two spring brooks that feed the river, and after a few minutes rapid walking came to the oak which spreads above the limpid silvery pool, the abode of Mine Enemy.

"As long as I have sunk to the level of a pothunter," said I, treading softly over the moss, "I might as well do the thing thoroughly."

Very cautiously I produced an angle-worm from my box, baited my hook, cast the infernal machine into the pool, and then, placing my rod on the bank, put a flat stone on the butt and sat down to smoke. When I had finished my cigarette I lay down, stretching out on the moss under the oak tree.

And as I sprawled on my back looking skyward, I was aware of a pair of stockings,—black stockings,—hanging from a limb directly over my head.

Astonished and indignant I lay perfectly still, staring at the stockings. They had been wet but now were rapidly drying, swinging gently in the warm June wind.

"This is pleasant!" I thought; "some credulous country wench has taken my pool for a foot-bath. I'll not put up with it, by jingo! Have fishermen no rights? Is this a picnic ground? Is that river a resort for barefooted giggling girls?"

If there were any people splashing and paddling about among the stones down the river, I knew that every trout within range would be paralyzed with fright. I sat up and tried to see through the foliage which bordered the shallow river where it curved into the woods.

"They're down there," I muttered, "and I bet they've done the business for every trout between here and the falls. Idiots!"

I looked up at the stockings. They were certainly silk, I could see that. The sun bronzed the pointed toes, now almost dry. And while I looked there came a faint sound of splashing close by, just where the river narrows to curve into the woods. Something bright was glistening down there between the branches, something white that moved slowly up stream, nearer and nearer, now plainly in view through the leaves.

It was a young woman in a light summer gown with a big straw hat on her head, and she was slowly and deliberately wading through the shallow water toward my pool.

She seemed to be enjoying it; the swift water rippled around her ankles dashing her skirts with spray, as she lifted her wet pink feet carefully over the sharp rocks and deeper channels. Her skirt, gathered naïvely in both hands, fluttered perhaps a trifle higher than it might have done under other circumstances. It was a pretty innocent picture, but it was out of place in my trout pool, and I stood up, determined to expostulate. After a second I sat down again, somewhat suddenly. The black stockings waved triumphantly above my head. I looked at them, bewildered, utterly upset. The young lady in the water was Miss Thorne.

Before I could decide what to do, she came in sight around the trees, stepping daintily over the sandy shallows. I dared not move. She did not look up.

"What the mischief shall I do?" I thought, keeping very still so that no movement should attract her eyes to the oak on the bank above. I could not retreat and leave my rod, I dared not creep to the pool to recover it. Besides, I didn't want to go away.

She had sat down on a sunny rock, just below me, and was stirring the sandy bottom with her little toes. It was, as I said, a pretty picture, sweet and innocent, but utterly fatal to my peace of mind. I wondered what she'd do next, and lay silent, scarcely breathing.

"If she turns her back," I thought, "I'll get up and go. I'm no eavesdropper, and I'll go,—only I hope she won't give me the chance."

She had drawn a book from the folds of her skirt, and, as I lay there without sound or motion, she began to read, repeating aloud to herself the passages that pleased her.

> "I am the magic waterfall
> Whose waters leap from fathomless and living springs,
> Far in the mist-hung silence of the Past."

She paused, turning the leaves with languid capriciousness, then:

> "I fill the woods with songs; the trees,
> Through whose twigs flow prophecies,
> I deck with vestments green."

And again she read:

> "The shower has freshened the song of the bird
> And budded the bushes
> And gilded the maple and tasselled the linden and willow,
> Staining with green the forest-fringed path."

She sat silent, idly touching the fluttering pages. Then she raised her head, singing softly odd bits of songs to herself—to the thrushes around her. A great belted kingfisher flashed past, a blurr of blue and white against the trees. His loud harsh rattle startled her for an instant.

And, as she turned to watch his flight along the winding stream, I rose and slipped noiselessly into the forest. Before I had taken a dozen steps, however, I remembered my rod, and halted irresolutely. Looking back through the thicket fringe, I saw that she had turned my way again, and it was out of the question to recover it without being seen.

"If she only had her stockings on," I sighed. Should I wait, taking discreet observations occasionally? Should I go and let the rod take care of itself? Suppose the big trout should seize hold and drag it into the river? Suppose Miss Thorne should step on the barbed hook with her bare little feet! At the thought I turned hastily back in my own tracks, halted again, started on, wavered, took one irresolute step, and stopped. I could see her now quite plainly without being seen. She had tossed her book up on the moss, and was picking her way along the ascending bank, holding on to branch and root.

"She's coming for her stockings, that's what she's doing," I thought.

Until she had safely passed the pool where the hook lay, I kept my eyes on her. After that I waited until I saw her reach up to the oak-limb for the stockings; then I looked the other way. I gave her ten minutes to complete her toilet, holding my watch in my hand.

Once she sang pensively that puzzling but pathetic old ballad:

> "'Mother, may I go out to swim?'
> 'Yes, my darling daughter,
> Hang your hose on a hickory limb,
> But don't go near the water.'"

The ten minutes were up at last. "Now," said I to myself, "shall I look? No—yes—no indeed!—I don't know,—I'll just see whether—"

I turned around.

She had left the shelter of the oak and was hurrying down the bank toward my rod, with every appearance of excitement.

"I'll bet there's a fish on it," said I to myself; "by jingo! there is!—and it's bending and tugging as if a porpoise had the line! It'll be into the river in a moment! There! It's gone!"

But I was mistaken, for Miss Thorne grasped it just as it slid over the edge of the bank.

"She'll break it! I'll bet it's my big fish! There! She's pulling the fish out— she's trying to drag the fish up! I can't stand this! It's no use—I've got to go."

When she saw me hastening down the slope she did not cry out, neither did she drop the rod, but her blue eyes grew very large and round. And as I hurried up she gave one last convulsive tug and hauled up, over, and on to the bank an enormous trout, flapping and bouncing among the leaves.

In a second I had seized the fish—it took all the strength of my arm to hold him—and the rest was soon over. There he lay, a monarch among trout, glistening, dappled, crimson-flecked. I walked down to the water's edge, washed my hands mechanically, and slowly climbed back again.

"I didn't know it was your rod," she said. "I only saw a big fish on it, and I pulled it out."

"I—I thought you had left Clovermead," I stammered.

"I thought you had also," she said; "all the others have gone. To-morrow I go; my guardian is coming."

"To-morrow?"

"Yes; at eight o'clock in the morning."

There was an awkward pause. I glanced askance at the fish, already ashamed of my work, dreading to know what she thought of a man who fished with bait.

"It is a large trout," she said timidly; "it is a wonder that I didn't break your rod and line. You see I never before caught a trout."

"And—and you would not—you don't think less of a man because he fishes with bait?" I asked, red with shame.

"I? Why, no. What else would you use?"

"Flies," I said, desperately. "You know it."

"Flies? Can you catch enough?"

"I mean artificial flies," I said. "You don't understand, you can't conceive the depth of depravity that leads a man to catch a trout as I've caught this,—can you? It's simple murder."

"But," said Miss Thorne, with a puzzled glance at the fish, "I thought that I caught him."

"I—I baited the hook," I faltered.

"Then," said she, "it's a clear case of collusion, and we're both responsible."

We looked at each other for an instant. She sighed, almost imperceptibly.

"I am very sorry for what I said that night," I began. "You can't think how it has troubled me ever since. I have suffered a great deal—er—and I 'm deucedly miserable, Miss Thorne."

"I forgive you," she said sweetly. "Why did you not ask me before?"

"Because," said I, "being an idiot I didn't dare."

"It made me very unhappy," she said. "I should not have spoken so—"

"Oh, you were quite right!" I cried; "it was my fault entirely."

"No indeed!"

"It was, really."

"And to think I should have spoken so after the trout you gave me and the serenade"

"If the music had been as good as the trout—"

"It was,—it was charming; and you said some things that first afternoon under my window—"

"I meant them!—I mean them now a thousand-fold!"

The crimson stained her cheeks. She half turned toward the river.

"I think," she said, "that I am late for luncheon."

Very humbly I produced my flask of Bordeaux, my cold chicken, bread, and hot-house pears. She looked at them, her head on one side.

"It is not very much," I ventured,—"for two."

"I think it will do," she said reflectively; "there are some cresses by the brook. I am fond of cresses. Have you pepper and salt?"

I rummaged in my pockets, produced the harmonica, a package of tobacco, a spare reel, a knife, a steel hunting watch, a cigarette case, a box of dry flies, a match-case, a box of leaders, and finally a neat little parcel of pepper and salt.

She watched me with perfect gravity.

"If you please," she said, "you may go and play on your harmonica under that oak tree while I arrange the table. Will you?"

"Can't I help you?" I murmured, giddy with happiness.

"No. Go and play 'Sir Daniel O'Donnell.'"

I watched her, tooting fitfully the while, and presently she called to me that luncheon was ready, and asked me to lend her my handkerchief to dry her hands.

We drank in turn from the flask, gravely begging pardon for the *goutte sans façon*.

But the luncheon! There never was such a luncheon served in the palaces of Stamboul! I ate ambrosia—some name it chicken—and I drank nectar—foolish people would have called it Bordeaux, and I sat opposite to and looked in the blue eyes of the sweetest maid in the world.

And so we sat and chatted on, I knowing little of what was said save that it was her voice, always her voice in my ears and every word was melody. The swift droop of the long lashes on the pure curved cheeks, the gentle caress in every movement, the light glinting on tawny hair, on stray curling strands blown across her eyes—these I remember.

The shadows came and laid their long shapes on the sands of the shore, the trees darkened where the massed foliage swept in one unbroken sheet above the moss; the red west blazed.

Once a fish splashed among the weeds; a wood-duck steered fearlessly past, peering and turning, sousing its gorgeous neck in the shallow stream.

At last she sprang up, touching her hair with light swift fingers, and shaking her skirts full breadth.

"I must go."

"So soon?"

"Yes. Shall I say good-bye now for to-morrow?"

"Say it."

"Good-bye, then."

"Is that all?"

"Good-bye—"

"Nothing more?"

"Oh, what—what else?" she murmured; "I can say no more."

"I can," said I.

"You must not—ah, do you mean it?"

"Yes. I love you."

"Then we will go back—together," she said, innocently, and came close up to me, laying her white hands in mine.

"Ah," said I, as we entered the road by the dormitory, "the trout is a noble one, but, May, it was murder that was done on Clovermead water."

"And theft," she said, with a faint smile, "where is my heart, if you please?"

And we looked long, smiling into each other's eyes.

It all happened years ago. I have never touched bait to hook since, but I confess that I do still, at times, play "Sir Daniel O'Donnell" on the harmonica. May permits it, especially when the children beg me; and, as they are teasing me now, I shall probably play it to-night.

FROM
BARBARIANS

ROBERT W. CHAMBERS

MAROONED

I

So this is what happened to the dozen-odd malcontents who could no longer stand the dirty business in Europe and the dirtier politicians at home.

There was treachery in the Senate, treason in the House. A plague of liars infested the Republic; the land was rotting with plots.

But if the authorities at Washington remained incredulous, stunned into impotency, while the din of murder filled the world, a few mere men, fed up on the mess, sickened while awaiting executive galvanization, and started east to purge their souls.

They came from the four quarters of the continent, drawn to the decks of the mule transport by a common sickness and a common necessity. Only two among them had ever before met. They represented all sorts, classes, degrees of education and of ignorance, drawn to a common rendezvous by coincidental nausea incident to the temporary stupidity and poltroonery of those supposed to represent them in the Congress of the Great Republic.

The rendezvous was a mule transport reeking with its cargo, still tied up to the sun-scorched wharf where scores of loungers loafed and gazed up at the rail and exchanged badinage with the supercargo.

The supercargo consisted of this dozen-odd fed-up ones—eight Americans, three Frenchmen and one Belgian.

There was a young soldier of fortune named Carfax, recently discharged from the Pennsylvania State Constabulary, who seemed to feel rather sure of a commission in the British service.

Beside him, leaning on the blistering rail, stood a self-possessed young man named Harry Stent. He had been educated abroad; his means were ample; his time his own. He had shot all kinds of big game except a Hun, he told another young fellow—a civil engineer—who stood at his left and whose name was Jim Brown.

A youth on crutches, passing along the deck behind them, lingered, listening to the conversation, slightly amused at Stent's game list and his further ambition to bag a Boche.

The young man's lameness resulted from a trench acquaintance with the game which Stent desired to hunt. His regiment had been, and still was, the 2nd Foreign Legion. He was on his way back, now, to finish his convalescence in his old home in Finistère. He had been a writer of stories for children. His name was Jacques Wayland.

As he turned away from the group at the rail, still amused, a man advancing aft spoke to him by name, and he recognized an American painter whom he had met in Brittany.

"You, Neeland?"

"Oh, yes. I'm fed up with watchful waiting."

"Where are you bound, ultimately?"

"I've a hint that an Overseas unit can use me. And you, Wayland?"

"Going to my old home in Finestère where I'll get well, I hope."

"And then?"

"Second Foreign."

"Oh. Get that leg in the trenches?" inquired Neeland.

"Yes. Came over to recuperate. But Finestère calls me. I've *got* to smell the sea off Eryx before I can get well."

A pleasant-faced, middle-aged man, who stood near, turned his head and cast a professionally appraising glance at the young fellow on crutches.

His name was Vail; he was a physician. It did not seem to him that there was much chance for the lame man's very rapid recovery.

Three muleteers came on deck from below—all young men, all talking in loud, careless voices. They wore uniforms of khaki resembling the regular service uniform. They had no right to these uniforms.

One of these young men had invented the costume. His name was Jack Burley. His two comrades were, respectively, "Sticky" Smith and "Kid" Glenn. Both had figured in the squared circle. All three were fed up. They desired to wallop something, even if it were only a leather-rumped mule.

Four other men completed the supercargo—three French youths who were returning for military duty and one Belgian. They had been waiters in New York. They also were fed up with the administration. They kept by themselves during the voyage. Nobody ever learned their names. They left the transport at Calais, reported, and were lost to sight in the flood of young men flowing toward the trenches.

They completed the odd dozen of fed-up ones who sailed that day on the suffocating mule transport in quest of something they needed but could not find in America—something that lay somewhere amid flaming obscurity in that hell of murder beyond the Somme—their souls' salvation perhaps.

Twelve fed-up men went. And what happened to all except the four French youths is known. Fate laid a guiding hand on the shoulder of Carfax and gave him a gentle shove toward the Vosges. Destiny linked arms with Stent and Brown and led them toward Italy. Wayland's rendezvous with Old Man Death was in Finestère. Neeland sailed with an army corps, but Chance met him at Lorient and led him into the strangest paths a young man ever travelled.

As for Sticky Smith, Kid Glenn and Jack Burley, they were muleteers. Or thought they were. A muleteer has to do with mules. Nothing else is supposed to concern him.

But into the lives of these three muleteers came things never dreamed of in their philosophy—never imagined by them even in their cups.

As for the others, Carfax, Brown, Stent, Wayland, Neeland, this is what happened to each one of them. But the episode of Carfax comes first. It happened somewhere north of the neutral Alpine region where the Vosges shoulder their way between France and Germany.

After he had exchanged a dozen words with a staff officer, he began to realize, vaguely, that he was done in.

II

"Will they do anything for us?" repeated Carfax.

The staff officer thought it very doubtful. He stood in the snow switching his wet puttees and looking out across a world of tumbled mountains. Over on his right lay Germany; on his left, France; Switzerland towered in ice behind him against an arctic blue sky.

It grew warm on the Falcon Peak, almost hot in the sun. Snow was melting on black heaps of rocks; a black salamander, swollen, horrible, stirred from its stiff lethargy and crawled away blindly across the snow.

"Our case is this," continued Carfax; "somebody's made a mistake. We've been forgotten. And if they don't relieve us rather soon some of us will go off our bally nuts. Do you get me, Major?"

"I beg your pardon—"

"Do you understand what I've been saying?"

"Oh, yes; quite so."

"Then ask yourself, Major, how long can four men stand it, cooped up here on this peak? A month, two months, three, five? But it's going on ten months—ten months of solitude—silence—not a sound, except when the snowslides go bellowing off into Alsace down there below our feet." His bronzed lip quivered. "I'll get aboard one if this keeps on."

He kicked a lump of ice off into space; the staff officer glanced at him and looked away hurriedly.

"Listen," said Carfax with an effort; "we're not regulars—not like the others. The Canadian division is different. Its discipline is different—in spite of Salisbury Plain and K. of K. In my regiment there are half-breeds, pelt-hunters, Nome miners, Yankees of all degrees, British, Canadians, gentlemen adventurers from Cosmopolis. They're good soldiers, but do you think they'd stay here? It is so in the Athabasca Battalion; it is the same in every battalion. They wouldn't stay here ten months. They couldn't. We are free people; we can't stand indefinite caging; we've got to have walking room once every few months."

The staff officer murmured something.

"I know; but good God, man! Four of us have been on this peak for nearly ten months. We've never seen a Boche, never heard a shot. Seasons come and go, rain falls, snow falls, the winds blow from the Alps, but nothing else comes to us except a half-frozen bird or two."

The staff officer looked about him with an involuntary shiver. There was nothing to see except the sun on the wet, black rocks and the whitewashed observation station of solid stone from which wires sagged into the valley on the French side.

"Well—good luck," he said hastily, looking as embarrassed as he felt. "I'll be toddling along."

"Will you say a word to the General, like a good chap? Tell him how it is with us—four of us all alone up here since the beginning. There's Gary, Captain in the Athabasca Battalion, a Yankee if the truth were known; there's Flint, a cockney lieutenant in a Calgary battery; there's young Gray, a lieutenant and a Prince Edward Islander; and here's me, a major in the Yukon Battalion—four of us on the top of a cursed French mountain—ten months of each other, of solitude, silence—and the whole world rocking with battles—and not a sound up here—not a whisper! I tell you we're four sick men! We've got a grip on ourselves yet, but it's slipping. We're still fairly civil to each other, but the strain is killing. Sullen silences smother irritability, but—" he added in a peculiarly pleasant voice, "I expect we are likely to start killing each other if somebody doesn't get us out of here very damn quick."

The staff captain's lips formed the words, "Awfully sorry! Good luck!" but his articulation was indistinct, and he went off hurriedly, still murmuring.

Carfax stood in the snow, watching him clamber down among the rocks, where an alpinist orderly joined them.

Gary presently appeared at the door of the observation station. "Has he gone?" he inquired, without interest.

"Yes," said Carfax.

"Is he going to do anything for us?"

"I don't know. . . . *No!*"

Gary lingered, kicked at a salamander, then turned and went indoors. Carfax sat down on a rock and sucked at his empty pipe.

Later the three officers in the observation station came out to the door again and looked at him, but turned back into the doorway without saying anything. And after a while Carfax, feeling slightly feverish, went indoors, too.

In the square, whitewashed room Gray and Flint were playing cut-throat poker; Gary was at the telephone, but the messages received or transmitted appeared to be of no importance. There had never been any message of importance from the Falcon Peak or to it. There was likely to be none.

Ennui, inertia, dry rot—and four men, sometimes silently, sometimes violently cursing their isolation, but always cursing it—afraid in their souls lest they fall to cursing one another aloud as they had begun to curse in their hearts.

Months ago rain had fallen; now snow fell, and vast winds roared around them from the Alps. But nothing else ever came to the Falcon Peak, except a fierce, red-eyed *Lämmergeyer* sheering above the peak on enormous pinions, or a few little migrating birds fluttering down, half frozen, from the high air lanes. Now and then, also, came to them a staff officer from below, British sometimes, sometimes French, who lingered no longer than necessary and then went back again, down into friendly deeps where were trees and fields and familiar things and human companionship, leaving them to their hell of silence, of solitude, and of each other.

The tide of war had never washed the base of their granite cliffs; the highest battle wave had thundered against the Vosges beyond earshot; not even a deadened echo of war penetrated those silent heights; not a Taube floated in the zenith.

In the squatty, whitewashed ruin which once had been the eyrie of some petty predatory despot, and which now served as an observatory for two idle divisions below in the valley, stood three telescopes. Otherwise the furniture consisted of valises, trunks, a table and chairs, a few books, several newspapers, and some tennis balls lying on the floor,

Carfax seated himself at one of the telescopes, not looking through it, his heavy eyes partly closed, his burnt-out pipe between his teeth.

Gary rose from the telephone and joined the card players. They shuffled and dealt listlessly, seldom speaking save in monosyllables.

After a while Carfax went over to the card table and the young lieutenant cashed in and took his place at the telescope.

Below in the Alsatian valley spring had already started the fruit buds, and a delicate green edged the lower snow line.

The lieutenant spoke of it wistfully; nobody paid any attention; he rose presently and went outdoors to the edge of the precipice—not too near, for fear he might be tempted to jump out through the sunshine, down into that inviting world of promise below.

Far underneath him—very far down in the valley—a cuckoo called. Out of the depths floated the elfin halloo, the gaily malicious challenge of spring herself, shouted up melodiously from the plains of Alsace—*Cuck-*

oo! Cuckoo! Cuckoo!—You poor, sullen, frozen foreigner up there on the snowy rocks!—*Cuckoo! Cuckoo! Cuckoo!*

The lieutenant of Yukon infantry, whose name was Gray, came back into the room.

"There's a bird of sorts yelling like hell below," he said to the card players.

Carfax ran over his cards, rejected three, and nodded. "Well, let him yell," he said.

"What is it, a Boche dicky-bird insulting you?" asked Gary, in his Yankee drawl.

Flint, declining to draw cards, got up and went out into the sunshine. When he returned to the table, he said: "It's a cuckoo. . . . I wish to God I were out of this," he added.

They continued to play for a while without apparent interest. Each man had won his comrades' money too many times to care when Carfax added up debit and credit and wrote down each man's score. In nine months, alternately beggaring one another, they had now, it appeared, broken about even.

Gary, an American in British uniform, twitched a newspaper toward himself, slouched in his chair, and continued to read for a while. The paper was French and two weeks old; he jerked it about irritably.

Gray, resting his elbows on his knees, sat gazing vacantly out of the narrow window. For a smart officer he had grown slovenly.

"If there was any trout fishing to be had," he began; but Flint laughed scornfully.

"What are you laughing at? There must be trout in the valley down there where that bird is," insisted Gray, reddening.

"Yes, and there are cows and chickens and houses and women. What of it?"

Gary, in his faded service uniform of a captain, scowled over his newspaper. "It's bad enough to be here," he said heavily; "so don't let's talk about it. Quit disputing."

Flint ignored the order.

"If there was anything sportin' to do——"

"Oh, shut up," muttered Carfax. "Do you expect sport on a hog-back?"

Gray picked up a tennis ball and began to play it against the whitewashed stone wall, using the palm of his hand. Flint joined him presently; Gary went over to the telephone, set the receiver to his ear and spoke to some officer in the distant valley on the French side, continuing a spiritless conversation while watching the handball play. After a while he rose, shambled out and down among the rocks to the spring where snow lay, trodden and filthy, and the big, black salamanders crawled half stupefied in the sun. All his loathing and fear of them kindled again as it always did at sight of them. "Dirty beasts," he muttered, stumping and stumbling among the stunted fir trees; "some day they'll bite some of these damn fools who say they can't bite. And that'll end 'em."

Flint and Gray continued to play handball in a perfunctory way while Carfax looked on from the telephone without interest. Gary came back, his shoes and puttees all over wet snow.

"Unless," he said in a monotonous voice, "something happens within the next few days I'll begin to feel queer in my head; and if I feel it coming on, I'll blow my bally nut off. Or somebody's." And he touched his service automatic in its holster and yawned.

After a dead silence:

"Buck up," remarked Carfax; "think how our men must feel in Belfort, never letting off their guns. Ross rifles, too—not a shot at a Boche since the damn war began!"

"God!" said Flint, smiting the ball with the palm of his hand, "to think of those Ross rifles rusting down there and to think of the pink-skinned pigs they could paunch so cleanly. Did you ever paunch a deer? What a mess of intestines all over the shop!"

Gary, still standing, began to kick the snow from his shoes. Gray said to him: "For a dollar of your Yankee money I'd give you a shot at me with your automatic—you're that slack at practice."

"If it goes on much longer like this I'll not have to pay for a shot at any-body," returned Gary, with a short laugh.

Gray laughed too, disagreeably, stretching his facial muscles, but no sound issued.

"We're all going crazy together up here; that's my idea," he said. "I don't know which I can stand most comfortably, your voices or your silence. Both make me sick."

"Some day a salamander will nip you; then you'll go loco," observed Gary, balancing another tennis ball in his right hand. "Give me a shot at you?" he added. "I feel as though I could throw it clean through you. You look soft as a pudding to me."

Far, clear, from infinite depths, the elf-like hail of the cuckoo came float-ing up to the window.

To Flint, English born, the call meant more than it did to Canadian or Yankee.

"In Devon," he said in an altered voice, "they'll be calling just now. There's a world of primroses in Devon. . . . And the thorn is as white as the damned snow is up here."

Gary growled his impatience and his profile of a Greek fighter showed in clean silhouette against the window.

"Aw, hell," he said, "did I come out here for this?—nine months of it?" He hurled the tennis ball at the wall. "Can the home talk, if you don't mind."

The cuckoo was still calling.

"Did you ever play cuckoo," asked Carfax, "at ten shillings a throw? It's not a bad game—if you're put to it for amusement."

Nobody replied; Gray's sunken, boyish face betrayed no interest; he continued to toss a tennis ball against the wall and catch it on the rebound.

Toward sundown the usual Alpine chill set in; a mist hung over the snow-edged cliffs; the rocks breathed steam under a foggy and battered moon.

III

Carfax, on duty, sat hunched up over the telephone, reporting to the fortress.

Gray came in, closed the wooden shutters, hung blankets over them, lighted an oil stove and then a candle. Flint took up the cards, looked at Gary, then flung them aside, muttering.

Nobody attempted to read; nobody touched the cards again. An orderly came in with soup. The meal was brief and perfectly silent.

Flint said casually, after the table had been cleared: "I haven't slept for a month. If I don't get some sleep I'll go queer. I warn you; that's all. I'm sorry to say it, but it's so."

"They're dirty beasts to keep us here like this," muttered Gary—"nine months of it, and not a shot."

"There'll be a few shots if things don't change," remarked Flint in a colourless voice. "I'm getting wrong in my head. I can feel it."

Carfax turned from the switchboard with a forced laugh: "Thinking of shooting up the camp?"

"That or myself," replied Flint in a quiet voice; "ever since that cuckoo called I've felt queer."

Gary, brooding in his soiled tunic collar, began to mutter presently: "I once knew a man in a lighthouse down in Florida who couldn't stand it after a bit and jumped off."

"Oh, we've heard that twenty times," interrupted Carfax wearily.

Gray said: "*What* a jump!—I mean down into Alsace below—"

"You're all going dotty!" snapped Carfax. "Shut up or you'll be doing it—some of you."

"I can't sleep. That's where I'm getting queer," insisted Flint. "If I could get a few hours' sleep now—"

"I wish to God the Boches could reach you with a big gun. That would put you to sleep, all right!" said Gray.

"This war is likely to end before any of us see a Fritz," said Carfax. "I could stand it, too, except being up here with such"—his voice dwindled to a mutter, but it sounded to Gary as though he had used the word "rotters."

Flint's face had a white, strained expression; he began to walk about, saying aloud to himself: "If I could only sleep. That's the idea—sleep it off, and wake up somewhere else. It's the silence, or the voices—I don't know which. You dollar-crazy Yankees and ignorant Provincials don't realize what a cuckoo is. You've no traditions, anyway—no past, nothing to care for—"

"Listen to 'Arry!" retorted Gary—"'Arry and his cuckoo!"

Carfax stirred heavily. "Shut up!" he said, with an effort. "The thing is to keep doing something—something—anything—except quarrelling."

He picked up a tennis ball. "Come on, you funking brutes! I'll teach you how to play cuckoo. Every man takes three tennis balls and stands in a corner of the room. I stand in the middle. Then you blow out the candle. Then I call 'cuckoo!' in the dark and you try to hit me, aiming by the sound of my voice. Every time I'm hit I pay ten shillings to the pool, take my place in a corner, and have a shot at the next man, chosen by lot. And if you throw three balls apiece and nobody hits me, then you each pay ten shillings to me and I'm cuckoo for another round."

"We aim at random?" inquired Gray, mildly interested.

"Certainly. It must be played in pitch darkness. When I call out cuckoo, you take a shot at where you think I am. If you all miss, you all pay. If I'm hit, I pay."

Gary chose three tennis balls and retired to a corner of the room; Gray and Flint, urged into action, took three each, unwillingly.

"Blow out the candle," said Carfax, who had walked into the middle of the room. Gary blew it out and the place was in darkness.

They thought they heard Carfax moving cautiously, and presently he called, "Cuckoo!" A storm of tennis balls rebounded from the walls; "Cuckoo!" shouted Carfax, and the tennis balls rained all around him.

Once more he called; not a ball hit him; and he struck a match where he was seated upon the floor.

There was some perfunctory laughter of a feverish sort; the candle was relighted, tennis balls redistributed, and Carfax wrote down his winnings.

The next time, however, Gray, throwing low, caught him. Again the candle was lighted, scores jotted down, a coin tossed, and Flint went in as cuckoo.

It seemed almost impossible to miss a man so near, even in total darkness, but Flint lasted three rounds and was hit, finally, a stinging smack on the ear. And then Gary went in.

It was hot work, but they kept at it feverishly, grimly, as though their very sanity depended upon the violence of their diversion. They threw the balls hard, viciously hard. A sort of silent ferocity seemed to seize them. A chance hit cut the skin over Flint's cheekbone, and when the candle was lighted, one side of his face was bright with blood.

Early in the proceedings somebody had disinterred brandy and Schnapps from under a bunk. The room had become close; they all were sweating.

Carfax emptied his iced glass, still breathing hard, tossed a shilling and sent in Gary as cuckoo.

Flint, who never could stand spirits, started unsteadily for the candle, but could not seem to blow it out. He stood swaying and balancing on his heels, puffing out his smooth, boyish cheeks and blowing at hazard.

"You're drunk," said Gray, thickly; but he was as flushed as the boy he addressed, only steadier of leg.

"What's that?" retorted Flint, jerking his shoulders around and gazing at Gray out of glassy eyes.

"Blow out that candle," said Gary heavily, "or I'll shoot it out! Do you get that?"

"Shoot!" repeated Flint, staring vaguely into Gary's bloodshot eyes; "you shoot, you old slacker—"

"Shut up and play the game!" cut in Carfax, a menacing roar rising in his voice. "You're all slackers—and rotters, too. Play the game! Keep playing—hard!—or you'll go clean off your fool nuts!"

Gary walked heavily over and knocked the tennis balls out of Flint's hands.

"There's a better game than that," he said, his articulation very thick; "but it takes nerve—if you've got it, you spindle-legged little cockney!"

Flint struck at him aimlessly. "I've got nerve," he muttered, "plenty of nerve, old top! What d'you want? I'm your man; I'll go you—eh, what?"

"Go on with the game, I tell you!" bawled Carfax.

Gary swung around: "Wait till I explain—"

"No, don't wait! Keep going! Keep playing! Keep doing something, for God's sake!"

"Will you wait!" shouted Gary. "I want to tell you—"

Carfax made a hopeless gesture: "It's talk that will do the trick for us all—"

"I want to tell you—"

Carfax shrugged, emptied his full glass with a gesture of finality.

"Then talk, damn you! And we'll all be at each other's throats before morning."

Gary got Gray by the elbow: "Reggie, it's this way. We flip up for cuckoo. Whoever gets stuck takes a shot apiece from our automatics in the legs—eh, what?"

"It's perfectly agreeable to me," assented Gray, in the mincing, elaborate voice characteristic of him when drunk.

Flint wagged his head. "It's a sportin' game. I'm in," he said.

Gary looked at Carfax. "A shot in the dark at a man's legs. And if he gets his—it will be Blighty in exchange for hell."

Carfax, sullen with liquor, shoved his big hand into his pocket, produced a shilling, and tossed it.

A brighter flush stained the faces which ringed him; the risky hazard of the affair cleared their sick minds to comprehension.

Tails turned uppermost; Flint and Gary were eliminated. It lay between Carfax and Gray, and the older man won.

"Mind you fire low," said the young fellow, with an excited laugh, and walked into the middle of the room.

Gary blew out the candle. Presently from somewhere in the intense darkness Gray called "Cuckoo!" and instantly a slanting red flash lashed out through the gloom. And, when the deafening echo had nearly ceased: "Cuckoo!"

Another pistol crashed. And after a swimming interval they heard him moving. "Cuckoo!" he called; a level flame stabbed the dark; something fell, thudding through the staccato uproar of the explosion. At the same moment the outer door opened on the crack and Carfax's orderly peeped in.

Carfax struck a match with shaky fingers; the candle guttered, sank, flared on Flint, who was laughing without a sound. "Got the beggar, by God!" he whispered—"through the head! Look at him. Look at Reggie Gray! Tried for his head and got him—"

He reeled back, chuckling foolishly, and levelled at Carfax. "Now I'll get you!" he simpered, and shot him through the face.

As Carfax pitched forward, Gary fired.

"Missed me, by God!" laughed Flint. "Shoot? Hell, yes. I'll show you how to shoot—"

He struck the lighted candle with his left hand and laughed again in the thick darkness.

"Shoot? I'll show you how to shoot, you old slacker—"

Gary fired.

After a silence Flint giggled in the choking darkness as the door opened cautiously again, and shot at the terrified orderly.

"I'm a cockney, am I? And you don't think much of the Devon cuckoos, do you? Now I'll show you that I understand all kinds of cuckoos—"

Both flashes split the obscurity at the same moment. Flint fell back against the wall and slid down to the floor. The outer door began to open again cautiously.

But the orderly, half dressed, remained knee-deep in the snow by the doorway.

After a long interval Gary struck a match, then went over and lit the candle. And, as he turned, Flint fired from where he lay on the floor and Gary swung heavily on one heel, took two uncertain steps. Then his pistol fell clattering; he sank to his knees and collapsed face downward on the stones.

Flint, still lying where he had fallen, partly upright, against the wall, began to laugh, and died a few moments later, the wind from the slowly opening door stirring his fair hair and extinguishing the candle.

And at last, through the opened door crept Carfax's orderly; peered into the darkness within, shivering in his unbuttoned tunic, his boots wet with snow.

Dawn already whitened the east; and up out of the ghastly fog edging the German Empire, silhouetted, monstrous, against the daybreak, soared a *Lämmergeyer*, beating the livid void with enormous, unclean wings.

The orderly heard its scream, shrank, cowering, against the door frame as the huge bird's ferocious red and yellow eyes blazed level with his.

Suddenly, above the clamor of the *Lämmergeyer*, the shrill bell of the telephone began to ring.

The terrible racket of the *Lämmergeyer* filled the sky; the orderly stumbled into the room, slipped in a puddle of something wet, sent an empty bottle rolling and clinking away into the darkness; stumbled twice over prostrate bodies; reached the telephone, half fainting; whispered for help.

After a long, long while, the horror still thickly clogging vein and brain, he scratched a match, hesitated, then holding it high, reeled toward the door with face averted.

Outside the sun was already above the horizon, flashing over Haut Alsace at his feet.

The *Lämmergeyer* was a speck in the sky, poised over France.

Up out of the infinite and sunlit chasm came a mocking, joyous hail— up through the sheer, misty gulf out of vernal depths: *Cuck*-oo! *Cuck*-oo! *Cuck*-oo!

THE END

ROBERT W. CHAMBERS BIBLIOGRAPHY

In the Quarter (1894)
The King in Yellow (1895; stories)
The Red Republic (1895)
With the Band (1896; poetry)
A King and a Few Dukes (1896)
The Maker of Moons
    (1896; stories)
The Mystery of Choice
    (1897; stories)
The Haunts of Men
    (1898; stories)
Ashes of Empire (1898)
Lorraine (1898)
Outsiders (1899)
Cambric Mask (1899)
The Conspirators (1900)
Cardigan (1901)
The Maid-at-Arms (1902)
The Maids of Paradise (1903)
In Search of the Unknown (1904)
A Young Man in a Hurry and
    Other Short Stories (1904)
The Reckoning (1905)
Iole (1905)
The Tracer of Lost Persons (1906)
The Fighting Chance (1906)
The Tree of Heaven (1907; stories)
The Younger Set (1907)
The Firing Line (1908)
Some Ladies in Haste (1908)
Special Messenger (1909)
The Danger Mark (1909)
Ailsa Paige (1910)
The Green Mouse (1910)
Adventures of a Modest Man
    (1911)
The Common Law (1911)
The Streets of Ascalon (1912)
Japonette (1912)
The Gay Rebellion (1913)

The Business of Life (1913)
Blue-Bird Weather (1913)
Quick Action (1914; stories)
The Hidden Children (1914)
Anne's Bridge (1914)
Between Friends (1914; stories)
Who Goes There! (1915)
Athalie (1915)
Police!!! (1915; stories)
The Better Man (1916; stories)
The Girl Philippa (1916)
Barbarians (1917; interconnected
    war stories)
The Dark Star (1917)
The Restless Sex (1918)
The Laughing Girl (1918)
In Secret (1919)
The Moonlight Way (1919)
The Crimson Tide (1919)
The Slayer of Souls (1920)
A Story of Primitive Love
    (1920; story)
The Little Red Foot (1921)
Eris (1922)
The Flaming Jewel (1922)
The Talkers (1923)
The Hi-Jackers (1923)
America, or the Sacrifice (1924)
Marie Halkett (UK: 1925;
    US: 1937)
The Girl in Golden Rags
    (UK: 1925; US: 1936)
The Mystery Lady (1925)
The Man They Hanged (1926)
The Way of Dionysia (1926;
    Red Book Magazine serial)
The Drums of Aulone (1927)
The Gold Chase (1927)
The Rogue's Moon (1928)
The Sun Hawk (1928)

The Happy Parrot (1929)
Painted Minx (1930)
The Rake and the Hussy (1930)
Beating Wings (UK: 1930;
   US: 1936)
War Paint and Rouge (1931)
Gitana (1931)
Silver Knees (1931;
   Liberty magazine serial)
The Whistling Cat (1932)
Whatever Love Is (1933)
The Young Man's Girl (1934)
Secret Service Operator 13
   (1934; stories)
Love and the Lieutenant (1935)
The Fifth Horseman (1937)
Smoke of Battle (1938;
   completed by Rupert Hughes)

PLAYS/MUSICALS

The Witch of Ellangowan
   (1897; aka Meg Merrilies)
Iole (1913; musical comedy based
   on the novel)
Sintram and His Companions
   (opera libretto)

CHILDREN'S BOOKS

Outdoorland (1903)
Orchard-Land (1903)
River-Land (1904)
Forest-Land (1905)
Mountain-Land (1906)
Garden-Land (1907)

ART

Washington: or The Revolution
   (1895) [text by Ethan Allen]
Halifax in Wartime (1943)
   [text by Frank W. Doyle]